Designated Protector

DESIGNATED PROTECTOR

HOPE ABROM
AMANDA ABROM

Designated Protector

Cover Design by Stefanie Saw (Seventhstar Art)

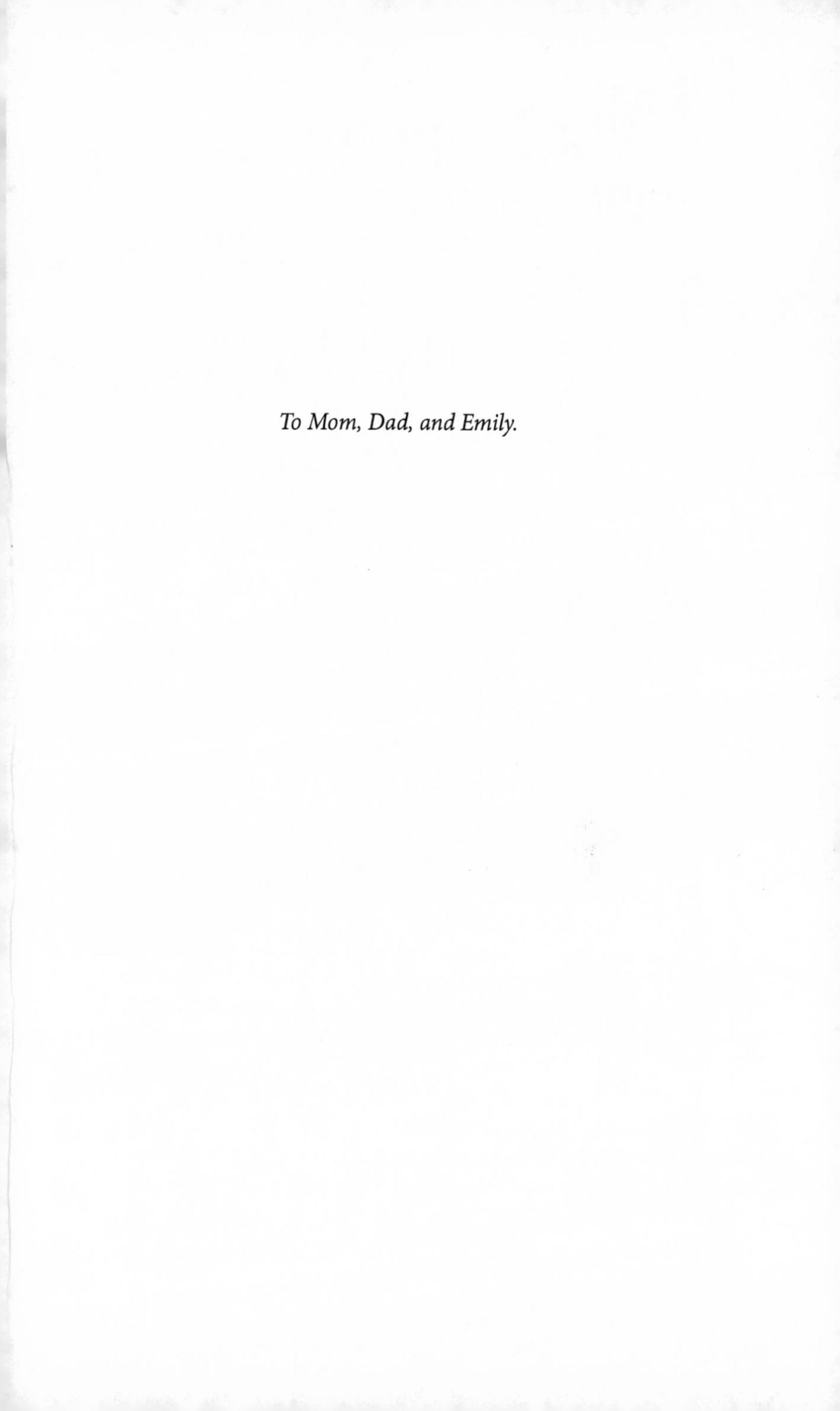

To Mom, Dad, and Emily.

Grovia

Vorinder

Klover

Madris

Wonitu

Morbaeda

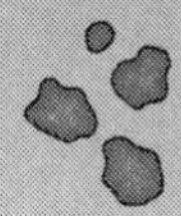

Kapitale

Solaris

Ulodae

North
Castle

Dyrstig

Larkesh

Sun Castle

Captain's Palace

Taville

Tamir

Lost Lands

Wicz

Lost Castle

THE PROPHECY

When the lineage of darkness begins from beyond
The designated protector is forced to abscond
With only a teardrop of blood as defense
The sword wins the war at a friend's expense
When companions turn hostile and extinguish the light
When droplets of sun must hide in plain sight...
...One key per heir, a thought unforeseen
Until light and dark congeal, and the world is serene

27 YEARS BEFORE THE DEATH OF KING SUN

Prologue

A crisp wind blew the bedroom curtains. They danced in the breeze, extending inwards to a ghostly, stone room located on the high floors of Sun Castle. The beacon at Sun Spire cast a glowing aura through the open window, creating an orange outline on the bedroom floor. The wind was sharper than usual for the dry moorland, signaling that something was rushing in from the horizon.

The distant crying of an infant rang throughout the room. Despite the exhaustion that ate away at every limb, Landon's eyes shot open. He fixated on the ornate canopy that concealed the bed. He jostled himself awake and sat up, stealing a glance at his wife beside him.

Anastasia shifted, hearing the call of her child from the nursery.

Landon placed his hand on her shoulder. "Stay here."

Anastasia gave him a tired smile before pulling the blankets higher.

Landon stood up from the bed. Through the windowpane, the lights surrounding Sun Castle sparkled against the night sky. Another sharp gust of wind blew, rattling the wooden frame that held the curtains.

He crossed to the nursery door, guided by the light from the outside. When he reached the door, his daughter's crying ceased.

Landon entered the nursery, remaining quiet. He slid into the room before shutting the door behind him, letting his wife remain asleep.

The nursery was spacious. Ornaments hung from the ceiling, dangling above the cribs on one side, and a large window was on the opposite wall.

The silhouette of a man was at the window, his back to Landon. The figure was shrouded in a veil of fog as if he was made of smoke.

The sight poisoned Landon with fear, his heart dropping in his chest.

"Who are–"

"Shhh..." the man said as he turned around, revealing himself to Landon. He held Landon's daughter in his arms, bouncing her gently. She was wrapped tightly in a pale, pink blanket and was only a few months old.

The man was young and muscular, with a sharp jawline and pale skin. The fog continued to ripple down his legs, pooling at his boots. His bottomless eyes pierced through Landon like arrows. If it weren't for the sledgehammer strapped to the intruder's back, the man's resemblance to Landon was uncanny.

His brother.

"Mortimer?" Landon finally spoke.

"I did it," Mortimer said. "I found the Shadow of Eclipse."

Landon stiffened. "What?"

Mortimer's eyes glistened with darkness. His lips curled upwards. "The royals lied to us. The magic was never a myth – it was a man."

Landon's eyes widened. "A man?"

"Yes," Mortimer said, "and I killed him."

Fear surged through Landon's body. His palms began to sweat, and his heart beat faster.

Landon extended his arms out toward his brother, gesturing to the child. "Let me hold her."

"Don't you understand?" Mortimer ignored Landon's request. "They kept the truth of our ancestors from us, hoping that we would never find out. Well, it's time that the royals die for their heinous atrocities, including the lies that put them on the throne."

"What lies?"

"That we…that *I*…am supposed to protect Morbaeda." The fog swirled around his figure as though it were alive, increasing in speed to match its master's emotions.

Landon shook his head. "I won't let you kill the royal family."

"You will help me, or else." Mortimer lifted his hand to touch the baby's cheek, the lifelike darkness extending from his fingers like talons.

Landon's voice escaped him. He could sense the power devouring his brother's body, ensnaring Mortimer in its grasp and transforming him into an other-worldly being. He couldn't allow Mortimer to overthrow the royals.

Landon took a step forward. "Please, don't hurt my child," he pleaded.

"I'm going to make you a deal," Mortimer said as he bounced the baby. The smoke followed him, remaining transfixed around his body. "Since the king has the Teardrop, I can't get close enough to him to take the key," Mortimer explained, "but you can."

"I'm not making a deal with you," Landon said.

"You will," Mortimer responded, certain. "If you get me the key…," he paused to look down at the baby in his arms, "I will give you the child."

"Don't do this. Please, give her to me!"

Landon raced forward, hoping to save his child from the dark fog surrounding her. With a raise of his chin, Mortimer summoned a telekinetic force. An invisible wave threw Landon back, and he landed a few paces away. His breath was knocked out of him, and he clutched his chest as he lay flat on his back, his mind trying to process the magic that had occurred.

"I don't need you!" Mortimer shouted. "I can make anyone else get me what I need, but I'm giving you a chance."

Landon struggled to regain his breath. He remained on the floor and shook his head. "I'm going to kill you."

Mortimer laughed. "No, you won't," he said. "Now, is it a deal?"

Landon was silent. He stared at his child in Mortimer's hands. Tears started to burn his eyes, but he bit his tongue, holding them back.

Mortimer noticed the elongated pause. "It's a deal," he answered his own question. "Until we meet again, brother."

The black smoke swirled around Mortimer. The wind blew the curtains and ruffled Landon's hair, forcing Landon to squint against the sharp air.

"Stop!" Landon found the strength to get to his feet. He rushed forward, extending his arms outwards to hold his child, but Mortimer's telekinetic force pummeled into Landon's chest once more. He was thrust backward again.

"Oh, one more thing." Mortimer called out over the howling of the wind. "If you don't do what I ask, I will kill the child, and you will never see her again."

The smoke thickened and began swallowing Mortimer, consuming Landon's child.

The door burst open, and Anastasia stood there, her eyes wide.

The fog had entirely devoured Mortimer. He evaporated into black smoke along with the baby. The black mass swirled harshly before traveling out the window and vanishing into the night.

"No!" Anastasia screamed, running to the window. She watched the cloud as it traveled across the moor, disappearing into the darkness.

Landon pulled himself to his knees, feeling his rib cage pulsing in pain.

Another baby began crying. It screamed from its crib, flailing its arms aimlessly. But the baby's twin sister was gone.

Anastasia whipped around and went straight for the crib with the crying child before picking it up, trying to soothe it. Tears streamed down her cheeks, but her full attention was on the child in her arms.

Landon struggled to stand, clutching his side in pain. "I need to warn the king."

Anastasia froze. "You need to get our child back."

Landon searched for words, his mind racing. There was no doubt the Shadow army would go for the royals, even if Mortimer couldn't get close himself. Landon needed to warn them – he needed to protect the newborn prince.

He needed to protect the key.

"You're helpless," Anastasia said. She took a step forward, extending the child toward Landon. He was forced to scoop the baby out of her arms and cradle it.

Anastasia's eyes narrowed. "I'm going to save *my* daughter."

She whipped to the door and stormed out of the nursery.

"Anastasia!" Landon called, but she was gone.

She couldn't face Mortimer by herself.

The baby continued to cry, the wailing piercing Landon's ears. He looked down at the child.

Landon crossed to the crib and set the baby down, disregarding the cries. Then he turned his back on his child and left.

10 YEARS BEFORE THE DEATH OF KING SUN

- 1 -

Kaison

Kaison Ruiz was 17-years old when he escaped Grovia.

On that day, Kaison sat in the back of a rowboat. He dipped his oar into the marsh and pulled it back through the weeds. His ears were alert to the sounds of the swamp and the water lapping around the edges of the tiny boat. Faint, pulsing ripples echoed in the air. Birds and insects chirped throughout the marshland, emitting faint whispers. He was surrounded by a labyrinth of cypress trees that created cage-like structures with their roots, which cast menacing shadows onto the water. Beyond the web of trees, the sun was setting over the horizon, casting a yellow glow on the swamp.

The foliage was typical for the isle of Grovia, located deep in the Republic of Vorinder, which neighbored the island of Salix. An intricate web of trees and marshland served as protection for the towns on the islands, dubbed by the locals as the Albufera. There was no going to the Albufera before or after dark, and only the most skilled hunters could navigate the Albufera in the moonlight.

They were running out of time. Dusk would shine on the Albufera for a few more moments, and then they would be left in darkness. Kaison gripped onto his oar firmly and used his muscular upper body to propel the boat forward. The floating object moved sluggishly through the wild plants.

The man at the front of the boat held up his left hand as a signal for Kaison to stop rowing. In his other hand, he gripped a faded parchment.

"Here," the man said.

Kaison obeyed his father, drawing the boat to a stop. He pulled the oars from the water and let them rest at the bottom of the rowboat.

"I can do it this time," Kaison said.

Arthur nodded. He pulled a satchel off his shoulder and handed it to Kaison. They could only collect what they could discreetly carry past the harbormaster.

Kaison rose to his feet, feeling the boat rock gently, as he took the satchel from his father's grasp. He pulled it over his head, letting the strap rest against his chest.

"Be careful," his father instructed. "You won't be able to see down there."

"I can do it," Kaison reiterated.

The setting sun reflected brightly off the water, creating a shining prism of orange and yellow rays. Despite the debris floating on the top, the water acted as a perfect mirror. In the direction where Kaison was staring, the Albufera opened up into a large, circular pool. The open area was wide and deep, perfect for lurking animals. In the center of the open marshland was a single cypress tree, and around the edges of the open water was a tangled maze of trees.

Arthur reached down and picked up his staff, bracing himself for any predators nearby. It was a beautiful golden staff, with three gemstones at the base.

After taking a sharp inhale, Kaison jumped off the side of the boat and plunged into the water. The foliage clung to his body, and he yanked it aside as he resurfaced. The icy water seeped through his clothes and chilled his entire body, but he ignored the freezing temperature. Steadying his breathing, he exhaled before descending into the murky water.

He clawed past the foliage, diving deeper. His eyes burned, a green haze clouding his vision. It was almost pitch black at the bottom of the Albufera, and he extended his hands before him as he reached his destination.

A circular object protruded from the sandy bottom, and Kaison couldn't tell if it was made of iron or steel. It had an entirely different texture, and he scraped away the moss to inspect it more clearly. As he followed the outline, his hand reached the ground. Whatever it was, it extended deeper into the sand. How deep was it buried?

A smaller object glistened beyond his reach. Kaison propelled his body farther before scooping it into his palm. It was barely larger than his thumb and was connected to a chain.

A pain throbbed at Kaison's chest as he searched for air.

Kaison shoved the necklace into his satchel before bracing himself against the Albufera floor. Pushing off, he ascended above.

When he broke through the surface of the water, he gasped for breath, instantly feeling relief.

"Kaison."

The tone in his father's voice was sharp, and Kaison snapped his head in the boat's direction.

"It's buried deeper than we thought," Kaison explained.

"Get out of the water."

Arthur's voice didn't waver, and Kaison knew better than to object. Kaison swam back toward the boat, kicking past the plants that tried to hold him back.

Arthur kneeled at the boat's edge, extending a hand in Kaison's direction. With his father's help, Kaison hoisted himself back in the boat, water dripping from his clothes. Arthur remained on one knee, staring out at the water.

After Kaison caught his breath, he followed his father's gaze. There was something underneath the surface. The shape was changing the pattern of the water. Every passing moment, it moved closer and closer toward the boat.

Arthur gripped his staff tighter, watching the silhouette move.

Kaison knew exactly what the figure was and didn't know how his father had remained so calm when ordering him to return to the boat.

Selfishly, he wanted to show his father he was capable of handling the predator himself.

Kaison retrieved his harpoon from beside him, preparing to strike. The animal was approaching swiftly, like an arrow cutting through its target. Two beady eyes punctured the surface of the water.

In one swift movement, Kaison launched his harpoon deep into the water. The shape withered as it was pierced with the end of the blade and thrashed until it fell limp. Kaison still held the end of the rope in his hand and began pulling the harpoon back toward the rowboat. The rope was heavy, and it took all of Kaison's strength to lure the animal toward him without tipping the boat over. When the animal was close enough, Kaison's father reached into the water and pulled the large creature into the boat. Kaison assisted him with the heavy animal.

A black caiman.

Kaison carefully removed the end of the harpoon from the caiman's head, and a bloody residue remained.

"Nice job," Arthur said.

Kaison tried to hide the smile that formed from the compliment. But it wasn't a lucky shot. He knew the singular way to kill a caiman.

Knowing he had his father's attention, Kaison brought up his proposal. "We should convince the council to increase the hunting hours. If we can hunt more caiman, it will prevent them from reaching the village."

A smile appeared on Arthur's face. "Leave it to you to want to go to the council and change everything." He added a laugh. "We're supposed to keep the village fed. Killing more than we need is unnecessary and affects the population."

Kaison didn't fully agree. "Aren't the hunters supposed to keep the village safe?" Kaison inquired.

Arthur shook his head. "You can't control nature, no matter how many hunters we send to the Albufera."

Kaison shrugged. "So, when the caiman overrun the village, it's not our problem?"

"They won't," Arthur said warmly. "Besides, there are worse things to fear than caiman."

Kaison nodded. Then he reached into the satchel and withdrew the necklace. "I found this," he said, holding it out so they both could see. "Whatever is down there is bigger than we thought."

Arthur inspected the necklace. It was a ball chain with a rectangular, silver object clasped to the end of it. He flipped it over to see words written there:

MILLER
TOM J.
523-55-4468 AF
0 NEG

"It looks like an identification," Arthur mused. "I've never seen anything like it before."

"What are the numbers?" Kaison asked.

"I'm not sure. Could it be a shipwreck?"

Kaison's brow furrowed. "I don't think so," he admitted.

"Let's head back," Arthur said.

"But–"

"It's getting dark."

Arthur rose to his feet, but he didn't waver as the rowboat lurched from side to side. He grasped his staff in his hand, and a new expression flooded his square face. He had a faint mustache, and thin facial hair covered his strong, lower jaw. His boxy eyebrows accentuated his dark brown eyes, which were set deep into his face and emphasized his harsh features. Like Kaison, he had dark, tan skin and brown hair.

Kaison was a mirror image of his father – except for the mustache.

Arthur's eyes drifted out toward the single cypress tree that lay in the center of the open marshland. He turned his staff over in his hand. "We will come back tomorrow."

Kaison concealed the necklace in the satchel. He shook out his wet hair, splattering water, before reaching for the oars.

They had seconds of daylight left, and they were alone. All of the other hunters had already headed back. Kaison and his father were in an area of the marsh called the Reflecting Grounds – known for its bright water and single cypress tree in the middle of an open pool. It was one of the only open spaces in the entire Albufera, and most of the other hunters didn't go there. Arthur, unlike the others, always pushed Kaison to explore more and to venture farther away from the village of Grovia.

Kaison knew it was because of the secrets that were under these waters. What they were uncovering could date all the way back to the War of Worlds. They couldn't risk the other hunters knowing what was underneath the surface.

Kaison began rowing, leading them in the direction of Grovia, using all of his strength to maneuver through the branches and weeds that created a layer of debris. Meanwhile, his father readied the basket full of fish and cleaned the blood from the caiman. The boat traversed underneath the dark trees, until it was concealed in the overgrown plants and foliage. The water was black with weeds and vines wrapping up around the outside of the tree trunks. The air was still, and a light fog floated above the waterline.

Soon they passed under a curtain of weeping willow trees. Tiny lights from the fireflies twinkled throughout the willow branches. Kaison turned the boat to the right and paddled in the direction of their home.

The two continued traveling through the Albufera. It grew darker as they pulled away from the Reflecting Grounds. Here the brush was even thicker, and the trees blended into one hopeless maze. The plants grew closer together, but the boat easily maneuvered between them. While Kaison paddled, Arthur used his staff to push the foliage out of the way so that they could pass.

The fog thickened, swirling upward to the sky like hot steam. It was no longer transparent, but a murky white. The lights from the insects were the only twinkles that cut through the darkness.

No one else was on the Albufera, but soon the faint vision of lanterns could be seen in the distance. Kaison rowed even faster, and his father hastily tore away the brush. Then they disappeared once more under a blanket of willow branches and emerged upon their hometown.

The town of Grovia was perched above the marsh on wooden posts. The docks and platforms surrounded a central marketplace. Above the marketplace, the platforms twisted upward in many layers, with many ladders connecting them. The residents lived above the docks and marketplace in treehouses. The homes were built into the canopy of large forest trees, with rickety bridges creating pathways between them.

Kaison spotted a familiar face waving from the dock.

It was his sister – Theadosia. She was leaning up against the railing at the dock where they were heading.

A dozen hunters were on the dock, already selling their catch after a day of hunting. At the end of the docks were larger hunting boats that could hold up to ten hunters. Their wooden oars were the length of willow branches, and the bows rose upward into the shape of weeping willows. These boats didn't travel to the Albufera but went toward the other side of the islands until they made it to the outskirts of Vorinder and the ocean. On all sides of these boats hung sagging nets full of ocean fish that wiggled as they flapped aimlessly on top of the others.

It was here that the marsh ended, and they found themselves on solid land.

Kaison pulled his boat up to one of the docks, and his father jumped out onto the pier. Arthur stopped the rowboat, letting it gently reach the wooden dock, before he grabbed a rope at the edge of the boat and tied it in place. Then Kaison threw Arthur both of their weapons. Finally, Kaison stood up, steadied himself, and grabbed the basket full of fish. He leapt up onto the dock to join his father, leaving the caiman in the boat.

"I'm going to go make a sale for the caiman," Arthur said before he walked toward a group of fishermen and merchants.

Theadosia was making her way over to Kaison. Her chestnut hair was pulled back into a bun, and her bangs fell across her plain, round face. She wore a long, cotton vest over her white tunic, with a leather belt wrapped around her waist. Her dark brown pants were tucked into high leather boots. Water dripped from the edge of her long vest, landing in little droplets next to Kaison. She left watery footprints on the dock as she approached.

Theadosia's arms were crossed, and her brows furrowed downward. She sank into her left hip and frowned as an exasperated sigh escaped her lips.

"You left without me," she said, pausing before adding, "again." Theadosia kept her arms crossed and used her head to gesture toward the boat.

"I know you wanted to come, but caimans are dangerous," Kaison said.

"No, they aren't," Theadosia corrected, "and now you've robbed me of another opportunity to try out my new blades."

"By plague, you're so dramatic." Kaison laughed.

"Well, I guess I have to go tomorrow with Lucas then?"

Kaison knew she was only saying that to get under his skin. He didn't let her. He brushed past her and walked away. In truth, he knew his sister, as well as everyone in Grovia, was perfectly equipped to handle themselves, but he didn't like the idea of his younger sister hunting with the boys in the village, let alone Lucas.

Footsteps clanked behind him, and his sister caught up to him.

Kaison flashed back to his earlier conversation with his father in the boat and added, "You never know what could happen. You can't control nature."

Theadosia crossed her arms, walking beside him. "Don't use father's words against me," she jeered. She knew the phrase like the back of her hand.

"I'm protecting you. Think if the giant caiman learned to climb trees and came into our house–"

Theadosia hit her brother on the shoulder. "I will push you off this dock." She pointed a finger in his face.

Kaison hoisted the basket up higher in his grasp. "I wouldn't want you to spill the fish."

Theadosia opened her mouth to speak, but she broke into a laugh. "I'll take the boat out myself tomorrow."

Then the two reached the edge of the dock and emerged into the marketplace. It was lively with chatter as everyone finished their purchases for the day. Kaison headed directly to the fish stand, the stench something he was used to by now. He set the basket down on the counter, waiting for the seller to finish with his last purchase. The seller seemed to be in a heated dispute with the hunter, which meant it may be a while.

Theadosia pushed aside another customer to stand directly next to Kaison. "So?" she inquired, tapping the satchel that hung from Kaison's waist. "What did you find?"

Kaison shot her a wide-eyed glare.

She frowned before letting out a huff. "You better show me later."

Kaison gave a curt nod as the merchant approached. He extended a ticket toward Kaison. "Where's your father?"

"Selling a caiman."

"A caiman?" The merchant's eyebrows raised. "How far were you out on the Albufera, son?"

Kaison didn't know how to answer that question without telling him they were at the Reflecting Grounds.

Theadosia cleared her throat loudly. "I'll take that," she said, reaching out and snatching the ticket from the merchant's hands. "Pleasure doing business with you."

"I'm the only one–"

"As I said, thanks," Theadosia cut him off. She grabbed her brother by the arm and pulled him away from the stand. Through the crowd, which was a sea of green and brown clothing, they saw their father approaching.

"Sold the caiman for forty-two willows," Arthur said.

Theadosia muttered something under her breath in the language of Mysticism.

Arthur inclined his head while he tried to hide a smile.

"What?" Kaison looked from his younger sister to his father.

Ignoring Kaison completely, Theadosia set off toward the center of the marketplace. "Let's go to dinner. Mom's waiting," she called over her shoulder. When she noticed her brother and her father hadn't followed her, she turned back around. "I can't help that you two decided to stay out late, and she had to do your job."

"She won't be happy," Kaison said under his breath.

Arthur shook his head. "Nope."

The family continued through the crowded marketplace. The wooden stands were pressed closely together and residents weaved between them. None of the tables had awnings or covers, for the tree leaves created enough shade for the merchants. Most of the stands held fish from the day's catch. The rest displayed baskets with herbal remedies, spices, and plants from the marsh. Each basket was a bright new color, more vibrant than the one before. All stands were marked with a flower from Vorinder to signify what each merchant was selling.

It was one of the best feelings to be in the marketplace. Kaison enjoyed returning from the day's catch and negotiating with the townsfolk. It was never overwhelming, but rather comforting to build relationships with his neighbors, even if it was over the sale of smelly, cold fish.

They reached the giant cypress tree in the middle of the crowd. The cypress soared the height of a large hill, with a trunk so thick it would take thirty men to wrap their arms around it. The tree supported a staircase that spiraled around the outside of the tree trunk and soared into the canopy.

They ascended the circular staircase that weaved around the cypress. Soon, they reached the upper level of the trees. They climbed one more spiral staircase until they were on the fourth platform in the air. From their vantage point, the people in the marketplace were like tiny insects.

Theadosia led the way over a wooden, rope bridge. It dipped under their weight and swung in the air as the trio crossed it. The only railing was a single rope on either side. When they reached the opposite side of the bridge, they found themselves on a circular platform that extended around another cypress tree. They walked around the tree until they came to a second rope bridge. Their own home was across the planks.

Finally, they reached their cypress tree and the treehouse that was perched in the large branches. Theadosia passed between the leaves that created a covering over the front door, and the three emerged into the kitchen. In one corner was their rustic, carved countertop, decorated with vegetables and fruit. Herbs hung from the ceiling. Adjacent to the kitchen was a circular table raised two feet off the ground with four pillows as seats.

Their mom was in the middle of the room bringing plates over to the table. "There you all are," Dianna said, her voice similar to that of Theadosia's. She had a round face and dark hair that was pulled back into a bun. She had a clear complexion and dark, tan skin like the rest of the family.

"What can I help with?" Kaison asked.

"Nothing now," Dianna said, eying her son. She was going back and forth from the hearth and placing clay dishes on the table. It was one of the family's favorites, and a popular meal in Vorinder – a baked corn cake filled with meat, vegetables, and hard-boiled eggs. She had also made a large stew filled with different kinds of seafood, that had been cooking for hours to blend the flavors. However, this was considered to be a dish from the mainland.

Arthur closed the curtain behind them. He hung his staff and Kaison's harpoon on a hook near the front door and went over to his wife, giving her a gentle kiss.

"Hi, honey." Dianna greeted him.

Arthur smiled. "Sorry, I'm late. How was work?"

"We will talk later." Dianna gave him a warm smile, but her gaze was set on their children.

Kaison placed his hands on his younger sister's shoulders. "Too bad we aren't having caiman for dinner."

Theadosia pushed her brother away. "Sod off," she said.

"Theadosia, language," Dianna scolded.

Theadosia shot her older brother a glare. Then she turned and ascended the stairs, pushing her older brother out of the way, so she could go up to her room. Once she had disappeared, Kaison made his way over to the table, helping to serve the rest of the food.

"And what happened to you?" Dianna looked Kaison up and down. He was still soaked from his dive in the marsh.

Arthur was the first to take a seat at the circular table, and Kaison and Dianna followed his lead.

Kaison removed the satchel from around his body, withdrawing the necklace he had found. He placed it on the center of the table for his mother to see.

After one glance at the necklace, Dianna gave her husband a disapproving look.

"How long are you going to keep this up?"

It was an argument they had had before. Arthur let out a deep breath before calling up the stairs, "Thea, it's time for dinner!"

Dianna returned her attention to Kaison. "There are *present* things that require attention," she said. "You should focus more on the government and politics of today rather than trying to uncover what happened centuries ago. Have you read the book I gave you yet?"

Kaison paused, wondering whether or not to lie. "I started it."

Dianna wasn't convinced. "Thea already finished the book."

"Good for her," Kaison responded. "I don't see the need to learn a new language, let alone a dying language."

"You should learn Mysticism," Arthur said.

"I could count on my hand how many people in Grovia speak Mysticism, and you three are over half of them," Kaison objected.

"It's more common on the mainland than you know."

Kaison was taken aback by his father's determination. "I…" Kaison searched for words. "Mysticism is only spoken in the Lost Lands. When will I ever go there?"

"It's not," Arthur said.

"Right," Kaison muttered, "You and Thea have your inside jokes in Mysticism."

"Kaison," Dianna scolded.

Kaison bit his tongue. His parents were only trying to help him. They only ever were.

Their conversation was interrupted by the sound of quick foot-steps. Theadosia scampered down the staircase and stopped at the bottom, staring wide-eyed at her family.

"There's something coming from the west bridge," she said, her breath short. "Fast."

Arthur jumped to his feet.

"Daddy caiman brought an army to find you?" Kaison laughed.

"You're an idiot," Theadosia snapped. "I'm serious."

Arthur stepped out onto the balcony at the front of their home. Kaison was right behind. They peered over the railing, down past four levels of treehouses, to the marketplace below. The townspeople were shouting in the direction of the far bridge on the edge of the marketplace. It stretched out over the marshland and to the adjacent islands. On the bridge were dozens of men on horseback, charging toward the center of Grovia. Their clothes and horses were black, and a dark mystical fog dripped off their bodies. The mist wrapped around the horses' hooves, making it appear as if they were gliding through the air on clouds. The thundering hooves shattered the peaceful aura of the marsh.

"By plague," Arthur said under his breath. He grabbed his son by the shoulders. "Inside, now." Arthur ushered Kaison inside, much to his objection.

Dianna rose from the table.

Arthur locked eyes with his wife. "They're here."

- 2 -

Kaison

The Shadows?" Kaison asked. He had heard stories of the Shadows that had been terrorizing villages on the mainland. He had never suspected they were true, and he never suspected they would come to a free republic.

A scream echoed through the dense marsh.

Immediately, Dianna pushed past Theadosia and raced upstairs. Arthur went for his staff, taking it off the wall. He then took Kaison's harpoon off the hook and threw it over to his son.

Kaison caught the harpoon in one hand. "Is it the Shadows?!" Kaison shouted.

Arthur's face was grim, and it was enough of an answer.

More screams erupted outside. People shouted from their balconies, and footsteps thundered across the bridge.

Theadosia scampered across the room and joined Arthur at the wall with their weapons. Below, sitting in a basket, were a variety of blades. She picked up a wristband with a hidden blade from the basket. Then she strapped the leather band around her wrist. The blade retracted and was concealed under the sleeve of her tunic. Then she strapped another blade onto her other wrist.

Theadosia threw two gloves over to Kaison. "Put these on."

Kaison obeyed, strapping on the fingerless gloves. Then he made sure his rope was correctly attached to the spring at the end of his harpoon.

Arthur's eyes fell on his children. The screams from outside continued to ring in the distance. "I should have told you sooner, but I didn't think they would find us." Arthur gripped his staff in his hands. He then pressed one of the gems at the base of the weapon, and it transformed.

The staff expanded, making Kaison jump back in alarm. An axe blade and spearhead extended from the top, transforming what used to be a staff into a golden halberd. Sparkles of golden dust fluttered from the blade. The three gemstones remained at the base of the long weapon.

It was stunning – almost as tall as Arthur himself. And Kaison knew he had witnessed magic for the first time.

Kaison's mouth was agape, and Theadosia was the first to curse, "By plague!"

Arthur's expression was apologetic. "Do you trust me?"

All Kaison could do was nod. He had a thousand questions at that moment.

"Whatever happens out there, keep running," Arthur ordered. Then he ran to the bottom of the stairs. "Dianna!" he called.

Kaison looked at his sister.

She started, "Did you–"

"No." Kaison shook his head. His father hadn't once transformed the staff into the halberd out on the Albufera. How had he never known about the magic?

Dianna returned with a satchel strapped across her body, a pack of arrows on her back, and a bow in her hand. She jumped over the last three stairs and landed on the treehouse floor.

A violent explosion shook the home. Kaison's stomach lurched as the platform below his feet shifted underneath his weight. The house trembled, making the family stumble to catch their bearings.

Theadosia's eyes were wide. "What was that?"

Another explosion sounded outside, followed by heightened screams.

"Let's go!" Arthur shouted, strapping the halberd onto his back.

Kaison was the first to burst out the front door and onto the balcony of their home. Havoc and devastation ravaged his hometown. The sight made his heart sink, and his whole body flushed with fear.

Far below, horses were galloping across the wooden piers throughout the marsh, trampling the townspeople. The Shadows set fire to the posts that held up the homes in the canopy. On the bridges below them, men in black armor were scaling the ladders, coming for the residents. On a perpendicular bridge to the one leading away from Kaison's house, villagers were gathering with their spears, sending them raining down on the intruders.

"Follow me!" Arthur called.

Arthur began running to the left, across the bridge to another platform. Kaison and Theadosia followed him, and Dianna took up the rear. Right before they reached the next platform, another explosion shook the marshland.

Kaison clutched onto the thin railing on the rope bridge and braced himself. A snapping noise rang through the canopy. On the family's left and a story below, a tree that served as the center point for two homes began to tip. Kaison watched the tree cascade to the ground, pulling down adjacent bridges with it. People clung onto the bridges until the supports snapped, and the villagers fell to the ground far below. Whoever was left in the homes had been crushed.

A fire ignited in the marketplace, sending smoke and ash into the canopy, causing Kaison to choke.

The bridge underneath Kaison began to crack. Terror shot through his entire body, and for a moment he wondered if he would survive the dash across the bridge. His head clouded, and his thoughts spun as fear consumed him. His father's voice rang loud and clear, breaking Kaison out of his stupor. His dad was yelling something up ahead.

Kaison started forward once more, chasing after his father and sister, knowing his mother was right on his trail. His legs moved mechanically, and his body took control over his mind. The next platform was only a few feet away. That's when he felt the bridge underneath him break. Behind him, the ropes connecting the bridge to his home had snapped.

Theadosia and Arthur were already on steady ground on the next platform. Kaison jumped out toward them, and he sprung away from the bridge as the planks shook underneath his feet. He landed on the platform next to his sister and father. He had barely made it to safety before the bridge he was on smashed aggressively into the tree in the center of the platform. The bridge was hanging by a thread.

"Dianna!" Arthur called, dropping to his stomach and reaching his hand down toward her.

The rope bridge hung aimlessly in the air. Dianna clung to the wooden planks with both of her palms, a few feet away from her husband's extended hand. Her bow fell, descending into the fiery pits below.

Dianna began pulling herself upward, but the rope snapped.

Kaison dropped his harpoon and flattened to the ground as quickly as he could. He grabbed one end of the rope, his father holding the other. The weight of the bridge caused the rope to slip from his grasp, burning the inside of his palms through the gloves.

Dianna gained the strength in her arms to continue climbing, but it was too late. A rain of arrows from the story below flew toward the family.

Kaison shielded his face with his forearms, releasing the rope. It didn't matter that he let go. Dianna was struck with an arrow through the side of her ribcage. Her tight grasp on the bridge released, and she fell.

Arthur, still holding onto the rope, screamed her name. Kaison watched as his mother plummeted, landing on the bridge below her. The intruders that had shot the arrows approached her with swords in hand.

A man stepped toward their mother, appearing to be the leader of the raiders. He walked inside of a black cloud. Smoke fanned out and away from his frame in the form of a cape, leaving a trail of darkness behind him. His shoulders were broad and his skin ghostly. He held a long sledgehammer, which was dripping with crimson blood. The weapon drew a splattered trail of red behind him. When the man reached Dianna's crumpled figure, he stopped dead in his tracks and widened his stance. He extended his weapon to her and fixated his grasp on the handle of the weapon. They wouldn't take any prisoners.

"No!" screamed Kaison.

The leader's head snapped in their direction, his eyes fixated on Arthur and Kaison.

Arthur yanked his son by the arm and pulled him up. "We have to move," he said.

Kaison grabbed his harpoon from the ground. They turned to run across the platform to the only other bridge leading them to safety.

Theadosia was leaning up against the trunk of the tree, holding her shoulder. An arrow was lodged into her flesh, causing oozing blood to leak from her skin. She was gasping, more from shock than from pain.

Arthur ran up to his daughter and cupped her face in his palms. "You're going to be alright," he said. "I need to get it out."

Theadosia gave her father a blank expression, unable to say anything. Her eyes were beginning to water.

Arthur placed one hand on her arm and wrapped the other around the arrow. Without giving a warning, he yanked the arrow from his daughter's shoulder, causing her to let out a yelp of agony.

"I'm sorry," Arthur said, letting the arrow fall to the ground. "We have to move."

Arthur picked his halberd up from the ground before leading his children to the other side of the platform. They had to cross one more bridge to reach the ladder leading down to the marketplace.

Theadosia grabbed her shoulder, attempting to stop the bleeding, and Kaison made sure that she kept up with their father's quick pace. But Arthur stopped dead in his tracks at the start of the next bridge.

On the platform at the opposite end of the bridge were men in black armor. They were scaling up the ladder. They were blocking their escape route!

Kaison ran over to the railing and peered down. There was a platform underneath them. It was on another tree a few paces away, but it was too far of a jump.

Kaison fixated on the tree at the center of the platform. He could use his harpoon.

Stepping back as far as he could, he gave a running start before launching his harpoon in the direction of the tree. As it flew through the air, the rope extended, slipping from Kaison's grasp. The speared end lodged into the center of the distant tree, and Kaison held the end of the rope with both hands.

"Thea, come on!" Kaison urged. He tied the end of the rope around the tree beside him, pulling it firmly to check the durability.

"That won't hold my weight," Theadosia objected.

Arthur clutched his halberd in both hands, facing the men who were starting across the bridge. "Thea, go!" he said.

Theadosia obeyed. Using her belt as a tool to zipline across, she leapt from the ledge. She soared through the burning air, whipping across the rope at a great speed to the platform on a lower level. She released her grasp seconds after she reached the platform, collapsing to the ground with a loud thud.

The men were halfway across the bridge now.

Kaison leapt into the air, barely clutching the rope. The rope burned through his gloved hands as he scaled down to the lower platform. He was almost across when the rope snapped. Kaison's heart lurched in his chest. He reached out for the platform as far as he could, the momentum taking him the last bit of the way. His ribcage slammed into the side of the platform with a hard thud, and he grasped onto the edge.

Theadosia grabbed her brother's hands to prevent him from falling. She struggled to yank him high enough so that he could hoist his body up the rest of the way.

Another explosion sounded, sending a waft of smoke into Kaison's face. The platform he was on started shaking. They had to go now.

Kaison struggled to his knees and looked back to his father. To his dismay, the intruders had nearly reached his father, and he had no escape. A colossal cloud of black smoke was traveling up the tree trunk. It trickled up the bark like a serpent and floated up onto the platform.

"Dad!" Kaison called, attempting to warn him.

Instead of bracing himself against the warriors, Arthur turned in Kaison's direction. "Catch!" he called before tossing the halberd with as much power as he could.

"Wait!" Kaison objected, unable to comprehend why his father wasn't going to defend himself. But the halberd was already flying through the air. Kaison had to twist his body in order to grab the staff and avoid the blade at the end. The weight of the weapon tipped him forward.

"The library at Sun Castle!" Arthur shouted.

Kaison was hardly able to hear him over the screaming. "What?"

The pillar of smoke was forming into a distinct shape. A man appeared out of the smoke, holding a sledgehammer.

"The library!" Arthur insisted.

Kaison and Theadosia stared in horror. Their father stood facing the man that had floated onto the platform like a ghost. But they weren't fighting – they were talking to one another.

Suddenly the man snapped his head toward Kaison. He extended his palm outward, latching onto the halberd with a telekinetic force.

The halberd started slipping from Kaison's grasp. "Thea!" he yelled for help. He used all his strength to close his fingers around the metal, but the monster's power was too strong. Kaison was being dragged toward the end of the platform.

Theadosia was at his side, and they both held the weapon together. They struggled to gain traction on the wood and continued nearing the edge.

Then the invisible force vanished and Theadosia and Kaison fell, tumbling on top of each other. The halberd clanked onto their laps.

Arthur had knocked the man with the sledgehammer backward. Immediately, the Shadows retaliated.

"Dad!" Theadosia screamed.

The sledgehammer rose through the smoke, and their father was taken out in one swift blow.

Kaison scrambled to his feet. A gut-wrenching feeling ate away at him as he watched his father's body fall off the side of the platform. He stood frozen for a long moment.

An arrow whizzed past the siblings, barely missing Kaison's ear. He turned around to see three of the residents from Grovia shooting arrows toward the man and the raiders on the platform above.

"Run!" Kaison yelled.

The whole village was quaking. There was no escape from the fire, and townspeople were jumping from their balconies, falling to their deaths. Ash rose all around them and below was a dark layer of smoke.

Kaison picked up the halberd in one hand. It was much heavier than the harpoon he was used to. Then he grabbed Theadosia's wrist and pulled her away from the platform edge. "We have to go!" Kaison shouted.

The siblings reached the rope ladder and started making their descent. Theadosia went first, heading down into the smokey marketplace.

Theadosia landed with an ungraceful thud on the piers, and afterward, Kaison landed beside her. All around them was a frenzy of people, and the Shadow charged down the center of the marketplace on stallions, tearing down the burning structures.

Kaison tore off through the remnants of their town. There was a sharp ringing in his ears. A nauseating feeling ate away at his core. He couldn't tell if his vision was blurry or if there was too much smoke. He staggered forward into the ashes, stumbling in one direction. The world spun aimlessly around him. The loud ringing pierced his temples, growing stronger.

"Look out!" Theadosia screamed.

Theadosia grabbed her brother by his shirt and pulled him back, and an enormous cypress collapsed in front of him, smashing through the planks and sinking into the swamp. Their pathway was cut off. On either side of them, the fire was blazing, consuming the posts that held up their town.

The siblings turned around to run in a different direction, but they were faced by a man in dark armor. A masked helmet covered his face, and he held a long sword in preparation to slice them in two.

Kaison prepared his father's halberd, bracing himself, and stepping between the man and his sister. Hardly another moment passed before the man charged.

Kaison blocked the oncoming slash, stumbling backward from the man's aggressive blow. He clutched the halberd with both hands, preparing for another attack, when he heard a large snap from above. A flaming branch and rope bridge were falling down. Kaison tried to dodge, but he wasn't fast enough. A burning plank raked down the front of his chest, and he let out a yell of agony.

The branch smashed against the back of the Shadows's helmet, and he stumbled forward. Theadosia lunged and drove her hidden blade into his neck.

Kaison watched as the Shadow collapsed to his knees and started to disappear. His armor and his flesh dissipated into thin air, mixing with the black smoke from the fires around them, and eventually vanishing altogether.

The smoke was beginning to close Kaison's airway. He searched for another escape, but the thick fog masked his vision. Planks and branches were still falling from above. Children were running one way, animals were scampering around the town square, and he could hear horses somewhere in the distance.

"This way," Theadosia said behind him.

She was facing the cypress that had blocked their path earlier. Without waiting for Kaison's response, she jumped down on the bark, sliding across it, before leaping the rest of the way into the marsh.

Kaison followed his sister's lead. He held the halberd in two hands and dropped to the bark of the cypress a few feet down. He skidded down the wood before jumping into the swamp.

Once on the ground, his heavy boots were pulled down deep into the mud. The water reached his knees and splashed against his body. He tried his best to keep the halberd out of the water so that it wouldn't sink and be buried in the mud below. He wasn't going to lose his last memory of his father.

At that moment, a loud screech alerted them. Two golden mares were tied to a cypress tree, frantically crying. Their reins had tangled and snagged on a branch, making them unable to run. They were splashing in the swamp, trying to free themselves and escape from the burning village.

Kaison raced over to the horses, trying to calm them. "It's all right!" he shouted over the snapping branches and loud screams.

Kaison untangled the horses' reins but made sure to hold them firmly.

"Get on!" Kaison shouted.

Theadosia pushed her way through the swamp and reached the horses' side. She launched herself up onto the back of one horse while Kaison hoisted himself on the other one.

They tore off as fast as they could through the swamp, escaping the chaos and leaving the lives that cascaded down from the canopies.

- 3 -

Kaison

The siblings remained in silence while they rode away from Grovia. They were lost somewhere in the swamp, riding through the tangled trees and marsh that provided cover all around them. Kaison had never been alone in the Albufera after nightfall. He had always hunted with his father. Usually, this place was a peaceful sanctuary that provided him some comfort, but today, for the first time, the landscape made his chest tighten and his hands shake. Tension built in his neck and shoulders, for he remained on high alert in case any more raiders lurked in the shadows. He continued to grip the halberd, ensuring it wouldn't fall into the water. Each step he took only confirmed his parents' absence.

The moon was directly overhead when he and his sister finally decided to slow their pace. They reached a bank and stopped to get out of the shallow water. Kaison dismounted first, landing roughly in the tall grass and setting down the halberd. After Theadosia dismounted, she clutched her shoulder from where the arrow had pierced her earlier. Then she collapsed to the ground, holding her face in her hands.

Kaison took the reins and tied them to a nearby branch. Then he sat on the ground beside her. The wet earth soaked right through his clothing, causing a chill to run up his spine. He placed his hands into the dirt and clenched as hard as he could into fists. He still couldn't breathe after witnessing the attack. Everything flashed before his eyes once more. It was as if he could still hear the screaming. His clothing reeked of smoke, and a dusting of ash ran down his arms.

Theadosia sniffled beside him. She was staring off into the marsh, but she wasn't crying.

They must have run far, to the outskirts of the island of Grovia. The docks with ships to the mainland had to be close by. Maybe there were people there. However, if they went to the mainland, they would be foreigners in another kingdom. There was nowhere for them to go. The other option would be wandering the dangerous marsh until they stumbled upon another Vorinder village.

"The library…" Theadosia breathed beside him.

"What?" asked Kaison.

"The library at Sun Castle. Those were father's last words to us. He wants us to go there."

Kaison tried to disregard the sickening feeling of grief that ate away at his core. "Sun Castle is across the channel…days away," he said. "We've never even been to Solaris."

Kaison's eyes fell on Theodosia's shoulder. She was still bleeding. "How does it feel?" he asked.

Theadosia pulled back the loose fabric, still wet with a crimson coating. She winced. "It hurts," she said.

Kaison scooted closer to her. "By plague," he said under his breath, grimacing at the sight.

He would have to take care of it to prevent infection, but there was hardly anything he could do with no resources. Kaison took off his thin shirt, feeling the cool night air against his chest, before wrapping it around his sister's arm.

Theadosia squirmed as the pain rippled down to her hand. "What are we going to do?" She brushed her bangs out of her eyes, and said, flustered, "We should try to find a nearby town, or they're going to come after us too."

"I don't know where we are."

"Neither do I."

Kaison finished the makeshift bandage and brought his hands down to his lap. "There."

Theadosia examined her arm judgingly before her eyes scanned Kaison's bare chest.

"By plague…" she let out.

On Kaison's chest was a deep burn mark running from his left pec all the way down to his abdomen.

"I'll be fine," he replied, ignoring the pain.

Kaison fixated on the tree line, knowing the Albufera was dangerous at night. The moon had shifted, and now it was hard to see more than a few feet in front of them. They had to make a new plan. They had no idea what villages were safe in Vorinder, or on Morbaeda. If the Shadows had attacked Grovia, they could attack any village. They had to get somewhere where there was enough security to ensure that no one would target them again.

"Why did father toss us his halberd instead of using it to fight off those warriors?" Theadosia interrupted his thoughts.

"He saw my harpoon fall," Kaison said. "I'm sure he wanted us to have the weapon."

Theadosia looked unconvinced. She gestured toward it, lying on the wet earth beside them. "Let me see."

Kaison obeyed his sister and handed the halberd to her. The shaft was black with gold decal running down it. Both the axeblade and the spearhead were a myriad of gold hues, getting darker toward the tip of the blades. The handle at the base of the staff was also gold. On the shaft were three beautiful jewels in sparkling colors: red, green, and purple. It was a beautiful weapon. But that evil man – that smoke thing – somehow knew Kaison's father and had tried to take the halberd from them. That must have been why they attacked.

"The library at Sun Castle," Kaison spoke aloud before taking the halberd back from his sister.

Theadosia's eyes widened, but she was looking past Kaison. Something had caught her attention. She rose to her feet.

"Kaison…" she said.

Kaison followed her gaze. The trees were moving, separating to show an overgrown willow tree. The leaves of the willow tree twinkled in the moonlight, illuminating a white light across the marsh. The halberd in Kaison's hand began to glow simultaneously, and Kaison could feel a slight pull toward the tree.

The willow tree's branches continued to expand, floating elegantly out toward Kaison and Theadosia. Then the branches dropped downward, grazing the water's surface. The tree grew upward and outward until it reached higher than any of the other foliage in the Albufera. As it grew, the white light only became brighter until Kaison and Theadosia were forced to look away.

Kaison used his forearm to shield his face. He called to Theadosia, "Are you seeing that? Am I losing my mind?"

"I see it," Theadosia said under her breath. She was quick to jump up and untie the reins from her horse. "Come on!" Without waiting another moment, she pulled one of the horses toward the magical willow tree.

"Wait!" Kaison called, grabbing the other horse and untying the reins before running after her.

Theadosia disappeared under the long branches of the willow tree.

Kaison squinted in the bright light as he pushed aside the branches, walking underneath the tree. He sloshed around the marsh, for a moment feeling lost in a white abyss as he moved the branches out of the way. He clutched the halberd strongly in one hand and the reins of his horse in the other.

He put his arm out in front of him to try and brace himself. He couldn't see anything. He moved slowly, careful not to hurt his sister or the horse with the halberd's exposed blade, but they had vanished in the white void.

Something caught his foot, and he tripped forward. His heart clenched as he steadied the halberd. Looking down, he noticed that the marsh had ended, and he was now on solid ground. Kaison pushed away the last branch and emerged from underneath the tree. It took a few moments for his eyes to adjust, and he took in the new landscape.

Kaison and Theadosia were on a moorland that stretched on for twice the length of the Reflecting Grounds. A magnificent castle towered in the center of the moor. It was constructed with tan and earth-colored stones, with tiny lights all spaced perfectly across the bricks, making it seem like the castle blended into the starry sky. At the front was a drawbridge passing underneath a brick arch. On the second level of the castle was a balcony that stretched all around, with openings in the rocks to allow for knights to send their arrows flying down on the moor. In the center of the structure, a single tower rose in the shape of a triangular spire. It shone brightly above all of the other structures, and another light beamed from the window, acting as a beacon. Around the edge of the spire was another balcony – the highest point in the valley.

A town sat at the base of the castle, outside the gates.

Kaison had never seen a place with such an open and clear sky. Stars glimmered above them, and the moon shone brightly on the grass on the moor. They were no longer in Vorinder.

"Is that..." Theadosia started, "Sun Castle?"

Kaison couldn't find the words to express his emotions. He was too bewildered. There was no way they had been transported from Vorinder to the Kingdom of Solaris. Usually, it would take a week-long journey to the main island, a ship-ride across the channel, and another long trek to Sun Castle. He turned around, anticipating to see the glowing willow tree, but there was nothing behind him but dark forest.

Finally, Kaison found his voice. "The fact that we're here is impossible," he said.

The halberd radiated in Kaison's palm, illuminating the area around them. It seemed to get dimmer as he held it. His fingers grazed across the gemstones. They were losing their vibrant colors as the magic retreated.

The red jewel shifted under his touch. Curiously, Kaison examined the scarlet gem. He noticed that it was looser than the others. Kaison pressed down onto the jewel, and the red gem contracted until he heard a click. The blades began contracting into the staff.

"Thea, look!" He urged her to see the magic transpiring before them.

The halberd's blade contracted completely, and the staff itself began shrinking. It shrunk until it was no longer a halberd, rather a short staff the length of a sword. It was still beautifully decorated in ornate gold, with the three dazzling green, purple, and red gemstones. Kaison held it firmly, staring in awe.

It was back to normal – the staff he had known his father to carry with him everywhere.

"The halberd is magical," Theadosia said. "How else can you explain it?"

Kaison latched the transformed halberd to his belt in the place of a normal sword. "Why didn't father tell us sooner?"

Theadosia gestured to the castle before them. "Father told us to go to the library at Sun Castle. We'll find answers there."

Kaison couldn't wrap his mind around the idea. It would be dangerous to enter a foreign castle and snoop around their library. They knew nothing about Sun Castle, except the fact that their own kingdom Vorinder used to be a part of Solaris territory before seceding two decades ago. The knights at Sun Castle wouldn't be too happy to see seceders at their gates asking for help.

"Alright. We have no choice. Especially if father's halberd brought us here. We have to honor him and go. We have to try to get inside," Kaison finished.

His sister nodded.

The two mounted their horses, and with a snap of the reins, they raced across the moorland to the castle. Once they started riding, they realized how far away the castle was and how big it must have been to have been seen from such a far distance. Every stride they took, the castle grew larger on the horizon. Its massive reach spanned the center of the moor, and its windows acted as a lighthouse for those traveling by.

As the two continued riding, the town on the outside of the castle walls came into view. It was a small town with sand-colored, square homes that sat upon large stone foundations. The bottom half of the two-story homes had a rock exterior, and the top was built from light wood. The houses were pressed together in clean, neat rows. At the center of the town was a belltower, rising into the night sky.

The siblings made their way forward toward the town on horseback. When they reached the edge of the houses, they slid down from their horses and continued on foot.

The streets were clean and colorless. Not many people were outside at night, but those that were stood outside their doorways drinking and singing. A raised stage nearby had a jester, entertaining a large crowd.

Unlike Grovia, the paths they walked on were pressed with perfect, tan stones. All of the houses were symmetrical, with two tiny windows on either side of a brown door. Pink and gold decorations hung across the windows and were strewn out across the paths, providing a cheerful passageway to the front of the homes. Between each of the houses were rows of flowers. Above them hung banners with the image of a pink laurel and flame. Elements of pink provided the only splash of color in the area.

Kaison didn't take much longer looking around the town. Instead, he stopped the man beside him who was heading toward the jester's stage. "Do you know where the inn is?" Kaison asked.

The man examined Kaison but didn't comment on his appearance. "First building on the right around the corner." He pointed before letting out an obnoxious hiccup.

"Thanks," Kaison replied.

Kaison and his sister continued toward the inn. They maneuvered through the partiers and late-night stragglers making their way back to their houses. The people seemed easy-going, laughing loudly and screaming at their friends in the street. They were dressed in muted jewel tones, but Kaison noticed that not a single person was wearing green, the signature color of Vorinder. Also, the women wore dresses instead of the long tunics and trousers like Theadosia wore.

Soon they rounded the corner and saw that the inn had an area dedicated for the horses. Kaison and Theadosia tied up their horses before continuing to the door.

The inside of the inn made it feel more spacious than it appeared. At the center of the room was a desk with a boy sitting at it. On either side of the desk were staircases, leading up to the second floor. Behind a large railing on the second floor Kaison could see many doors and a singular hallway leading deeper into the inn. Behind the desk was an archway that led into a dining hall. It was loud with chatter and cheering.

The boy looked up from his book when he noticed the siblings enter. His blonde hair fell past his shoulders, and he had chocolate eyes that twinkled against his tan skin. Closing the book, he stood from his chair. He was maybe eight years of age, give or take.

"Hello," he said, his voice chipper.

"Hi," Kaison responded.

The boy's eyes flicked rapidly from Kaison's burn mark across his bare chest to Theadosia's bloody bandage on her shoulder.

"We're looking–"

"Are you all right?" the boy asked.

Kaison ran his hand through his hair and sighed. "We will be," he said, forcing a smile on his face for the child. "Is there someone in charge of the inn?"

"My mother," the boy said, clasping his hands behind his back.

"Where is she?" Theadosia asked.

"In her room." The boy shifted back and forth from the balls of his feet to his heels. Then he froze. "Oh! You want me to go get her? I can do that." The boy swirled around and started for the door at the bottom of the staircase. He entered without knocking, leaving the door partially open as he disappeared inside.

"After we get a room, we should find something to take care of that wound," Kaison said.

Theadosia's eyes showed lingering pain, but she didn't answer.

The boy entered the room as quickly as he had exited. Behind him, a woman appeared. Her apron was smudged with food and dark circles sagged underneath her eyes.

"I apologize for Erik. I wasn't expecting anyone," the woman said as she came up to the desk.

The boy's face turned a bright shade of red.

"I'm Madame Winters." The woman added a smile.

"I'm Kaison," he introduced himself, "and this is my sister Theadosia."

"Welcome to Tamir," Madame Winters said. She went over to the desk and flipped open a large, leather-bound book.

Erik took a step forward. "What can I do mom?" He twirled his thumbs as he spoke.

"Not right now, Erik," she said. "Did you make a reservation?" the woman asked Theadosia and Kaison.

"Um…no," Kaison replied.

She glanced up from the notebook with raised eyebrows. "Well, with the Harvest Banquet we simply don't have any more rooms available. Where did you come from?"

"Grovia," Theadosia answered

"All the way from the Republic of Vorinder?" she asked, startled. Only then did Madame Winters see the bloodied shirt wrapped around Theadosia's shoulder. "Do you need a doctor?"

"We need a place to stay," Theadosia replied.

"I'm sure we can find something," Madame Winters said. "Come in." She motioned to the doorway underneath the staircase. "Erik, take their weapons to the weapon rack."

Erik walked forward, prepared to take the staff from Kaison's belt, but he stopped short. "What is that? That's not a sword."

"Oh, it was a gift given to me by my father," Kaison said, attempting to be as polite as possible.

The woman studied Kaison with a blank expression. "A gift?" She stole another glance at the staff at Kaison's side. Kaison was sure that she could see the three gemstones glittering from the transformed halberd. It would be worth a fortune here.

Her sharp stare made Kaison uncomfortable. He cleared his throat, searching for words.

"On second thought," the woman said, "I don't think I'm able to help you, but the infirmary at the castle should be able to take a look at your wounds."

"The castle?" Theadosia was taken aback. "We need a place to stay tonight."

"You can try to go to Elistalia," said Madame Winters with a shrug. "It's for people like you."

Kaison and Theadosia exchanged glances.

Madame Winters continued, "It's a place for those who've had their homes destroyed. Go to the castle. Ask for Dux Nikodemus, and tell him I sent you. He can decide if you will be admitted to Elistalia, and the castle infirmary can also tend to your wounds."

Dux Nikodemus? Kaison was familiar with that name. Nikodemus was head knight of Solaris. The siblings had learned about him in school back in Grovia.

Kaison tried to decipher the quick change in the woman's intentions. One moment she wanted to help them and the next she was sending them to the castle. Her demeanor had changed when she had seen the transformed halberd. Did she know it was magical? She at least knew it was valuable. However, if it were true that the castle would take them in, they were one step closer to the library.

But how did she know their village had been destroyed?

"Erik, show them the way," Madame Winters ordered.

Erik nodded, obeying. "Follow me," he said, walking around Theadosia and heading out the front door.

"Thank you for your time," Theadosia said to the woman behind the desk.

Her eyes were intent on Kaison. As the siblings were leaving, she added, "Welcome to your new home."

- 4 -

Kaison

Erik led Kaison and Theadosia in the direction of the castle, speaking the entire time they walked. Erik was asking many questions of the siblings and would move onto the next question without even waiting for an answer. Then he told them about the castle and the surrounding mystical forest. He also relayed his excitement for the upcoming Harvest Banquet. Kaison had heard of the banquet before – a holiday in Solaris that celebrated the best harvests around the kingdom.

All of Erik's chatter became a blur to Kaison. He only grew more apprehensive as they approached the castle, wondering what they would find inside. The knights wouldn't be pleased to see citizens from Vorinder. He wasn't sure if they would be safe here or if they would be allowed to stay as Madame Winters had suggested. It didn't seem plausible that Sun Castle would open its doors to strangers. But they had to find a place to stay for the night.

Also, Kaison's secondary mission was at the forefront of his mind. He was determined to find out why the library at Sun Castle was so important. Why would his father choose those words as his last?

The siblings guided their horses as they followed Erik. Erik and his mother seemed genuine in their offer to take them to the castle, but Kaison remained suspicious.

As they approached the castle, the tallest tower above grew bigger. Even though Sun Castle had many smaller towers, there was one that stretched up like a golden spire, far larger than the rest. The lights on the outside of the castle glowed bright up close, and the brick walls were illuminated with torches. All of the lights that dotted the outside of the walls began melding into one huge beam. Kaison couldn't keep his eyes off the mesmerizing structure. He had never seen a building stretch higher than cypress trees.

"What are you looking at?" Erik bobbed up and down as he walked.

"The tower," Kaison replied. "I've never seen anything like it."

"That's Sun Spire!" Erik exclaimed.

"What is that?" asked Theadosia. She was gently leading her horse along beside her.

"Only the highest point in the kingdom. They say you can see the entire world from the top."

The three rounded the corner. At the end of the road was an iron gate blocking the entrance to the castle. The gate had horizontal and vertical beams crossing over one another, creating small squares that revealed an inner courtyard. Erik came to a stop and gestured to the gate in the distance.

"That's the entrance to the castle grounds," he said.

"Thank you so much, Erik." Theadosia smiled warmly.

"I hope to see you both soon!" Erik added before swirling

around and heading back to his home. Before disappearing around a corner, he turned around and waved to the horses.

Kaison took a deep breath before pulling his horse forward toward the gate. He didn't have to share his apprehension with Theadosia, for he could sense her nervous energy beside him. As they approached the sandy tunnel that led to the gate, a rush of cool air tore past them. The cool breeze stung the burn mark running across Kaison's chest.

A whistle sounded, and Kaison looked to the top of the gates, seeing guardsmen in the watchtowers. No doubt they were notifying the watchmen at the gate of the strangers' approach.

Momentarily, they stood at the entrance to the castle grounds. Kaison gawked at the central spire that stretched to the heavens. He realized that Solaris's citizens must be able to see the spire from wherever they lived. Solaris was much bigger than Vorinder, but with all of the lights, the citizens would always have something to guide them home.

"Who's there?"

A deep voice startled Kaison. On the other side of the bars, a tall, silver-haired man appeared from out of the night. His eyes were bottomless, and his skin was pale. His hair was slicked back perfectly into a long, ponytail. A scar ran down the left side of his face. Consequently, his left eye was disfigured and grey. He wore metal armor with a pink crest on his chest, and a sword hung from his belt. It was so long that it touched the grass.

"Answer me, child," the man ordered.

Kaison cleared his throat. "My name is Kaison," he started, realizing that his mouth had dropped open, "and this is my sister, Theadosia."

"Do you have business with Sun Castle?" the knight demanded.

"If not, then get out of the street."

The knight's face was partially hidden in the shadows, but even so, Kaison could sense his harsh scowl. However, Kaison didn't blame him for the judgmental glare. Kaison was shirtless and covered in ashes, and Theadosia had a bloody shirt wrapped around her arm.

"We were sent here to find Dux Nikodemus," said Kaison. "We were told there's an infirmary inside the castle, and my sister needs medical treatment."

The knight scoffed. "Find medical assistance elsewhere."

"Please, our village was destroyed," said Theadosia.

"Our intelligence hasn't reported a village attack for days," the knight replied.

Kaison exchanged a glance with his sister out of the corner of his eye. Should he reveal that they weren't from Solaris?

The knight continued, "Go find somewhere else to beg."

"Emmett!" A voice sounded from the gardens in the courtyard.

The tall, silver-haired man turned around to see another knight emerge out of the darkness.

"Yes, Dux Nikodemus?" Emmett groaned.

"Let them go to the infirmary," Nikodemus said. "Tomorrow they can be taken to Elistalia."

Emmett remained in the same position.

Nikodemus reached Emmett's side. He had a combed, white beard and silver hair, contrasting his dark skin, but he didn't look a year older than forty-five. He was shorter than Emmett, but didn't slouch, making him appear larger than his counterpart. His metal chest plate also bore the pink crest. Upon closer inspection, Kaison could see that the crest was a semi-circular laurel with a flame inside. It was the same one that was spread across the village.

"You must forgive him," the head knight said. "I'm Dux Nikodemus." His hands moved when he spoke, floating elegantly while a new gesture accompanied each word.

"I'm Theadosia, and this is my brother, Kaison."

"It's an honor," Kaison stammered, bowing his head in respect. "Madame Winters said you could help us."

"Madame Winters?" Nikodemus questioned. He maintained a pensive expression on his face for a moment. "Certainly. Emmett, open the gate."

There was an elongated pause before Emmett let in and crossed to the pulley system. He shouted out instructions to other knights standing at the watchtower on top of the gate.

"What happened to you both?" Nikodemus asked.

Kaison's mind spun. "Our village was attacked. We're from Grovia. In the Republic of Vorinder."

Nikodemus's face twisted in distress, and his eyes shied away from the two. "They've made it to Vorinder," he said under his breath.

Emmett returned to Nikodemus's side as the iron bars rose upward.

"You have to send knights there to see if there are any other survivors," pleaded Theadosia.

"Vorinder is not our responsibility," Emmett said in annoyance.

Nikodemus's face softened. "We will send a messenger to your leadership, but I'm sure they've already been notified about this atrocity. Kaison, you can stay in the West Wing while we take Theodosia to the infirmary. In the morning, you can go to Elistalia together."

Emmett scoffed.

"What's Elistalia?" asked Theadosia.

"A place for all the vagabonds we take in from the streets," said Emmett.

Nikodemus's jaw shifted, but he disregarded Emmett's statement. Then he said, "It's a place of refuge for all the people that have had their homes destroyed."

Once the gate had opened, Kaison and Theadosia led both of their horses inside.

Inside the gates, night had suddenly turned to day. The torches illuminated the sandy brick walls, casting a glow on the interior garden. Before them was an open space of flat land – the size of a jousting field. Wide paths cut through the grass, dividing the green space into perfectly square plots of earth. On these plots were bright, pink flowers arranged in a circular pattern. In the center of the circles were fountains that sprayed water higher than the knights. The walls boxing in the plots of flowers were detailed with white marble and gold-leaf decal. The lanterns around the garden were all covered with different fabrics, making each square plot of flowers and water glow a different color. The colors delineated a striped pattern on the flat moorland garden. More gold-leaf detailing was twisted into the shape of the laurels and created a border on the wall that surrounded the entire area.

The center path cut straight through the garden and led over a cobblestone bridge up ahead. Then it ended at the front doors of the castle, which was still a jousting field away.

"What are their names?" Nikodemus motioned to the horses.

Kaison snapped out of his trance to see Nikodemus petting Theadosia's horse on the muzzle. Meanwhile, Emmett was ordering the guards to close the gate behind them.

"Sapphire," Theadosia answered. "And that one's Alice." She had made the names up on the spot, and Kaison didn't argue.

Nikodemus addressed them both. "I'll take them into the stables for you. They're east of the gardens," he explained. "You'll find them there in the morning."

"Thank you," Kaison replied.

"Your weapons." Nikodemus gestured to the staff at Kaison's belt.

Kaison froze. "This isn't a weapon."

Nikodemus tilted his head. "We consider it as a weapon."

"But this is my father's," Kaison protested.

"I won't lose it."

"You can't have it!" Theadosia took a step closer to the knight.

Kaison grabbed his sister's wrist and pulled her back. "It's alright, Thea," he said. They had to get into the castle. They had to find out why their father's dying words were to find the library in Sun Castle. They were desperate for a place to spend the night, and this was the only way. Also, they couldn't alert the knights that there was anything particularly special about the staff.

Kaison unlatched the staff from his belt and handed it over to Dux Nikodemus. Nikodemus grasped it in both hands, examining the craftsmanship. He ran a finger down the three gemstones. He was silent for a moment before looking up at the siblings.

"I will take good care of this," Dux Nikodemus stated.

"Should I search them further?" asked Emmett.

Kaison knew that Theadosia was still wearing the hidden blades underneath her sleeves. If the knights found them, it would instantly arouse suspicion.

"No need," answered Nikodemus. "I'll see you both in the morning."

Then the head knight grabbed the horses by the reins and led them through the winding gardens. He held their father's transformed halberd in his other hand. Before long, he was out of sight, taking the magical halberd with him.

Theadosia's brow furrowed as she mouthed, *"What did you do?"*

"Don't worry," Kaison whispered, but he was mainly trying to reassure himself.

"At least I have some protection," muttered Theadosia, referencing the hidden blades tied to each of her wrists.

Emmett double-checked the lock on the gate before turning back to the two siblings. "Follow me," he spoke deeply and started off toward the castle doors.

They walked straight ahead on the torch-lit, cobblestone path and noted that the grounds wrapped around the sides of the castle. The territory of the castle spanned the length of dozens of jousting fields, and the foliage masked the practice areas, stables, and armory.

The trio made their way across the vast gardens and arrived at the main entrance to Sun Castle. The double doors rose two stories high, and four knights were positioned outside. Emmett nodded at each one of them in turn, and the knights opened the doors for them, revealing the grand entranceway.

The grand hall, positioned on the south end of the castle, was a circular room with a high ceiling supported by four marble columns. Before them, was a staircase leading upward. A chandelier hung from the ceiling with teardrop-like crystals. A stained-glass window covered each of the four ends of the circular room. The ceiling created a dome, and the image of an azure night sky and a sun was painted above. On the ground of the grand hall was a mosaic. There were many different tiles placed perfectly throughout the floor to create a map. Green tiles formed the moorland, while tan tiles depicted Sun Castle. All around the artistic valley were tiny houses, representing villages. The land stretched beyond the valley and mountains, and around the edges was a large body of water, making Solaris seem like a single island in Morbaeda. Vorinder was nowhere to be seen.

Emmett stopped someone on their way across the grand hall.

"Cheyenne," Emmett said, "can you take this girl back with you to the infirmary?"

The girl had olive skin and black hair that fell in subtle, earthy waves. Bright, turquoise eyes flashed against thickly, penciled eyebrows and full lips on a pear-shaped face. Her make-up was exaggerated...at least, more exaggerated than Kaison was used to. She was young, around Theadosia's age, but wore a plain dress and apron.

Cheyenne examined the appearance of each one of the siblings in turn. "Of course," she eventually replied. Cheyenne turned on her heel and retreated down a corridor. Theadosia was quick to follow, and Kaison started behind them.

Emmett held out an iron hand to stop Kaison. "Not you."

"Why not?" Kaison asked.

"Ladies only."

"I'm not leaving my sister," he said.

"I'm fine," Theadosia assured her brother.

Kaison was hesitant, but eventually let in. The friendly nurse seemed like she would take care of Theadosia. Besides, Theadosia was quick with her blades.

Emmett called out to Cheyenne. "Bring her back in the morning. The queen will see them."

His words were jarring. The queen? Why would Emmett take two lost teenagers to see the queen? Surely, they weren't important enough to gain an audience with Queen Benedict. Her ascent to the throne was the reason that Vorinder had seceded from Solaris. Kaison suddenly regretted revealing where they had come from.

Kaison kept his attention on Cheyenne and Theadosia as the girls walked down a hallway. Cheyenne hadn't turned back or acknowledged Emmett's request. Soon, they disappeared around the corner and were out of sight.

"Come, child," Emmett said before starting up the grand flight of stairs. Kaison was forced to follow.

They walked quietly, passing doors and turning around corners. It was impossible to keep track of exactly where Emmett was taking Kaison.

Finally, Kaison and Emmett ascended another flight of stairs, and the hallway ended. They stood in an open space that served as a seating area. There were six couches and tables set up in smaller, distinct pods. A few boys were seated together and others walked around in the room. When Kaison and Emmett approached, everyone fell silent. Each one of the boys turned in Kaison's direction, their burning gaze falling on the newcomer. Feeling exposed, he covered his bare, ash-covered chest in embarrassment. After a long pause, the silence ended and was followed by whispers.

Emmett approached two boys on a nearby couch.

"This boy is going to stay in your room," Emmett announced, his statement directed at one of the two. "You still have an open bed?"

The boy Emmett had gestured to was stocky with broad shoulders that appeared much wider than his waist. His arms were large and muscular, and even though he was sitting, Kaison could tell that he was much shorter than the other knights he had seen in the castle. His black hair curled around his brows, and his smile created sharp dimples on his dark skin.

He didn't move or straighten when they entered the room. Instead, he relaxed back into the couch, his one leg crossed over the other. "Yeah," he said.

"Good," Emmett said.

The knight turned to Kaison and gave him one last look. His eyes were narrow, as though his mind was deep in thought. The disfigurement of his face sent a chill down Kaison's spine.

"Don't get too comfortable," Emmett said.

Kaison didn't know if Emmett's words were a threat. He didn't feel the need to respond. If it was up to Emmett, Kaison would still be out on the streets.

With that, Emmett left.

Swallowing the lump in his throat, Kaison gave the two boys on the couches an awkward smile. "I'm Kaison," he said.

"Louie Netherand," the stocky one who Kaison would be spending the night with answered. Louie gestured to his friend on the couch adjacent to him, expecting him to introduce himself.

The second boy's lips curled into an alluring smile, and indiscernible thoughts swirled behind his turquoise eyes. He tilted his head to the side and let out a long breath, parting his mouth to reveal perfect, white teeth. The stubble of his facial hair created a slight shadow on his face. His shirt was halfway unbuttoned, revealing his bare chest and flawless olive skin.

The boy spread both of his arms out along the back of the couch and expanded his presence. His deep voice let out a sneer. "This is why I have my own room," he said, one side of his mouth twisting slyly. "I don't have to accommodate swine."

Kaison blinked, and his head jerked backward in surprise.

"Great Sun, sod off," Louie groaned. He rose from the couch and approached Kaison. He was forced to look up at Kaison for he only reached his shoulders. "I can show you to my room."

Louie's friend stood next. He sauntered toward the other two, flexing his muscles in a surprisingly casual way. His facial expression emphasized his sharp jawline. "You're not going to tell us your story?" he asked.

Kaison stood still. "No. I don't answer to swine either," he stated.

The boy's eyes narrowed to slits.

"By plague," Louie laughed. "I like you, Kaison."

The boy glared at Louie before his sharp gaze returned to Kaison. "Watch yourself." Then he turned and headed to his room, disappearing down a corridor.

Louie shook his head. "That's the great Julian Xy'tier."

"*The great?*" Kaison asked.

Louie patted Kaison on the shoulder. "Everything I say is sarcastic, my friend," he said before walking away.

Louie led Kaison through a doorway and into a dark hallway. They both headed down the corridor before entering Louie's room.

Inside were two beds along with two tables and matching dressers. A trunk was at the bottom of one bed with clothing spilling out of it.

"That bed's mine," Louie said, pointing to the one in the center of the room.

Kaison followed him inside and shut the door behind them. Seeing the other bed in the corner made Kaison realize how exhausted he was.

"So, knights have their own wing in the castle?" Kaison asked.

"I'm not a knight. I haven't officially had the ceremony yet. Technically, I'm still an apprentice," Louie answered. "But yes."

Kaison walked over to the bed in the corner. Every limb in his body ached. It took all his strength not to collapse onto the bed and bury his face in his hands.

Louie crossed to the trunk and pulled out clean night clothes before throwing them over to Kaison. Then he plopped on his bed. "Shouldn't you get that checked out?" He gestured to the burn mark on Kaison's chest.

"I'll be fine," Kaison answered. He pulled the clean shirt up over his head and began removing his shoes.

"Was your village attacked too?"

Kaison nodded before plopping down on the bed, feeling a sudden rush of relief.

"Where are you from?" Louie asked.

"Grovia," Kaison answered.

"I'm from the Republic of Vorinder too," Louie said, his face twisting in concern. "I had no idea the Shadows had started attacking Vorinder. I thought they were only after Solaris villages."

Kaison was surprised to hear this. "They let citizens of Vorinder become knights? They hate us."

"It was arranged before I was born," Louie confessed, "and before we became a separate kingdom. My family is close to Bastian Alegria."

Kaison understood. Bastian Alegria was the leader of the council in Vorinder.

Louie continued, "Why aren't you at Elistalia?"

"My sister is at the castle infirmary," Kaison said.

"Is she alright?"

"She was struck by an arrow."

"Great Sun," Louie said.

Kaison placed his elbows on his knees and held his face for a moment. He brushed his hands over his cheeks and let his eyelids droop. "At times I think she's stronger than I am."

Louie smiled. "I'll have to meet her." He turned to blow out the candle before leaving Kaison alone to sleep, but paused. "I guess I'm supposed to watch you but it's not like I'm getting paid."

Kaison cleared his throat. "You don't have to worry about me."

"Blessings," he said. "Goodnight," he finished, and blew out the candle. Then he retreated to the doorway and went out to rejoin the other knights.

With no light in the room, Kaison was consumed in darkness. He laid back on the bed and focused on the ceiling. Suddenly the grief began to eat at him. Both his parents were dead. In fact, everyone from Grovia that he knew or loved was gone.

Sorrow pulled at his aching heart, flooding his entire body with a wave of depression. He could barely move, and he shut his eyes tight, fighting back tears. The adrenaline was quickly fading away and fatigue consumed him. What was he doing here? Why did he let that knight take his halberd and separate him and his sister? He knew nothing about Solaris – except for the fact that it was a dangerous place overrun with raiders. Villages burned at every corner. Solaris wasn't safe. And above all that, the royals hated the people of Vorinder.

He let out a shaky exhale as he clung to his last sliver of hope – his father's last words:

The library at Sun Castle.

- 5 -

Osiris

The evening air was cool, and a breeze carried the salty smell of the ocean. A crescent moon lit the sky, and stars dotted the night. Aside from the distant crashing of the waves, there were no other sounds in the air.

A girl scaled the side of a building, hidden in the shadows. Her dark clothes were molded to her figure, and a cloth mask covered the bottom half of her face. Dual daggers were sheathed to her leather vest, and black gloves protected her hands. A satchel was strung over her shoulder, the bag dangling at her hip.

Taville was the main port city of Larkesh, home to the Captain. The multi-story city was connected by pathways on the rooftops and bridges. The Captain's Palace was poised on a cliff edge, overlooking the ocean beyond. Osiris was farther down the coast, at the residential area for the upper class.

Osiris hoisted herself over a railing, landing on a private balcony. Her boots made no sound on the wooden lookout. It was positioned only one story above an adjacent roof, but was still considered one of the higher manors of the town. Crouching, she crossed the balcony to the glass doors. Pressing her ear against the glass, she listened to the other side.

She could faintly make out voices.

Her mind flashed to the blueprints she had seen earlier that day of the wealthy, top-story home. She knew exactly where she had to go.

Reaching her hand up, she grabbed the handle, expecting it to be locked, but to her surprise, the handle turned. Slowly, she opened the door, only enough for her to slip through.

The foyer was decorated with an array of paintings and potted vases. Golden sconces and stained glass lanterns adorned the walls and ceiling, illuminating the area. A settee was in the center of the room. On the table were three teacups next to a pot. The staircase on the left had a multicolored runner going down the center.

The voices sounded like they were coming from the double doors straight ahead. According to the blueprints, that was the bedroom. A gaggle of girls squealed from the other room before breaking out into laughter.

Turning her attention to the sand-colored door on her right, Osiris snuck toward it.

Locked.

Withdrawing the two lockpicks from the front of her vest, Osiris knelt before the handle. She inserted the picks into the lock, testing the pressure and sounds of the device. Within moments, the handle shook and clicked.

Osiris concealed the two lockpicks before entering the room.

The study beyond was small, but no less extravagant than the foyer. A life-size painting hung behind the main desk, and the burgundy curtains were tied back with tassels, displaying the town on the horizon. The bookshelf towered overhead, embellished with gold plating.

Osiris closed the door behind her before tending to the task at hand. She crossed to the bookshelf, drawing from past experience. She examined the floor at the base of the shelving. There were no scuff marks to prove that the bookshelf moved. Double-checking her theory, Osiris pressed her shoulder into the side of the bookshelf before pulling it.

It didn't budge.

Osiris crossed to the desk. She opened each one of the drawers in turn, finding nothing but scattered papers and ink.

A golden letter-opener rested on the center of the desk. Swiping it with her gloved hand, Osiris shoved it into the pocket on her thigh.

Another laugh broke out in the distance.

Osiris's mind churned, and she scanned the room once more. Her eyes fell on the painting.

She drifted toward it and ran her hands along the golden frame. First across the top, then down the side, and along the bottom. As her fingers traced up the last side, she felt a switch.

Her lips curled into a smile, concealed by her mask.

Shifting the piece beneath her fingers, the painting popped open like a door. Osiris pulled it back, uncovering a hidden shelf. Coin purses, an ivory crossbow, and a box of letters rested on the shelves. In the center was a small chest.

Reaching out, Osiris released the latch and opened the chest, revealing a diamond necklace. The jewelry sparkled on a velvet cushion. It was stunning.

A squeal pierced Osiris's ears, and she heard the bedroom door open on the other side of the wall.

Slamming the chest shut, Osiris swiped it from the shelf and shoved it to the bottom of her satchel. She snatched one of the coin purses, tying it to her belt, before closing the painting. A mechanical click notified her that it had been sealed.

Osiris darted across the room, reaching the study door. Pressing her ear to the wood, she listened attentively.

The women were chatting over each other, each one louder than the next. The thudding of heels started to become less audible.

Osiris opened the door, peering out. She barely saw the back of the women's heads as they descended the staircase. However, one remained at the top of the stairs.

"Get home safely!" she called, the high-pitch tone striking Osiris's ears. "I will see you all at the next Tournament!"

Without hesitation, Osiris dashed to the balcony doors while the woman's back was turned. Making close to no sound, she turned the latch and escaped onto the balcony. After she closed the door behind her, the woman turned around.

Osiris jumped back into the shadows, away from the glass doors. Turning around, she planted one hand on the railing before swinging her legs over the balcony edge. Osiris fell to the roof below, landing first on her feet before rolling out of the fall, protecting her knees from the impact. As soon as she was upright again, she took off across the rooftops, escaping into the dark of the night.

- 6 -

Kaison

In the morning, Kaison received clothes and had a chance to bathe. He tried to shake off yesterday's events, but he still saw the final images of his parents. The painful memories burned into his mind on a repeating cycle. A tense urgency clutched his chest and throat. His only respite was the thought of finding Theadosia and the library. They had to find it before the knights decided that they were no longer welcome inside the castle walls.

Kaison snuck out of the room before Louie woke up. He wanted to find his sister. He made his way through the corridors and out into the main entryway. Then he retreated from the knights' wing and found his way back to the great hall with the dome and the floor mural.

The room was bustling with activity. Servants and nobles darted through the space. The nobles showcased their lush jewels, which dripped off their shirts, headpieces, and wrists. Some stood together in pairs next to the four columns, the ladies lifting their chins to demonstrate the golden gemstones that dangled from their necks. The men spoke with large gestures and booming voices, projecting loud laughter throughout the room.

Kaison spotted Theadosia across the gilded entryway. She wore a burnt, rust dress that covered both shoulders. The fabric stopped above her wrists. The neckline was rigid and perfectly straight across her chest, and like the other nobles, a looped golden chain dangled in a t-shape down the front of her sternum. The orange skirt fanned out around her in a perfect circle, cinching at a belt made from tiny, metal petals.

Theadosia approached her brother. Her face twisted uneasily as she avoided the hem of her new dress, and she brushed her bangs out of her eyes, for her hair was down today.

"By plague...," Kaison couldn't believe she was wearing a dress.

"Don't laugh," Theadosia snapped when she reached Kaison's side.

"I'm not laughing. It actually looks nice." He acknowledged the expensive golden pieces hanging from her neck, wrists, hair, and waist.

"I can't breathe," Theadosia complained. "What do people eat here?"

"You look great. How was the infirmary?"

"Fine," she responded.

"Are you all right?"

"No," Theadosia replied. "I can't stop thinking about mother and father."

Kaison let out a sigh. "We have to find this library."

"I asked Cheyenne about it," said Theadosia. "Apparently it's on the third floor, and it's locked at night. What about the halberd?"

Kaison hadn't considered how they were going to get it back.

Maybe, if he re-grouped with the knights in training, they would be able to take him to an armory.

Suddenly a sharp voice penetrated the space behind Kaison:

"Sharing secrets are we?"

It was Emmett.

Emmett's face was stone-cold. His cadaverous frame shifted side to side on the balls of his feet, making his long sword scrape across the mosaic. It was clear that on the scarred side of his face, his eye was glazed over as if it wasn't looking at anything in particular. The red tint to the scar contrasted his pale skin.

Emmett continued, "The queen wants to see you."

Emmett didn't give the siblings a chance to object and began crossing the grand entryway. The scraping of the sword continued, sending an eerie chill up Kaison's spine. They had no choice but to follow.

The siblings sprang to action and briskly hiked up the staircase once more. Emmett walked in front of them, his silver ponytail bouncing up and down behind him. He seemed to be floating like a statue across the hallways, for his upper body was perfectly still.

The queen's royal study was behind a set of ethereal doors. The wall opposite the doors was lined with floor-to-ceiling windows, overlooking the courtyard outside.

"Stay here," Emmett instructed. He nodded at the knights guarding the queen's study, and they allowed him to enter. Kaison and Theadosia waited outside, watching the doors close behind Emmett and leaving the siblings in the hallway with the two stoic knights.

"This doesn't feel right," Kaison said. "I doubt the queen meets with everyone whose village was destroyed."

Theadosia dropped her voice to a whisper. "I think the halberd brought us directly to the castle father wanted us to find for a reason.

We should be grateful."

Kaison eyeballed the knights to make sure they weren't eavesdropping, but they remained in statuesque positions. Their heads fixated on the windows before them.

When he was sure the knights weren't listening, Kaison said, "Do you think the innkeeper and Dux Nikodemus acted strangely after seeing the halberd?"

Theadosia shifted her weight to the other hip, considering the question. "You think they know it's magical? Or maybe they like the valuable gems?"

Kaison shrugged. "Either way, we have to be careful."

Footsteps echoed along the corridor, alerting the two to an approaching knight. Dux Nikodemus emerged at the end of the hallway. He walked with a powerful determination, carrying the staff – the transformed halberd – in one hand.

"Good morning," Nikodemus said when he was in earshot. The guards bowed to their superior when he reached the grand doors. They each opened a door to let him pass, but Dux Nikodemus didn't enter and addressed the siblings instead. "Come in," he said with a gentle smile.

Kaison's step fell in line with the head knight, and the siblings passed into the queen's chamber. They were inside a square room. The walls around the outside of the room were covered in four bookshelves that stretched upward toward the sky, coming together in a dramatic, vaulted ceiling. Between each of the bookshelves was a marble archway, leading outward from each side of the square. Four long tapestries hung from ceiling to floor in the archways. They were pink with the emblem of the flame within a laurel. The silk tapestries fluttered like curtains and allowed a clear passage into the rest of the royal chambers.

In the center of the room was a pink table. Behind it sat a woman dressed in magenta. Her golden hair was tied up in a bun, and a sparkling crown with jagged spires sat on her oversized head. Her sleeves draped off her arms elegantly. Upon hearing the siblings enter, she straightened up regally, her nose pointed in the air, and looked downward with her eyes.

Emmett stood beside the desk, his arms clasped behind his back.

Kaison and Theadosia stepped across the marble flooring dotted with speckles of pink. They reached a lounge before the queen, but they remained standing. Were they supposed to bow? Was there a certain distance they had to observe between themselves and the queen?

"Sit down," the woman said, referencing the velvet lounge in front of her desk. She hardly had to move her head because her eyes ordered the two to their places.

Kaison obeyed, and his sister sat beside him. The velvet seating arrangement was lifted on an angle, forcing them to sit awkwardly in order to not lean against one another.

"I'm Queen Benedict," the woman spoke.

"Kaison Ruiz."

"Theadosia Ruiz."

"How pretty." Queen Benedict raised her eyebrows. The queen paused a moment before continuing. "Dux Nikodemus explained you two came here seeking refuge? How awful that your village was destroyed...in Vorinder nonetheless." She grabbed a piece of paper off her desk and began writing. "I'm surprised he's taken such an interest in you – considering thousands of refugees come to the gates." She picked up another paper, adding a signature, before moving to the next.

"You're safe here," Dux Nikodemus urged from behind them.

He still held their father's staff in his hands, out in the open for both Emmett and Queen Benedict to see.

Kaison paused and cleared his throat before speaking. "Honestly, Your Majesty, I wasn't expecting to stay."

Benedict covered her mouth, but it didn't hide the yawn. Her pen flicked across the pages. Then she said, "Dux Nikodemus is a good advocate. That's why we're having this little meeting. To talk about you staying here permanently."

"Stay here?" Theadosia asked.

"What was your profession in the Republic of Vorinder?" Benedict directed her question to Kaison, ignoring Theadosia.

"I was a hunter."

"And you hunt with a scepter?" Benedict asked, her eyes snapping to the transformed halberd. "I didn't realize that those from Vorinder preferred blunt force weapons."

"No," Kaison replied. "My main weapon is a harpoon."

Benedict nodded. "I'd like to see what you can do, hunter. Fighting *people* this time. You can join the practice now with the knights, and Dux Nikodemus can determine if you're fit to train."

"Train?"

"You'll be a knight, of course." She signed three more papers and threw the pages to the side.

Kaison's stomach flipped. "No offense, Your Majesty, but I'm not even from this kingdom. I don't want to be a knight," Kaison answered. He only needed to stay here long enough to fulfil his father's wishes, and then they would rightfully return to their own kingdom.

Benedict put down the pen and locked eyes with Kaison. She leaned forward in her chair, placing her elbows on the desk in front of her. "I have people dying left and right in nearby villages that are being attacked. I need more men." There was a slight pause before she scoffed. "It's not like you two have anywhere else you intend to go?"

The queen was presenting Kaison with the opportunity to stay long enough to search the library. It wasn't like this was a binding contract.

"We'll fight," Theadosia answered for them both.

"I'm not offering this option to you. However, if your brother is interested, it will help." She leaned back in her chair and tapped her fingers on the desk. "But if you don't want to stay, Kaison, then both of you can feel free to see yourself out of the castle and off the grounds of refuge at Elistalia."

"He will stay," Theadosia said almost too quickly. She gave Kaison a snide eye as she kicked him inconspicuously. Kaison could hear her trying to give him a telepathic signal about the library.

"Let's hear it from the man himself," said the queen.

"I'll go to training today," said Kaison.

Benedict smiled. "Wonderful," she said. "Elistalia is a wonderful location I think you will enjoy, Theadosia. Your brother will stay with the other knights."

"I can't go with her?" Kaison asked.

"No, you'll stay with the knights," Benedict replied.

Kaison nodded. The siblings rose from their seats, but Nikodemus stood in their way. Nikodemus stopped Kaison with a hand on the boy's chest.

"Here," Nikodemus said, extending Kaison's father's staff out to the boy. "I'll see you on the training field."

Kaison nodded, taking the transformed halberd from the knight. Relief overcame him as he gripped the staff in his hands. "Thank you," Kaison responded.

Then the two siblings exited, heading back to the grand hall.

- 7 -

Emmett

Sir Emmett watched the doors close behind the two Ruiz siblings, and the adults were finally alone to talk about them in private. Emmett stood next to the queen, his hands folded behind his back and his chest puffed out to assert dominance.

The head knight brought his attention away from where the children had exited, returning his gaze to the queen, but before she had a chance to speak, Emmett interjected. "I can't believe you gave the halberd back to him."

Nikodemus was unaffected by Emmett's tone of voice. "He needs to trust us."

"They don't know any better." The queen straightened the paper that was lying on the center of her desk. "Children are so easy to manipulate."

Emmett was growing impatient. "We should take the halberd now," Emmett said, "We don't need him."

Benedict pointed a finger at him. "We don't know that yet."

Nikodemus took a few steps closer. "Don't touch him, Emmett."

Emmett scowled.

"Besides, we don't have everything we need yet."

"People are dying," Emmett insisted.

"We need the Ademantum first," the queen said.

"It's only a matter of time before he realizes it's magical," said Emmett, "and then he'll be back in Vorinder before we can stop him."

"He's not going anywhere," said the queen, "Right, Nikodemus?" she inquired of her head knight.

Nikodemus nodded.

A low growl rumbled at the back of Emmett's throat. His jaw shifted as he bit his tongue.

Benedict brushed Emmett aside. "It's time that we focus on strengthening ourselves, so that when the time comes to take the halberd, we won't be exposed." She stood up from her chair and crossed to a map of Morbaeda. It hung on the wall between two large windows. "I've sent word to my brother, and he's assured me he has complete control over the North."

"He isn't queen," Nikodemus reminded, "and the people will listen to you before listening to him."

Benedict flipped a loose strand of hair out of her eyes. "Northerners have always wanted a man to rule, and Rupert fills that void for them." She cleared her throat, returning to her speech. "What are our plans for Larkesh?"

"Their positions at our borders haven't moved," said Emmett.

"I know. They see us as weak. It won't be long before they attack."

"What do you propose?" Nikodemus asked.

"We attack them first. Take the territory Solaris has never been able to claim."

Emmett knew the unlikelihood of that. Larkesh was known to

have underground dealings and unconventional class structures. They were rumored to have prisoners put through a death tournament as a show. Some Solaris citizens referred to them as barbaric.

Nikodemus and Emmett exchanged a glance behind the queen's back.

Benedict continued, "I want to know their weaknesses – points of attack. Their captain should have all the information."

Nikodemus nodded. "There is a thief in Larkesh I discovered that could execute something of that scale."

Emmett shifted his weight. "Is he trustworthy?"

"*She,*" Nikodemus corrected, "is supposedly the best."

Benedict's lips pursed. "Do your research. Offer her a deal she can't decline."

Nikodemus bowed his head slightly. "You can count on me, Your Majesty."

"At least I can count on one of you." Benedict fired a glare at Emmett.

Emmett swallowed the anger and remained calm.

"That will be all. I need to prepare for my speech." She started back toward her desk, and her voice shifted in tone before saying: "Get out."

- 8 -

Kaison

Kaison and Theadosia were escorted back to the grand hall by a second-knight named Sir Chadwick. He walked at a brisker pace compared to his melancholy counterpart, Sir Emmett, making the journey back to the grand hall seem shorter than before.

Kaison clutched the transformed halberd that hung from his belt. Now, it merely looked like a short staff shaped in a cylinder, with a flat surface on each end. The others might wonder why he hung a blunt weapon on his belt, especially one that didn't resemble a mace, flail, or club, but Kaison was determined to never let it out of his sight again. He still needed to discover how to activate its magical powers.

As they walked, he mentally prepared himself for the training to become a knight. Kaison had never fought someone before. His heart beat nervously and perspiration glistened on his forehead. The knights here would be highly-trained and well-prepared to counter any attack Kaison could muster. He didn't want to go up against them, and he didn't want to ride into battle. The trauma he had experienced in Grovia was enough for a lifetime. Besides, Kaison had never held a sword before – the preferred weapon of those from Solaris.

When they reached the grand entryway, Sir Chadwick stopped at the top of the stairs. He gestured to the crowd below. "Here you are," Chadwick said.

"Thank you," Theadosia answered before starting down the stairs, trying not to trip over the front of her new dress.

Kaison was lost in thought, but nevertheless, he followed his sister down the stairs.

When they reached the lower level, Theadosia said, "Let's go to the library." She nodded in the same direction in which Cheyenne had taken her to the infirmary last night.

"Now? I don't know when training starts."

"You're actually going to go?" Theadosia's mouth dropped open.

"I thought..." Kaison searched for words. "If we don't find what we need in the library, they will have to trust me to let us stay longer."

Theadosia's lips thinned, but she nodded in agreement.

"By plague, look who's back," an unfriendly voice sounded on the siblings' left.

Julian stood before the siblings with his elbow propped on Louie's shoulder. His olive skin glowed under the light seeping in through the windows, and his turquoise eyes were mischievous. His other hand was poised on his hip. His blue tunic was neatly pressed, all the way up to a stiff high collar, but the deep v-neck exposed half his bare chest.

"Can I help you?" Theadosia asked, taking a step toward them, but her tone wasn't inviting.

Julian's eyebrow raised in judgement.

Louie stood with his feet wide, and his chest puffed outward. He had noticeably shifted his weight to the balls of his feet to make himself look taller. His black hair fell in spring-like ringlets against his dark skin. He smiled at Kaison. "I was only kidding when I said I had to meet your sister," Louie said.

"Yeah well," Kaison began, "looks like we're here to stay for the time being."

Julian laughed, but it was more mechanical and suave than genuine.

"At least for the day," Kaison added.

"Well," Louie said, shifting out from underneath Julian's elbow as he stepped toward Theadosia. "I'm honored to meet the fearless warrior." He bowed to Theadosia extravagantly.

Theadosia crossed her arms. "And you are…?"

"Louie," he said. "Louie Netherand."

"I don't know what my brother told you," Theadosia gave a side eye toward Kaison, "but my name is Theadosia."

"Tell us, love," Julian said, taking a step closer to Theadosia. He touched his fingers to her cheek and slowly ran them down to her neck. "How did it feel when the arrow penetrated your perfect skin?"

Theadosia's face went pale.

Kaison was frozen in shock when Louie intervened

"Sod off!" Louie shoved Julian's hand away from Theadosia. "She's barely been here a minute," he scolded.

Julian raised his hands defensively. "Fine," he said, "I'll wait… but only for a minute." He flashed a wink at Theadosia.

"Listen." Kaison stepped toward Julian, but a strong cologne stung Kaison's nose, making him recoil. "I don't know who you think –"

"Stop." Theadosia silenced her brother, placing a hand on his chest and making Kaison back away. She then returned her attention to Julian. She lifted her chin and said, "He's not even worth my energy."

Julian straightened out his tunic. He opened his mouth to respond, but Theadosia spoke over him.

"So Louie," she said, "where are you from?"

"Madris," Louie replied. "I came to Solaris about a year ago."

Theadosia's eyes softened. "We were from Grovia."

"That's what we need," Julian growled. "More people from Vorinder who don't believe in the monarchy. You three will never be true Solaris citizens, like me."

Louie fired Julian a glare. "I serve Queen Benedict."

"You disagree with the Republic?" Kaison inquired. He hadn't met someone from Vorinder who didn't agree with seceding from Solaris after the death of the previous queen.

Louie shrugged. "I'm not sure I believe that the queen has to be destined by fate. And who's to say Benedict isn't?"

"Fate or not," Julian intervened, "it's about being a good ruler."

"Theadosia!"

Kaison was surprised to hear his sister's name being called from farther away. Two girls approached the group, heading toward Theadosia. They pushed their way through the crowd. One of them Kaison recognized from yesterday.

It was the nurse Cheyenne, who had escorted Theadosia to the infirmary. Her black, straight hair was plastered to either side of her olive face.

The girl beside her was mesmerizing. Beautiful brown curls bounced in big circles as she approached them. Her skin was pale and her green eyes were doe-like. She wore a purple flowered dress that extended to the floor and pink bows in her hair that matched her rosy, full lips.

"Hi, Cheyenne," Theadosia said.

"How are you feeling?" Cheyenne inquired.

"Better."

"Are you all waiting for the speech?" Cheyenne looked at the rest of the group.

Theadosia crossed her arms. "What speech?"

"The queen's announcement." Cheyenne seemed surprised. Then she acknowledged the girl beside her. "This is my friend, Pandora," she told Theadosia.

Pandora's eyes twinkled.

"This is my older brother, Kaison," Theadosia responded, grabbing his arm and pulling him closer.

Kaison stared blankly at Pandora, unable to look at Cheyenne. Pandora's eyes met his, and she flashed an enchanting smile.

"Oh, Pandora, my sweet." Julian took Pandora's hand and pulled her close.

Louie shook his head and shoved his hands in his pockets.

Julian continued, "Why do you bore yourself with such low individuals?"

Pandora giggled.

"Sod off, Julian," Cheyenne snapped.

Louie said, "Cheyenne and Julian are twins – in case you couldn't tell."

They did look strikingly similar with their olive complexion and dark hair. Both were tall and attractive, with sharp jawlines.

"Lucky me," Cheyenne groaned.

Julian held Pandora tightly. "I'm the more likeable one," he said.

Pandora pushed Julian away playfully. "I like Cheyenne more than I like you," Pandora teased.

Julian's lips curled into a smile. "I can fix that."

Pandora bit her lip and turned to look at the siblings again. "It's nice to meet you both, Kaison and Theadosia." She smiled. Her voice was melodic. "What brings you to Sun Castle?"

"Our village was attacked," Kaison explained.

Pandora's tone changed, and her doe-like eyes drooped. "That's so sad."

Kaison didn't want to talk about the attack, so he changed the subject. "The queen wants me to join the knights this afternoon."

"What?" Julian scoffed.

"Another one?" chimed Cheyenne at the same time.

"By plague," Louie said under his breath. "You didn't say you had a private meeting with the queen."

"It wasn't private," Kaison replied. "Dux Nikodemus and Sir Emmett were there."

"That's even more of a big deal," Louie said, his mouth agape.

"Also, back up," Julian said. "You're going to join the knights this afternoon? This isn't a horse race. Being a knight is a prestigious honor that takes years of training and sacrifice. I've worked my entire life to get here and so has every other knight. Why should you get to take someone else's spot?"

"Are you scared he will take yours?" Cheyenne jeered at her brother.

"No," Julian answered defensively.

"I don't want to take someone's spot," Kaison said. "We had no choice when our village was destroyed. We came to Sun Castle as a place of refuge, and now the queen is forcing me to be one of her knights or else I'll be on the streets. I don't have a choice."

"Cry me a river," said Julian. "Towns all over Solaris have been destroyed. Do those men get to become knights?"

Kaison looked around the circle to see if anyone would defend him, but Julian did have a point. Why was the queen determined to put him in her royal guard?

The conversation couldn't continue because a roar of applause echoed throughout the grand hall. The group of six turned to the staircase to see Queen Benedict appear at the top.

"Hello everyone!" Queen Benedict called from her position on the upper floor. Her voice boomed in a lighter tone than earlier. Dux Nikodemus and Sir Emmett were on either side of her.

"As you know, the Shadows have been making their way across Solaris. I want to assure you that as long as I am queen, you will always be safe at court here at Sun Castle."

Kaison hardly recognized the queen. The woman at the top of the staircase was nothing like the woman he had met with earlier. Her eyes locked intensely on the nobles, and her voice was hopeful, dripping in forced happiness. She delicately placed her hands in front of her and used no gestures as she spoke.

"As we approach the Harvest Banquet, I want to encourage all of you to set aside your grief for the betterment of the kingdom. The Harvest Banquet is an important celebration where we show the Northern Horizon, Vorinder, and Larkesh the unwavering strength of Solaris."

Ignoring people's grief? It was certainly not something Kaison would consider saying if he were a monarch.

Queen Benedict continued, "The Harvest Banquet will be followed by the Harvest Ball as we do every year. However, this year, as a display of Solaris's generosity and compassion, it will be open to the people of Elistalia."

A few hushed whispers rang through the crowd, coming from the elite members of court.

"I know some of you believe they are not true members of Sun Castle, but it is important that those who have lost their homes are able to integrate into this community. We must ensure that they feel welcomed," Benedict said. "We don't know how many more villages will be destroyed. Sun Castle, and the shining beacon that is Sun Spire, will always be a place for the lost."

Julian shifted his stance in front of Kaison, and once again Kaison's senses were clogged with Julian's strong cologne radiating from his clothes. "Here we go again. She won't say anything about the knights that have died." Julian whispered into Louie's ear.

"How many this time?" Louie kept his gaze on the queen as he spoke to Julian.

"This morning Nikodemus told me that two hundred of our own knights were massacred along the borders of the Lost Lands. The Shadows are only getting stronger."

"Great Sun..."

Julian continued whispering to Louie, "Won't be long before we're deployed to save Solaris. Better write home before this woman gets everyone killed."

Nikodemus stepped forward to address the crowd. When he did so, the nobles gave a slight bow in his direction. It was more than they had given the queen.

Nikodemus cleared his throat. His somber face dropped toward the Solaris citizens. "I want to brief all of you on the security measures that will occur during the time of the Harvest Banquet. First, I must start this briefing by being honest with all of you. The Shadow of Eclipse continues to terrorize our land. We have also received intelligence that the Shadow of Eclipse is no longer in Solaris, but has terrorized multiple villages throughout the Republic of Vorinder," Nikodemus explained. "It is only a matter of time until he moves onto the Northern Horizon. This means we must take every precaution to ensure the security of Sun Castle."

Nikodemus continued explaining the new security protocols, all of which didn't make any sense to Kaison. However, hearing about the man who killed his parents only made Kaison more concerned about leaving Sun Castle. Once they found out why their father had sent them here, where would they go? The Shadow of Eclipse knew their father and that monstrous entity would find them. Maybe, Kaison's only option was to be a knight.

But that didn't change his burning feeling inside that wanted to avenge his parents' death. The Shadow of Eclipse was a monster.

Louie turned around and whispered, "Do you know if your village was the first one in Vorinder to be attacked?"

"I don't," Kaison replied, his voice low.

Louie's face softened. "I need to contact my family."

Beyond the perils of Vorinder, another pressing question was on the forefront of Kaison's mind. Was the man who killed his parents – who had so brutally wielded the sledgehammer – the leader of the Shadows or an insignificant general? Was he the Shadow of Eclipse? Or was there something more to fear?

He could almost hear his father's words as they hunted together for the last time on the Reflecting Grounds. The words echoed in his head once more:

There are worse things to fear than caiman.

His father had known.

I'm sorry I didn't tell you sooner.

Kaison's father's words continued to circulate in his mind. His father knew that the halberd was magical and that someone was out there, waiting to kill him for it. Now that Kaison and Theadosia had escaped, the Shadow of Eclipse would continue to kill until he found them again.

Kaison touched the staff at his belt – the transformed halberd. He had to protect it with his life.

Kaison tuned back into the speech.

"Those are our best courses of action to retaliate against the Shadow forces," Dux Nikodemus was saying from the staircase. "Until we quell the attacks, we will continue to provide a refuge for any and all who are displaced. Thank you."

With that, the crowd rose into another bout of applause.

"The castle will be opened tomorrow morning for additional guests that are traveling to the Harvest Banquet." Queen Benedict spoke over the nobles, who were already dispersing in the entranceway. She shouted a few more instructions, before Sir Emmett held out his hand and led her away from the group. Nikodemus followed behind them both, before turning down another passageway.

The great mass in the grand hall was now fully disassembling. The room filled with clamoring chatter, and the court's guests plunged back into chaos.

"Alright." Louie placed his hands on Kaison's shoulders. "It sounds like we need training now more than ever. Are you ready to join us?"

"Honestly, I'm not sure," Kaison answered. They needed to go to the library. Now. He looked at his sister. "Where will you be?"

"I would offer that she can come with me," Cheyenne said, "but the infirmary is crowded right now, and I have a lot of work to do."

"You can come with me," Pandora said, taking Theadosia's hand. "I have a fun job," she gave Theadosia a wink.

"I don't know what that means," Theadosia laughed, "but sure."

Julian grabbed both Pandora and Theadosia's interlaced hands and kissed them gently on the back of the palm. "Until later, my sweets," he said, his baritone voice seductive. "Let's go," he motioned to the boys to join him. He gave his sister Cheyenne an indiscernible look before storming through the crowd toward practice.

- 9 -

Kaison

The moor was more heavenly in the daytime. The boys crossed into the picturesque garden and weaved through the shining flowers and crackling fountains, which blasted water high into the air. Julian led the three over the stamped stone pathways, toward the back of the castle. He walked with an annoying saunter to his step. When they rounded the corner, the polished flower plots disappeared, and the radiant landscape faded into a scorched, brown wasteland. Beyond that was a practice field, armory, and royal stables. A tan archway depicted the path for the rest of their stroll.

Once they were far enough away from the girls and servants that roamed the gardens, Julian turned to Kaison. "Your sister is cute." He grinned. Then he strolled away.

Kaison bit his lip, feeling his entire body tense in frustration.

"Don't let him get to you," Louie advised.

"I just met him, and I can't stand him," Kaison said.

"Think of how long I've had to deal with Xy'tier – I mean Julian,"

Louie replied. He puffed out his chest and examined the training fields. "But we have to focus on training now." Louie bounded after the others, assuming that Kaison would eagerly follow.

Kaison had never coveted those that were the warriors in Vorinder. They were an offensive bunch, running straight off into battles and cunningly striking others down with hidden blades and poisonous substances. Kaison preferred to be the one that stayed behind – on the defensive – protecting those that needed him the most. It was why his role as a hunter and provider had made so much sense when he had selected it in front of the town council three years ago. He wondered more about Louie's story, and if becoming a foreign knight in Solaris was Louie's first choice for a trade.

Kaison headed after Louie, determined to ask about the best methods for adapting his Vorinder training to the new practice arena. As he ducked under the arch, he slammed against someone, knocking a young girl right off her feet.

"Sorry!" Kaison blurted out before even making eye contact with the girl.

"Watch where you're going!" she shouted. She was on the brown grass in front of Kaison, glaring up at him with reptile-green eyes. She had tight red curls that flew wildly in all directions, and a blue book with a sparkling diamond on the front rested right beside her.

"Sorry," Kaison repeated, squatting down in front of her. He picked up the book and brushed it off before reaching his hand out to help the girl.

"Don't touch my stuff!" The girl snatched the book from Kaison's hand and she bounced to her feet.

Kaison rose to a standing position. He towered almost a foot above her.

The girl rubbed her pale, freckled forehead with the ball of her hand while clutching the journal tightly to her chest. She openly judged Kaison with her stare.

Kaison shoved his hands in his pockets and forced a welcoming expression. "I'm new," he said.

"Obviously."

Kaison struggled for words. "I'm Kaison."

"I don't care."

"And you are...?"

The girl's nose wrinkled in disgust. "Mind your own business."

"I was–"

"Excuse me," she said, hardly letting Kaison back away before she stormed past him. She bumped him on the shoulder aggressively as she passed before charging toward the castle.

Kaison rubbed his shoulder, watching the girl go.

"That is Maeve," Louie spoke from a few feet away. He was up ahead on the path. "She never fails to be rude."

Maeve. The girl with the fiery hair, reptile eyes, and a diamond journal.

Kaison shrugged off the encounter and joined Louie on the stone path once more. Directly ahead of them was the large jousting field with wooden stands constructed on either side. The outside of the jousting field was lined with a circle of sand and fenced in with wooden panels. The rose-gold panels delineated Queen Benedict's crest – the laurel and the flame.

Louie led Kaison to a smaller stable at the head of the jousting field. It had a gaping wooden doorway for knights to prepare their horses before charging down the field to meet their opponents. They passed under a silk banner with another crest and entered the room.

On the polished walls were foreign weapons – everything from spring-loaded daggers to broadswords to crossbows. The entire room would have held the marketplace in Grovia with ample room to spare. Kaison noted that each boy had gravitated to a designated table and bench in the room, preparing their armor and weapons. At the far end, thick smoke roared from a blacksmith's fire, coiling up through a hole in the thatched roof.

All eyes fell on Kaison when he entered the room. Julian was surrounded by a posse of men, and he watched Kaison, shaking his head. As he did so, all the others imitated their leader in their own way. Kaison had to keep reminding himself that this was all a long-winded excursion to uphold his father's final wish. There was something here that his dad wanted him to find.

Kaison crossed to the wall of weapons. His face dropped when he stared at a variety of different swords. Then, out of the corner of his eye, Kaison spotted a solution. Hanging on the end of the row of weapons was a spear. Kaison's hand instantly flew to the staff at his belt, which he knew could transform in front of his eyes. This was no place to show off a magical halberd. But maybe…he could learn how to use a spear or equivalent during this training. That way, he would be able to use his father's weapon when the time came.

The thought was daunting. He knew the weapons weren't the same and didn't weigh the same. But it was the only way to hide the magic.

The boys dressed in armor and picked out their weapons and shields. Then they returned to the moorland. Julian was the only boy that had brought his weapon from home, meaning he didn't have to borrow gear and armor from Sun Castle. Julian had a jewel-inlaid sword, easily more expensive than the meat of a dozen caiman.

Kaison struggled to stand underneath the weight of the armor, but when he looked around, he noticed that it was normal to all the knights. There were about thirty boys in the clearing, all with their eyes on the head knight of Sun Castle.

"Welcome again, knights in training," Dux Nikodemus began. "As you know, our forces are continuing to deplete. We've lost many valuable knights in this war with the Shadow of Eclipse." Nikodemus's hands moved as he spoke. "Every one of you is important moving forward, and you must be well prepared."

The boys were sullen and didn't rally under Nikodemus's encouraging words.

"With a new knight joining us, we should return to the basic one-on-one combat," Nikodemus stated. "The Shadows excel in one-on-one combat and never tire. Don't think for a second you can be over prepared."

Kaison's mind returned to the Shadow Theadosia killed in Grovia. Did all the Shadows evaporate into thin air?

"Find a partner and take up space. Remember, this is warm-up, I don't want any broken bones," Nikodemus called out. "You need to be fresh for the battlefields."

At the sound of Nikodemus's command, the boys began to pair off.

Kaison looked to Louie but was confronted with the awkward realization that Louie and Julian were a pair.

"Uh…," Louie stammered, glancing at Julian. "Simon never has a partner. You can train with him?"

"There's a reason he never has a partner," Julian groaned under his breath.

Kaison looked around. "Who's Simon?"

"Come on," Louie stated. He bounded off in one direction, forcing Kaison to follow quickly behind.

They were approaching a tall, pale boy who was fixing his shoulder pad while he stood off to the side of the field.

"Hey, Simon!" Louie called as they approached. "How are you, my man?"

Simon stopped fixing his shoulder pad.

"I think this is the first time you have spoken to me since last year," Simon said, his voice monotonous. His eyes were dark and bottomless, and his black hair fell in straggly pieces across his forehead. His skin was fair, as though it was never touched by the sun.

"Nah." Louie laughed.

Simon didn't flinch. "Yeah…"

"Good one." Louie's laugh trailed off. Then he patted Simon on the shoulder, messing up the shoulder pad.

Simon's eyes narrowed. "Can I help you?" He once again fixed his armor.

"Well, this is Kaison, he's new."

Kaison nodded in acknowledgement.

Simon's face was indiscernible. "Welcome," he said unenthusiastically. Simon's bottomless eyes peered at the transformed halberd with the three jewels, examining it in wonder.

"Kaison doesn't have a partner, and you never do, so I figured I'd introduce you two," Louie said. His voice was peppy, as if he wasn't offending Simon with his blunt comment.

Simon's gaze was set on Kaison. "Sure," he said.

"Great!" Louie beamed. "Have fun!"

With that, Louie bounded away toward Julian, his sword swaying.

Kaison cleared his throat. "I honestly don't know why I'm training to be a knight," he said in warning.

Simon shrugged. "They do that to boys who lose their hometown. Why else did the queen welcome a stranger with open arms?" Then Simon extended his hand forward. "To a fair fight," he said.

Kaison was hesitant, but eventually nodded. "To a fair fight," he replied before shaking Simon's hand. He felt something metal underneath his palm, and when they released, Kaison noticed a large silver band around Simon's middle finger.

Without delaying any longer, Kaison brought his spear in front of him and braced himself for Simon to attack.

"You sure you don't want a sword?" Simon gestured to Kaison's unusual choice of weapon.

Kaison grabbed the old spear tighter. "I'll be fine…"

Simon charged at him. Kaison blocked, the sword hitting the handle of the spear above Kaison's two hands. Then Kaison returned the attack against Simon. It was the first time he was practicing one-on-one combat. Luckily, the spears he had used in Vorinder were similar enough to this one – only half the weight. How did these knights make fighting look so easy?

Simon and Kaison continued to strike against one another, neither advancing nor taking the lead in the fight. Mainly, Kaison was trying to understand the weight distribution of the spear and how he could possibly use this as a weapon to fight with in battle.

Kaison couldn't help but notice Dux Nikodemus watching him the whole time. It was to be expected. Somehow, Kaison had to prove himself so that he would be allowed to stay here.

After about an hour of warming up, Dux Nikodemus called them back to the center of the field. Kaison returned to stand beside Louie and Julian, as sweat dripped down his temples.

"How'd it go with Plague Boy?" Julian snickered.

"Simon," Louie clarified.

Kaison was still out of breath. "Do you have a rude name for everyone?"

Julian scoffed and shook his head. He smiled slyly, "I only speak the truth."

"The truth?" Kaison asked.

Louie exchanged a glance with Julian, worry flashing in his eyes. He twirled his sword in his hand nervously, wondering if he should speak up.

"Are you going to tell him or should I, Netherand?" Julian asked angrily.

Louie started, "There's not much–"

"We hate him." Julian cut him off. "Everyone does."

Kaison paused. "Why?"

"If you want to be respected around here, don't go near Plague Boy." Julian stopped upon seeing Louie's chastising expression. Then Julian corrected himself. "Don't go near Simon."

Then Julian brushed past Kaison, knocking him square in the shoulder as he passed.

Louie shrugged apologetically.

"Like Julian's much better than Simon." Kaison shook his head.

Louie spoke sincerely, "There's nothing wrong with him, he's a fine knight to practice with. He just has a bad reputation."

Before Kaison could reply, he heard the head knight calling them all back to the center of the field, and all the boys raced in Nikodemus's direction.

"Alright!" Dux Nikodemus was summoning their attention. "I'd love for us to do a one-on-one battle simulation and provide our own input to help our fellow knights. Julian, would you start us off?"

Julian smiled before crossing the small distance to the center of the field.

"Of course," Louie said under his breath.

Kaison flashed a confused glance at Louie.

"Dux Nikodemus likes to do this thing where he picks two people to test, and it's an elimination game. Whoever wins continues to battle more people in the training until everyone has done at least one battle," Louie explained. "Julian's already going to be a first-tier knight, and yet he still gets to go first in this game. No one else can prove that they can fight because he beats everyone."

"Oh," Kaison remarked. "Well, good for him."

Louie shot Kaison an annoyed glare.

"Kaison!"

Kaison felt his heart plummet as he heard his name.

"Come join us," Dux Nikodemus said.

Kaison blinked.

Louie's mouth dropped open. "By plague, you're first." He laughed.

Kaison forced himself out of his frozen position and crossed the field to where Dux Nikodemus and Julian were standing. Kaison couldn't make out the expression on Julian's face.

"We will have you two start us off. Kaison, all you have to do is try to beat Julian," Dux Nikodemus said. "Whenever you're ready."

Dux Nikodemus backed away from the two boys to give them space. Julian withdrew his sword while Kaison readied his spear.

Julian glanced down at the weapon hanging from Kaison's belt. His eyebrow rose upon inspecting the three gemstones. "Don't know how to fight with your own weapon?" Julian inquired.

Kaison gripped his spear tighter, ignoring him. He couldn't be kicked out of the training as quickly as he was thrown in, losing his only chance to find what his father wanted him to find.

Kaison's heart lurched when Julian charged. Kaison quickly put his spear in front of him and blocked Julian's attack, but the impact from the blow threw Kaison off balance. Julian spun around and slammed the flat part of his sword into Kaison's side, intentionally so as to not hurt him. In a real battle, it would have been a death blow. Kaison stumbled, attempting to catch his bearings, when Julian kicked his hip, sending him crashing down onto the ground.

"Stop!" Dux Nikodemus called.

Kaison could feel the grass underneath him. Dirt was plastered to the side of his cheek.

"Let's reset," Nikodemus ordered.

Kaison struggled to stand up to his feet, feeling as if the kick had already bruised his hip bone. The spear was heavy in his grasp.

"Reset?" Julian asked. "We never reset."

"Julian," Nikodemus scolded.

Nikodemus's eyes were hopeful, as if he was anticipating Kaison to be better the next time. But Kaison's wrists were already in pain, and his biceps were shaking from the length of the warm-up.

Kaison barely had time to readjust his grip on the spear before Julian lunged again. This time, Kaison dodged the oncoming sword and thrust the spear at Julian's upper thigh, but Julian blocked.

Kaison bounced backward and prepared himself again.

Julian rushed him, slashing his sword down through the air. Kaison blocked, and Julian turned his sword handle as soon as his sword hit Kaison's weapon, causing Kaison to struggle to keep a sweaty grasp on his spear. In one swift movement, Julian grabbed the center of the spear and wrenched it out of Kaison's palms. Hardly a moment passed before Julian kicked Kaison in the stomach. As Kaison keeled over, Julian sent his elbow straight into Kaison's temple.

Kaison collapsed to his stomach, feeling a burning pain pulsing at the back of his eye. Julian kicked him in the stomach to roll him on his back. Julian planted his foot on Kaison's chest and drew his sword up to Kaison's neck.

"You're dead," he said. A smirk creased his face. "Again."

Kaison could hardly breath under the pressure of Julian's foot. The tip of Julian's sword dug into the bottom of his chin, causing a droplet of blood to form.

The boys circling the field began clapping. Only when he heard the praise did Julian release Kaison and turn to the crowd. "Who's next?" he called, not even slightly out of breath.

Kaison rolled on his stomach once more, pushing himself up to his feet. Pain ate away at his body.

"That's enough!" Dux Nikodemus called, silencing the crowd. He walked out into the center of the field and took Kaison's spear out of Julian's hands. "Simon is next."

Simon made his way forward as the crowd of boys fell silent.

Kaison reached out toward Nikodemus to take his spear back, but Nikodemus kept a firm grasp on it.

"Walk with me," he said, starting off the field.

Kaison uneasily followed. The boys backed out of the way, letting Nikodemus step through them, and Kaison was on his tail. Once they had distanced themselves from the boys surrounding the practice battlefield, Nikodemus came to a stop and turned to face Kaison, the spear in both hands.

"We have a lot of work to do with you," Dux Nikodemus started. "You have years of training to make up."

Kaison rubbed his temple, still in pain from where Julian had hit him. "I'm a hunter," Kaison reminded him.

"Animals and people aren't that different," Nikodemus said.

Kaison shrugged, disinterested.

Nikodemus reached into his trouser pocket and pulled out a piece of fabric. He unraveled it in front of Kaison, showing a symbol of a glowing sun. "Do you recognize this?" His voice had dropped to a whisper.

Kaison inspected the wrinkled fabric. "I mean, it's the sun." Kaison shrugged.

"No, this particular sun," Nikodemus said. His eyes were urgent and invested, waiting for a certain answer.

"No, sorry," Kaison admitted.

A cheering roared from the crowd of boys, signaling that the next practice battle had been won. Nikodemus cleared his throat before shouting in their direction, "Alexander, next!"

Nikodemus hastily wrinkled the fabric and shoved it deep into his pocket as if he wasn't allowed to be seen with it.

"And this spear," Nikodemus clutched it in his palms, "do you think you can fool me with your choice of weapon?"

Kaison didn't understand the question.

Nikodemus gestured to the transformed halberd in its staff form, hanging from Kaison's side. "If you're trying to keep the halberd a secret by grabbing this pitiful spear, then you've failed." Nikodemus threw the spear to the side like it was as light as a flower.

Kaison's heart lurched. "This staff is my father's. It's not a halberd."

"Of course." Nikodemus didn't sound convinced. "Take my advice and hide that halberd immediately."

"It's not a – "

"Kaison, I know," Nikodemus said. "Right now, I'm the only one that knows, and let's keep it that way. Hide the halberd."

Kaison's heart started to beat faster in his chest.

Nikodemus dropped his voice even quieter, taking a step closer. "You should go to the library after class today."

Kaison's blood turned to ice.

"Look at a map," Nikodemus said. "See how far your hometown is from Sun Castle. If you don't believe the maps, climb Sun Spire."

Kaison stared back at the knight, completely distraught. Did he know he was transported from Grovia? Did he know what Kaison was searching for?

Nikodemus straightened up and cleared his throat. "Trust me," Nikodemus said. He glanced down at the staff hanging from Kaison's belt once more. "Hide it." He turned back to the crowd of boys and walked away before Kaison could respond.

Kaison stood frozen, his mouth agape, completely dumbfounded. How did the head knight of Solaris know about the halberd? Who else did?

Exhaling, Kaison returned to the crowd. His hands moved to the transformed halberd at his side, attempting to cover the jewels, but he knew the boys had already seen it. There was no hiding it now. His best bet was to conceal that it was anything but a beautiful, family scepter.

Kaison approached Louie. Louie stood watching the present battle, but nodded in Kaison's direction after seeing him approach. "What did Dux Nikodemus want?"

Kaison didn't hear Louie's question, completely disregarding it. "You need to take me to the library," Kaison said. "Now."

- 10 -

Kaison

Louie led Kaison through the depths of the castle. The entire time, Kaison was replaying his conversation with Dux Nikodemus in his head. The head knight knew about the magical halberd, which meant the queen and the unsettling Sir Emmett must know too. For some reason, the unlikely trio had chosen to give the transformed halberd back to Kaison rather than confiscate it. Either they didn't care, or they were waiting for Kaison to lead them to the answer.

Kaison shuddered. They had to figure out why the library was so important and get out of here fast.

"Why are you so determined to go to the library?" Louie asked beside Kaison. He was leading the newcomer deeper into the castle.

"Nikodemus told me to look at a map of Morbaeda," Kaison answered.

"And why is that so important? Specifically, now…during dinner."

"I need answers about my hometown."

Louie nodded, skeptical, but feeling a sense of obligation to assist the new knight. "Well, you're lucky I'm friends with the best scholar in training to help us."

A set of grand doors, stretching two stories into the air, came into view. Only by looking through the open doorway and seeing the foyer light pour onto colorful books did Kaison recognize the room as the library.

Louie led Kaison inside. There were no guards or attendants to greet them.

The bookshelves inside were dark oak and outlined in gold trim. The shelves stretched upwards three stories into the air, where the dark oak transitioned into square paneling that covered the ceiling. The ceiling was flat, but a stained-glass window in the shape of a sun cast a pool of yellow light in the center of the room. The yellow light expanded outwards to many chaises and tables. An upper balcony looked out over the center circle below where couches and tables were placed.

Kaison looked at the sun on the ceiling, freezing. It was the same sun Nikodemus had asked him if he recognized.

"I need to find my sister," Kaison said.

Louie smiled, his dimples showing. "I'm sure she's still with Pandora."

Kaison followed Louie through the library, looking around in amazement. The grandiose nature of the environment mixed with the near silence created a type of haven inside the castle walls. Unlike the scroll rooms in Vorinder, the books at Sun Castle were packed in perfectly neat, color-coded rows. Not a single book lay open on the tables scattered throughout the space.

The boys crossed through the center of the room, passing through the yellow light, and came to a door on the back wall, underneath the second-floor balcony.

Louie knocked on the door and waited to hear a female voice before he opened it.

Inside, Theadosia and Pandora were standing beside each other leaning over a tall table. Books lined the wall, but on smaller shelves that contained bottles and other trinkets. Parchment was plastered throughout the room with a bunch of different writings and formulas.

Louie closed the door behind Kaison, separating them from the public library.

"Louie Netherand." Pandora smiled. "To what do I owe this honor seeing you twice in one day?"

Louie flipped his tight curls away from his face and puffed his chest out before placing his hands in his pockets. "Kaison needed something, and I figured you'd be a better help than me in this library."

Pandora glanced at Kaison, her pearly eyes wide.

Kaison's chest tightened. She was stunning.

"You thought correctly," Pandora said.

"Come look at this," Theadosia said, beckoning for her brother to come over with a wave of her hand.

Kaison obeyed, and Louie followed him over to the table. They stood across from the girls on the other side. There were a few manuscripts scattered between them alongside potions in flasks and beakers.

"It's a little thing." Pandora blushed. "I've been practicing."

Pandora held out her palm over the table. She closed her eyes and took a deep breath through her nose. With an exhale, a light began forming at her fingertips. Slowly, the brightness increased in intensity, and before long, there was a glowing white orb hovering over her palm. She opened her eyes and witnessed the light before her.

Kaison's jaw dropped. "You're a magician?"

Pandora smiled, but her gaze was set on the light before her. "I've been learning magic my entire life."

"She's not a magician," Louie said, not sounding impressed. "She's an upgraded candle."

Instantly Pandora closed her fist around the light, extinguishing it.

"You're jealous," Theadosia teased.

"If only," he said. "Did she tell you magic is forbidden?"

"Louie..." Pandora said under her breath.

"I thought you were being careful," Louie said. "Now you're showing two strangers?" He looked at each one of the siblings in turn. "No offense or anything."

"You're the only people that know," Pandora said. "Also, they're new and nobody would believe them if they started saying I practice magic." She gestured to the siblings.

"Julian knows too," Louie added.

"No..." Pandora responded. "He doesn't know I'm still practicing."

Kaison's mind was on the magically transformed halberd hanging at his side. "Why is magic forbidden?"

He was under the impression that any magic originated in Solaris.

Pandora's eyes filled with sorrow. "Light magic was locked away the night King Arturo disappeared almost two decades ago. People are convinced any magic today is connected to the darkness, but that is not correct."

Kaison remembered the story his parents had told him. Almost two decades ago, King Arturo had escaped the castle when his wife, the queen, was killed. Kaison had never realized that the king was also responsible for locking away light magic.

"Then how are you summoning light magic that's locked away?" Theadosia asked.

"It is not all locked away," Pandora explained. "After the queen died, King Arturo only concealed the light magic that is the most powerful – the offensive spells. Also, he destroyed the more advanced spell books so as not to create chaos and mass distribution."

"Or, you believe what everyone else does: Queen Lidia died and the light magic died with her. King Arturo had nothing to do with it," Louie said. "There are no magicians left from his time."

"He hardly had any magicians," Pandora countered.

"Maybe there's a reason for that," Louie said. "You could be thrown in jail, Pandora. What if Julian finds out you're still practicing and tells someone?"

"Julian would never do anything to put me in jail," Pandora objected.

"I…think I agree with Pandora," Kaison said, "that not all magic existing today is dark magic."

Pandora smiled hopefully.

Louie looked at Kaison, his eyebrows strewn together in skepticism. "Why do you say that?"

Kaison looked across the table at Theadosia. She raised an eyebrow in her brother's direction, warning him to not disclose information about his halberd.

"I don't know for sure…" Kaison tried to retrace his steps. He changed the subject. "Is there a map of Morbaeda here?"

Pandora frowned but didn't ask further questions before crossing to the wall. She took down a large piece of parchment containing numerous formulas and revealed a map of Morbaeda behind it.

Kaison crossed the room to join Pandora. Theadosia and Louie followed behind them at a slightly slower pace.

Kaison used his hand to scan the map. He stopped over a large castle at the center of the map.

"Sun Castle," Pandora chimed before Kaison could ask.

Morbaeda was divided into four sectors. The Lost Lands, Larkesh, Solaris – which was what Queen Benedict ruled – and the Republic of Vorinder. Solaris spanned the majority of the peninsula, the Lost Lands occupied a small territory in the southern mountains, and Vorinder was a collection of islands off the western coast. Larkesh was another foreign nation in the East, a comparable size to Queen Benedict's territory.

"I've never seen a map like this before," Kaison admitted. He eyeballed the map in disbelief. Grovia was in the western part of the Republic of Vorinder. The distance between Grovia and Sun Castle was easily three days' travel, excluding the small body of water between them. And yet, Kaison and Theadosia had arrived at Sun Castle in minutes.

"It's probably different from what you're used to in Vorinder," Pandora explained. "Queen Benedict gave the land in the North to her brother, so technically they co-rule, but they both have their own territories. King Arturo was responsible for everything before he disappeared." Pandora told the story in her sing-song voice and brushed her palm against the map on the wall.

"Except for Larkesh," Kaison noted, "I heard no one negotiates with their kingdom. Vorinder doesn't."

"Neither does Solaris," admitted Louie. "The people of Larkesh are more technologically advanced, but at the same time terribly backward. They divide society into classist groups and make them compete to the death in awful tournaments."

"What?" gasped Theadosia. "Why have we never heard about this before?"

"They cover it up well, but my family is close to Vorinder's ambassador," Louie explained. "You overhear a lot of stuff you might not want to hear."

Pandora cleared her throat. She motioned to the Lost Lands in the south. "This is where the Shadow of Eclipse resides."

Kaison's teeth clenched in anger. The Shadow of Eclipse was responsible for killing his parents and terrorizing their village, let alone many towns across all of Morbaeda. "Why doesn't the queen send a force after him?" he asked.

"They can't stop him," Pandora replied in a shudder.

"You know, 'Until light and dark congeal, and the world is serene,'" Louie said, quoting the ancient prophecy they all knew too well.

Theadosia crossed her arms. "We all know that's a nursery rhyme."

"Exactly," Louie said. "If it were real, basically the apocalypse has to happen before our world can live in peace." He put his thumbs into his pockets and leaned up against the edge of the table behind him.

"It is real," Pandora insisted. "The night King Arturo disappeared, a new lord came to power. A new Shadow of Eclipse."

"Are you sure King Arturo wasn't killed?" Kaison asked.

"His body was never found. It's possible he was kidnapped."

"By the Shadow of Eclipse?" Theadosia asked.

Pandora nodded, and her large curls bounced up and down.

"No way," Louie intervened. "Supposedly there's an object of light magic that protects the king from the Shadow of Eclipse," he explained. "Someone in the castle must have killed the royal family.

The Shadow of Eclipse couldn't have gotten close to the king."

"That object is a myth," Pandora said.

"Your kidnapping theory is a myth," Louie countered. He remained leaning up against the table casually. "I think someone in the castle killed King Arturo, and everyone is blaming the Shadows cause that's the only answer they have for an unsolved mystery."

"Don't you want to solve that mystery?" Pandora had excitement in her eyes.

Louie paused, choosing his words carefully. "Why would that make a difference? We serve Queen Benedict now."

"Which isn't the true bloodline. King Arturo was the one from the prophecy who was 'forced to abscond.' We could still be waiting for the true queen!"

Louie shook his head. "The prophecy could have already been fulfilled, it could be about a future daughter of Queen Benedict," Louie was using his fingers to demonstrate the number of options, "it could be happening far in the future, or it could be fake." Louie waved the four fingers he was holding up in Pandora's face.

"Louie, the prophecy is–"

"Alright!" Kaison cut them off. "While you two argue, I'm stealing Theadosia."

Kaison crossed between Louie and Pandora to his sister's side. The two of them seemed unfazed and continued their discussion – or argument – about the prophecy. Kaison took Theadosia's arm and pulled her toward the opposite corner of the small room.

"Did you get a good look at the map?" Kaison whispered.

Theadosia nodded, pulling away from Kaison's grasp. "We both know the halberd is magical. If people find out, they may think it's dark magic, and we may be in trouble."

"It could be dark magic," Kaison said. "How do we know?"

"Uh..." Theadosia raised her eyebrows upon hearing the assumption. "Maybe because the tree was glowing and sparkling. Isn't dark magic like...dark?"

Kaison ran his hands over his face and let out a deep breath. "Dux Nikodemus knows about the halberd. He told me to hide it."

Theadosia bit her lip. "How does he know?"

"I have no idea," Kaison said.

"Would he tell someone?"

Kaison was hesitant. "Let's find what we came for in the library and get out of here as soon as possible."

Theadosia agreed. "Let's split up. We have no idea what we're looking for."

His sister was right. The library was enormous, and it could take weeks to search every shelf and book. But they didn't have time. Kaison was determined to stay in this room day in and day out – even if it meant forgoing his sleep and his training as a knight.

Theadosia brushed past Kaison and headed back over to where Pandora and Louie were standing. "Louie, do you want to give me a tour of the library?"

Louie stared. "Um...Pandora knows more about the library than I do. Also, it's dinnertime, and I'm hungry."

Theadosia tilted her head. "Please?"

"Give her a tour," Pandora said, nudging Louie on the arm.

"Fine," Louie said. He made a grand gesture toward the door. "After you, my lady."

"Thanks." Theadosia flashed him a smile before starting out of the backroom. Louie followed her and within moments they were both gone.

When Pandora and Kaison were alone, they stood in silence. Kaison's heart fluttered.

"Why did you want to see the map?" Pandora asked. She returned to the table in the center of the room and began to clean up.

"I wanted a reminder of how far my sister and I came," Kaison said, peering over his shoulder at the large map. Suddenly he caught himself. It was the most horrible lie he had ever heard. She would see right through him.

"Right." Pandora's voice faded. Then she said, "Sorry if I made you uncomfortable with all the talk of magic."

"I wasn't uncomfortable."

"Your expression said otherwise."

"Well…," Kaison's thoughts began churning in his head. Maybe Pandora could help him learn more about the halberd if she was one of the few people practicing and believing in light magic.

"Yes?" Pandora inquired.

"I know that light magic exists."

Pandora clasped her hands behind her back. "How?"

Kaison walked up to the table and placed his hands down on it, leaning in toward Pandora. "For dinner last night I was in Grovia, my hometown," Kaison said as he pointed back at the map, "and by nightfall I arrived here. I believe this took me here," Kaison said. He pulled the staff off his belt and placed it down on the table. It clanked on the wood before it gently glimmered in the light.

Pandora studied the staff on the table before her. There was a long silence until Pandora finally returned her attention to Kaison.

"The stick brought you here?" She tilted her head, her voice unamused.

"It's not a stick."

"Fine, the scepter."

"It's not a scepter, it's magic!"

"Are you making fun of me?"

"No!" Kaison blurted out. "I'm serious!"

Pandora was silent for a moment. "Why would you tell me?"

Kaison ran his fingers through his hair. "I need to know where it came from and how it works, and according to what I heard, you're the only one that is practicing light magic."

Pandora brushed her brown curls behind her shoulder and clasped her hands on top of the table while she stared down at the staff. "Tell me what happened."

"Honestly, it was a blur," Kaison said. "I was holding the halberd, and a sparkling tree appeared –"

"A halberd?" Pandora cut him off.

"Yes…," Kaison realized his story was beginning to sound more crazy. "This staff transforms into a halberd. Then the sparkling tree appeared, and I felt drawn to the tree by some invisible force. Theadosia and I passed underneath the tree branches, and we were here."

Pandora's big eyes widened. "How peculiar. If you let me, I would love to look into it. I am sure with a little research I can find something in the books about a magical halberd that can transport you across Morbaeda."

"By all means," Kaison said, although he wasn't sure if she was being facetious. He took the staff off the table and replaced it at his belt. "Please…don't say anything."

Pandora smiled. "No one would believe me if I did."

Kaison's face reddened. "Thanks."

Pandora picked up the stand of vials off the table and went to put them on a shelf in the corner.

"There's something else," Kaison added.

Pandora set the vials down before turning around, her brown curls flying over her shoulder, and her dress fanning around her.

"Yes?"

"This library...what do you know about it?"

"First your sister wants a tour, and now you want to learn about it. You two are awfully interested in this library for your first day."

Kaison forced a smile. "We're both academics." He tried to shrug it off.

"Mhmm," Pandora said. "Well, follow me. I'm certain I'm better at giving tours." Pandora led the way out to the public library, and Kaison followed. Then Pandora turned down the pathway on her right. She gestured toward the central area with the two front doors.

"This is the main entrance way. Supposedly, the library was shut down for years when Queen Benedict came to power," Pandora explained. She clasped her hands behind her back as she walked, her large curls bouncing. "It's prettier from the second floor."

Pandora weaved around a bookshelf and arrived at the central stairs. They were doubled in width and had a large pink runner down the center.

Kaison tried to take in his surroundings. Why would his father bring him here? He peered up at the chandelier, scrutinizing the number of candles. Then he started reading each title above the bookshelves. There had to be something hidden here. It wouldn't be in plain sight, right?

The two ascended the staircase. Once they had made it to the second story, they could properly view the stained-glass windows on their right and tapestries on their left.

Pandora led Kaison to the East Wing of the library. They continued weaving in and out of the bookshelves while Pandora described small historical details about artifacts and manuscripts. She pointed out each book she had read as she continued the tour.

Nothing seemed too extraordinary. The stained-glass windows

were solid-colored panels and did not delineate any sort of scenes or patterns. Opposite the windows were tapestries hanging from floor to ceiling. Underneath these tapestries were velvet-lined benches built into the wall.

Then something caught Kaison's eye.

Along the wall of tapestries was a maroon cloth draped from the ceiling. It was symmetrical to the other tapestries along the wall, but in the center, was an embroidered weapon that Kaison recognized.

It was a halberd.

- 11 -

Kaison

Kaison stopped dead in his tracks. His breath left him. Could it be this easy? He walked forward, getting a closer look at the stitching.

Pandora snapped her head around. She was many paces ahead in the tour. "Kaison?"

Kaison stood before the tapestry of the halberd. It made sense. His father had given him a halberd and told him to come here. The halberd was the connection.

Kaison looked around. "Thea!" he called. He needed to find his sister. What if this was it?

"What is going on?" Pandora's eyes were wide.

"I need to find my sister," Kaison said. "Thea!" He called again, this time louder.

"Shh!" Pandora scolded.

Kaison took off down the aisle. He turned the corner and crashed into his sister.

"By plague!" Theadosia squealed in alarm. "What is it?"

Louie was directly behind her. His brow was wrinkled with an expression of concern.

"Come, look at this," Kaison said with a wave.

He led Theadosia back to the tapestry, a quickness to his pace. Then he gestured to it, waiting for Theadosia's approval. Pandora was still standing beside them, her arms up beside her in a shrug.

Theadosia stared, her mouth agape. She reached out and ran her fingers down the embroidery. "A halberd," she said.

"Exactly," Kaison replied.

"Well, did you look behind it?"

"Not yet," Kaison said.

With a nod at each other, Kaison took the edge of the tapestry in his hands and pulled it to the side.

There was absolutely nothing on the other side of the tapestry but a blank, stone wall.

"Oh, look," Louie said. "The wall."

"This doesn't make any sense. This has to be it," Kaison muttered.

"What is going on?" Pandora asked, her voice rising to an even higher pitch.

"They've lost their minds," Louie said.

"Our father sent us here to find something," Kaison confessed without thinking twice. "This has to be it." He pressed the stone wall behind the tapestry, hoping for something to move.

Louie scanned their surroundings, making sure no one was watching, before he said, "Maybe it's the wrong tapestry?" He ended with a shrug, looking at Pandora in hopes that she would have an answer.

"Wait," Theadosia said. She took the tapestry in both hands, pulling it away from the wall so that Kaison could continue to investigate, before stretching it out. "There's something on the back."

Before Theadosia had a chance to say anything more, Kaison felt a stone moving underneath his palms. Using his fingernails, he scraped at the corners and slowly loosened it from its position in the wall. With a sharp tug, he pulled the stone from the wall.

"You're not supposed to do that," Pandora said.

Kaison peered inside the hole. At the back of the opening was a large open space in the shape of a diamond.

"Found it," Kaison said, a smirk crossing his face. Kaison stood up tall and took a step away. "It's a keyhole."

"What?" Louie asked in shock. He raced forward and bent over to get a look himself. "By plague, it is."

"Where do you think it leads?" Pandora's doe-eyes were wide.

"And where's the key?" Louie added.

"Wait." Kaison shook his head. "I didn't mean for you two to get involved."

"Well, it's a little late for that." Pandora clasped her hands.

"Kaison, look," Theadosia urged again. She was still holding the tapestry in her hand and studying the back.

Kaison peered over her shoulder and saw what she was referring to. On the backside of the tapestry was another image.

It was still the halberd, but this time, the halberd was upside down. The staff was shortened, and the end opposite the axe blade was taken apart. The pieces of the staff were embroidered next to the halberd. It was as if the tapestry revealed how to disassemble the staff…

"Hold this," Kaison said, giving the stone that he had removed from the wall to Louie.

Louie didn't object and took the stone from Kaison's hands.

"Tell me, how did you know there was a hidden keyhole here?" Louie asked.

"Luck, I guess." Theadosia raised her eyebrows.

"It wasn't luck," Pandora said. "You both were searching for something from the start." However, her voice wasn't cold, but laced with intrigue.

Kaison took the staff off of his belt. Kaison started to manipulate the staff, trying to move different pieces of it. He picked at all three of the jewels one by one – first the red one, then the purple, and then the green. He started fidgeting with the bottom of the scepter, seeing if it would turn one way or another.

"What are you doing?" Theadosia asked.

"I'm trying to get it to match the illustration," Kaison replied.

Louie scanned the tapestry. "Um…am I not getting something here? That's a halberd on the tapestry. And you're holding some fancy staff."

Kaison continued to try and bend the staff, but to no avail.

"Try hitting it on something?" Louie said.

"No!" Theadosia shot Louie a glare. "Don't break it."

Kaison proceeded to push at different parts.

"Don't break it," Theadosia ordered.

"I'm not," Kaison said. He moved his hands to the base of the staff and pulled at the edge. Suddenly, the end of the staff popped off like a cork in a bottle.

Theadosia and Pandora gasped simultaneously. Louie's mouth dropped open.

Kaison rotated the transformed halberd in his hands and peered inside the staff. He held it up to his eye. Sure enough, there was a thin piece of paper rolled up and tucked inside. Kaison carefully reached his fingers down the inside of the staff and pulled out the note. After withdrawing the miniature scroll, Kaison gently unraveled the old parchment.

Theadosia let the tapestry fall, concealing the keyhole, and leaned in closer. Pandora and Louie both moved closer as well, trying to read the message on the parchment for themselves.

Kaison read:

"The crimson tear I lay to rest,
Beneath reflection far northwest.
Under the tree, inside a chest,
The key you seek to start your quest."

Kaison skimmed the parchment, scanning the words over and over again.

"It's a riddle," Pandora said.

"But what does it mean?" Louie asked.

"That's the point of riddles, Louie," said Pandora. "You're supposed to figure it out."

Theadosia crossed her arms and sank into her hip. "Our father brought us all the way here only to find something in the weapon he gave us? It doesn't make sense."

"No," Kaison said. "He wants us to follow this riddle and get the key for whatever is behind there." He ended with a point toward where the hidden keyhole was.

"No offense..." Louie started, "why couldn't your father give you the key?"

"He didn't have time," Theadosia replied.

"He had time to create a treasure hunt."

"Louie," Pandora warned.

Suddenly a creaking noise sounded from around the other side of the library. Kaison's ears were alerted, and he stiffened. He craned his neck in time to see a figure slip around the side of the bookcase.

Louie hid the rock behind his back.

"Hello?" Kaison called.

"Someone was listening to us!" Pandora said in a forced whisper.

Kaison grasped the staff in his hands and darted down the row of tapestries as fast as he could. When he reached the bookcase, the figure had disappeared. He whipped around the shelf. The aisle was empty.

But there was no doubt – someone had been watching them.

- 12 -

Osiris

Osiris stood on the ledge outside her destination. The window was shut, but it was nothing Osiris couldn't break into.

Leaning forward, Osiris planted her gloved palms firmly against the glass. Pressing against it, she opened it a crack. Then she slipped her fingers underneath and forced the window open the rest of the way.

Silently, she slipped one leg inside before ducking her head underneath the frame, entering the window.

The office was dimly lit by a candle in the corner. A man was backlit by the candle and his seated silhouette spanned widely within the space. However, his back was to her. The room wasn't nearly as ornate as the top-tier home, but this man certainly still had money.

"I have a door, you know," he said.

"And I can't get caught," Osiris replied.

The chair scraped against the ground as the man rose to a standing position. He crossed the room, coming into view. A thick beard covered his face, and a bright orange sash draped around him, indicating that he used to be a soldier.

"Would you like some tea?"

Osiris pulled the satchel off over her head and extended it to him. "I would like my money."

"Ahh..." he sang, "all business." He took the satchel from her, revealing the chest. Prying open the latch with his thick fingers, he uncovered the diamond necklace.

His eyes lit up, widening. A twinkle glistened against his iris. "You don't disappoint," he said. He reached into his pocket, withdrawing a velvet pouch. It jingled, the coins inside bouncing against one another. With a light toss, he threw it up in the air and caught it again in his palm. "What did we agree on again?"

Osiris didn't flinch. They had already made the deal, and he couldn't back out now. She kept her voice steady as she said, "Two-hundred silver."

"Right," the man spoke. He shifted his body back toward his table, carrying the chest with him. "I think that's a lot of money, don't you?" He shoved the coin purse back into his pocket.

Osiris felt her shoulders clench. This is why she didn't like working with new contractors. "You made the offer. You hired me."

"No...." he said, "*I* didn't. I'm just the middle man."

Osiris shifted her weight, trying to maintain her composure. "Pay me two-hundred silver, or give me back the necklace."

The man set the chest down on his desk, his back turned to Osiris. "I don't care what my superior said," the man spoke. "He's not from Larkesh. I am. And I don't work with Vynx."

Osiris sensed the attack before it happened. The man whirled around, drawing a crossbow from the shadows. He aimed it directly at Osiris, and it fired.

The world seemed to move in slow motion. The arrow whizzed through the air, the sound reverberating through the room. She could see where the arrow was moving in a faint white outline, as if she could predict the pathway of the weapon.

Osiris reached her hand up and grabbed the arrow out of the air. The room snapped back to normal. Anger burned through her limbs, and her fist tightened, snapping the wood into two pieces. The broken arrow fell to the ground pitifully.

The man lowered the crossbow as his eyes widened. "Y-You Vynx aren't human. You're evil!" He struggled to find another arrow amidst the papers on the desk, shuffling around in the dim light.

"I only want the money," Osiris said. "Give it to me, and I'll leave."

The man couldn't find another arrow. He glowered at Osiris, masking his fear. He let out a yell as though it were a battle cry. He charged forward, raising the crossbow in the air to use it as a blunt weapon.

Osiris cocked her head to the side, evaluating her options. She tried to refrain from fighting him, but she had no choice.

Osiris dodged the initial blow, stepping to the side. She withdrew one of the daggers from her vest in a swift motion. With a singular foul swoop, she spun around and plunged the dagger into the man's back.

He let out a shriek, collapsing down to his knees. The crossbow clanked to the ground. "Y-You can't outrun the Tournament forever. You Vynx will…"

Osiris yanked the dagger out of his back. A cry escaped his lips as he fell forward, his cheek meeting the ground. He choked, gasping for air.

Letting out a sigh, Osiris looked down at her dagger, which was drenched in his blood. She cleaned the blade against her thigh.

"It didn't have to come to this," she said, sheathing the dagger.

But the man had stopped choking. His body was still.

Osiris knelt down, pushing the man over to flip him onto his back. Then she withdrew the coin purse from his pocket. She hesitated for a moment, staring at his lifeless eyes.

Her attention shifted to her wrist. She pulled back her sleeve, revealing a symbol branded to the inside of her forearm. The symbol of two overlapping diamonds with a line through the center was burned into her dark skin. She was a Vynx, and it was branded on her so that everyone would know. Her chest tightened, and she hastily pulled her sleeve back down.

"Keep the necklace," she said as she stood. She tied the coin purse to her belt. "I keep my word."

Turning away, she started back for the open window when her body froze.

A silhouette vanished from the window frame. It was so quick, Osiris second guessed that she had seen it in the first place.

Osiris dashed to the open window. Ducking underneath the frame, Osiris peered out, but the figure she had seen a moment earlier was no longer there. She couldn't have imagined it.

There was no doubt that someone was there. Someone had watched her commit a murder.

- 13 -

KAISON

Kaison, Theadosia, Louie, and Pandora quickly scampered out of the library, careful to return the stone in the wall and make sure the tapestry looked untouched. At dinner, they continued to think about the riddle over and over, but it didn't make sense. Kaison still didn't understand why his father had brought them here. Even if they were connected to Sun Castle – which was highly likely at this point – why didn't his father come out and tell him the truth? Why didn't his father give him this mysterious key long ago?

His father had to know about the library at Sun Castle and what was behind the wall. Nikodemus also knew about the halberd. What was the connection there? Did Arthur use to work with Nikodemus? Was he a knight at one point in his life?

Before long, the sun had set, and the dining hall closed. It was time to escort Theadosia to Elistalia. Pandora explained that there was a woman that ran Elistalia named Madame Lucia and that the complex was located outside of the castle walls on the outskirts of

Tamir.

Kaison and Theadosia said goodbye to the others and made their way to the grand entryway. Then, they stepped outside to the overbearingly pink gardens and flowers, and crossed to the gate. The knights were happy to lift up the gate and see the two Vorinder natives leave the castle's protection for the time being.

The siblings retraced their steps exactly the same way Erik had taken them and followed the directions to Elistalia.

"Who do you think was watching us in the library?" asked Theadosia.

"Whoever it was knows about the riddle now," answered Kaison. "Why did you tell Pandora about the halberd?"

"I thought she could help," Kaison said, flustered. He let out a huff and ran his fingers through his hair.

Theadosia scoffed. She stopped on the path and sunk into her hip. "Are you sure it's not because you find her attractive?"

"I do not."

Theadosia raised an eyebrow.

"She knows about magic!" Kaison said.

"Sure." Theadosia started walking once more and Kaison matched her stride.

"And don't come at me when you were flirting with Louie."

"What?"

"When you asked him for a tour."

Theadosia laughed. "That wasn't close to flirting, trust me."

Kaison covered his ears. "I don't want to talk about this."

Theadosia was shaking her head, continuing to laugh. "Don't worry, he's not interested in me."

"How do you know?"

Theadosia shot him a glare. "You're so dumb."

Kaison shrugged. "I'll take your word on it. But back to Pandora, she said she would research it."

"Fine. Please promise me you will hide it somewhere and not keep carrying it around for everyone to see."

"I promise," Kaison admitted, but he wasn't sure that leaving the transformed halberd in his room unguarded was the best option either.

They arrived at Elistalia, which was a large barn illuminated by a dozen torches. There were no windows on the outside of the building, and they had to step over a pile of tangled weeds to make it to the front door. The main entranceway of the barn had been cleared of livestock and transformed into a communal dining hall. However, the faint scent of barn animals still lingered, and the humid air was laced with the smell of sweat. Kaison and Theadosia stood in the center of a group of tables, surrounded by dozens of guests. Children scampered past them, almost crashing into the two as they chased each other. A baby squealed from the nearest table at a high-pitched tone.

"You shouldn't have to stay here while I'm at the castle," Kaison said. There were no guards or knights stationed in his view.

"It's a refuge," Theadosia said. "Did you expect the queen to put us all up in a manor?" She turned to her brother, and when she saw the dissatisfaction remaining on his face, she added, "It's only until we find out what's behind the wall in the library."

When Kaison still hadn't responded, Theadosia let out a huff.

"Come help me find this Madame Lucia woman."

Kaison began to follow Theadosia through the people. He looked at each one of them in turn, wondering about their individual stories. Each one of them had been attacked by the Shadow of Eclipse and his army. Each one had barely escaped with their lives. Each one probably had seen their family members die. The thought made Kaison shudder. Who was to say the Shadow of Eclipse wouldn't return here and finish the job?

"Excuse me," Theadosia stopped a person crossing their path. "Where is Madame Lucia?"

The stranger pointed off in a random direction.

"Thank you," Theadosia said.

Before long, someone stuck out from the crowd. She was a petite woman with graying-black hair pulled back into a tight bun. Unlike the others in the building, she wore a vibrant pink apron over her clothes. She had a scroll in front of her and scribbled down words as she scanned the area, calling out to everyone that crossed her path by name.

Theadosia approached her. "Are you Madame Lucia?"

Her eyes lit up as she glanced up from her scroll. "Yes I am." She smiled. "You are?"

"Theadosia Ruiz," she introduced.

"Kaison."

Madame Lucia straightened in her posture. "Dux Nikodemus told me about you two. All the way from the Republic of Vorinder!"

Theadosia forced a smile.

"Yes," Kaison muttered. "My sister is staying here tonight."

"I know," Lucia said. "Room twelve."

"Where can I find that?" Theadosia inquired.

Something caught Kaison's attention. A woman on his right was kneeling on the ground, praying, and she had a shawl wrapped around her. On the shawl was an image of a sun. It wasn't an ordinary sun. It was the same insignia that Dux Nikodemus had shown him that morning and asked if he recognized it.

It was the same symbol on the ceiling in the library.

Kaison snapped back to the conversation happening before him.

Lucia was pointing at an upper loft. "Second door closest to the stairs on that side," she said. "Let me know if you need anything."

Theadosia smiled. "Thanks."

Theadosia started off in the direction of her room, pushing through the crowd. Kaison looked to where he saw the woman with the symbol, but she seemed to have vanished. Quickly, he picked up the pace to reach his sister.

They headed toward the staircase to the upper level. The warehouse seemed to be getting quieter, but maybe that was Kaison adjusting to the loud noise of indistinct chatter.

As they ascended the stairs, Kaison looked down at the main gathering space. He tried to find the woman with the shawl once more, but she was completely gone. That symbol meant something. He needed to know what.

When Theadosia reached room twelve, she entered. It was a small space filled with three bunk beds and two chests. A large family seemed to have claimed two of the bunkbeds. They had five children, three of them playing some game that involved them rolling under the bed, and the other two were already curled up on a top bunk. The mother looked drained, and she attempted to calm down the three children that were awake, but they weren't listening.

The other bunk bed had a girl sitting on the top, busy writing in a blue journal. Kaison recognized her immediately. It was the girl from the gardens. Her fiery red hair was impossible to miss.

Maeve.

Theadosia proceeded to the bunk. "Is this taken?" Theadosia asked, gesturing to the lower mattress.

Maeve withdrew her attention from her journal to see who had spoken to her, but her eyes fell on Kaison.

"I don't feel safe with a strange boy in the room," Maeve said.

"I'm not staying," Kaison said.

"You better not be," she replied. Finally, her attention went to Theadosia. "No, it's not taken. I welcome you to the best place ever." The sentence dripped with sarcasm.

An obnoxious squeal sounded from one of the kids, causing Kaison to tilt his head from the pain in his ear. He had been in the room for a moment, and it was already horrible.

"You don't have to stay here," Kaison said to his sister. "I can find you somewhere in the castle."

Theadosia shook her head, letting out a deep breath. "What makes me more special than all these people?" she asked. She looked down at her dress before continuing. "I'm going to ask if they have any nightgowns or something. Or maybe some pants. I can't stand these clothes."

"Do you want me to come with you?" Kaison offered.

"What are you, my bodyguard? I'll be right back." Theadosia exited the room.

One of the children hit their sibling, and a bout of tears followed. It was more screaming than crying. Then the two on the top bunk woke up, and the family began shouting at one another. Kaison thought his ears were going to bleed from their high-pitched screams. Deep down, he had sympathy for the pain the family was going through, but Kaison was certain he couldn't stay in this room for one night.

He took a step closer to the bunk. "How long have you been here?" he asked Maeve.

Maeve scanned Kaison up and down before returning to her journal. Her quill pen gently brushed against the paper.

An uncomfortable silence passed between him and her, despite the squealing from the children.

Kaison cleared his throat.

"I'm Kaison, originally from Grovia."

Maeve closed the journal. "So?" she said. Her eyes were a brilliant shade of green.

"I thought…" Kaison stopped. "Obviously you're here because you lost your village. My sister and I lost ours too."

Maeve rolled her eyes before she scooted on her bed closer to Kaison. "If you're looking for someone to hold your hand and wipe away your tears, that's not me."

Kaison's mouth parted as he searched for words. "No, I…" he struggled to answer. "I was looking for a name."

Maeve looked unconvinced. Finally, she seemed to relax as she leaned up against the wall. "Maeve."

Kaison smiled. "Kaison."

"You already said that." Maeve rolled her eyes and reopened her journal.

"May I ask how long you have been here?"

"No."

Kaison ran his hand through his hair. She wanted nothing to do with him, it was clear. He tapped his foot on the ground impatiently as he waited for his sister to return.

"A few months."

"Months?"

Maeve's eyes narrowed. "Did you not hear me?"

"N-No, I heard you. I'm just…surprised. How many people from your village survived?"

Maeve hesitated. She closed her journal once more and held it to her chest. "Two of us."

Kaison shook his head. "I didn't realize how many people the

Shadow of Eclipse had killed."

Maeve flipped a curl out of her eyes. "My village wasn't attacked by the Shadow of Eclipse."

Taken aback, Kaison's mouth parted as he searched for a response.

The door opened again, and Theadosia reappeared. "They didn't have anything," she spoke as she entered, closing the door behind her.

Maeve went straight back to writing in her journal, and Kaison couldn't ask her any more questions. He glanced at the hysterical children before speaking to his sister. "You sure you will be alright here?"

"Yes," Theadosia smiled. Then she dropped her voice to a whisper. "We have to solve the riddle. Meet tomorrow?"

Kaison nodded.

- 14 -

Kaison

The night air fluttered against Kaison's face. During his time at Elistalia, the sun had completely set, leaving the moorland dark and still, except for the shining beacon of light pouring out of Sun Spire. His mind was churning with thoughts as he proceeded across the open field. His fingers clutched around the transformed halberd once more. He knew his sister would be fine by herself in the refuge, but he still wished that they hadn't been separated from one another.

Kaison decided to take a short cut through the practice fields, instead of circling back to the front entrance of the town and taking the main road up to the front gates. He made his way to the gate at the western edge of the castle and passed underneath it, nodding to the knights in turn. Then he continued on his way.

Soon Kaison was near the stables on the western side of the castle so that he could take the west entrance to his chambers without going through the main hall. He hoped he had the pathway memorized correctly.

There was no one around the training fields, as everyone had reported back to the knight's quarters for the evening, so Kaison took it upon himself to walk slowly so that he could think. He needed to decode the message inside the halberd. He could hear his father speaking the riddle in his mind:

The crimson tear I lay to rest,
Beneath reflection far northwest.
Under the tree, inside a chest,
The key you seek to start your quest.

Far northwest...what was far northwest? The riddle obviously pointed him to the key for the library. He had to figure out where it was.

His stomach churned in grief. Why couldn't his father be here to help him?

Kaison continued to walk, focused on the tall grass in front of him. That's when he noticed a second shadow beside him.

He turned around to face a wooden beam flying down from the sky. Instantly, Kaison blocked with his forearms, feeling the pain from the blunt weapon ripple through his wrists. A sudden adrenaline shot through him, and he looked at his attacker.

This figure was shorter than Kaison and wore all black. A scarf was wrapped around their head and mouth, masking their appearance completely. An oversized shirt tucked into trousers made it impossible to tell what size they were.

The attacker was already preparing for another blunt hit. They raised the wooden pole straight above their head, but Kaison acted fast, punching his knuckles across the attacker's jaw.

They stumbled backwards, surprised, but it only made them

move faster. They raised the wooden beam up in the air and thrust it forward.

Kaison barely had time to move his face out of the way, and the weapon came down with a tremendous blow to his shoulder. Kaison let out a scream as he stumbled on the ground. Quickly, he reached to his belt to unlatch his transformed halberd, but as he was drawing it forward, the attacker thrust their boot into Kaison's stomach.

The wind was knocked from Kaison as he fell onto his back, the staff clanking roughly on the ground beside him.

The attacker sent their boot straight into Kaison's side, causing an unbearable pain to ripple through his ribcage. Kaison clutched his side in agony, unable to brace himself against the punches to his face.

"Help!" Kaison screamed.

Silhouetted by the stars, Kaison saw the wooden beam coming down once again. Kaison braced himself, holding his arms out before him. The wooden beam slammed against his palms. Kaison ignored the electrifying pain, and he clenched his fists tightly. He tore the beam out of his attacker's grasp. He flung it off to the side, knowing if he was hit in the face then it could be the end.

The attacker didn't stop even though their weapon was gone.

The punches came so fast. One after another. All Kaison could do was bring his arms up to his face, attempting to block. He couldn't open his eyes for more than a moment to try and get a better look at his attacker. The pain was overcoming him, and he could taste blood.

Then suddenly, the attacks stopped. A pounding headache burned against Kaison's temples, and he rolled to his side, clutching his stomach in pain. He coughed up blood. Hardly able to open his eyes, he saw the figure bend over and pick the staff up off the ground.

The halberd!

Then the attacker pressed down onto the red gem, and the blade shot out the top while the staff extended downward. The glittering gold halberd was magnificent in its full form, and the moonlight reflected off the metal that was about to be Kaison's execution.

"No!" Kaison cried, another sudden wave of adrenaline shooting through him.

He reached out and grabbed the center of the staff of the halberd, immediately pulling the attacker back toward him.

The figure then took hold of the weapon with both hands, but Kaison countered and did the same. The halberd was horizontal between them, and they both tugged against it. They were in a deadlock. Kaison's sweaty palms began to slip.

Then the attacker planted their boot on Kaison's chest to provide more leverage. "Give me the halberd!" the attacker screamed.

It was a girl.

Kaison's moment of shock didn't last long, for another looming figure appeared behind the girl. With one swoop, the man's arms grabbed the girl around the waist and swiftly yanked her backward. The girl lost her grip on the halberd, causing it to come crashing down on Kaison's chest, knocking the wind from him once more.

Kaison's rescuer threw the girl to the side, and she landed roughly on the grass. The man widened his stance, hovering over her. He reached out to pull off the scarf hiding her identity, but she had already scrambled away. She crawled to her feet and scooped up her wooden beam before tearing off in the direction of the castle. Within a few moments, she had completely vanished into the night as if she was never there.

The tall figure extended a hand toward Kaison. "Are you all right?" they asked.

Kaison blinked, regaining his senses. His eyesight was still blurry, and pain throbbed deep within his head, but the moonlight cast enough light to reveal his rescuer.

Simon was hovering over him, his face indiscernible.

"I'm fine..." Kaison managed to say, his voice raspy. He reached up and grabbed tightly onto Simon's hand.

Simon pulled Kaison to his feet, but almost instantly an overwhelming pain pounded against Kaison's ribs, and he collapsed forward.

"You're not fine," Simon said, pulling Kaison upright and slinging his arm over his back. "I'll take you to the infirmary."

"No," Kaison said. He couldn't trust anyone at the castle. "Can you help me to my room?"

Simon gave a curt nod. He picked up Kaison's halberd for him, and he helped Kaison walk back to Sun Castle. The magnificent weapon was still in it's full form and was almost as tall as Simon.

Kaison limped the entire way, putting a lot of weight against Simon for support and clutching his ribs with his other hand. Dizzying black specks clouded his vision, forcing him to depend entirely on Simon for direction.

He was lucky that Simon had shown up. It was clear that the girl had intended to kill him and steal the halberd. A shudder went up Kaison's spine at the thought.

Simon led Kaison through the servant's entrance to try and remain hidden before leading him up the stairs to the knights' wing. The stairs were harder to ascend than Kaison thought they would be.

Only a few knights were still awake and in the main foyer. A few glances were shot in Kaison and Simon's direction, but no questions were asked.

Finally, Simon reached Kaison's room. Without knocking, Simon thrust the door open with the heel of his boot.

"Great Sun!" Louie's voice was heard. He shot up from his bed.

Simon continued to help Kaison in the room before finally letting him collapse down onto his bed.

Kaison fell flat on his back, an ache rippling through the side of his ribcage. He tasted blood. His veins bulged in his head as thundering blood pulsed through them.

"By plague, what happened?" Louie asked, standing up from his bed.

Simon returned to the door and slammed it shut. "Someone attacked him," he stated.

"Who?"

"We don't know. They were masked," Simon said. He held the halberd upright in both of his hands. "They were trying to steal this."

Louie's eyes flicked between Simon's face and the halberd. He opened his mouth to speak, but suddenly stopped short. Then he crossed the room to reach Kaison's side.

"Are you all right?" Louie asked.

Kaison was staring up at the ceiling, his mouth slightly open. He let out a groan of pain. "I think I'll be fine," he said. "Only because Simon intervened."

Louie questioned Simon. "You were conveniently there at the time of the attack?"

Simon was silent, his expression blank.

"Louie...," Kaison mustered, his voice barely audible. "He saved my life."

Louie puffed his chest out before sharply exhaling. Then Louie held out his hand toward Simon, gesturing for the halberd. "I can take care of it from here," he said.

Simon was still. His thin face was shadowed in the dim light, but his bottomless eyes glimmered. Finally, he took a step forward and placed the halberd in Louie's grasp. "Take care of yourself, Kaison,"

Simon said before exiting the room.

The door closed behind him with a loud thud.

Louie carefully placed the halberd at the foot of Kaison's bed. "We should get you some help," he said.

"No," Kaison replied. "I don't trust anyone here."

"Then I'll get Pandora," Louie said.

"No," Kaison repeated.

"Kaison, you need–"

"A girl attacked me," Kaison blurted out.

Louie hesitated. He leaned up against the wall and crossed his arms. "You think it was Pandora?"

"No…I…," honestly, Kaison had no idea. "I don't know. She's the only one that knows about the halberd."

"Speaking of which, where did the halberd come from?"

"Remember when I found the note in the staff?"

Louie nodded.

Kaison waited for Louie to connect the dots. It hurt too much to talk.

Louie's eyes suddenly widened. "Blazing Sun! The staff is the halberd? There's no way!" He threw his hands in the air before shoving them in his pockets and letting out a huff. "Well, it wasn't Pandora who attacked you," he said. "She can't fight."

"And you know that for sure?" Kaison asked.

Louie didn't respond.

Kaison was at a loss. Who would attack him for his halberd? Did they want it for its transportation magic? Nikodemus had told him to hide it, and he had been right. Anyone on the practice field would've seen it, and the queen and Emmett knew about it too.

Kaison closed his eyes. His mind churned with thoughts. Maybe whoever attacked him wanted it for the message inside. Kaison's father was leading him somewhere, and he had to be the first to get there.

Far northwest…beneath reflections…

Pieces of the note echoed in and out of his mind.

Kaison shot up in bed, ignoring the pain that surged through his body. "I know where we're supposed to go," he said.

Louie jumped. "Where?"

"The letter in the halberd," Kaison clarified. "My father and I used to hunt at a place called the Reflecting Grounds, right next to my hometown."

"Why do you think we have to go there…?" Louie's eyebrow was raised high on his forehead.

"The grounds are far northwest," Kaison continued. "We must be looking for a chest beneath the water at the Reflecting Grounds. That has to be it!"

"The letter is leading us to the Republic of Vorinder?" Louie said, straightening his posture as his eyes widened.

Kaison nodded. "I'm supposed to return home."

- 15 -

EMMETT

Sir Emmett waited in the darkness of the hallway. Anticipation burned inside of him. He tapped his foot impatiently as he waited for the person he was meeting. The only solace now was thinking of the woman he so longed for. He closed his eyes and pictured her. Her voice taunted Emmett with every soft, velvet word that left her lips. If only he could reverse time, maybe she would still be alive.

Reality traversed through his mind like a sharp dagger.

A figure was approaching him from the end of the hall. It was the girl he had been waiting for. She was disguised in an acceptable outfit, but it wasn't something Sir Emmett would have worn to attack someone. In fact, it was hardly an acceptable outfit for any woman.

The girl continued to approach him. A hood covered her face and masked her appearance. She walked briskly, her fear exuding from her body.

Emmett waited until she was within a few paces from him. She came to a stop, her arms on either side of her, empty.

"Where is it?" Emmett's voice was already booming.

The girl unwrapped the scarf from her face, letting it fall on her shoulders. Emmett immediately could see by her face that he had fought back.

"Simon showed up out of nowhere." Her voice wavered as she spoke.

"Simon?" Emmett took a step forward, and the girl immediately countered.

"I'm sorry!"

"You disappoint me," Emmett stated. He changed his tone of voice and expression, a mask to hide his next intentions.

She cowered back further, clasping her hands in front of her chest. "Please, give me another chance!"

Sir Emmett growled. "You don't understand the situation, do you?" He withdrew a paper from his back pocket, unfolding it in front of the girl. He shoved her against the wall with his forearm and put the piece of paper in her face. "Look!"

The girl was trembling underneath him. Her lip quivered as she fought back tears.

On the paper was a landscape she had never seen before. Various angular buildings stretched into a cloud-filled sky. A body of water surrounded the buildings, and they seemed to twinkle with added rectangular flames.

"What is that?" she asked.

"The question you should be asking is: how do we get there," Emmett answered. He stepped away from her, regaining his composure and refolding the paper. Then he shoved the drawing back into his pocket. With a huff, he finally said, "It's time for phase two."

- 16 -

Osiris

Osiris continued through the alleyways. The city of Taville was starting to wake up with the rising of the sun. Osiris pressed onward, acknowledging the villagers that glanced in her direction.

She remembered the figure at the window – the one who had witnessed the murder.

She remained cautious as she watched everyone, wondering if any of these people could've been the mysterious silhouette.

Rounding the corner, Osiris continued past the marketplace where merchants were beginning to set up. She entered the building on her right, and the doors were already propped open.

The woman at the counter was rolling a piece of orange cloth. The fabric store was overflowing in colors and styles. Everything from wool to leather filled the shelves on the wall, organized by color.

"Moriah," Osiris greeted the girl. She went directly to the table, standing across from her.

"Good morning," Moriah spoke, but kept her attention on the

fabric in front of her.

Osiris untied the coin purse from her belt and plopped it down on the counter.

Moriah scrutinized Osiris, her face flashing from underneath her bangs. Her hand extended toward the velvet bag before scooping it up from the table. She shoved it into a drawer behind the counter. Then she returned to the fabric.

Osiris glanced over her shoulder at the open doorway, making sure no one was about to enter. Then she headed into the backroom, passing underneath a curtain of beads. She knelt down at the carpet, pulling back the corner and revealing a trap door. She hoisted the trap door up from the ground, and it creaked open with a shriek. Then she scaled down the ladder into the darkness beyond.

Dropping to the concrete floor, Osiris landed in the cellar. It was expansive, far larger than a normal cellar. It was set up with rows of bunk-beds. The mattresses were cheap and deteriorating, and the blankets were thin. Almost two dozen people were crowded in the basement. The grates on their right led to the tunnels, eventually out to the ocean.

Only a few people were awake, and every once in a while, Osiris heard a cough. As she passed through the center of the room, something fell in her peripheral vision. A stuffed doll had fallen from an upper bunk.

A small child on the upper bunk sat upright, looking over the edge.

Osiris knelt to pick up the doll before extending it back to the girl.

"Thanks, Osiris." The child reached out for the doll, the Vynx symbol flashing on her wrist. She grabbed the toy and pulled it close to her chest before resting her head back down.

Osiris gave the girl a smile before continuing through the cellar. She reached the beds beside the grates that led to the tunnels. A strong draft blew through the grates.

At the end of the row of bunk beds, there were three mattresses set up directly on the ground. That was where Osiris slept, in case anything came through the tunnels.

Feeling her limbs ache, Osiris plopped down on her mattress, letting her back rest against the cool stone. She exhaled, her mind racing with thoughts.

The boy on the mattress across from hers shifted. He flipped onto his other shoulder before propping himself up on his elbow. His russet hair was a mess. His skin wasn't as dark as Osiris's, but rather a deep bronze. Reaching into his pocket, he withdrew a golden pocket watch. Flipping it open, he checked the time, before his eyes settled on Osiris.

"I'm curious where you've been all night when we had no contracts." His voice was calm in an attempt to mask his discontent.

Destrian was the one who had brought her to this hideout years ago. Ever since, they worked as accomplices for any gig they were assigned.

It was no use lying to him. "I knew you wouldn't approve of the deal," Osiris stated.

"And why is that?"

"Because it was someone we haven't worked for before."

Destrian blinked multiple times, and he sat upright, concealing the pocket watch in his pocket. "Is it someone we will consider working for in the future?" He leaned his elbows against his knees.

"No." Osiris flipped her braid over her shoulder.

Destrian shifted on his mattress. "Well, may he rest in peace."

Osiris scanned Destrian's appearance. His boots were on, with one lace untied. The mud was still fresh. "And where have you been all night?"

Destrian's nose flared. He scratched the back of his neck. "I made contact with a soldier who has access to the trading ships. With the right persuasion, he could get us passes."

"It won't work," Osiris said. "They'll check our wrists at the gate."

Destrian's head jerked into a tilt. "The right people can be bribed."

"How much do we have saved?" Osiris asked.

"Not more than they would receive to turn us in."

Osiris let out a deep breath. "Besides," she paused to look over at the line of bunk beds in the cellar, "how do we leave everyone behind?"

Destrian followed Osiris's gaze. "The city is filled with Vynx in hiding. We can't save everyone."

"I disagree."

A bell rang upstairs.

Immediately, Osiris shot up to a standing position, her heart plummeting in her chest. It was the bell Moriah was supposed to ring when soldiers came to the hideout looking for Vynx. They hadn't been forced to use it before.

Destrian rose in front of her, only slightly taller than she was. His eyes spoke for him: "Go!"

Destrian tore off toward the ladder to the fabric store. The people startled awake, and he reassured them as he passed.

Osiris wrenched the grate from the tunnel, the loose screws rattling as they bounced on the ground. She threw the grate to the side before charging into the tight space. She was forced to crouch as she darted through the tunnel. It was pitch black, but she was familiar with the exit. It was how she and Destrian snuck in and out while the fabric shop was closed.

Her boots splashed against the shallow water at the bottom of the tunnel, soaking through the leather. Her hand traced the wall, feeling for her next turn. She whipped to the right, turning down another passage before reaching a metal ladder. She scaled the ladder, seeing another grate at the top. Beams of light shone through the grate in rectangular patterns. Osiris didn't slow down her pace as she ascended the rungs.

Reaching the grate, she used her forearm to push it up and to the side. Osiris hoisted herself onto solid ground in a back alley. She glanced up and down the alley, but saw no one except for the people on the cross street beyond. She replaced the grate on top of the opening, concealing it to look like a sewer, and darted toward the side of the building.

Getting a running start, Osiris ran up the side of the building before extending her hands to the story above. Her gloved palms gripped the ledge of the roof just as gravity pulled her back down. She struggled to find traction along the wall, and she used her legs to help her onto solid ground. Once on the second story, she used the grooves in the clay walls to help her scale to the rooftops. Her fingers burned, and she felt her body shaking as she forced herself to ascend. When she was closer to the top, she was able to grab onto the wooden posts that held the marketplace flags. Using those to leverage herself, she managed to reach the roof.

The tunnel had taken her across the street to the buildings opposite the fabric store. She knelt at the edge of the rooftop, peering down at the scene below. Moriah was talking to two soldiers in the doorway of her shop, her arms flying aimlessly as she yelled at them. The soldiers stood out amongst the marketplace crowd that was now beginning to stir. The Larkeshi army's orange and rust colors were hard to miss.

One soldier tried to push past Moriah, but she instantly pressed a palm against his chest, holding him back. They were looking for Vynx in hiding.

Then Osiris saw Destrian exit the shop, slipping out through the fabrics. The soldiers paid him no mind, thinking he was one of the villagers in the marketplace browsing through the shop. Osiris watched him as he started down the street, his hand tight around a small pouch.

Osiris scanned the rooftop for the chest she had left up there. Sure enough, it was only a few paces away. She darted over, opening the chest to reveal her supplies: a bow with a single arrow, flint and iron. The end of the bow was wrapped, concealing a stash of gunpowder.

Osiris raced back to the edge of the roof, her eyes scanning for Destrian once more. She saw him farther down the street, near where it opened up into a plaza.

Destrian watched a group of people pass him, giving them a nod, before he placed the pouch on top of a barrel.

Getting to work, Osiris began to set the fire arrow ablaze with her tools. After a few simple strikes, a spark lit the end of the arrow, igniting a blue flame. She nocked the arrow and drew the bow, aiming at the ignition materials Destrian had planted. Destrian was walking away from the barrel, his strides calm.

For a brief moment, Osiris felt the world slow. She could see the trajectory of the arrow as though it were a faint glow. Exhaling, Osiris released the arrow.

Her surroundings snapped back to normal as the arrow hit its target. An explosion lit the street, the sound piercing Osiris's ears. Screams erupted from the marketplace, and a bright red glow danced through the street.

The soldiers immediately sprang into action, leaving Moriah behind and forgetting about their interrogation.

Osiris dropped the bow in the chest, slammed it closed, and made her escape. Using a pole on the backside of the building, she dropped over the edge of the rooftop and slid down it. She felt the rush of the wind, her braid flying, and her stomach flipping.

Right before she reached the bottom, Osiris gripped the pole tighter to slow her descent. Landing with a hard thud on the cobblestone, Osiris regained her composure and started walking down the alley. Behind her, screaming rang through the streets, and Osiris headed in the opposite direction.

She sensed someone approaching, and only a moment passed before Destrian fell in stride with her, their shoulders almost touching.

They neither said a word nor looked at one another as they proceeded down the road, leaving the screaming and the flames behind them.

- 17 -

Kaison

Early the next morning, Kaison rose from the bed, careful not to wake Louie. He couldn't sleep, not with the pain of the injuries. He could feel caked blood on his cheek and wondered if there was an open wound.

Pulling on a clean shirt, Kaison started for the door.

He paused, glancing back at the halberd that rested at the bottom of his bed. It would be safe for a moment alone, especially with Louie asleep there.

Then Kaison snuck out of the room.

He made his way down the corridor, his mind racing. His father wanted him to return to Grovia. It was so simple. But what did his father want him to find that he couldn't have given him back home? There was so much his father had kept hidden from him. Now, Kaison wasn't only fulfilling his father's wishes, he was looking for answers.

He passed a few knights on the way to the infirmary, none of which paid him any attention. Once he reached the infirmary, he noticed the doors were propped open, and he let himself in.

Rows of white cots lined the walls, and only one seemed to be occupied. Kaison assumed whoever it was was asleep. A sheet draped from the ceiling hid a back area.

A throbbing pain burned deep within his head, and Kaison could taste blood at the back of his mouth. He clutched his ribcage and parted the curtain, stepping inside the backroom.

There were two empty cots and glass cabinets along the walls. A white table rested between the cabinets, cluttered with bottles and herbs.

Kaison crossed the room, quickening his pace. He had to take something before a nurse arrived.

Scanning the bottles, Kaison read each label. He wasn't familiar with over half of them, and the other half weren't going to help him.

"Talamine...," Kaison muttered under his breath, looking for the specific herb he was after. If he couldn't find ointment, he could at least take the pain reliever.

He went to the glass cabinets where piles of herbs were organized. There was one shelf that was unlabeled. Kaison's heart lurched when his gaze settled on a deep blue leaf, thick with thorns. Brixann antidote?

"Can I help you?"

He nearly jumped out of his shoes and whipped around to face a girl. She was holding back the white sheet curtain, her eyebrows raised.

It was Cheyenne Xy'tier, the nurse who had helped Theadosia the first night. Her jet black hair cascaded down her back, and her short-sleeve dress revealed her olive skin.

Kaison raised his hands defensively. "I'm sorry, I was looking for–"

"You're stealing." It wasn't a question.

Kaison swallowed the lump in his throat. "I..." He couldn't lie.

There was no doubt an uncomfortable tension settled in the air while Kaison searched for words.

Cheyenne gestured to the cot. "Sit down."

Kaison didn't move.

"It's fine. I won't tell anyone you're here."

Relief flooded through Kaison, and he lowered his hands, crossing to the cot. Exhaling, he hoisted himself up on the bed, feeling the pain immediately ripple through his side. He had to bite his tongue to hold back an audible groan.

Cheyenne started for the cabinets. The pace to her stride implied she knew exactly what she needed to treat him.

Kaison knew she would inevitably ask what had happened. The prior night flashed before Kaison's mind, causing his breath to catch in his throat. He searched for plausible lies, but he hadn't looked in a mirror yet to see how poorly he actually appeared.

Cheyenne stood at the table, grinding together herbs. Her back was to him.

Kaison tried to see around her to examine what she was mixing together, but her body was blocking the pestle and mortar from his view.

"You don't have to steal," Cheyenne said. "I don't know where you come from, but we aren't barbarians here."

Embarrassment flooded through Kaison's body. "It won't happen again."

After draping a cloth over her forearm, Cheyenne picked up the mortar and a bowl of water before approaching Kaison on the cot. She stood directly in front of him, almost touching his legs that dangled from the side of the table with her body.

Now that the girl stood before him, something caught Kaison's eye. There was a small gash on her lower lip that appeared to be a recent wound. Unless it was always there, and he had never noticed? Aside from that, Kaison was able to see the resemblances she had to her twin. They both had flawless skin and sharp jawlines. It was annoying on Julian's face, but Kaison could admit Cheyenne was beautiful.

Cheyenne set the mortar and water down beside Kaison before dipping the cloth in the water. "Hold still," she said. She brought the cloth to Kaison's face to wipe away the dried blood. As soon as the fabric made contact with his skin, Kaison winced, jerking away.

Cheyenne froze, and her turquoise eyes twinkled back at him.

"Sorry," Kaison muttered under his breath. He forced a smile as he sat up straighter, still clutching his ribcage with one hand.

Cheyenne continued to take care of his wound, wiping away the dried blood. "Are you going to tell me what happened?" As she dipped the cloth back in the water, the clear liquid turned a murky pink.

"If you tell me what happened to you." The sentence escaped Kaison's lips before he thought twice.

Cheyenne's free hand flew to her mouth, covering her lip. Her eyes were wide at first, but then she regained her composure. "Julian and I got into a fight."

She returned to cleaning Kaison's face.

It struck a nerve. "Julian hit you?" Kaison clarified.

The pressure of the rag on Kaison's face intensified, and it didn't go unnoticed. "You know how siblings are," said Cheyenne.

Kaison grabbed Cheyenne's wrist, and she froze once more. "I would never hit my sister."

Cheyenne yanked her hand free from Kaison's grasp. "Well, isn't she lucky." Cheyenne scowled. She dropped the rag in the water basin, causing the tainted liquid to splash against Kaison's clothes. Then she picked up the mortar. Dipping two fingers in, she drew some ointment from the mixture before extending her hand to Kaison's face.

A wave of unease rippled through Kaison as he watched Cheyenne. How could Julian hit his own sister? Kaison hated him even more.

Cheyenne's fingers touched Kaison's temple, but it was gentle. The ointment was cool and soothing to the touch. Slowly, she worked the mixture into Kaison's skin, her fingers traveling from his temple and down his cheek. As she reached his lips, Kaison felt the sting as the medicine cleaned his wounds.

"What is that?" Kaison asked.

"The ointment? Clahrn."

Kaison nodded. "I hadn't thought of that."

"Are you a doctor?" Cheyenne mused.

Kaison smiled. "No."

Cheyenne met his gaze, and her hand drifted away from his lips.

"Thank you," Kaison said.

"Don't thank me," she said. "Lift your shirt."

"What?"

"Let me put some on your ribs."

Kaison was startled. "How did you know?"

"You haven't let go of them since you sat down." Cheyenne tilted her head. "It doesn't take a genius to know you're in pain." The tone of her voice reminded him of Julian.

Kaison obeyed, wincing as he pulled up his shirt and revealed his bare chest.

Cheyenne grimaced when she saw the bruise extending up his side. "Ouch," she said before proceeding to scoop up more ointment. She was gentle when massaging it into his skin, but even the lightest pressure caused Kaison to bite his tongue in pain.

Kaison turned his head to the side, trying to keep his distance. A perfume filled his senses, reminding him of the cologne on Julian. But this time, it wasn't overbearing and stiff, but floral and light.

Then Kaison felt a finger on the center of his chest. His breath caught in his throat, and he jerked back.

"Looks like a nasty burn," Cheyenne said.

Kaison looked down at his chest. The burn mark from the flaming plank in Grovia was fiery red, his skin aggravated. "Everything else hurts worse."

"That's not a good answer." Holding the bowl in her hand, she went back to the table against the wall, picking up a burgundy glass bottle. When she returned to Kaison, she held out the bottle to him. "Drink this."

Kaison didn't argue, popping the cork and downing the liquid. It was a bitter flavor with a sour aftertaste. He tried to hide the grimace as he set the bottle down on the cot beside him.

Once Cheyenne was done treating him, she wiped her hands on her apron before stacking the bowls. "Next time, ask me before trying to treat yourself?" she said.

Kaison pulled his shirt back down, feeling it stick to the ointment. "I will," he said bashfully. He scooted off the table, landing on his feet before Cheyenne. "Thanks again."

Cheyenne's grip tightened on the bowls. "Take care of yourself." Then she turned and went back to the table, setting the bowls down and proceeding to clean up.

Kaison stayed a moment longer, watching her until his father's note came to the forefront of his mind. Then he exited the infirmary.

Kaison returned to his room to get the staff. He had to find Theadosia and get back to Grovia. As he was walking down the corridor, he was surprised to see the door to his and Louie's room wide open. There were voices coming from inside.

After Kaison rounded the corner, Theadosia, Louie, and Pandora came into view. Louie was leaning against the wall, his arms crossed, while Pandora was pacing the center of the room. Theadosia sat on Kaison's bed, holding the staff in her lap.

When Kaison came into view, the three fell silent and their heads shot in his direction.

"Kaison!" Pandora exclaimed first. "Are you alright?" She came to stand directly in front of him, examining the bruising on his face.

Kaison gave her a smile, though he could still feel the pain. "I will be."

"I told them everything," Louie stated.

"Do you know who it was?" Theadosia asked.

An odd sense of discomfort flooded through Kaison. He stepped away from Pandora before crossing to his sister. "No, but whoever it was, she was skilled."

"Like an assassin…" Louie nodded his head as if he experienced the attack himself.

Kaison gave his full attention to his sister, dropping his voice to a whisper. "We're running out of time."

Theadosia sat up straighter. "I think I figured it out – the riddle."

"The Reflecting Grounds?"

Theadosia leaned back, startled. Her brow furrowed, almost disappointed that he had figured it out too, but then she nodded. "We have to go now." She handed the staff to her brother.

"I'm coming with you," Louie said from across the room.

Kaison latched the staff to his belt. "You don't have to do that."

"I want to," Louie said. "I haven't been back to Vorinder in a long time, and I'm a little too invested in your father's scavenger hunt."

Theadosia scowled. "It's not a scavenger hunt."

Pandora interjected next, "I'm coming too."

That took Kaison by surprise.

"Now that I realize the halberd is magical, I want to know more. I've been researching transportation spells and haven't found anything that explains a willow tree. I want to see it for myself."

Kaison invited the company. There was no way Pandora was the one who had attacked him the night prior, right?

Kaison announced, "Then let's go."

Once Kaison had fully recovered from the attack, the four met in the stables to ride to Grovia. Pandora explained she had her own horse and had gone to saddle it, while Louie was busy collecting snacks for the ride.

Theadosia and Kaison were preparing their two horses they found initially in Grovia.

Soft footsteps alerted the siblings that someone was approaching, and they looked up to see Simon at the entrance to the stall. He stood tall, his skinny structure making him appear even taller. His dark eyes were wide, and the dim light in the stable accentuated his bony cheekbones.

"How are you?" Simon asked, the tone in his voice made him sound disinterested, but Kaison was beginning to realize that the boy always sounded monotonous.

The attack flashed before Kaison's eyes. If Simon wasn't there, it could've ended entirely differently.

"Alright," Kaison replied. "I never properly thanked you."

Simon shrugged. "Glad I was there." He then turned his attention to Theadosia. "I don't believe we've met."

"Theadosia Ruiz," she said.

"My sister," Kaison added.

Simon remained steadfast on Theadosia. "I'm Simon."

Theadosia smiled. "Thank you for saving my brother. You're a hero."

Simon's face reddened. "Just a coincidence." Simon then acknowledged the horse. "Are you going somewhere?"

"For a ride," Theadosia replied. She stroked the horse once more.

"You aren't staying for the Harvest Banquet?"

Theadosia shifted her weight. "We will be back soon."

"Maybe I'll see you there," Simon offered.

Theadosia smiled.

"Are you ready?"

Kaison jumped out of his skin at the sound of someone behind him. He whipped around to face Pandora and Louie. Pandora had a hold of a white Clydesdale. Its huge stature took up almost the whole width of the aisle. The horse had emeralds beaded into its mane, and the saddle was embroidered with the name 'Xy'tier'.

"Does Julian know you're taking his horse?" Simon asked.

Pandora fired him a glare, her hair flipping over her shoulder. "Don't you have something to do?"

Simon nodded, realizing he wasn't welcome in the group. Hunching his shoulders, he started away, leaving them behind.

Kaison eyed Pandora. He hadn't heard her with that tone of voice before.

"I'm not riding Giselle, I don't want Julian to kill me," Louie stated.

“Well, I don’t know how to ride a horse,” Pandora admitted. “So, I’ll ride with someone on Giselle.”

Kaison was hesitant, but Louie wouldn’t budge. He finally said, “I’ll ride Julian’s horse then. Let’s return to Grovia.”

- 18 -

Kaison

The three horses set off across the moor. Louie and Theadosia rode the two horses from Grovia, while Kaison and Pandora rode Giselle, the large Clydesdale. Louie had taken a spear from the armory, and it was latched in place on the side of the horse's saddle. Theadosia had tied her hidden blades underneath her wrists.

Today the moor was packed with hectic travelers. Artisans and merchants had set up pink, striped tents where they were preparing to sell goods at the upcoming Harvest Banquet. The atmosphere was abuzz with the anticipation of a new sale, and the villagers from across Solaris shouted across the pathways to their fellow companions in spirited tones. Kaison could smell freshly fried pastries mixed with the scent of seafood, cheese, and beef. Hot steam rose from grills and large pots of stew.

The sounds of rattling metal goods combined with frantic shouting mixed in the air, jostling memories in Kaison's mind. He thought of the marketplace back home, stretched out along the docks of Grovia. He flashed to an image of the sunsets where he sat in their family's designated stand, listening to his father impart his usual advice. Those moments seemed like forever ago.

The horses maneuvered in and out of the stands, rushing toward the outskirts of Tamir and the forest beyond the moor. Once they had passed Tamir, they broke into a gallop across the open field. The cool wind whipped in Kaison's face and flooded his throat and nostrils with fresh air. They pressed onward, knowing they had to travel far out of sight from any castle guards in order to use the halberd. As they rode, Kaison grew skeptical if the halberd's magic would activate in the same way it had done before. When they had escaped Grovia, he didn't summon any magic, and the willow tree had materialized out of thin air.

Kaison's mind churned with thoughts about the key that would open the passage in the library, the halberd, and his recent attack. But those thoughts were broken when he felt Pandora's fingers slip tighter around his waist. She pressed her body closer to his and leaned her chin on the top of his shoulder.

"Are you alright back there?" Kaison raised his voice so she could hear him.

"Yes, I'm fine," Pandora admitted. "I'm more curious than I have been in a while. I hope we can make it to Grovia and back like you say."

Kaison sighed. "I hope we can too."

"If you can channel that kind of power, you're special. You must know that."

Kaison didn't think of himself that way. The fluttering feeling in his stomach didn't shake the fact that a girl had attacked him a few nights ago. As much as he didn't want to admit it, Pandora could be a threat.

Pandora continued, "At least, I think you are."

They reached the edge of the moor as the sun was peeking over the horizon, casting a morning glow around them. They slowed their pace to a steady trot as they entered the pine forest, concealing themselves entirely from anyone on guard at Sun Castle. Then Kaison came to a complete stop.

"We're here," he said.

Theadosia and Louie pulled their horses to a stop on either side of Kaison.

"Are you lost?" Louie asked. When no one answered he stifled a laugh. "The passage to the docks is in the opposite direction." They were standing before a row of trees leading into the thick forest.

"He's not lost," Theadosia said.

Kaison wasn't paying attention. He took the transformed halberd off his belt. The staff shone in the light that cast through the trees, and the three glittering jewels appeared even brighter under the shadows of sunrise. He held the staff off to the right, and he pressed his thumb down onto the central, red jewel. The bottom of the staff extended and so did the top. Then an angular blade shot out of the side of the staff. Tiny, frosted particles fell to the grass like dust, leaving the space around the horse in a thin coating of gold.

"Whoa...," Louie murmured from his horse.

Kaison turned to look back at Pandora. Her doe-like eyes were bigger than he had ever seen.

Kaison pointed the halberd over the Clydesdale's beaded mane. Taking a deep breath, Kaison thought back to his hometown of Grovia, praying desperately that the willow tree would appear once more. He wasn't sure if it was going to work.

Kaison let out a deep breath, holding the handle of his halberd tighter. He squeezed his eyes shut. Then, the trees began to shake.

Leaves and pine needles fluttered around them, and the ground before them shifted as a tree sprouted out of the ground, growing exponentially. The deciduous trees separated, their roots manipulating the earth. Then a willow tree magically sprouted, its branches peeling over into a canopy of shimmering light. The magnificent willow tree extended high into the sky, and its leaves touched the ground as though they were a curtain.

Pandora gasped, and her eyes locked on the magic transpiring before her.

Louie's mouth was agape. "Great Sun..." he said.

The glimmering willow tree radiated strongly in the middle of the forest. The light streamed toward the halberd, creating a clear pathway that led from the end of the weapon to the willow tree. When Kaison's horse trotted forward, the tree faded slightly, becoming translucent and revealing the lands of Grovia beyond.

"Let's go!" Theadosia was the first to initiate movement. With a tap of her heel, she led her horse through the cascading willow branches. She disappeared under the leaves, and sparkles floated down from where she had vanished.

Kaison let Louie go next, making sure the gateway remained open.

Louie followed Theadosia's path. He clutched the reins tightly and leaned backward as the horse traversed through the willow branches.

After Louie disappeared, Pandora spoke, "That's light magic."

The brilliance of the tree before Kaison was undeniable. "I know that now," he said. He tapped his heel against the Clydesdale before hunching over to tunnel under the branches. The light became brighter, causing him to squint. The leaves swallowed him before he emerged in the open space on the other side.

Kaison pulled the horse to an immediate halt. He was positioned again between Louie and Theadosia on their respective horses.

Rain sprinkled from the sky, hitting Kaison's cheeks with tiny droplets which consequently streaked down his face. The three horses were positioned on a bank, looking out across a clearing. Before them was the town of Grovia.

The town was crumpled into one heaping pile. Giant cypress trees had collapsed on top of one another, creating dangerous balance beams. On every side, houses that were once held strongly in the tree canopies were now piles of soggy wood sinking into the swamp. There were no visible fires, having been extinguished by the rain and the marsh, but smoke still rose from the center of the town. Ash accompanied the rain, falling from the darkened sky.

Grovia appeared smaller in one pile. Originally, it was spread vertically through different levels, but now it had all crumpled down in a mound. What remained of the platforms teetered from side to side in the wind, as if the trees or the mounds of wood would collapse into the marsh at any moment.

A tight lump caught in Kaison's throat as he gazed at the image before him. Somewhere among the rubble was his former life. His childhood. He was trying to bury the grief that crept in on him. He didn't want to look at Theadosia, knowing her expression would probably make him feel more emotional.

Slowly, Kaison pressed his thumb into the red gem. The halberd transformed once more back into a staff, and Kaison returned it to his belt. He ran his hands over his forehead and through his hair, taking a few deep breaths before he was able to speak. "The Reflecting Grounds are north of town." With a snap of the reins, he started off toward the location he was convinced the letter in the halberd was referring to.

Kaison continued toward the hunting ground. As he rode, he felt Pandora's grasp tighten around his waist.

The horse stumbled, causing Kaison's stomach to drop. He helped the horse regain its footing before continuing on as the rain started to pick up. The horse struggled to walk in the marsh, the weight causing them to sink deeper. A thick fog created a blanket that masked where the marsh sunk into deeper pockets.

The hunting ground was close to the town of Grovia, but this time, they were traveling on foot rather than by boat. They would have to go around the opposite way, staying in the shallow areas of the marsh and approaching from the other side of the Reflecting Grounds. This was the only area where the marsh was shallow enough to approach by land.

As they rode, Kaison looked to Theadosia. They locked eyes, and Kaison felt more comfortable than before. "Are you alright?" he asked, knowing she was processing the same grief he was.

Theadosia nodded.

"I can't believe the attacks made their way to Vorinder," Louie mused from his horse. Then he straightened up taller. "I need to get in touch with my family."

"Have you heard from them recently?" asked Theadosia.

"No." Louie shook his head. "I sent them messages, but they haven't replied in a while. It's been too long."

After the four traveled for a few more minutes, the marsh opened into a wide clearing. The trees that had been protecting them from the rain were no longer there. Before them, sat the large reflecting pool that stretched on for longer than the eye could see, disappearing into the fog. A faint cawing of birds was heard somewhere in the distance.

Kaison came to a halt on the bank before the pool of open water.

He swung his leg over the horse and landed roughly on the ground. His boots squished on the earth, and he sunk down into the mud.

Both Theadosia and Louie brought their horses to a halt just behind. They also dismounted while Pandora remained on her horse.

"This is the Reflecting Grounds?" Louie asked.

"Yes," Kaison answered.

All four of them stared out at the Reflecting Grounds. In the center of the hunting ground was a singular cypress tree. Its branches swayed in the wind and dripped with rain onto the water below. The cone-shaped roots at the bottom disappeared into the green water.

The single cypress tree was prominent in the middle of the water. Something was out there. Somewhere at the base of that tree. They would have to dive to the bottom of the marsh to find a chest wedged somewhere between the tree's roots.

Kaison was fixated on his goal. "I'll swim out there."

"I'm coming with you," Theadosia added.

"It will be dark out there, and there's no way you will be able to see the bottom of the marsh," Pandora said from her spot on the horse.

"I've done this before. You stay here," Kaison told her. "Make sure the horses don't scare."

"Scare?" Pandora's face flushed.

Kaison shrugged. "Snakes."

Louie unstrapped the spear from the side of the saddle. He pointed a few feet out in the water as a slithering ripple pulsed from underneath the surface. "Like this one."

Pandora squealed.

"That's a redbelly snake. It's harmless," Theadosia said.

But Louie had already prepped his spear and plunged it into the water, perfectly impaling the thin water snake.

"I said it was harmless!" Theadosia scolded.

Louie pulled his spear back and flipped it up, letting the snake flop at the end of the blade. He examined it closely. "Harmless, but it makes a good snack."

"Come on." Kaison redirected Theadosia's attention back to the cypress. "Louie, if you see anything moving in the water, yell." He unlatched the transformed halberd from his belt, knowing the staff would drag him down, before handing it to Louie.

Louie chuckled as he took the halberd from Kaison. "You seriously are going to swim out there?"

"I have to," Kaison finished.

Kaison waded out a few steps into the thigh-high water. Each step he took, the water climbed higher on his body, before the ground dropped off beneath him. He cautiously let himself continue forward until his whole body was submerged.

He was instantly chilled by the cold temperature. He started to tread, making sure his sister was beside him, before swimming for the cypress. It wasn't too far out, and the closer he got, the larger the tree seemed to grow.

Rough plants brushed against his feet and ankles, tangling underneath him. The water moved unnaturally around him, altering him to the fact that other fish and animals were swimming close. With only a few more strokes, he reached the cypress tree.

Theadosia swam up beside him. The branches on the tree were too tall to hold onto, so Theadosia grabbed one of the grooves at the bottom of the tree and attempted to prop her foot on one of the roots underwater.

"Let's hope that this is the right place," Kaison said.

Theadosia continued treading water, but like Kaison, she knew what they had to do.

With that, both siblings took a deep breath before diving underwater. They scaled down the side of the cypress, using it to help them dive deeper. The water was murky and a dark green, allowing little light. The deeper they descended, the harder it was to see. They were at the base of the cypress, where the thick roots branched out in multiple directions. Both Kaison and Theadosia blindly reached underneath the roots, hoping to grab onto something.

Kaison's chest tightened, and pains ached around his ribcage. His throat clenched in agony as he fought back the urge to take a breath. He pulled his hand out from between the twisted roots and pushed off the marsh floor, swimming back to the surface.

He emerged from the water with a gasp. Moments later, Theadosia broke through the surface. Her bangs were plastered to her forehead.

"Anything?" Kaison asked.

Theadosia shook her head, catching her breath. The rain seemed to be picking up.

"Find anything?" Louie's voice called from the bank.

"It's too dark!" Kaison called back.

"I'm trying again." Theadosia panted. Then she disappeared under the water once more.

Kaison was about to follow her lead when a dim light began shining from the bank. Pandora was crafting what looked like a glowing orb between her palms. She still sat on the horse, not wanting to step down onto the soggy earth.

"Hold out your hand!" she called.

Kaison obeyed. He held his palm out above the surface of the water.

Slowly, Pandora extended her hand over the mane of the horse. The glowing orb floated effortlessly, traveling across the distance between Pandora and Kaison. It hovered over the surface of the water, reflecting against it, before it reached Kaison. Kaison was awe-struck by the glowing magic. As soon as it was hovering over Kaison's palm, it dropped, landing in Kaison's grasp. It felt like a light-weight ball.

Theadosia emerged from the water and took in another gasp of air, startling Kaison. She saw the glowing orb almost immediately, and her eyes widened in shock.

"What is that?"

"Pandora's magic."

Theadosia reached out and took it in her hand. As she did so, she bobbed lower in the water. She flipped it over, examining it on all sides. The rain had no effect on its glow.

"Let's go." After taking a large breath, she dove back under the water.

The two siblings descended into the murkiness below. The orb magically glowed underneath the surface. The rays cut through the haze in the swamp and cast sharp beams on the tree.

Kaison pushed past a plant and grabbed onto the roots of the cypress. He used his upper body strength to pull him deeper, grasping at the roots to launch himself forward. Theadosia held onto the other side while holding the orb before them. It illuminated the root structures that created a nest all around them.

A fish suddenly escaped out from underneath the cypress and dodged between the siblings, making Kaison flinch backward. Sharpening his senses, Kaison peered underneath the cypress.

The base of the cypress tree formed into a dome. Its roots encapsulated the area like a jail cell. Buried partly underneath the earth at the center of the opening was a metal box. It was larger than Kaison anticipated, large enough to hold a crown. It sparkled as it reflected the magical orb.

Kaison reached between two roots and hastily dug at the mud holding the chest down. Theadosia tried to hold the light as close as she could. Pulling back some moss and algae, Kaison was able to reveal the box. He reached in so he could grab it with two hands and tried to pull it out, but it got caught between the roots. Kaison tugged again, digging his boots into the earth for leverage, but it seemed too large to fit between the roots of the cypress.

The light flickered as Theadosia began to resurface. Begrudgingly, Kaison followed her. He was so close.

Both Theadosia and Kaison broke the surface and took in a deep breath.

Theadosia spoke, "It's stuck."

Kaison kicked the water to stay afloat. "I can dig it out."

Theadosia looked skeptical, but let in. She took in a huge breath of air before diving.

Theadosia used the orb to light the way. As soon as they returned to the chest, Kaison reached underneath the cypress. He grabbed both sides of the metal box and turned it before pulling again. It wedged between the roots, getting stuck once more.

Anxiety built inside Kaison. He dug his heels into the sandy marsh floor, and he pulled the box back with all his strength.

The box slid from between the roots, almost with enough momentum to slip out of his hands. Kaison began swimming to the surface, but Theadosia grabbed his shirt, stopping him. She pointed above them.

Floating at the surface of the water, silhouetted by the light from the sky, was a huge caiman. It rested elegantly, as if waiting for Theadosia and Kaison to resurface.

- 19 -

Kaison

Kaison and Theadosia watched the caiman. It was on the opposite side of the cypress from the bank, which meant they might be able to escape to where Pandora and Louie were without crossing its path.

Kaison looked back at Theadosia and nodded his head in the direction of the bank where the horses were.

Theadosia's eyes flooded with concern, and she shook her head.

Then a silhouette of a spear flashed across Theadosia's face. A spear bounced off the hard shell of the caiman before landing in the water and slowly beginning to sink.

The caiman stirred, now angry, and would be charging toward the bank.

The siblings propelled themselves forward, hoping to reach the bank before the predator. Kaison tucked the metal box under one arm while he used one hand to propel him forward. Theadosia released the glowing orb so that she could swim faster.

The ground beneath them began to rise, and they were nearing the shoal. Muffled shouting could be heard above the water.

Kaison broke through the surface, gasping for air. Louie and Pandora were shouting inaudible words. Pandora was still on the horse. Louie had Kaison's halberd gripped between both his hands, in its full form, bracing himself for the oncoming caiman.

Theadosia coughed as she emerged from the surface. She stumbled through the brush, pulling herself up to her hands and knees.

Kaison held the box tighter. It was ten times heavier out of the water. He grabbed Theadosia's arm with his other hand, pulling her forward. The plants clung to his ankles, trying to drag him back down. He snapped his head back over his shoulder to get a glimpse of the caiman. The caiman was moving now, rapidly closing the distance between them.

"Move!" Louie screamed, gripping the halberd. He was bouncing from one foot to the next, uncertain whether or not to sprint forward and help them.

Kaison waded through the marsh, struggling to move against the knee-high water. Then they reached the bank. Kaison gave the box to Theadosia and grabbed his halberd from Louie's hands.

Kaison barely had time to brace himself before the caiman lunged.

Right before the caiman had a chance to snap its jaws shut, a sparkling flash of light lit the marsh. The caiman smashed against a frosted gold wall that was now between Kaison and the predator.

Kaison stumbled back in awe. He watched the caiman lunge again, and its snout bashed into the invisible wall one more time. Each time it happened, a flurry of gold sparkles shook from the frosted barricade.

Kaison turned around to see Pandora. She had gotten down

from the horse and was now standing a few feet away, her arms outstretched in front of her. Her arms seemed to shake, and her eyes were dead set on the shield.

"By plague," Louie said. He was standing beside Theadosia, and she leaned against him as she tried to catch her breath.

Kaison was awe-struck, frozen in his shoes.

The pounding stopped. The caiman gave up as quickly as it had attacked. With a quick turn, the caiman tore back off into the swamp. For such a large animal, it moved with speed. Once in the swamp, it became almost invisible except for its eyes poking out above the water. The four watched it until it completely disappeared into the fog.

Pandora let out a breath as her arms fell beside her, the shield vanishing in a flurry of twinkling gold. She panted heavily, clutching her chest as she gasped for breath.

Kaison went over to her side.

Pandora still couldn't speak.

"That was incredible," Theadosia stated.

"I didn't know you could do that," Kaison spoke.

Pandora finally met his gaze. "Honestly," she said, "I didn't either."

Theadosia hoisted the metal box in her arms. "This is it," she said.

Kaison retracted the halberd and clipped it to his belt, while all four crowded around the box they had risked their lives to find.

Theadosia scraped at the moss that covered the lock. Then, she forcefully pulled up the latch, and it snapped with a clunking noise. The box popped open slightly.

Kaison couldn't wait. He opened the lid of the box all the way while Theadosia held it in her arms.

Inside the tightly sealed box was a pile of ash. On top of the ash was a small scroll, similar to the one Kaison had found in his halberd, and a pouch.

Kaison held back every instinct to grab the pouch, and instead, picked up the scroll. It was perfectly dry.

After Kaison unraveled the scroll, he read the words out loud.

"Kaison,

If you find this letter, it means I had to give you my halberd, and the Shadows found us. I knew you could decipher the message I left behind. It had to be cryptic in case anyone else opened the halberd. Please take this letter with great heed, as you are in danger.

You must take care of your mother's necklace – the Crimson Teardrop. I'm sorry I didn't tell you sooner, but your mother died when you were young, and I wanted you to treat Dianna as your real mother, and Theadosia as your full sister. Please leave your mother's ashes in Grovia.

Now that you have the halberd, you will be hunted by the Shadow of Eclipse. Be strong, my boy. You are the halberd's designated protector. The pendant will protect you and Theadosia as long as it can.

Go to Sun Castle and find the key in Sun Spire where the northern gold carries the flame. There are so many secrets you must see and learn for yourself. Sir Landon and Dux Nikodemus will help you. Trust them with your life.

I love you both. Everything I did was for the greater good. To protect this world and beyond.

Now it is your turn.

-Dad."

Kaison's breath caught in his chest. At first, he didn't know what to say. His eyes burned into the parchment before him, and his hands shook.

Gently, Pandora brushed her hand against his and took the scroll from him. She reread the letter silently.

Theadosia looked at her brother. "We are...," she tried to form her words, "we don't have the same mother?"

Kaison opened his mouth to speak, but no words formed at the tip of his tongue. The intensity of the situation was only beginning to sink in. The knowledge that Theadosia was his half-sister wasn't what troubled him the most. It was his father's words that shook him to the core.

He was the halberd's designated protector.

What did that mean?

"Wait...," Louie started. "Our world's evil lord – the Shadow of Eclipse – is hunting you for your halberd?"

"Your father knew Dux Nikodemus?" Pandora asked, rereading the letter.

"But who is Sir Landon?" Theadosia asked another question.

"We should head back," Kaison interrupted. "Maybe there are answers behind the secret door, and the key is in Sun Spire."

"Then what is in the pouch?" Pandora questioned.

Kaison took the velvet pouch in his grasp. Delicately, he opened the pouch and reached inside.

A glossy object brushed against his fingertips. He withdrew his hand to reveal a medallion necklace. The chain was thin and gold. Hanging from it was a teardrop-shaped ruby, held to the necklace by a swirling golden clasp.

Kaison's heart pounded in his chest as he held it.

"This must be the pendant my father referred to," Kaison said.

"My mother's necklace."

"How is that supposed to protect you from the Shadow of Eclipse?" Louie asked.

Kaison put the ruby necklace on, hiding it underneath his shirt.

"There must be answers in the library," Theadosia said.

Kaison nodded. "Then let's go get the key."

Kaison felt the necklace against his chest. If it protected him from the Shadow of Eclipse's magic, then that meant he could hold his own in a fight against him.

That meant he could avenge his parents' death.

- 20 -

KAISON

The group returned to Solaris when the sun was at its highest point in the sky. After discovering the pendant, Kaison and Theadosia scattered Kaison's mother's ashes in Grovia, letting her rest alongside their father. Then they retraced their steps until they found an open clearing. Kaison used the halberd once more to summon the willow tree, and they passed underneath it until they were back on the outskirts of Sun Castle.

Once they were back in Solaris, they made their way to the stables. On the moor, almost all of the colored tents had been set up. Even more travelers had put their harvests on display. The contestants would be entered into a competition and a winner would be crowned. It was a well-known celebration of Solaris, and promoted agriculture across the kingdom.

They all dismounted and pulled their horses through the crowd. It was too congested to ride through the moor now. They moved elbow-to-elbow through the marketplace. As they walked by, Kaison noted the abundance of corn, oats, cheese, beef, fish, fruits, and wine. The fresh smell of pressed apple ale from the North, and Solaris' cinnamon drink with pressed peaches and wheat barley, clogged Kaison's senses. His father had always cooked things from other lands, and now suddenly, Kaison knew why.

His father was from Solaris. He must have been a knight with Dux Nikodemus a long time ago. It was the only thing that made sense.

Louie was grabbing practically every free sample along the way. "Thank you." He grabbed a cake pastry stuffed with cheese and shrimp and then another stuffed with ground beef and onion. "Thank you." He grabbed the peach punch in his other hand.

"Why don't we have a Harvest Banquet in Vorinder?" He directed his question toward Theadosia and Kaison.

"Because the council doesn't have to have a festival to stuff everyone with food. They do that already," replied Theadosia. "Besides, they don't have to flaunt food around to show their wealth. They do that in other ways."

"Controlling the medicine trade." Kaison nodded.

"Animal skins for clothing," Theadosia added.

"True...," Louie nodded, "but maybe I will suggest this to the Alegrias next time I see them." He mentioned the name of the family that oversaw the council. He grabbed a piece of cheese off the next table of samples.

"What do they do to welcome people that travel to Vorinder?" asked Pandora. "Do you have balls?"

"No," Louie said. "Feasts. Hunting and fishing trips."

"Don't forget the swimming and boating competitions," Theadosia said.

"Oh right," Louie said. "Now *that* is something they should get rid of."

Everyone laughed.

They soon reached the royal stables. To Kaison's dismay, Julian was sitting on a haybale at the stable doors. He twirled a piece of straw between his fingers in boredom as if he had been sitting there for a long time.

"Curses," Kaison said under his breath as he continued to lead Julian's horse toward the stables. When he was within a close distance to the barn doors, he brought the Clydesdale to a halt.

Julian's jaw clenched upon seeing his horse. He was quick to his feet.

"You!" Julian exclaimed.

Theadosia pulled Sapphire to a halt beside her brother, while Louie pulled the third horse to a stop.

"Listen," Kaison began, watching Julian storm toward him, "we only–"

Julian's fist swung across Kaison's jaw, sending a rippling pain up the side of his face.

"Hey!" shouted Louie.

"Julian!" Theadosia and Pandora exclaimed simultaneously.

"You stole my horse?" Julian's voice was raised in anger.

Kaison held the side of his face in pain and slowly regained his footing so he could face Julian once more.

"It wasn't my idea," Kaison said.

Pandora and Theadosia had crossed over to the boys.

Julian clenched his fists again. "You know I had to miss the harvest jousting tournament?" he said before shoving Kaison backward.

"Julian!" Pandora yelled, grabbing one of Julian's arms, attempting to pull him away.

Theadosia had run up to Kaison and stepped between him and

Julian. "Stop!" she shouted.

"I borrowed Giselle!" Pandora yanked Julian hard enough that he was forced to turn to her.

"What?" Julian stared at Pandora, his jaw clenched.

"It's my fault. It wasn't Kaison's," she said, speaking quickly.

Julian glared at Kaison again. "Well, he was leading her! And most obviously riding her!"

"So was she!" Kaison gestured toward Pandora.

"Kaison, stop," Theadosia said.

Pandora pulled Julian's arm harder. "Listen, I'm sorry I borrowed Giselle." Somehow, her voice was calming.

"Why would you do that to me?" Julian asked.

"I completely forgot about the jousting tournament. I'm sorry," she continued. She let her hand fall from Julian's cheek and placed it on his chest.

"I was going to win!"

"I know you were," Pandora said, "but you'll win next year. And the year after that."

Julian let out a slow, deep breath. He scowled once again at Kaison, his turquoise eyes burning with anger.

Pandora placed both her hands on the side of Julian's face, forcing him to look at her. "It's only a game," she said.

Julian released his clenched fists. After he contained himself, he slowly pulled away from Pandora and scanned her appearance. Her dress was soaked and tinted green, and her shoes were caked in mud. The stench of the marsh remained.

"What in Solaris happened to you?" He wrinkled his nose from the smell.

"I'll tell you all about it after I get cleaned up," Pandora said.

Julian agreed. "You do that."

Then Julian turned away from Pandora and walked over to his horse. He shook his head in disgust, seeing his dazzling horse also coated with the same swampy stench. When he reached the horse, he petted her forehead.

"Let's get you away from these terrible people, Giselle," Julian whispered. He took her bridle, and after one last glare at Kaison, he led Giselle into the stables.

The four of them waited for Julian to disappear inside.

Louie cleared his throat and patted Alice's muzzle. "See why I chose not to ride Giselle?"

"Are you hurt?" Pandora asked Kaison, her doe-like eyes genuine.

Kaison shifted his jaw, still feeling a lingering ache. "I'll be fine," he said.

"I'll clean up the horses, you all go change, and I'll meet you at the library," Theadosia said. "Go get the key."

"I should go have a heart-to-heart with Mr. Tough Guy." Louie nodded his head in the direction Julian had left. "I'll meet you there as well."

Kaison didn't object. The argument with Julian made his blood boil, and he didn't want to be in the stables anywhere near him. He touched his chest, feeling the ruby pendant underneath his shirt.

At least they had the pendant.

- 21 -

THEADOSIA

Theadosia watched Pandora and Kaison head up the hill to Sun Castle before she led Sapphire and Alice into the stables. Louie walked beside her, extending his last pastry in her direction.

"Hungry?" he offered.

"No, thank you."

Louie popped the pastry into his mouth, and a dusting of frosting coated his chin.

When they entered the stables, they saw Julian up ahead with Giselle, yelling at Simon.

"I told you, you can't wash her inside," Simon was saying.

"I don't have to listen to you, Plague Boy!"

"Hey!" Theadosia called.

Julian turned around. "What do you want?"

"The horses should be washed outside," Theadosia said, her voice strong.

Julian let go of Giselle's bridle and threw his hands in the air.

“Fine,” he said. “You do it. Be my guest.”

“Xy’tier,” Louie’s voice was sullen.

Julian scowled. “What, Netherand? You’re a part of this. You didn’t stop them from stealing my horse.”

Julian went for the exit, muttering curse words under his breath.

“Come on!” Louie called, bounding after him. Soon, the two were out of sight.

Theadosia brought her attention back to Simon. “He’s always angry for no reason it seems,” she said.

Simon did not move his bottomless eyes. He then gave a curt nod before extending his hand. “I can take your horses.”

“I got it,” Theadosia replied, giving Simon a gentle smile.

Simon’s expression didn’t change, nor did he say anything. He simply took Giselle’s reins and began leading her toward the back exit.

Theadosia followed, leading Sapphire and Alice. She felt uncomfortable in the awkward silence that took place between them, and she searched for conversation starters.

“How long have you been working in the stables?” she asked.

“Since I arrived at the castle,” he replied.

The two exited the stables momentarily. Theadosia left Alice by the exit so she could take care of one horse at a time. She followed Simon’s lead and brought the other horse up to the water basin.

They both attended to the separate horses, removing the gear and placing it on the side to be washed later. Theadosia set the saddle down, and Simon handed her a brush.

“Thanks,” she smiled again, hoping to get some sort of reaction from Simon, but he didn’t give her anything. He simply dipped his own brush in the water before scrubbing the mud off of Giselle, starting from the horse’s shoulder and working down to the hoof.

Theadosia dipped her brush into the basin before beginning to wash Sapphire. "You don't talk much," Theadosia said.

There was a moment of silence before Simon replied, "Most people don't care what I have to say."

"I don't think that's true," Theadosia said.

She waited for Simon to respond, but he continued to wash Giselle in silence. He was bent over, scrubbing down one of the horse's back legs. He was the first person she wasn't able to have an engaging conversation with.

She dipped one of her hands in the water basin before flicking the water in Simon's direction. The water splattered against his shoulder, and a few droplets landed on his cheek.

Simon slowly turned his head to look at Theadosia. His dark eyes burned into hers, and his expression was unreadable.

Theadosia flashed him a smile.

The silence continued.

The smile slowly faded from Theadosia's face. "It was a joke...," she muttered.

Uncomfortable, Theadosia began to clean the horse faster. She was about to move to the other side when water splattered the side of her face.

Her mouth dropped open in shock. Simon was leaning forward against the water basin. His expression was still curiously indiscernible. He gave a simple shrug as if tempting Theadosia to splash him again.

Theadosia grinned before taking both her hands and tossing a cupful of water at Simon. It soaked the entire front of his shirt. Theadosia covered her mouth, not realizing how much water she had splashed against the boy, but this time Simon didn't hesitate to splash Theadosia back. The two continued in a playful game, completely forgetting about the horses for a moment.

Theadosia was certain she saw a glimpse of a smile from Simon. They continued splashing the water against each other, until they were completely soaked.

"You win, you win!" Theadosia exclaimed.

"Sorry," said Simon, upon noticing her appearance.

"Don't worry…I…," Theadosia's voice ran quiet. Simon had already returned to his job. Theadosia sighed and continued to the task at hand.

Finally, Theadosia finished cleaning the horses, including Julian's horse, and she said goodbye to Simon. He was still working outdoors in the inner corral. She went back inside the stables to make sure that the horses were securely locked in their pens. Finally, Theadosia made her way down the central aisle and to the entrance.

When she reached the stable entrance, before she stepped out into the sunlight, a figure moved into her path.

It was Sir Emmett.

"Theadosia." Emmett's lips shifted into a crooked smile. "I was looking for you."

- 22 -

Kaison

Kaison ran his hands through his hair impatiently. He was standing outside the entrance to Sun Spire, positioned a distance away from the door so that he didn't raise any suspicion.

All he could think about was finding the key and returning to the library. Deep down, the answers to his burning questions were so close. He and his sister only needed one more day to ensure that they found what their father wanted them to find. Then they could return to Vorinder and try to make a new life for themselves there. Theadosia could continue her studies to be on the town council, and Kaison could continue to hunt and uncover artifacts in the Albufera.

If the Shadow of Eclipse was going to come after them for the halberd, staying at the largest castle with the brightest beacon in Morbaeda wasn't exactly a secret place to hide.

Looking up, Kaison saw Pandora round the corner. She looked much different than earlier. No longer was she coated in mud and drenched from head to toe, but rather she looked like a princess. She wore a pastel purple dress and had matching ribbons running down her hair.

"You clean up nicely," Pandora said.

Kaison blushed. He couldn't think of a compliment to respond with, so instead he peered down the hallway to the entrance to Sun Spire. "Let's go get the key."

Both Kaison and Pandora started off down the corridor.

"What do you think is behind the door in the library?" Pandora asked as she walked beside Kaison.

Kaison's mind churned with thoughts, but it was impossible to know exactly what his father could be leading him to. Everything they had discovered so far had been a complete surprise.

"Answers," Kaison eventually admitted.

"Answers to what?"

"About my father, about the magic, and about why he told me I was some sort of protector."

Pandora stopped walking. "Kaison, I know you want answers about all of that, but you need to also protect yourself. I can tell you haven't taken the time to grieve, and you might not like what you find."

Kaison paused. "Why would you say that?"

Pandora shook her head. "I know what it's like to have your expectations shattered."

"How so?"

"When I came here to practice magic, I thought it would fulfill all my dreams. Now I find myself learning things here and there – darting into dark corners like I'm harboring some awful secret. I don't want you to feel like you have to keep any secrets either."

"I would rather be beholden to secrets than never learn the truth," Kaison responded.

Pandora's face softened. "You can say that now when you don't know the truth."

They both began walking again and arrived at the doors to Sun Spire. Kaison glanced up and down the corridor to make sure no one was watching. The Spire was open to everyone in the castle, but Kaison wanted to make sure their search would remain secret. Kaison reached his hand out for the door handle, but the door swung open. Startled, Kaison jumped backward before the door hit him in the chest. A girl stood before him.

Her fiery red hair made her instantly recognizable. She clutched her blue journal closer to her chest, as if she had been caught red handed.

"Maeve," Pandora muttered, seeing her standing in the doorway to Sun Spire.

Maeve's blue eyes were strikingly bright. She didn't blink. "Can I help you?"

Pandora gestured to the staircase behind Maeve. "You're in the way." She forced a smile, attempting to make the statement sound nicer.

"What were you doing in Sun Spire?" Kaison asked.

"What are you going to be doing in Sun Spire?" Maeve fired the question directly back.

The tone in her voice was unpleasant, but her eyes were sparkling brightly. They were almost...mesmerizing. Were they different from when Kaison had met her earlier? He tried to re-play their earlier conversations.

The book Maeve was holding glistened in the dim light of the corridor – almost in the same way as her eyes. Kaison's gaze was fastened to it in curiosity.

When Maeve noticed Kaison's gaze, she shifted her stance, attempting to cover the book. "Excuse me," she said before pushing past them, knocking Kaison on his shoulder.

As she forced her way between them, the journal dropped from Maeve's grasp, landing with a thud on the ground.

Pandora rubbed her shoulder, distancing herself, but Kaison saw the journal sprawled open on the stone floor.

Only a few words were on the page, and it was as if the ink was twinkling.

I wish I had...

Kaison leaned down to grab the open journal, and he had almost picked it up before something flashed in his peripheral vision. Maeve slapped him across the cheek, and a sharp stinging rippled down his face.

"Sod off!" Maeve shouted, causing Kaison to wince. He didn't think she was that strong because of how small she was, but the pain in his cheek made him realize otherwise.

Maeve scrambled to pick up the journal and held it even closer to her than before. With a huff, she turned on her heel and stormed off down the corridor.

"Are you all right?" Pandora asked.

"Fine," Kaison let out.

"She's so rude."

Kaison's face still stung from Maeve's slap. She had pulled the journal away from him so quickly. But Kaison had read the whole sentence before Maeve had swiped the journal away.

I wish I had blue eyes.

- 23 -

THEADOSIA

Sir Emmett's stern face and bottomless eyes seemed to peer into Theadosia's soul, and his greasy, silver hair was gelled back, revealing the scar on his face. His long sword touched the ground.

Startled, Theadosia said, "Excuse me," before attempting to go around the knight.

Emmett extended his hand, blocking her direct path once more. "I don't believe we had the opportunity to get to know each other." His raspy voice was unnerving.

Theadosia took a step back, distancing herself from him. "No offense..." Theadosia brushed her bangs back. "I don't really care to get to know you."

Emmett took a step closer to her, enough to slide the stable door shut behind him. It came to a close with a loud bang that reverberated through the rafters. He glanced at the surrounding area to make sure they were alone, before glowering at the girl before him.

"The guards told me that you arrived back at the gate this morning," said Emmett, "and now I'm here to claim something that I think you have."

Theadosia crossed her arms and sunk into her hip. "You've been spying on us."

"No, I'm merely concerned for your safety."

"Doubtful."

Emmett's face twisted. "Tell me what you discovered."

"What do you mean?"

"Your family heirloom."

Theadosia's blood turned cold. "What?"

Sir Emmett took a step closer, and Theadosia immediately countered, her back drawing nearer to the wall. "Let me help you remember," the knight said. "I'm looking for a ruby."

Theadosia instantly thought about the pendant. She forced a laugh. "I think we all would like a ruby."

Sir Emmett's fists closed. He swallowed hard before stepping closer to Theadosia. "You don't understand the severity of the situation."

"Sir, I–"

"I know you have it."

"I don't know what you're talking about."

"Don't play dumb with me!" Sir Emmett's voice boomed. He grabbed her shoulders and shook her. "Don't lie to me, girl."

Theadosia shoved his hands off her. "Excuse me!" she said, ducking underneath his arm and going for the door behind him.

Emmett reached out and clamped his hand around her wrist, turning her back around. "This is no time for games," Emmett said, his breath beating down on her face.

Theadosia attempted to free herself from his grasp. "I told you, I have no idea what you're talking about! Let go!"

"There are consequences for lying to a first knight," Emmett said. His fist continued to close tighter around her wrist, and Theadosia could feel her hand pulsing.

"Are you threatening me?"

"Take it as you will."

"How dare you!" With one swift kick, Theadosia slammed her boot against Emmett's shin.

He released the grasp on her wrist immediately, and he keeled over in pain.

Theadosia pulled her hand to her chest, feeling the circulation begin to return to her fingertips. Turning on her heel, she went for the door, but Emmett was fast. With one lunge, Emmett reached forward and grabbed Theadosia's neck.

Emmett slammed Theadosia against the stable door, his grasp tight around her throat.

Theadosia gasped. She clawed at Emmett's arm, trying to force him to let her go. She still had the hidden blades spring-loaded under her sleeves, but she knew the consequences for killing or harming a knight of Solaris could be deadly.

"If you or your brother want to live, you *will* give me the ruby!" Emmett's voice roared in Theadosia's face. His expression twisted again, the scar on his face disfiguring, and he drew closer to her neck. He spoke:

"And the halberd."

He continued to crush his fingers into her neck and push her into the wall. When she didn't respond, he spoke menacingly. "This is the last time I'm going to repeat myself," he said. "Tell me where the ruby is, or I'll kill you."

Theadosia clawed at Emmett's wrists. Dark spots danced in her vision. She had to activate her blades.

"Let her go!" Another voice sounded in the stables.

Instantly, Emmett relinquished his grasp on Theadosia's neck and whipped around to face the source of the voice.

Theadosia gasped, clutching her neck, her chest heaving up and down. She scampered away from Emmett to the wall, distancing herself from the knight.

Simon was storming the central aisle of the stables.

"How dare you lay a finger on her!" For the first time, Simon's voice was the opposite of monotonous. It rang with power.

Emmett fixed his collar. "A simple conversation," he said.

"That's not what I saw."

"You should forget what you saw, boy," Emmett stated. He then turned to Theadosia. "Have a good time at the festivities this weekend, Lady Ruiz," he finished, and opened the stable doors. The blinding sunlight streaked in from outside, and Emmett vanished.

Simon kept his distance from Theadosia. "Are you all right?"

Theadosia cleared her throat, her breathing steadying. "I will be." She let out a sigh before meeting Simon's gaze. "Thank you."

Simon had returned to his statuesque form, his face unwavering. Only the slightest dip of his chin, attentiveness in his eyes, showed his concern.

"Are you sure you're alright?"

"I think so," she replied, massaging the front of her neck. "I should go." Theadosia straightened up and started for the exit, wanting to get back to the castle.

"May I…" Simon's voice trailed off.

Theadosia stopped at the doorway and turned over her shoulder, flipping her bangs out of her eyes. "What was that?"

Simon hesitated. "Would you like me to escort you back to the castle?"

A moment of silence passed between them.

Then Theadosia nodded. "I'd like that."

- 24 -

Kaison

Pandora and Kaison burst through the door at the bottom of Sun Spire. Before them was an ascending spiral staircase that disappeared around the corner. The small, stone staircase was barely wide enough for the two of them to squeeze through side by side.

"This way," said Pandora. She began ascending first.

At each turn, there was a small slit in the stone that acted as a window, allowing light to stream inside and illuminate their path. Besides the tiny cracks, there were no other torches lit in the staircase.

Kaison hauled his body up more stairs. There must have been hundreds. Story after story he climbed, following Pandora closely behind. As soon as he was beginning to feel pains in his chest, he saw a wooden door at the top of the staircase.

Kaison let out a sigh of relief.

Pandora reached out to touch the handle and pulled the door out toward them. Then the two stepped inside.

They emerged into a circular room. The floor was covered in checkered, marble stones, and the walls were tan like the outside of the castle. Four windows covered separate sides of the round space. The windows spanned the entire height of the walls, stretching from the marble floor to the ceiling. They met in a four-starred point at the top of the tower. In the center hung a golden chandelier, and on the outside of the room were four sconces that held lit torches.

"There's nothing in here," said Pandora. She stepped farther into the room and circled around. Her dress flowed outward from her frame as she spun.

"There has to be. We have to find it," said Kaison.

"What did the letter say again?" asked Pandora.

Kaison took a moment to remember. "The northern gold carries the flame."

Pandora nodded in response.

"Northern," Kaison mused. "Which way is north?"

"That way." Pandora pointed to one of the windows.

Kaison darted toward it and stood directly in front of it. The light streaming in from the full window touched his entire body. It cast a large pool of light on the floor behind him.

Outside, Kaison viewed a wide open plateau. To the right, if he squinted, he was able to see mountains on the horizon. However, nothing outside appeared to have the image of a flame. In fact, technically they were standing in the Sun Spire – the beacon of light that directed everyone toward Sun Castle. Wasn't Sun Spire the flame?

Pandora was at his side. She examined the fields below where the marketplace was set up with colored tents and stands, specifically for the Harvest Banquet. The sun was high in the sky.

Pandora let out a sigh. "I don't see anything from this window. Even if there was a pattern in the grass on the moor, there's no way we would see it now because of the tents." She clasped her hands behind her back and twirled back to the center of the tower. She gave Kaison a half-defeated smile.

Kaison couldn't help but smile back before his mind re-focused on the task. Kaison peered around the room once more. There were no objects. The flames coming from the torches on the wall barely lit the room.

The flames…

Kaison focused on the four golden sconces that were holding the torches.

"Pandora, look!" he pointed to the golden sconces.

"The northern gold carries the flame…," Pandora mused.

Kaison stepped closer to the sconce on the north side of the tower. He strained himself on his tiptoes to try and reach it, but his fingers barely grasped the gold.

Pandora hurried over to him. "Help me up there."

Kaison bent down to his knee and clasped his hands together to make a platform for Pandora to stand on. Pandora placed her hand on Kaison's shoulder and held her dress up in the other hand. Then she placed her foot into Kaison's makeshift platform and stepped up. When she was fully balanced on Kaison's knee, she reached out toward the sconce.

"I don't see anything," Pandora said. Her right hand grabbed the torch and pulled it out of the sconce.

"Do any parts of it move?"

Pandora lifted her other hand off Kaison's shoulder that she had been using to balance. Then she yanked hard on the golden sconce, pulling the metal down. A loud clank echoed through Sun Spire. The force caused Pandora to stumble, and her foot slipped out of Kaison's grasp. Kaison reached out to catch her, and Pandora fell into Kaison's embrace, her chest against his.

Kaison's face was close to hers, and he stared deeply into her big, doe-like eyes.

Pandora paused before standing upright. She brushed her hands against her skirt, as if she was brushing off non-existent dirt.

Kaison turned his attention back to the sconce and rose to his feet. The golden sconce had been pulled downward away from the wall. Below the sconce, a stone panel had popped open. Sitting directly inside was a silver key the size of Kaison's palm.

Kaison reached his hand inside the opening to grab the key. He turned it over in his palm. The diamond shape resembled the keyhole in the library.

"We found it!" he exclaimed.

Pandora cheeks lifted. "Let me see," she said eagerly, holding out her hand.

Kaison passed her the key.

She flipped it over, a soft grin appearing on her face. "I can't believe it," she said. "I want to be there when you find out whatever is behind the tapestry."

Kaison took the key back from Pandora. "You will be. Let's go." Kaison turned to go, but Pandora stopped him.

"Who else did you tell about the tapestry?" Pandora questioned.

Kaison was taken aback. "No one."

"We need to be careful. Do you have any idea what's behind it?"

Kaison wasn't sure if she was curious or scared. "It won't be dangerous," he tried to reassure her. "My father wanted Theodosia and I to solve this riddle."

"I'm not scared to explore, but you were attacked. Someone wants to hurt you, and I don't want to see you get hurt again," said Pandora.

Kaison breathed a sigh of relief, running his hands through his hair. "Well, that was before I knew you had magical shields."

"My shields can't always protect us," Pandora said. "Whatever is behind that tapestry, you need to be prepared to be hunted for it – or worse."

Kaison tilted his head. "What do you think is behind the tapestry?"

Pandora wrinkled her nose. "Well…"

The door to Sun Spire opened abruptly, causing Kaison and Pandora to jump. Louie entered the room with Theadosia right beside him.

"Sir Emmett attacked Theadosia," Louie blurted out.

"Threatened me." Theadosia corrected Louie. "Well…it would have been worse if Simon wasn't there."

"Hmm," Louie mused. "Plague Boy seems to be saving you two a lot."

Theadosia snapped her head in Louie's direction. "Don't call him that."

"Sorry…bad habit."

"Attacked you? What happened?" Kaison insisted.

"He's after the pendant," Theadosia stated. "The halberd too. We have to keep them hidden."

Kaison felt the necklace against his chest. He nodded. "We will. Are you all right?"

Theadosia sunk into her hip. "I can handle myself, remember?" she said. "Now, did you find the key?"

Kaison held up his hand. "Found it."

"Then what are we waiting for?"

- 25 -

Kaison

The four made their way to the library doors. There were only a few people roaming the hallways of Sun Castle, for most of the nobles and knights were enjoying an afternoon browsing through the festival on the moor. Kaison was secretly grateful that they had been here during the national celebration because that meant the halls were almost bare. Nothing could deter him from finding what his father sent him to discover.

Kaison led the way into the library before starting for the back stairs. They remained nonchalant, careful not to draw attention to themselves. After Kaison ascended the stairs at the back of the room, he turned down an aisle, leading him toward the wall with the tapestries.

With one more turn, the halberd tapestry came into view. Kaison stopped before the maroon fabric.

"Let's try this again," he said, reaching into his trousers and pulling out the key.

Theadosia lifted the curtain and removed the loose stone from the wall, while Louie stood on guard, scanning the area intently to make sure no one was watching.

Taking a step closer, Kaison bent over and inserted the key into the keyhole. He let out a deep breath before turning the key. It turned easily in the slot, and a loud clanking sound was heard.

A lever popped out from the side of the wall, almost hitting Theadosia in the hip. She gasped and jumped back in surprise.

Kaison removed the key and put it back in his pocket before approaching the lever. He wrapped both hands around it before giving a sharp tug. A visible crack formed along the wall, showcasing a doorway. Then the door began to slide aside as though it were on a track, exposing a hidden room.

It was pitch dark inside, and Kaison couldn't see further than two feet in front of him.

Before anyone had to ask, Pandora raised her hand. Her palm faced the ceiling. With a slight exhale, a glowing orb formed at her fingertips. It was too bright to look at directly, causing Kaison to shy away from the brilliant rays.

"Let me," Pandora said, starting off into the hidden room.

Kaison's heart beat faster. He remembered what Pandora had said about expectations and about being in danger. Truly, he had no idea what to expect inside. After taking a deep breath, he entered alongside the rest of the group.

Once inside, the light from Pandora's glowing orb illuminated the space around them. The hidden room was a combination of a library and a storage room. It was filled with rows of shelving, scarcely covered in books and scrolls. The shelving continued past the circular pool of light, disappearing into darkness. Glass cabinets were filled with all sorts of trinkets: goblets, plates, jewelry, and even clothing. The cabinets farther in the distance were all covered by beige sheets that used to be white at some point in time. A giant table rested in the middle of the room, which was covered in artwork such as tapestries and giant portraits.

"What is this place?" Kaison asked, looking around the hidden room in awe.

"It looks like no one has been here in years," Pandora replied.

Louie was by the door, closing it so no one would know they were there. He left a sliver of light peeking through in case the door locked behind them.

Theadosia had reached the center table and picked up a piece of paper that was about the size of her hand. "Here you go," she said before reading it, "*All of King Arturo's belongings to be hidden for safe-keeping by order of Sir Landon*. Signed Dux Nikodemus."

"Who is Sir Landon?" Pandora asked. With a raise of her hand, the glowing orb that was floating near her ascended to the ceiling, acting as a chandelier over the central table.

Kaison shifted in his stance, continuing to scan the room. Artifacts…their excavations at the Albufera. What if their father was a historian or something of the like for King Arturo? That would explain how he knew Dux Nikodemus. He could have been sent to Grovia to continue his search. What if the halberd was something he had uncovered?

Theadosia's voice snapped Kaison out of his thoughts. "The letter from our father mentioned Sir Landon as well," she said.

"Does he still work at the castle?" Pandora asked. She looked at Louie.

"I've never heard of him," Louie said, "but I'm sure Dux Nikodemus would know."

Kaison agreed. "I'll ask him myself." He reached up and touched his chest, feeling the ruby pendant underneath his shirt, making a silent promise he would piece together the puzzle his father had assigned him to.

Theadosia picked up another piece of paper from the table. Kaison walked over to Theadosia's side and looked over her shoulder at the picture. It was a portrait of a young woman holding a baby.

"Is this the queen?" Kaison asked.

Pandora approached them to get a look at the picture herself. "Yes. I didn't think pictures of the royal family were saved."

"Well," Louie intervened, "nobody knew this entire room existed, yet here we are."

Kaison rounded the table and squinted his eyes to try and determine how deep the room actually went.

"We should split up to cover more ground," said Kaison.

"Two groups?" Pandora suggested. "Theadosia and Kaison, you would recognize anything from your dad, so you two lead the groups?"

"I'm staying by the door," Louie said.

Theadosia was picking up another piece of paper off the center desk. "I'll stay here too."

"Great," Kaison replied. He turned to Pandora. "Shall we go explore?"

With a smile, Pandora opened her palm and another glowing orb of light manifested in front of her. "Let's go," she said before starting off deeper into the hidden room.

The remainder of the hidden room was full of large bookshelves and furniture covered with beige sheets. Some of the shelves were completely empty, only taking up space in the room, and some contained one or two scrolls. All of the scrolls were covered in a filthy layer of dust. The shelves also held small statutes and trinkets. There were compasses, maps, goblets, and jewelry strewn in all directions, with absolutely no organization.

Kaison turned around a bookshelf and almost crashed into a suit of armor. He came to a halt before the suit. It was gold, and the chainmail glistened from underneath the breast plate. A red feather extended into the air from the top of the helmet. The model knight held a shield before him, and his other arm was outstretched on the diagonal. It was as if the other hand was meant to be holding something.

The shield entranced Kaison. A beautiful coat of armor was decorated with golden laurels and glistening gems. And in the center...

"Wait, Pandora!" Kaison called. Her magical light had flickered too far out of reach.

Pandora turned around to see Kaison was many paces behind her. "Did you find something?" she asked, quickly returning to Kaison's side.

Kaison pointed to the shield before him, and Pandora brought her palm forward to shine the light on it.

On the shield was a golden sun. It was the exact symbol that Kaison had been seeing all over Solaris.

Pandora's shoulder touched Kaison's, and she pondered the mannequin knight before them. "What's wrong?" she asked.

"I...," Kaison's voice ran off. He ran his fingers through his hair before continuing. "Do you know what the sun crest symbolizes?"

"The sun was the emblem for Solaris until Queen Benedict decided to change it to her family crest," Pandora said. "Why?"

"Dux Nikodemus asked me if I recognized it the day I got here."

"He was probably testing you to see if your parents were from Solaris or Vorinder," Pandora said.

"No," Kaison said, "it was more than that. It wasn't a passing comment."

Pandora clasped her hands in front of her while the orb circulated overhead. "Maybe he was being sentimental."

More questions overwhelmed Kaison's mind. "Why didn't Dux Nikodemus take the throne then after Queen Lidia's death and King Arturo's disappearance?"

"Because he believes in the fated queen. He was only protecting the throne until the rightful heir came along," Pandora stated. "Solaris is destined by fate to be ruled by the one who possesses the Ademantum, and Dux Nikodemus was still waiting for the heir to reveal themselves."

"I know about the Ademantum," Kaison replied. "That's why Vorinder succeeded. After Queen Lidia died, Vorinder didn't believe the Ademantum chose Queen Benedict – only that she was claiming to have it. They wanted Arturo's bloodline to continue until the true queen was found."

"The problem is, no one knows what the Ademantum is," Pandora said. "How can Queen Benedict prove something that may not even exist?"

"Do you believe in having a fated queen?" Kaison asked.

Pandora hesitated. "Well, no one else has claimed to have it." She said before continuing on through the room. Kaison was forced to follow her so he wasn't left in darkness.

Then Pandora stopped, her eyes settling on a specific artifact. Kaison saw it too. Mostly everything they had passed was traditionally ornate, delineated in gold and red hues, but this object was different. The sight of the black, metal object was jarring to their eyes.

"What is that?" Pandora asked.

Kaison took a step toward the case. The object inside was silver and sleek, reminding Kaison of a crossbow but with a handle on the bottom.

"I don't know," Kaison admitted, having never seen something like it before. He pressed his palm against the glass, curiosity overwhelming him. Then he lifted the lid slowly, revealing the object.

"Don't break it," Pandora warned. "There's a reason it's in a case."

"I won't break it," Kaison replied. He slowly reached forward, picking up the object. It was cool to the touch, and felt like a metal sword, but weighed far less than he had anticipated. There was certainly a trigger like a crossbow, but also a tiny lever on the side. Carefully, Kaison pushed the lever upwards.

The artifact made a soft click.

"What is this?" Kaison gasped.

"Put it back," Pandora said, her voice shaken. With wide eyes, she reached forward and flipped the tiny lever again.

Kaison obeyed, putting the artifact back where he had found it. He shut the glass carefully, making certain to return everything to how it was when he found it.

Pandora was already walking off, bringing the light with her. But Kaison was fascinated and wanted to spend more time looking at each item.

Pandora rounded a bend in the shelves before stopping. "Golden books?" Pandora said before scurrying over. "These are from King Arturo's library!"

Kaison went to stand before the shelf. About twelve books rested there, spaced unevenly. Pushing aside cobwebs, Kaison picked up one of the books in his hands and flipped it over to read the cover.

Land Beyond Solaris.

Kaison opened the book to the first page and read the synopsis:

"This book is the personal diary of the first expe-

dition team sent to the Land Beyond. It details their journeys through the iron tunnels, where snake-like monsters cut deeply through the underground and carry passengers in their bellies. It also discusses the metal beasts that plunge through the roads pressed with yellow and white lines. The maps of the Land Beyond detailed here will allow any future expeditions to navigate the pathways back to the door that reaches Morbaeda. This can be found on the Eastern part of the green moorland, underneath the museum where the payments of culture are made."

Kaison turned to the next page. It was a map with many small squares. The tiny squares were in the shape of an island running south to north. The squares were grouped around a large, green rectangle in the middle, which took up almost half of the map. Lines were drawn in haphazard directions across the map with the labels: green snake, purple snake, red snake, blue snake.

Kaison flipped the page over. The first entry was written over in thick black ink:

Redacted after the War of Worlds.

The War of Worlds? The book was centuries old!

Kaison replaced the book on the shelf and picked up another.

Meanwhile, Pandora was dusting off the book she was holding, keeping it at an arm's distance until it was clean. Then Pandora let out a high-pitched exclamation. She showed the book to Kaison so that he could read the cover.

"'*Protection Spells of Light*,'" Kaison read.

"Why doesn't the world practice magic anymore?" Pandora asked.

"Take it. No one's going to miss it."

Pandora's mouth dropped open. She was silent for a moment before she let out a laugh. "Very funny," she said as she put the book back on the shelf.

Kaison picked up another book to read the title.

The Teardrop, the Halberd, and the Ademantum.

Kaison's heart skipped a beat.

Kaison gently opened the hardcover book to the first page. He began the first sentence, but a sound reverberated from the other side of the bookshelf. He peered through the open shelves to the other side, but there was nothing there but another stone wall. Kaison strained his ears to listen more closely, and muffled voices sounded from deeper in the room.

"This says..."

"Shhh," Kaison silenced Pandora.

She looked at him, slightly offended at first, before noticing his expression.

"Do you hear that?" Kaison asked.

"It's probably Theadosia and Louie."

Kaison waited, but the sounds had quieted down. For a moment, he agreed with Pandora.

Seconds afterward, the wall on the opposite side of the bookshelf began to shake. A faint outline of a door cracked into the stone and grew bigger. A deep scratching sound accompanied the wall as the door slid to the side.

"Get down!" exclaimed Pandora. She extinguished the magical orb and dropped to the ground. Then she tugged Kaison's arm, pulling him down beside her.

The two crouched behind the bookshelf, watching the figures emerge from the passageway on the other side.

- 26 -

Kaison

The wall slid open and revealed two figures. A torch silhouetted them both in the blackness. A tall man had a hold of a girl's wrist, and he shoved her inside the hidden room containing King Arturo's artifacts. The girl stumbled over her own footing as she whimpered.

The tall man released her. Then he turned around and slid the wall closed, covering their tracks.

"Haven't I already done enough for you?" the girl asked. The voice sounded familiar for some reason.

The man scoffed. He turned around to face her, lighting the space between them with his torch. The fire's light flickered on the man's face, revealing his identity.

Sir Emmett.

"I've been delivering messages for half a year now. I'm done!" The girl's back was to Kaison and Pandora.

"Are you raising your voice with me?" Emmett took a step closer.

The anger in his bottomless eyes sent a shiver down Kaison's spine.

"I've been putting my life at risk to make these maps for you!" The girl waved a piece of parchment in Emmett's face.

Emmett ripped the parchment out of her hands. "You're not done until I say so," he growled. "Don't you care about your family?" Emmett inched closer, forcing the girl to counter. The light was drawing nearer to the bookshelf. If the light went any farther, there would be hardly any books on the shelf to hide Kaison and Pandora.

As if Pandora was thinking the same thing, she grabbed Kaison's arm. The two scooted backward into the shadows, but their eyes remained glued on the conversation before them. Their backs hit a dresser, forcing them to stop.

"It would be sad to lose Julian after all this now, wouldn't it?" Emmett threatened. Emmett's face was filled with an intensity Kaison had never seen before.

"Leave him out of this," the girl said.

"I will, if you do this new task for me."

"I'm not a murderer."

"This has to be a clean execution. We need to get Maeve's journal," Emmett insisted.

Both Kaison and Pandora tensed. Execution?

"Tomorrow night," the knight continued. "Everyone will be on the moor for the Harvest Banquet and festival. You have to draw her somewhere private."

The room was silent aside from the flickering of the flames.

Sir Emmett took a step closer. "Am I wasting my breath?"

"No," the girl said. "I'll get it for you."

"If you don't," Emmett paused, "I won't forgive you, Cheyenne."

Pandora gasped loudly, and her hand flew to her mouth.

Kaison's body clenched as he watched Sir Emmett's face twist in confusion. Emmett's eyes shifted from Cheyenne to the bookshelf behind her.

They would be seen if Emmett took one step closer. Kaison grabbed Pandora's arm before scrambling to his feet, pulling Pandora up beside him. Hardly able to see, and making a split-second decision, he slid between the two dressers behind them, pulling a white sheet overtop to mask their hiding spot.

A cascade of dust flooded on top of them, and Kaison caught his breath in his throat, trying not to cough. The two were pressed against each other in the small space between the dressers. He could feel Pandora's head against his shoulder, and she kept her hand over her mouth to try to stay as quiet as possible.

Kaison could hardly see through the sheet covering them.

Emmett rounded the side of the bookshelf, and the torch light in his hand became even brighter. When he reached the other side, he looked around. The heat from the flame was palpable, drawing closer and closer to where Kaison and Pandora were hiding. Emmett and the torch were right in front of the sheet.

Then Emmett leaned down and picked up a golden book. It was the book about the halberd. It had slipped from Kaison's grasp when they had scrambled to hide. Emmett flipped it over in his hands, reading the cover, and put the book underneath his arm.

"It's nothing," Emmett said. He rose back to his feet. "Since you're incapable, I guess I must get the halberd myself?"

A lump formed at Kaison's throat.

There was a moment of silence before Cheyenne continued. "What's that?"

Kaison shut his eyes tightly, knowing they were in danger. Pandora's chest stopped moving as she held her breath.

"It's light," Emmett said, his dark voice loud. "Someone's here.

Move."

Emmett began walking away, the torch following him. Kaison opened his eyes, attempting to make out what was happening on the other side of the sheet. All he heard was a bunch of scuffling, and the light from the torch faded away. Before long, the light completely extinguished.

Kaison remained frozen, completely blind and lost in an abyss of darkness.

Pandora shifted slightly before she spoke, barely audible, "Theadosia and Louie don't know he's here." Her breath was warm on Kaison's neck.

That was enough to encourage Kaison to move. Emmett had told Cheyenne to 'execute' Maeve. He would come after the halberd next. They were out of time, and every second they stayed here it was putting Theadosia in more danger.

Kaison pulled the sheet off them and let it fall to the floor. A flurry of dust made him choke. He slithered out of the hiding spot and into the aisle, feeling a slight bit of relief, but still unable to see anything.

Pandora was furiously brushing the dirt off her.

"Sir Emmett's gone," Kaison announced.

Pandora opened her fingers and let a dim light form at them. "How did he get inside?"

"I guess there's another entrance, and Emmett also has a key."

"There," Pandora whispered, pointing at a dim light in the distance. It was coming from the second orb she left with Theadosia and Louie.

"We should get out of here," Kaison stated.

Pandora's shoulder pressed against his. She ran her hand down his arm until she found his hand and grasped it tightly.

The gesture took Kaison by surprise, but a warmth flooded through him. Kaison interlaced his fingers with hers, feeling some sense of security.

The light at Pandora's fingertips brightened slightly.

Kaison and Pandora made their way back through the king's belongings, weaving around shelves and furniture. They rounded a corner and made it to the front part of the hidden room. Louie and Theadosia were behind a desk, and Theadosia was reading from a scroll. The two of them were whispering, making their conversation inaudible.

When Kaison and Pandora stepped out from the shelves, Louie whipped around.

"By plague!" he exclaimed, clasping his hand to his chest. "You scared the daylights out of me!"

Theadosia turned to face Kaison and Pandora. She eyed them in confusion before her gaze locked onto their interlaced hands.

Pandora pulled her hand away from Kaison's.

"You two look like you've seen a ghost," Louie said.

Kaison cleared his throat. His palms were sweaty, and his heart was still thumping against his chest. "We need to go," he said.

"Did you get into an argument?" Louie asked.

"We heard you from here," Theadosia added.

"That wasn't us," Pandora said.

"It was Sir Emmett and Cheyenne," Kaison said. "They're planning to murder Maeve."

"What?" Theadosia gasped.

"Cheyenne is the one who attacked me. It's the only thing that makes sense. And Sir Emmett is now planning an execution."

"I don't believe it," Pandora said. "Cheyenne would never murder someone."

Kaison ran his hands through his hair, staring at the floor as his mind swirled with thoughts. "It sounded like she was being blackmailed. Sir Emmett was threatening both her and Julian."

Louie was pacing and asked, "Sir Emmett…blackmail and murder? Why?"

"Something about a journal. It was all a blur," Pandora said, her breathing becoming shallower. She brought a hand to her chest.

"A journal?" Louie asked. "Like that journal Maeve carries around everywhere?"

"She literally sleeps holding that thing," Theadosia added.

"I refuse to believe Cheyenne would be able to kill anyone," Pandora repeated.

"She attacked me and left me for dead!"

"Are we not going to talk about the fact that they somehow appeared in the room?" Theadosia inquired. "We went through all that trouble to find a key."

"I guess this castle has a lot of hidden passageways," Pandora said.

"Or Emmett has a key of his own," Kaison added.

"There has to be another entrance because they didn't come in through the library," Louie said. Then he let out a sigh. "Who else knows about this room?"

"Dux Nikodemus and Sir Landon," Theadosia said, referencing the letter she had found earlier.

Kaison cleared his throat. "Sir Emmett is going to come for the halberd."

"We have to do something," Theadosia said.

"Hide it?" Louie asked.

"Sir Emmett will still come for Kaison regardless," said Pandora.

Kaison was at a loss for words. All he wanted was for his father to be here and give him all the answers. "What did father want us to find here?" Kaison asked. His mind returned to the book that mentioned a halberd which he had left behind. He cursed under his breath, for Sir Emmett had taken it with him. If anything, maybe Kaison could have found out more information about the object his father had entrusted him with.

"What if it wasn't about something," Theadosia said, "but someone. Both the letter and the statement to move all of Arturo's belongings mentioned Dux Nikodemus and Sir Landon. Maybe we should ask Nikodemus who Landon is."

Suddenly there was another creaking noise coming from deep in the room.

"We're leaving now." Louie took the scroll from Theadosia's hands and replaced it on the desk before taking off toward the door.

"Wait!" Kaison removed the staff from his belt. He ran over to one of the darkest bookshelves in a corner. Then he leaned down and placed the staff on the bottom shelf. He grabbed a sheet, choking from the dust, and covered the transformed halberd with the sheet. Then he placed a painting in front of the bookshelf.

"You can't let that out of your sight," protested Pandora.

"I can't wear it to the festival or the banquet either," said Kaison. He took a step back to make sure the halberd was hidden. "It's safe. They'll never think to look here, but I shouldn't have the key either."

Theadosia said, "Give it to me."

"No, you're in too much danger already. Emmett already attacked you."

Pandora held out her hand, palm up. "I'll take the key."

Kaison nodded, handing the key to the hidden room over to her.

She put it in her pocket before saying, "We're in this together."

- 27 -

Osiris

Osiris stood on a thin ledge. Her back was pressed to the outside of the building, and she shifted sideways, heading toward a metal pipe. The rain was beginning to lift, but the surfaces were still slick. Below, the city was starting to wake, even though the sun hadn't risen over the horizon.

Osiris grabbed the pipe and slid down. The metal was sleek against her boots and gloves, making her descent quick. Letting go within jumping distance from the ground, she landed in an alleyway, feeling the impact of the drop in her knees. She caught her balance, scanning the area for intruders.

The alley was empty.

She peered inside the satchel hanging over her shoulder. The golden mirror was safe. Osiris pulled her mask higher on her nose and started down the alley.

She and Destrian needed a plan. Though they hadn't been discovered, their hideout was compromised. It wouldn't be too much longer until the soldiers would return and find them.

Osiris continued to press on down the street, her mind whirling with thoughts.

But something wasn't right. She felt like there were eyes on her, watching her every move. She tilted her head slightly, enough to look behind her out of her peripheral vision. A hooded figure was at the opposite end of the alley.

Osiris's chest tightened. It was the same figure she had seen a few days prior when she made the exchange for the diamond necklace. This same figure had seen her murder the retired soldier.

Osiris quickened her pace, rounding the corner. She couldn't go home. She wouldn't lead this stranger there and put her people in danger. The street she was on was filled with crates and wheelbarrows, perfect for her to hide. But she didn't want to hide.

The splash of a puddle was heard behind her, and she knew the figure was still on her trail. They weren't even trying to hide themselves anymore.

Osiris cut the corner into the nearest alley. Seeing a nearby crate, she jumped up before using it as leverage to reach for the second floor ledge. Grabbing the edge of the stone, Osiris hoisted herself up, slipping into the shadows between two of the second story windows.

The figure rounded the corner, slowing their pace as they turned their head, no doubt looking for where Osiris had gone.

Osiris steadied her breathing, fixated on the person below.

They proceeded to prowl farther, passing underneath where Osiris was hiding. A distant lamp flickered, silhouetting their figure. They were tall and broad, suggesting they were male, but Osiris couldn't be certain due to their hood and the way the cape flared around their body.

Once they were far enough past her, Osiris made her move. Unsheathing one of her two daggers, Osiris leapt down from the shadowed ledge. She grabbed their shoulder before wrapping her other arm around their neck and pressing the blade up to their exposed skin.

They were taller than her, but Osiris forced them to bend slightly at the knee as she tightened her grip. "Who are you?" Osiris growled, her lips close to their ear.

They raised their hands on either side of their head, fingers spread, in a position of surrender.

"I'm not here to hurt you. I'm here to make a deal." The voice was male, but gentle. He sounded to be in his late thirties, give or take. "That is, if you are Osiris Saber."

Osiris could feel the bulge of their muscles underneath her grasp. This person was a fighter.

She brought the blade closer. "Why were you spying on me then?"

"Because I'm the man who hired that idiot you killed."

A chill flushed through Osiris's body. She pulled her dagger back, shoving him away in the process.

The man stumbled slightly on the cobblestone, his hand flying up to his neck to feel if she drew blood.

Osiris didn't loosen her grip on the dagger as she let her arm fall to her side, straightening her posture. "Who are you?" Osiris asked again, this time enunciating more clearly.

The man turned to face her as he pulled back his hood. He had dark skin and welcoming eyes. He had a short white beard that contrasted his young appearance, masking his real age. The clasp that held his coat closed with a jeweled brooch, containing a pink flame with a laurel.

With an upward tilt of his chin, he announced, "I'm Dux Nikodemus."

Osiris's breath caught in her throat. She didn't blink. "You expect me to believe you are the Head Knight of Solaris?"

Nikodemus widened his stance, clasping his hands behind his back.

"Explain yourself."

"Might we get out of the rain?" Nikodemus asked. "I can buy you a drink."

A laugh escaped her lips. "With Solaris coin? I don't think so."

"Oh, that's right," Nikodemus said, "I forgot you're not allowed inside taverns."

Instinctively, Osiris glanced down at her wrist, but her gloves extended underneath her sleeves. There was no way he had seen the symbol branded on her. How did he know? Unless he was testing her.

"If this is about your man I killed, it's only because he went back on his word," Osiris said. "I don't do business with liars, and I certainly will not accept less than the original price for a job."

Nikodemus shook his head. "I couldn't care less about him. That was all a test."

Osiris was confused, but her expression didn't change.

"I needed to make sure you lived up to the rumors. You have a… reputation…for being the worst thief in Larkesh. And to me, when people say you're the worst, that means you're the best."

If her reputation had spread all the way to Solaris, it would only be a matter of time before a bounty was placed on her head. If he could find her, anyone could. Maybe the head knight had a few more resources to expedite the process, but it was the same nonetheless.

"Is that so?" Osiris tried to sound uninterested, but the thought scared her.

"It wasn't my intention for that man to swindle the deal," Nikodemus said, disregarding the rhetorical question. "He was a miscreant I hired from the street. Again, that was all a test."

"Did I pass?"

"Yes."

Osiris shifted in her stance. Her wet clothes were clinging to her body uncomfortably, and she gripped the dagger tighter in her hands. "And what was the test for?"

"I know Captain Hondo has plans to attack Solaris. I need you to get those for me."

Osiris's brow furrowed. "What?" she blurted out. The Captain? It was a death sentence. "Absolutely not."

"I will give you anything you ask for."

"I would have to break into the Captain's Palace. Nothing you could offer would cover the price of –"

"Your freedom?"

Osiris's mouth was agape. She stared back at the knight, her breathing starting to increase in speed.

"We don't have rules against your people in Solaris," Nikodemus said. "I could offer both safe passage and residence there."

Osiris stared back at him. It was all she ever wanted – to live freely. She would never have to worry about being caught and thrown into the Tournament to be executed. But with the opportunity finally there, she felt like a coward. If she took the deal, she would leave all her people behind. She couldn't do that. She wouldn't escape like a coward and leave everyone to die.

"No," Osiris said.

Nikodemus's eyes widened ever so slightly, showing his surprise. "What if you could bring someone with you?" He tried to sweeten the deal further.

"I said no," Osiris stated. "I want silver."

"How much silver?"

Osiris had to start high. Whatever number she set would be negotiated down, but she was working with the head knight of Solaris. That meant he had money. Royal money.

Osiris tilted her chin up. "One thousand suns."

"Done," Nikodemus said, the inflection in his voice not changing in the slightest.

She had been certain there was going to be a negotiation.

Caught off guard, Osiris quickly added, "I can't do it alone. My partners will need to be compensated as well."

"What are their names?"

Osiris wasn't sure she could convince them to take this risk, but she couldn't possibly break into the Captain's Palace without help.

"Destrian Amir and Moriah Omanne."

Nikodemus nodded, memorizing the names instantly. "Done," he said. "I will be back in ten days time."

Osiris's heart plummeted. "Ten days? That's not enough time."

"Make it enough time."

"I can't," Osiris insisted. "I would need blueprints of the palace…to scout it out…maybe get a disguise –"

"I don't have time to waste," Nikodemus said, taking a step forward.

Osiris immediately countered. She bit her tongue, infuriated she showed him weakness.

"Ten days," Nikodemus said. "I'll find you." Then the head knight reached into his belt and pulled out a coin purse. "To incentivize you," he said. He didn't take a step closer, noting her grip on the blade tighten. Instead, he bent down and placed the coin purse at his feet. Coming back to a standing position, he straightened, standing tall once more. "One more thing…I know Captain Hondo has a diamond ring somewhere in his quarters. Find it, and it's yours."

Osiris's eyes narrowed. "How would you know that?"

Nikodemus reached for his hood and ignored her question. "Pleasure doing business with you." He finished with a gentle smile before pulling the hood over his head, casting a dark shadow on his face. As he turned to leave, and the cape fluttered around his body. The head knight proceeded down the dark alleyway until he was completely out of sight.

The cool rain chilled Osiris to the bone. She sheathed her dagger, her hand clammy, before striding forward toward the coin purse. She picked it up, surprised by the weight of it, before opening the bag. A gasp escaped her lips as she stared at the sparkling coin.

She had to be careful. Now she owed him, and owing someone was more dangerous than any deal.

Ten days.

- 28 -

Kaison

The following day, the Harvest Banquet was coming to a close. Awards would be distributed and dinner would be served in the evening. Kaison had spent the entire past twenty-four hours searching for Dux Nikodemus. He needed to tell Nikodemus about the plot against Maeve's life. At the moment, Nikodemus was the only person he could trust. However, Nikodemus was nowhere to be found. It was as if he wasn't even in Sun Castle, but lost somewhere on the moor, most likely monitoring all of the security for the festivities in addition to monitoring the Shadow army.

Kaison considered if he and Theadosia should leave everything behind, forgoing all danger. Kaison would have to live with the unanswered secrets, never fulfilling his father's last wishes or avenging his parents' deaths, but at least he and his sister would be safe. But for how long?

Something deep down drew him to the artifact room. There was years of knowledge there, waiting to be studied and revealed to the rest of the world.

Besides, Theadosia wouldn't let him leave when they had the ability to prevent a murder. Theadosia had gone back to Elistalia to search for Maeve, but Maeve hadn't spent the night in her room. Madame Lucia, the woman who ran Elistalia, told Theadosia that a room had opened up at the castle, and it was offered to Maeve. Theadosia pleaded with Madame Lucia to give her the location of the room, but Madame Lucia informed Theadosia that it was strictly off protocol – by the order of Sir Emmett.

So Pandora, Louie, Kaison, and Theadosia spent the entire morning and afternoon circling the moor, wandering around in the maze of tents and stands. Even more farmers had arrived that morning with fresh produce, creating a complex network of paths. No matter how hard they searched, they couldn't find Maeve, Cheyenne, or Emmett anywhere. The four ended up meandering slowly through the moor, entertaining Louie's every urge to sample a new snack.

The sun set early in the day, and the participants were directed to the royal banquet hall. The banquet hall was on the first floor of the castle, with large glass windowpanes stretching from floor to ceiling that rotated on central axes. This allowed the glass windows to be rotated open and for more tables to be set up on the moor underneath a large, white tent. The white tent connected to the castle, allowing people to move freely between the indoor and outdoor spaces.

All of the villagers, nobles, and friends of the court were invited into the large dining hall to enjoy the meals that had been prepared on the moorland. A large row of tables with pink tablecloths covered the majority of the indoor area, and a white table faced perpendicular to the others at the head. The white table was the place for the nobles that would be judging all of the food prepared by the villagers. One villager would be crowned Queen of the Harvest. An even fancier table sat on a raised platform for the mega-elite, but Queen Benedict had not yet arrived.

Kaison entered the room with Pandora, Louie, and Theadosia, hesitating for a moment as he took in his surroundings. The scene was overwhelming. The nobles were seated at the indoor part of the room, where there was a solid floor, while the villagers and townspeople were outside on the moor under the tent. In the inner space, large floral centerpieces rose high above the tables, adorned with pink roses. Stretched down the center of the tables were candles in tiny, identical glass cups. Each placemat was set with lavender plates. Above, twinkling lights hung from the ceiling down toward the tables, creating the same image of Sun Castle on the inside as on the outside. Pink garlands were laced between the lights.

People were already taking their seats for the banquet, and the first round of food was being served to the guests. Kaison and his sister instinctively followed Pandora and Louie, weaving through the crowd, until they reached a long table on the outskirts of the room. They had been granted a seat near the outdoor tent, but still on the floor meant for the inner court.

Kaison slipped onto a satin pink chair on Louie's side while the girls took a spot opposite them. The room was so loud with chatter, it was hard for Kaison to hear his friends, even though they were right beside him. He didn't know how much more time they had until Sir Emmett would come for him, or until Cheyenne would attack Maeve. Their only hope was to spot them at the banquet.

Louie let out a grunt. He craned his neck toward the servers. "I'm starving. When is it our turn?"

Pandora disregarded Louie completely. "Do you see Cheyenne?" She sat up taller as she scanned the room.

"I don't think talking to Cheyenne will do any good," Louie said. "Not if she's working with Sir Emmett."

"Sir Emmett was threatening Cheyenne and her family. Both she and Maeve are in trouble, and Sir Emmett could go after Julian next."

"Xy'tier can handle himself," Louie muttered. Then he simply turned to the nearest server and raised his hand, gesturing for them to come over. Before the server approached, he added, "Why is it our job to prevent this..." Louie's voice trailed off, and he mouthed 'murder' as he leaned in closer.

"I don't want to live with a guilty conscience," Theadosia said. "We have to report this to Nikodemus the first chance we get."

Suddenly Kaison saw exactly who they were looking for on the outskirts of the room.

Dux Nikodemus. He was next to the raised table for the elite, walking with his hands clasped behind his back.

"He's right there," Kaison told his friends before standing up from the table. Without waiting for their response, he quickly made his way through the room, weaving in and out of people and gently pushing around tables. He crossed to Dux Nikodemus, standing right in his path.

"Kaison," Nikodemus said in a greeting. "How may I help you?"

Kaison cleared his throat, making sure he worded his sentence correctly. His father had told him in the letter to trust Nikodemus. He had so many questions for Nikodemus about the halberd and about how he knew his father. But he knew that they could be running out of time, and Maeve's life was at stake.

"Have you seen Sir Emmett today?" Kaison asked. He had to ease into the part about the murder. Nikodemus and Emmett could be friends, and Kaison couldn't risk Nikodemus brushing aside the murder completely.

"A few times," Nikodemus replied. "He's been helping with the new security protocols."

"Right," Kaison said. He was about to continue, but Nikodemus cut him off.

"Where's the halberd?" Nikodemus looked at Kaison's belt.

"Safe. Don't worry."

"You're not supposed to let it out of your sight."

"I know, but I don't know why. You owe me an explanation about that. But…"

"You can trust me, Kaison."

"Thank you," Kaison said, "That's what my father said. He said I could trust you and Sir Landon, and I will."

Nikodemus's face melted in concern. He suddenly took Kaison by the arm and pulled him farther away from the crowd. They stopped under an awning of garland, and Nikodemus made sure that they weren't in earshot of anyone.

"How do you know that name?" Nikodemus asked.

Kaison remained cautious, curious how Sir Landon's name had provoked such a visible reaction from the head knight. "I've heard it around."

"That's a lie," Nikodemus replied immediately. "Be honest with me."

Kaison stared back at the head knight. His father did tell him to trust Nikodemus. Finally, he let out a sigh. "When my father died, he told me to come to Solaris. He wrote a letter that said that I could trust you and Sir Landon."

Nikodemus's eyes burned with intensity. "Can I see the letter?"

"I don't have it on me."

"What else did the letter say?"

"Not much," Kaison lied. "It talked about how my sister and I could find a safe haven here."

"Have you asked anyone else about Sir Landon?" Nikodemus inquired.

"No."

"Keep it that way."

"Why?" Kaison asked.

"Dux Nikodemus," a voice called from behind.

Nikodemus turned to see a knight waiting for him. "The queen would like to see you," the knight stated.

"One moment, Sir Chadwick," Nikodemus called back. Nikodemus dropped his voice to a whisper once more. "Sir Landon is dangerous. His brother is the Shadow of Eclipse."

"What?"

"You heard me."

"So, Sir Landon is in the Lost Lands?"

"No," Nikodemus was quick to respond. He looked up over Kaison's shoulder, his eyes on Chadwick. "He's here under an alias. Which is why you need to be careful who you talk to."

Kaison's brows furrowed on his forehead. "Why would my father tell me to trust him?"

Nikodemus let out a sigh. "We need to talk in private about everything. Your father…the halberd…" His voice was so quiet it was almost impossible to hear him.

"You did know my father."

"Yes," Nikodemus said, his eyes gentle, "but I can't go into it today with all the festivities, so give me the day."

Kaison eventually let in. "Fine."

Nikodemus smiled, but then his warm expression vanished. "For now, you cannot even mention Sir Landon's name. Do you understand?"

A silence passed between them before Kaison eventually nodded.

"Sir?" Chadwick called once more.

"Coming."

"Wait," Kaison said, "there's something else."

"Not now. After the banquet." Nikodemus gave one last nod at Kaison before joining Sir Chadwick and reporting to the queen.

Kaison watched Nikodemus leave, cursing under his breath. He had wasted his only opportunity to warn the knight about the murder by blabbing on about a stupid, unimportant knight named Landon. As soon as Nikodemus was out of sight, Kaison's mind spun even more vigorously. He grew up learning all about the dangers of the Shadow of Eclipse. Why would his father tell him he could trust a person related to him? Furthermore, why would Sir Landon – the brother of the Shadow of Eclipse – work with Dux Nikodemus to hide away all of King Arturo's items?

Confused, Kaison returned to the table, maneuvering through the crowd. He plopped back on the bench beside Louie. Four mugs were placed at the center of their trio. The smell of peaches fluttered inside Kaison's nostrils.

Theadosia shifted to the edge of her seat. "Did you warn him? What did he say?" she inquired, stirring the seeds at the bottom of her drink nervously.

Pandora leaned in, but Louie was busy slurping his drink loudly.

Kaison dropped his voice to a whisper. He didn't want to tell his friends that he had failed, so he said, "I asked Dux Nikodemus about Sir Landon, and Sir Landon is supposedly related to the Shadow of Eclipse. Landon is his brother."

Louie spit out his peach punch, splattering cinnamon across his plate. "What?"

Pandora's doe-like eyes were wide with fear. "If he's related to the Shadow of Eclipse, he's connected to the dark lineage."

"You think the dark and light lineages are real?" Louie asked, his voice dripping with skepticism.

"Of course," Pandora stated.

"Supposedly he's also here under an alias," Kaison continued, "so, we can't mention his name."

"But father said Sir Landon was one of two people we could trust," Theadosia stated.

The conversation fell silent, and their minds swirled with terrifying thoughts.

Louie placed his elbows on the table. "You're telling me no one else is named Landon?"

Kaison shrugged. "I guess it's possible, but from the sound of it, Nikodemus and my father are referring to the same one."

Pandora let out a sigh before sitting up straighter and folding her hands in front of her. "One step at a time," she said. "At least now Nikodemus can help us stop Sir Emmett and save Maeve. You did tell him, didn't you Kaison?"

Kaison shook his head. "No. It's up to us to stop this murder."

- 29 -

SERAPHINA

The serene image of Sun Castle could be viewed from the mountaintops. The moorland surrounding the castle was patterned with colored tents, contorting the image into a mosaic out of a painting. The sun had almost disappeared over the horizon, casting its evening rays across the celebration.

The Shadow of Eclipse sat perched on the mountain overlooking the moorland. Sun Spire extended high into the milky sky, stretching between fluffy clouds.

Billows of black smoke floated around the Shadow of Eclipse, running down the mountainside and to where a young girl was sitting. Her jet-black hair fell in front of her eyes, and her pale skin revealed her malnourished state. She wore a dark coat with trousers tucked into high boots.

“Do you know what you’re supposed to do?” the man spoke.

The girl cracked her knuckles as she daydreamed in the direction of Sun Castle. It would be the first time the man was letting her out of his sight outside of the castle.

"Yes, Mortimer," she replied, unenthused.

Mortimer's tone changed. "I asked you to call me father."

The girl turned to look back at the Shadow of Eclipse, the intensity in her eyes meeting his. "You're not my father."

Instantly, Mortimer's hand raised, and a purple hue shot from his palm toward the young girl's throat. However, the girl's reflexes were fast. With a slight tilt of her head, the purple hue split in two, going off in two opposite directions and never reaching her neck. She didn't blink, and she continued the unofficial staring contest with Mortimer.

"That's my girl," Mortimer spoke. "You're almost as powerful as I am."

"I am as powerful as you are."

"Don't get ahead of yourself," Mortimer said, his voice dark and intimidating.

"Don't challenge me," the girl replied.

Mortimer smiled before pulling a vial from his pocket. He extended it out toward the girl, and it floated effortlessly toward her with his powers.

She noticed it out of her peripheral vision. "What is this?" she asked.

Mortimer dropped it into her hand. "It will mask anyone from sensing your approach," he said.

The girl didn't think twice. She uncapped the vial and poured the indigo liquid down her throat. However, as soon as she swallowed, a burning sensation ate away at her chest. She gagged once, feeling it burn into the pit of her stomach. She dropped the vial, and the glass shattered on the mountain.

"Brixann?" She choked, tasting the flavor as it seeped into her bloodstream.

"A safety measure," Mortimer stated. He rose to his feet. "You better hurry and tend to your task. Only I have the cure."

With that, Mortimer was consumed in a cloud of black smoke. It wrapped around his body and swallowed him whole. He vanished before the girl could object, leaving nothing but a lingering puff of dark fog.

The girl clutched her throat, feeling the pain eating away at her insides. She quickly scrambled to her feet and fixated on Sun Castle. She extended her hand, attempting to form a dark portal before her, but she was stung with an excruciating pain that rippled up her spine. A gasp escaped her lips when she realized she would have to run there, complete the mission, and return to Mortimer before the poison overtook her.

The girl's eyes narrowed in anger before she started bounding down the cliffside, charging toward Sun Castle.

- 30 -

Kaison

Inside the royal dining hall, Kaison and his friends went over the plan. The only option that seemed reasonable – and the one that would draw the least amount of suspicion – was locating Cheyenne and Maeve and making sure they didn't get close to one another. They would split up on the moor in order to cover more ground. Coming to the banquet at all now seemed like a waste, for they had hoped to find the girls there. Neither were present.

As soon as they were about to rise from their chairs, Queen Benedict entered the room, her presence large. She wore a pink dress in the shape of a flower that was pointed downwards, and her hair was piled inside of her crown. The top of her dress had small patches of white rectangles, creating a checkered pattern of white and pink on her bodice. The entire long-sleeved dress was covered in sparkling lace. She extended her hands up into the air. "What a glorious celebration!" she called forth.

The villagers outside rose into a furious applause. Some people whistled and hollered, which made the more pompous citizens scowl.

"Let's go," said Kaison, "we don't have more time to waste."

Kaison rose from his chair, but was pushed back down by one of the knights. "No one stands during the Queen's speech."

Theadosia exchanged a worried glance with Kaison. "We don't have time for this."

The cheering began to die down while the queen continued. "I am pleased to announce that the citizens of Ulodae had the highest abundance of crop!"

A cheer went up from one of the tables, revealing where the people from Ulodae were sitting. The rest of the room applauded out of obligation.

The queen spoke, "This night is not over. Now we will all head to the moor where we raise our candles to the sky and present our wishes for the next harvest. There will be a fantastic display of fireworks!"

Another round of thunderous applause roared. Almost instantaneously, the crowd rose from their seats and began heading toward the doors. The sound of screeching benches echoed all around.

Kaison rose to his feet beside Theadosia. She was holding a mug of peach punch in her hands, swirling the liquid around. Her face crinkled as she tried to wash the taste off her tongue.

"Stop drinking that," Kaison said.

Theadosia shot him a glare, but she didn't protest. "Kaison and Pandora will find Cheyenne. Louie and I will look for Maeve," Theadosia instructed.

Pandora nodded, letting out a nervous sigh.

"One problem," Louie said. "We don't have a plan for after we find them."

The group was silent. They all looked to each other in turn, hoping one of them would come up with a plan or at least a rendezvous point.

Before they could come up with a solution, Julian approached the group. He was fitted in polished armor as opposed to the rest of the people at the banquet. The armor was almost as shiny as his turquoise eyes and unbearingly dashing smile.

"Hello Pandora, Louie, Theadosia," Julian said while acknowledging the three in turn. He purposefully passed over Kaison, his nose up in the air.

"Where have you been?" Pandora asked.

"On guard," he replied. Julian reached out and fixed one of the ribbons in Pandora's hair, making sure it was perfect. "I'm changing positions to the eastern gates, so unfortunately I can't join you at the romantic display."

A strange jealousy gnawed away at Kaison's stomach while he watched Julian place his hand on Pandora's lower back.

Pandora brushed her brown curls over her shoulder. She smiled before she completely changed the subject. "Where's your sister?" she asked.

Julian froze for a moment before shifting his stance. "I have no idea," he replied. "Do you know what happened to her lip?"

Pandora's brow furrowed. "No."

"She wouldn't tell me either, but whoever did it needs to be taught a lesson." Julian shifted his jaw, his anger palpable. "No one touches my sister."

"I'm sure it was an accident."

Kaison kept his mouth shut, now knowing that he had been the one to strike Cheyenne. He remembered the morning in the infirmary when Cheyenne had helped him tend his wounds. The cut on her lip had never been from Julian. How had he been so blind?

Then Julian addressed Louie. "Dux Nikodemus wants you to suit up and take over Alexander's post at the west bridge."

"I'll head over now," Louie said. Louie shrugged at the group apologetically, but it was half-hearted. He trotted away to report to the head knight, disappearing in the crowd.

Pandora gently pushed Julian away. "I don't want to miss the display, and you should go to your post."

"Don't miss me, sweetheart," Julian's smooth baritone voice whispered to Pandora. He flashed her a wink before heading off in the direction of the eastern gates. As he was leaving the group, he made sure to scowl at Kaison.

It took all of Kaison's energy not to react in anger.

"We need to hurry," Theadosia said. "I'm getting a bad feeling. I'll go check if Maeve returned to Elistalia."

Pandora offered a new plan, "I'll go out to the infirmary and see if Cheyenne is there. Kaison you take the castle grounds and the lantern display on the moor?"

The task seemed daunting.

Kaison nodded. "Whatever happens, protect yourselves first."

Theadosia and Pandora nodded before the trio split up, disappearing in their separate directions.

Kaison took one last look at the lingering crowd in the banquet hall. Almost everyone was heading out to the moor, and only servants were left behind to clean up after the guests. Kaison decided to follow the crowd that was still emptying outside. Kaison fell in line with the others, following them out of the banquet hall and onto the moor. The crowd continued all the way underneath the tent until they were in a large open space. The mass of people continued into the southern gardens. It was similarly decorated with pink flowers and fountains.

While the guests began to receive their lanterns, Kaison pulled off to the side. The fountains in the garden glowed with multicolored lanterns, which hung across the garden in neat rows. The pink flowers were in pristine condition in their perfect, symmetrical plots. A marble bench in the gardens created a perfect outlook, so Kaison made his way to the bench and stepped up onto it. He looked out across the people heading underneath the entranceway onto the moorland. It was dark, but the moonlight cast enough light to see distinct figures in the crowd. He figured it would be easier to spot Maeve than Cheyenne.

He stood up on the bench for a long time, and with each passing moment, he grew more discouraged. The last of the crowd exited the castle and was now gathering on the moor a far distance away. Everyone was lighting lanterns to release in the sky before the fireworks display.

Kaison grew more concerned. Neither of the girls were anywhere to be seen, and Sir Emmett could come for him at any moment. He was beginning to doubt his ability to save Maeve – or protect anyone for that matter. He took one last look around the gardens and then decided to head back inside the castle. Maybe the girls had veered off from the crowd.

Kaison hopped down from the bench and was startled by someone blocking his path.

Simon looked vacantly back at Kaison. His lanky structure was silhouetted slightly by the moonlight, and he held a lantern in either hand.

"Hello," Kaison stammered.

A moment of silence passed between them, and an awkward sensation filled the air.

"You're not going to watch the display?" Kaison asked, motioning toward the crowd in the far distance.

"Where's your sister?" Simon asked.

Kaison found it impossible to discern the reason for the question because Simon's tone was so enigmatic. "She's back at Elistalia."

"Oh," Simon said. He looked down at the lanterns in his hands before looking back at Kaison. "I got her..." He hesitated before choosing different words. "I had an extra lantern."

"Aren't you a little late? Everyone's on the moor."

Simon didn't have time to say anything, for Maeve bounded up from behind him, her red hair bouncing crazily around her face. She skidded to a halt at Simon's side, grabbing onto his arm. She still held the blue journal tightly in her other palm. The size comparison between Simon's height and hers was drastic.

Kaison's heart skipped a beat upon seeing Maeve.

"Simon," she panted. "I need your help."

Simon gave his full attention to Maeve. "You need my help? After –"

"I know, I'm sorry!" Maeve cut him off. She seemed to disregard Kaison's presence entirely. "Please, I'll make it up to you. I'll fix everything I did to you, but right now I need a horse!"

At that moment, the lanterns began rising in the sky above the moor. They were all brightly colored, and dotted the night with bright speckles. The rose in a line, like a pathway leading up to the moon.

Simon pulled his arm from Maeve's grasp. "I can't help you." He looked to the lanterns in the sky longingly before he set the two he was holding down on the ground.

Maeve took a step closer. "You work in the stables!"

"That doesn't mean anything," Simon replied.

"Please," Maeve pleaded.

"I'm not helping you," Simon said. "Remember what happened the last time we tried to help each other?"

Maeve's face melted in despair as she stared up at Simon.

"I have a horse," Kaison broke into the conversation.

Both Maeve and Simon turned to look at Kaison. Maeve's blue eyes were wide with fear. She clung to the journal in her hands.

"Can I have it?"

Kaison ran his hand through his hair. Luckily for him, Maeve seemed to forget their previous conversation. The memory of her stinging slap still crept in the back of his mind.

"By Sun!" Maeve exclaimed desperately. "I'm sorry to you too, can someone please help me?" Her voice shook, which sent an unnerving chill down Kaison's spine.

Then something caught Kaison's attention. A girl with jet black hair and olive skin was dashing underneath the opened castle gates as if a demon was on her trail. Immediately Kaison recognized her as Cheyenne.

"Kaison," Maeve tried to get his attention.

Kaison's breath caught in his throat as he watched Cheyenne skid to a halt and stare wide-eyed at Maeve. The two girls were only paces from each other. Maeve's bright red hair was impossible to miss even in the dark.

Suddenly a loud explosion lit the night sky. Kaison, Simon, and Maeve dropped to the ground, covering their faces. Simon was the first to stand, clutching the handle of his sword at his belt and spinning to look in all directions. Out on the moor, a fire was rising. Smoke billowed from the mass into the night sky, but it wasn't an ordinary explosion. As the smoke rose, it turned a glowing hue of purple and seemed to draw the floating lanterns toward it.

“Out of the way!” A call rose from a nearby knight. The knights guarding the front doors of the castle left their post, dashing out toward the moor.

Kaison rose to his feet and took a few steps forward in awe, Simon directly beside him. The lanterns began to congeal into words, slowly but surely. It was as if an invisible magic was moving them. Kaison could hear screams coming from the moor, but he was too frozen in shock to be able to move. Before long, the sentence forming from the glowing lanterns and smoke became apparent:

I'm done waiting.

“He's here!” Maeve let out, her voice shrill.

“Who's here?” Kaison turned around to Maeve, but she was already sprinting off toward the main castle entrance.

Kaison looked around for Cheyenne, but it was as if she had vanished.

“Maeve!” Kaison called.

Simon grabbed Kaison's arm, stopping him from running after her. “What's that?” he was pointing toward the east side of the castle.

Kaison stared off in the direction Simon had gestured, but didn't see anything. His heart beat furiously in his chest. He had both Maeve and Cheyenne, and now they were both gone.

“Look!” Simon urged.

Flustered, Kaison squinted, hoping to see whatever it was that Simon was insistent on. The dancing fire from the southern moor was radiant, allowing them to see further away from the castle.

Sure enough, Kaison locked on to what Simon was referring to. Outside the eastern castle gates was a lone figure, sprinting toward the castle at high speed. It was a person, and they were approaching fast.

“Come on,” Simon said before taking off in the direction of the approaching figure.

"But the fire!" Kaison objected, turning back to look at the billowing smoke.

"Everyone is going to the fire," Simon replied. "We could be under attack!"

Kaison opened his mouth to speak, but Simon had already taken off in the direction of the figure running on the horizon.

Kaison was torn. He snapped back to view the castle entrance where Maeve had disappeared. Then he looked to the glowing fire on the horizon. The distant screams wailed in the night.

In a split-second decision, Kaison tore off after Simon. Kaison's heart pounded against his chest as he charged across the gardens. His boots thumped against the cobblestone, and he pushed himself to catch up with Simon. Simon's long legs propelled him forward at a fast speed. Kaison dodged around a fountain and through the hedges in the gardens, making sure he didn't lose sight of Simon. His legs were starting to tire, but he surged forward regardless. On the mountainside beyond the castle walls, the figure had disappeared, which meant that whoever it was had arrived at the castle gates already.

Kaison burst out of the gardens and reached the east gate, stumbling over his own feet as he attempted to slow himself.

Simon was already cranking the pulley system, raising the iron bars.

"What are you doing?" Kaison asked. "You don't know who it is!"

Simon either ignored Kaison completely or didn't hear him.

Kaison stood a few feet behind Simon. He watched the figure quickly clear the distance between them and the castle wall.

As the person approached, their long hair became apparent. They didn't resemble that a soldier.

It was a girl.

Simon locked the gate in its upright position and took a few steps back, waiting for the girl to reach the gates.

The girl breached the walls, running straight underneath the opened iron gate, and collapsed to the ground in front of Simon. She skinned her knees and palms on the stone, barely catching herself. Her chest heaved up and down, and she gasped for air, as though she had sprinted the entire way down the mountain and across the moor.

Simon dropped to the ground beside her.

"What's your name?" he asked, careful not to reach out and touch her.

The girl fell onto her side, her face now against the cobblestone and her eyes glossy. She muttered something, but it was inaudible.

Kaison relaxed his stance and approached cautiously, wanting to hear what she had said.

"I need..." She was struggling to form the words in between thick gasps for air. She clutched her chest with her hands.

"You're safe here," Simon stated dryly, but his monotonous voice wasn't the most welcoming.

The girl was lying on her side, her cape sprawled around her. She wore trousers tucked into boots and a leather-bound corset. Her skin was pale, almost ghostly white, and she had jet black hair. Her bottomless eyes gaped blankly into the sky, and she struggled to breathe.

"What is your name?" Simon asked again.

"Seraphina." She managed to form the words. Her breathing seemed to be steadying. She reached out for Simon and grabbed him by the collar of his shirt, but he didn't flinch. "I have a message for someone. I must find them."

Kaison knelt down on the other side of her.

"What is the message?" Simon asked.

"No," she said. Her chest heaved as she coughed violently, and her stamina was slowly draining. "It is for one person only."

Simon exchanged a glance with Kaison before returning to the stranger. "Who is your message for?" Seraphina's eyes drooped, and her hand wilted down to her side. Before she lost consciousness, she said:

"My message is for Sir Landon."

- 31 -

Kaison

Sir Landon?" Kaison asked. He reached out and shook the girl by the shoulders, but her eyes were closed, and her breathing had ceased. Kaison continued pleading, "How do you know Sir Landon?"

"We have to get her to a nurse," Simon said adamantly. He scooped her up into his grasp, struggling to his feet.

Kaison jumped upright. Everything inside him was telling him that it was a bad idea to bring this mysterious girl into the castle, but so far, she was the only one who might have answers. If she died, there was no way he was going to learn anything about Sir Landon and why his own father knew the brother of the Shadow of Eclipse.

"Drop the gate," Simon ordered, holding Seraphina tightly in his arms.

Without objecting, Kaison approached the gate. He wasn't altogether sure how to lower it. He hastily released the lever, and the iron gate flew to the ground in one giant motion, taking Kaison by surprise. Quickly, he readjusted the lever. When he had finished, he noticed Simon was already paces ahead, close to the eastern castle entrance, holding Seraphina in his grasp.

Kaison sprinted to catch up to Simon, and they both reached the eastern doors. The doors were guarded by Julian and another knight.

"Open the doors. We need to get her to a nurse," Simon was saying.

"Who is she?" Julian asked.

"Curses, Kaison, open the door for me," Simon demanded, lifting Seraphina up higher in his arms. He struggled to hold her.

Kaison knew every moment counted to save this girl and find out what she knew about Sir Landon. He started for the door handle when Julian stepped in front of him, puffing out his large chest to keep Kaison from passing by.

"What happened to her?" Julian asked, more strength behind his question.

"Julian, move," Kaison spoke, shoving the boy out of his way. "She got hurt in the explosion!" He lied.

Julian's face flushed with anger, and he stumbled back from Kaison's abrasive push. "By plague!" he let out.

Kaison forced the handle and used his shoulder to open the heavy doors. He held it open wide enough for Simon to pass through while holding Seraphina.

"Blazing Sun," Julian continued to curse. "Chadwick, stay here," he ordered before storming inside, hot on Simon's heels. He shoved by Kaison, following Simon. "I know that girl wasn't at the banquet!" he yelled angrily.

Kaison let the door close before bounding up the staircase after Julian and Simon. The castle was empty with everyone on the front moor for the display. Almost all the knights had left their posts to attend to the fire, and the shrieks from outside could still be heard.

"Do you know her name? Where did she come from? What does she want?" Julian was asking. "Do you know how much trouble you're going to be in for letting a stranger pass under our gates without consulting Dux Nikodemus?"

"Her name's Seraphina," Simon answered gruffly, "and she has a message for Sir Landon. We can't get more information if she's unresponsive."

"Who in the name of Solaris is Sir Landon?" Julian asked.

Suddenly a scream pierced Kaison's ears. This time, the scream was coming from inside the castle. All three boys halted in their tracks.

"What now?" Julian asked, grabbing the handle of his sword out of instinct.

An eerie silence followed, and they waited for another sign so that they could gauge where the scream had come from. The corridors were still, and in the faint distance, muffled shouts came from the moor outside. The only other sounds were flickering torchlight and the rustle of cool air flowing through the stone hallways.

Kaison's stomach dropped in fear. The whole conversation between Sir Emmett and Cheyenne was replaying in his mind. Cheyenne was determined to kill Maeve tonight, and Kaison had lost them both on the moor. They could be anywhere.

There was a murder happening in the castle.

Another scream rang through the corridor, this time making it clear that it was coming from the hallway adjacent to them.

"Get Seraphina to the nurse!" Kaison ordered Simon before bounding off down the hallway in the direction of the scream.

Julian debated whether or not to follow Simon or Kaison, before throwing his hands up in the air. He took off after Kaison, his pace fast.

Both Kaison and Julian tore around the corner and came to a single door. It was a large, wooden door with a single, silver doorknob. There were no other signals on the outside to demonstrate what the door led to. Kaison didn't have any time to waste, so he billowed against the door and threw himself into the next room.

He skidded to a halt inside what appeared to be the servant's quarters. It was a spacious, low-quality dining room with a tall fireplace at the center.

Maeve was pressed up against the wall in the corner of the room, gasping for breath. Her red hair was sprawled in all directions on her head, and her dress was torn.

"Maeve!" Kaison called, running over to her. He dropped to the ground in front of her when he noticed the blood. She was clutching onto her shoulder as a thick crimson liquid oozed down her body.

Julian ran over to Maeve and hovered over them both. "What happened?"

"Look out!" Maeve screeched.

Both Kaison and Julian turned around at the same moment. Julian's reflexes were fast, and he dodged an oncoming attack from a glistening silver dagger. Julian grabbed his attacker's wrist and used the other to grab onto the attacker's throat.

"Cheyenne?" His face flushed in shock.

Julian relinquished the tight grasp on his sister, and she stumbled backward, coughing. Cheyenne's hair was plastered to her face, and sweat trickled down her temples. She repositioned the dagger in her hand and held it out toward Julian as she slowly backed away. The tip of the dagger dripped with fresh blood. The cut on her lip was swollen, and her cheek was red as if Maeve had put up a good fight.

The hand that wasn't fastened on the handle of the dagger was holding steadfast to something Kaison immediately recognized.

The diamond journal.

"Julian, what are you doing here?" Cheyenne asked, her voice shaking.

Kaison remained kneeling on the ground beside Maeve. His eyes flicked back and forth between the two twins.

"Drop the dagger," Julian ordered. He took a step closer, but Cheyenne countered a few steps farther away.

"Stay back!" she screamed. Her eyes were pearly with the onset of tears. "You can't stop me."

Julian was slowly inching toward her. "Lower the knife, and talk to me."

"He said he would kill us both," Cheyenne said. As she backed away, she rounded around one of the dining tables, creating distance between her and her brother.

Julian's fists clenched. "Who said that?"

"I don't want you to be involved."

"If someone is threatening you, I will kill them." Julian's voice was steady.

"I can take care of–"

Cheyenne's voice was cut short. The window shattered, and the noise reverberated throughout the small room. The glass crashed to the ground, and the curtains billowed in the harsh wind. The small torch was extinguished, leaving them all in the dim moonlight.

A dark smoke rushed through the window frame.

The sight of it made Kaison's blood turn to ice. He knew what it was. *Who* it was.

The fog swirled into a silhouette of a man before solidifying into a figure. Mortimer emerged from the darkness, the remaining smoke pooling at his feet and continuing to move as if it were alive. His pale skin contrasted sharply with his dark features. The sledgehammer at his back was nearly his size, and Kaison recognized it as the murder weapon that killed his parents.

Kaison was on his feet, but the Shadow of Eclipse was going for Cheyenne.

"I'll take that," Mortimer extended his hand, telekinetically grabbing the diamond journal from Cheyenne's grasp. The journal whizzed out of her hands and directly into Mortimer's palm.

Julian already had his sword withdrawn.

Then Mortimer's gaze shifted to the rest of the room, looking once at Maeve, before meeting Kaison's stare.

Kaison's body stiffened.

Mortimer tilted his head, and his jaw shifted. "You…," he said. It was clear that Mortimer remembered Kaison from Grovia.

There was an odd pull toward the Shadow of Eclipse coming from Kaison's chest.

Before either of them could say anything, Cheyenne screamed. "That's mine!" Cheyenne raced forward, dagger in the air, ready to stab the intruder.

"Cheyenne!"

Before Kaison could stop her, she attacked.

Hardly moving, Mortimer grabbed Cheyenne's wrist, stopping her before the blade reached him. He tightened his grip, his eyes narrowing slightly, before twisting her wrist and shoving her arm back toward her. The dagger drove straight through Cheyenne's chest, and she choked. Mortimer released his iron grip and Cheyenne fell, catching herself on the ground.

"Cheyenne!" Julian cried. He started forward, sword gripped tightly, as Mortimer's attention snapped back toward the two boys.

Kaison knew Julian would receive the same fate.

Without thinking, Kaison grabbed Julian's arm and pulled him back with all his might.

Mortimer extended his palm toward the two of them, but Kaison stepped directly in front of Mortimer, protecting both Maeve and Julian. He had no weapons, but only the glimmer of faith that the Crimson Teardrop would protect him.

A purple hue flashed at Mortimer's fingertips and shot toward Kaison. The magic flew across the room, and a glowing red light blinded them all. Kaison was forced to shut his eyes, bringing his forearms up to block his face. A tingling sensation flooded through Kaison's body from head to toe. A thunderous noise blasted through the room.

Mortimer stumbled backward, staring at his palm.

Kaison pulled his arms down from his face, staring back at the Shadow of Eclipse. That's when he noticed the pulsing red glow coming from the pendant around his neck. He was invincible to the Shadow of Eclipse's magic.

Mortimer's face hardened. Without trying to attack again, he raised his hand, summoning the black smoke to wrap around his body. The dark fog consumed him, and the twinkling blue book disappeared with him. Mortimer became one with the smoke, and he flew out the open window, disappearing into the night.

The glow from the pendant around Kaison's neck ceased.

"Cheyenne!" Julian shouted.

He raced forward, easily sliding over the top of the dining tables and reaching his sister's side. He scooped her up from the ground. The dagger was lodged right in the center of her chest.

She choked twice, blood filling her lungs. Another tear ran down the side of her face and into her hair. She suddenly stopped moving, her fear transforming into a blank expression of nothingness. Cheyenne fell limp, her head falling backward, and her arms falling to her side.

Julian shook her gently, panting in horror. "No..."

Maeve coughed from the corner of the room, pulling Kaison to his senses. "Kaison..."

At the sound of his name, Kaison returned his attention to Maeve. "You're going to be alright," he whispered, dropping to her side.

The blood had dripped down her forearm and coated her entire hand scarlet. Her face was slowly becoming paler as the blood drained from her. The gash was huge, like nothing Kaison had ever seen before.

Kaison quickly pulled his thin shirt off and rolled it into a ball before pressing it against Maeve's shoulder. She winced, attempting to scoot away, but didn't have the energy.

"We have to get you to a nurse," he said, attempting to pull her into his arms.

"My journal..." Maeve's voice was barely audible.

"Don't worry about that."

Maeve used the last of her strength to push away from him. "You don't understand." She dropped her voice to a whisper so that only Kaison could hear. "Whatever you write in that book..." she choked, her face wrinkling in pain.

Kaison helped her stay in an upright position. "What is it?" he leaned in closer.

Maeve struggled to speak. "Whatever you write...comes true."

Kaison's eyes widened, but Maeve couldn't continue. She fell unconscious, the pain becoming too much for her body.

Kaison hoisted Maeve up in his arms and scrambled to a standing position. He halted in his tracks when he saw Julian on the ground, holding his sister.

Julian was drenched in blood. He slowly used his fingers to close Cheyenne's eyelids before looking up at Kaison on the other side of the room. His eyes weren't watery with tears. His expression was indiscernible.

He only said two words: "She's dead."

- 32 -

Kaison

Kaison scooped up Maeve in his arms, holding her close to his chest as he raced through the castle corridors toward the infirmary. A trail of blood splattered the floor behind him. Maeve's head cocked back, and her eyes rolled into her head. The gaping wound at her shoulder ran deep and across her chest. Cheyenne had barely missed Maeve's neck.

The infirmary doors came into view at the end of the hallway. Kaison picked up speed, running as fast as he could under Maeve's weight. He had never wanted this to happen. They should have gotten help when there was still time, rather than thinking that they could protect the others. Kaison would never rise to the role of a protector. He had no idea what his father had entrusted him with, but it shouldn't have been this.

Kaison reached the end of the hallway and stood before the doors. With a forceful kick, he thrust them open.

"Help, I need a doctor here!" he shouted. He entered the infirmary and hoisted Maeve higher in his grasp.

To his dismay, it was entirely empty. Rows of empty cots lined one side of the room, while the other side of the room was covered by a white curtain.

"Please, is anyone here?" Kaison shouted again. They couldn't all be on the moor. They should have brought many patients in here by now. His heart fluttered even faster.

The white curtain flew open, revealing Madame Lucia, the woman from Elistalia. Her face sank when she saw Maeve in Kaison's arms.

"In the name of Solaris!" she exclaimed. "Set her down over here," Lucia instructed, pulling the curtain open wider.

Kaison obeyed, stepping behind the curtain. It revealed another area filled with more cots, shelves, vials, and baskets of herbs.

Simon was also behind the curtain in the infirmary, hovering over a cot where Seraphina lay unconscious. He straightened. "Maeve!"

Kaison set Maeve down on the nearest cot as gently as he could, his arms aching. His bare chest was now coated in dark blood. The crimson pendant hung exposed on his chest, matching the rest of his stained skin.

Madame Lucia grabbed a basket from the shelf. "Tell me what happened," Lucia said, wiping away the blood from Maeve's wound.

"Cheyenne attacked her. Then the Shadow of Eclipse killed Cheyenne."

Lucia froze. "By plague."

Kaison went to the shelves with the herbs as well. He frantically grabbed the baskets and pushed away the vials so he could get a good look at the herbs in the back of the cabinet. The glass vials clattered together, and one tipped over, rolling off the edge of the shelf and scattering its contents onto the floor. The glass and herbs were now mixed together in one pile.

"Great Sun!" Kaison cursed. He ignored the bottle on the floor and continued searching. His shaking hands picked up two bottles. "Do you have Yasmile?"

"No." Lucia pointed to a box on the counter. "Bring me that," she ordered.

Kaison did as she instructed. He grabbed the box, hearing objects clank around inside, before handing it to Lucia. Lucia went to work right away, attempting to heal the wound.

Kaison saw a nearby pile of rags and took one for himself. He started wiping away the blood smeared on his bare chest. His clean chest made the ruby pendant around his neck even more visible, along with the scarred burn mark from the Grovia attack. He pressed the rag to his chest, and his burn wound stung like fire.

His thoughts raced. Without Yasmile, he knew Maeve wouldn't survive. After throwing the rag in a waste bin, he went back to the medicine cabinet. "What about Talamine?"

Lucia snapped her head around. "This isn't Vorinder," she said. She gave him a look that made Kaison fall quiet.

"Maeve needs to rest," Lucia said, tearing off a bandage. She went over to the opposite counter and began to gather more herbs. "Her wounds are very serious. I can only do the best I can."

"What does that mean?" Kaison asked.

Lucia didn't respond.

"Help her too." Simon gestured to Seraphina.

Lucia's expression faded. "She's gone."

"Please try," Simon objected.

"I'm sorry, there's nothing more I can do for her," Lucia said.

"Wait." Kaison took a step forward. "She can't be dead!" The only point of bringing Seraphina into the castle was to discover her hidden message for Sir Landon. If she was dead, Kaison might never understand Sir Landon's ties to his father.

Lucia turned to Kaison. "Watch over your friend carefully." She pointed to Maeve, but her eyes were hopeless.

Kaison couldn't have another person die on his hands. He rushed back to the cabinet and rummaged through its contents one more time, but to no avail. His only thought was maybe Louie had brought Vorinder medicines from home. He was about to dart out of the room to go find his roommate, when he heard loud sounds coming from the other side of the curtain.

"Bring them in here!"

Kaison turned to the sound of the voice. Dux Nikodemus entered the room, and another man was hanging onto the head knight so that he could walk. The person had blood dripping from his shin and limped with the help of Nikodemus. Nikodemus set the man down on the nearest cot while more people began to file in. Both men and women came inside the infirmary, some being carried, others limping or on stretchers. The crowd flooded the room until there were more people that cots. The crowd's chatter grew in sound until the infirmary rang with indistinct noise.

Kaison searched for Theadosia, but she was nowhere to be seen. He could only hope that meant she was safe, along with Pandora and Louie. He should have never left them. Stopping this murder was never his fight to fight – and he might not even have stopped it. Cheyenne was dead, and Maeve had grave injuries.

Then Nikodemus came up to both Kaison and Lucia. His armor and face were splattered with blood.

"Are you all right?" Lucia stepped closer and reached up to Nikodemus's face, wiping away some of the blood with a rag.

"I'm fine," Nikodemus replied, taking her hand, "but we're going to need all the extra help we can get. The moor is still on fire, and the lanterns are exploding out over the sky. The knights are mostly uninjured, but I can't say the same for the villagers."

"Is it the Shadows?" asked Kaison.

"No, the work of the Eclipse alone." Nikodemus clutched Lucia's hand tighter. He was completely focused on her. "I have to go back out there."

"We need your help here too," Kaison stated. "Maeve was attacked by the Shadow of Eclipse." Kaison took a step back and pulled away the curtain, revealing Seraphina and Maeve lying on the cots beyond.

Nikodemus's brow rose. "Is she alive?" he asked firmly. Nikodemus stepped inside and Kaison followed, letting the curtain flap to conceal them once again.

"I'm treating Maeve now," said Madame Lucia. She returned to Maeve's side. "However, I'm not optimistic."

"Great Sun," Nikodemus breathed. "How did this happen?"

"The Shadow of Eclipse was here," Kaison said, "but I think Cheyenne was the one who stabbed Maeve… before Cheyenne was killed."

Nikodemus paused. He pointed to the pendant hanging at Kaison's neck. "Where did you get that?"

Before Kaison could answer, a loud voice rang out from the other side of the curtain. "Nikodemus!" The voice was that of Sir Emmett. Emmett was busy carrying someone inside the doorway who he let fall on the nearest cot. Emmett didn't have a scratch on his body. His silver pony-tail was perfectly gelled back, and his bloodless sword scraped on the floor.

"Coming!" Nikodemus called.

Sir Emmett's face flashed through the curtains. He pulled them fully away and stood blocking the exit. His bottomless eyes were dead set on Maeve.

Kaison took a step away from Emmett, feeling the hairs on the back of his neck rise. He knew the pendant was exposed now, and there would be no more hiding from the knight. At least he had hidden the halberd back in the artifact room, and in the hospital, there would be witnesses if Emmett tried to attack him again.

Nikodemus then noticed Seraphina. "Who is this?"

"She came from beyond the moor. We need to help her," Simon said.

"She's dead," Lucia stated.

Nikodemus tilted his head in curiosity. He put his fingers to Seraphina's neck and checked for a sign of life. Then he nodded. "She's gone. Who was she?"

Simon touched his fingers to Seraphina's neck himself to validate what Nikodemus had said. "She was alive!"

Nikodemus didn't seem fazed by the tone of Simon's voice.

Sir Emmett had now fully entered the room, moving closer to Maeve. Kaison watched him attentively, and equally countered to position himself closer to Maeve on the other side of her bed. Kaison instinctively reached for his halberd at his belt, but only grasped empty air. He cursed under his breath.

"Who was she?" Nikodemus repeated, gesturing toward the stranger.

Kaison became present once again. "Her name was Seraphina, and she was here to find someone named Sir Landon." The words had escaped Kaison's lips before he had a chance to think.

Nikodemus's body stiffened, and it was as if a cold air froze the entire room. The noise from the distant crowd seemed to fade away.

"Repeat yourself, child," Emmett commanded. His voice was unnerving.

Kaison was about to speak, but the anger on Emmett's face stopped him. Emmett's hands were clenched into fists, and his jaw was cocked to one side. His eyebrows were low, casting shadows over his cheekbones. Then his eyes shifted to Kaison's chest, to the ruby pendant, glistening in the dim lighting. His piercing gaze was equally as terrifying through his scared and lifeless eye.

Kaison swallowed the lump in his throat. "I said..."

"Kaison, leave," Nikodemus cut him off immediately.

"But I –"

Emmett started forward. Kaison dodged out of the way, thinking Emmett was coming for him, but Emmett went straight for Seraphina's cot. Emmett shoved Nikodemus aside and dropped to his knees beside the cot. He reached out to touch Seraphina's hand, but stopped suddenly, his hand shaking.

"Simon and Kaison," Nikodemus ordered, "leave us, now."

Kaison didn't move. He didn't want to leave Maeve where Sir Emmett could finish what Cheyenne had started. Simon, on the other hand, shuffled on his feet, torn between obeying the head knight and staying beside the stranger he was so interested in.

Then Emmett stood up from the cot in one sharp motion. He pointed across the room at Lucia, who was cowering in the corner.

"Bring her back." Emmett demanded.

"I can't," Lucia cried.

Emmett started for Lucia, and Nikodemus jumped to action. Nikodemus grabbed Emmett by the shoulders and pushed him against the wall, forcing Simon to dodge out of the way.

"Don't take it out on Lucia. The girl is dead," Nikodemus said.

"What if it's *her*?" Emmett roared.

"We don't know that," Nikodemus answered.

"I have to know!" Emmett shouted. He shoved Nikodemus away before taking his fist across Nikodemus's face. Nikodemus stumbled to one side, but regained his footing easily.

"Boys, go!" Nikodemus shouted at Simon and Kaison. Then Nikodemus forced Emmett backward once again, slamming him into the cabinet and shattering the glass vials. Nikodemus pinned Emmett with his forearm to the knight's throat.

Before Kaison had a chance to intervene, Simon had grabbed him by the arm and dragged him out of the backroom.

"It's her!" Emmett's voice was heard again.

"By plague, what are you doing?" Kaison tried to wrench his arm out of Simon's grasp, but Simon didn't let up.

Simon didn't answer or let go of Kaison's arm until they maneuvered through the infirmary and out into the hallway. Once they were out in the corridor and far enough away from the chaos, Simon let Kaison go. Kaison rubbed his arm in pain, and a red mark emerged on his skin from Simon's tight grasp.

"Dux Nikodemus wanted us gone." Simon's voice was unrattled by the fight they witnessed.

"We can't leave Maeve with Sir Emmett. He's the one that wanted to kill her," Kaison argued.

Simon shuffled backward, taken aback by Kaison's statement. He looked back in the direction of the infirmary, as if thinking about going back in, but nothing about his body language revealed his emotions.

"Cheyenne is the one who attacked me and tried to get the halberd. I believe she was doing so on orders from Sir Emmett," Kaison explained.

"Sir Emmett sent Cheyenne to jump you and then kill Maeve?"

Kaison ran a hand through his hair. "Listen," he started, not wanting to get into all the details. "I need Seraphina," Kaison said, beginning to pace. His heart beat furiously in his chest. "She had a message for Sir Landon, and I know he's important and connected to my father."

"I know the message."

Kaison froze in his tracks. He turned back to Simon.

Simon took a piece of paper out of his pocket and extended his hand to Kaison. "It was in her coat," Simon said, "as if she knew she wouldn't be able to finish delivering it."

Kaison took the paper from Simon's palm into his own hands. He didn't realize how sweaty his palms were until he opened the small paper. Only three words were written in black ink.

I'm done waiting.

Kaison stared in dismay before returning his gaze to Simon. "This is what was written in the sky," he said.

Simon nodded. "I know."

- 33 -

Kaison

Did Seraphina write the message in the sky?" Kaison asked. "The lanterns moved with magic."

"She is connected to it somehow," Simon replied. "You said Sir Emmett was planning to kill Maeve?"

Kaison nodded.

"He must know about her journal."

Kaison raised an eyebrow in suspicion. "Do you know about her journal?"

Simon returned the gaze. "Do you?" His question was monotonous.

Kaison didn't say anything more.

When Simon saw that Kaison wasn't going to answer he said, "We can't leave Maeve alone with them. I need to make sure she's all right."

Kaison agreed. "I need to find my sister. I'll be there soon."

Simon went back inside the infirmary to make sure that Maeve would be safe. Meanwhile, Kaison walked at a brisk pace down the hallway. He had to find Theadosia. As he walked, Kaison crossed his arms, covering his bare chest. He had given up his shirt to stop Maeve's bleeding, and now he had nothing to cover himself.

Kaison rounded the corner and found a collection of knights standing around the servant's quarters. Many other servants were gathered in the foyer alongside them. The atmosphere seemed to settle in a bleak silence. Kaison knew the room.

A girl standing near the group turned to see Kaison, her bangs falling into her eyes. She was directly beside Louie.

"Kaison!" she exclaimed.

A wave of relief overcame Kaison upon seeing his sister. She came over to him quickly with the intent to give him a hug, but stopped short when she saw the scarlet tint on his skin.

Theadosia's eyes flicked down to the crimson necklace plastered against Kaison's chest. "You have to hide the pendant," Theadosia whispered harshly. She put up her hand to cover it, but realized that it was a poor plan. "You're such an idiot. Put it away."

Kaison pulled the pendant up over his head and pushed it down firmly into his pocket. Then he said, "It doesn't matter. Sir Emmett already knows that I have it."

"By plague," Theadosia let out. "You know he threatened me earlier about it!"

"Kaison, are you all right?" Louie interjected, seeing the tint of blood on his skin. "We were looking for you everywhere on the moor."

"I found Maeve. The Shadow of Eclipse stole her book and murdered Cheyenne."

A gasp escaped Theadosia's lips.

"Great Sun," Louie shook his head. "What was so special about

Maeve's book?" he asked. "I thought the Shadow of Eclipse was after your halberd. That's what your father made it sound like."

Kaison knew exactly why the Shadow of Eclipse wanted the book. Whatever was written in that book came true. Anyone – including the Shadow of Eclipse – would want that incredible power.

Theadosia looked even more concerned. "How did the Shadow of Eclipse even get inside the castle?"

"He transformed into smoke," Kaison said.

"You saw him?" Louie asked.

"Yes," Kaison replied. "He tried to attack us but couldn't because I was wearing the pendant." He hesitated, his body turning cold, before looking up at his sister and adding, "It was the man we watched kill father."

Theadosia turned away from her brother, pacing to the other side of the hallway.

"And now Emmett knows you have the pendant!" Louie threw his hands up in his air.

Kaison's head was spinning, and he didn't know if it was from the adrenaline or from his sickening emotions. "Yes, he knows. We're in more danger than ever. Theadosia, we should never have come here."

"Are you serious?" Her mouth dropped open. "We're not leaving now. We're seeing this through to the end. Father wanted us to use the halberd for something. We have to go back to the artifact room."

Suddenly, the sound of the door to the servant's quarters creaked at a high-pitch. Two knights began carrying a stretcher out through the opening. On the stretcher was a body covered in a thin white sheet.

"Make way!" one of the knights proclaimed, heading in the direction of the infirmary. Theadosia and Kaison parted, letting the knights carry the stretcher between them and down the corridor.

Kaison took a step forward, standing next to one of the knights in the doorway, and peered into the room. In the corner, Julian sat on one of the benches, hunched over and leaning on his knees. He seemed void of emotion, but still fixated on the pool of blood that marked where his sister had died.

Pandora sat on Julian's side. Her hands were folded in her lap, but her shoulder was touching Julian's. She was saying something, but she was too far away to make out the words.

The sky was grey. Icy raindrops fell from the clouds. The moor was soft and muddy, and a mist settled over the horizon. The weather matched the gloomy atmosphere of the people that had gathered on the moor.

It was the following afternoon. Around one hundred guests were attending a funeral that was being held to honor those who had perished during the explosions at the Harvest Banquet. A dozen people had died from their injuries. Cheyenne Xy'tier was among the dead.

The guests stood in a semicircle on the outskirts of a raised platform where the caskets were held. They were draped with the pink flags of Benedict's family. These flags had laurels on the four corners, rather than at the center. In the center, families had laid gifts, trinkets, and flowers on the respective caskets.

A priestess stood in the center of them all. Next to her, stood the queen. The queen wore a long, fur cloak in her signature color, while the rest of the participants wore black to pay tribute to the dead. Neither of these colors were the colors that you would wear to a celebration of life ceremony in Vorinder.

Nevertheless, Kaison and Theadosia both wore all black out of respect. The siblings stood next to each other on the outer circle.

Aside from Cheyenne, Kaison knew no one else who had lost their lives. In a surprising turn of events, Madame Lucia had informed Kaison that Maeve had pulled through. She suggested that he see her immediately, which came as a surprise.

Kaison was glad that no one else had died that night. Seeing the graves, however, reminded him of the people he lost in Grovia. His parents had never gotten a proper burial and celebration of life ceremony. They had been lost to the ash and swamp in the chaos.

A slight distance away, Julian stood with his gaze directed at the priestess. His hands were drawn behind his back, and his stance was wide. His olive skin sparkled in the rain, and his coat was flattened to his body. He didn't shed a tear. On either side of him were Pandora and Louie, both comforting their friend.

When the prayers were over, the Queen was the next to speak. Queen Benedict's message was loud and clear, and her pink dress stood out pretentiously compared to the rest of the black attire. "This devastating attack won't diminish our spirits," Benedict said. "The Shadow of Eclipse cannot and will not destroy the livelihoods of Sun Castle. We have still gathered here from far and wide to celebrate the Harvest. The winners from last night's Harvest Banquet will receive their prizes, and we will proceed as planned with the Royal Ball in their honor. The work of the Shadows cannot bring us down. I invite and expect all of you to join me this evening in the Royal Ballroom. Tonight we will come together with new-found convictions and courage. Sun Spire's beacon will forever be the shining light of hope in Solaris."

Kaison was used to attending dances and celebrations after funerals in Vorinder, but in this case, Benedict's plans seemed out of place. She only received momentary applause that fizzled out within seconds.

Then Kaison spotted a figure in the distance. At the other side of the graveyard, there was a person kneeling at the foot of a grave. It wasn't a polished tombstone, but a simple wooden cross. Sir Emmett was kneeling before the cross. His back was to Kaison, and his hands were planted on the muddied ground beneath him.

The priestess began to recite poems and chants over the bodies. More time passed by. It seemed as if no one knew the poems the priestess was reciting. Julian's face in particular scowled upon hearing certain prayers.

Kaison couldn't get Sir Emmett out of his mind. It wasn't like the second knight to miss an opportunity to stand by the queen and appear even more ominous. Who was he mourning, separate from the others?

Calmly, Kaison removed himself from the ceremony, backing away respectfully. He headed in the opposite direction of the semicircle and approached the effigy across the graveyard. The soft ground moved underneath his boots, and the rain sent a chilling cold down his spine.

The closer Kaison drew, the clearer the scene became. A name had been sketched into the cross.

Seraphina

"You're at the wrong funeral, child," Sir Emmett spoke, his voice rumbling. Somehow he knew Kaison was behind him without even turning around.

Kaison cleared his throat. "Who was she?" Kaison asked, hoping Emmett would disclose more. She had been his only link to Sir Landon and to the answers he needed.

Emmett was silent for a moment. He turned his head slightly, showing his profile.

"This is all your fault," he said under his breath.

"What?"

Emmett rose from the ground and turned to face him. His silver hair wasn't tied back today. It fell across his forehead, dripping with rain. His bottomless eyes starkly contrasted his pale skin. Both his trousers and his palms were caked in mud.

"You heard me, child."

"I'm not a child. Stop calling me that."

"Don't you get it?" Emmett asked. "You're the reason why she died." The knight took a step closer to Kaison.

"I had nothing to do with her death!"

"You and your halberd."

Kaison's eyes widened. "My halberd?"

Emmett lunged toward Kaison and grabbed his collar. Then he pulled Kaison to him until they were face to face. "I will kill you," Emmett threatened him, "as soon as I get what I need."

Kaison was still. "I'd like to see you try."

They were both frozen, their eyes locked on one another. Emmett tightened his fist stronger around Kaison's collar. Kaison felt Emmett's bony grasp begin to choke him, but he wasn't going to show pain.

A voice sounded behind them. It was Nikodemus. The entire funeral procession was moving into the center of the graveyard, preparing for the internment.

"Is there a problem?" Nikodemus asked.

"No," Emmett spoke through gritted teeth. He released Kaison with a shove before he turned on his heel and stormed off.

Kaison pulled down his coat, fixing the wrinkles at the front.

"Meet me in my office," Nikodemus said. "It's time we talked."

- 34 -

Osiris

Osiris saw Destrian in the distance. They were underneath the pier, right where the sand met the ocean. The waves crashed against the shore, rising to the rocks and posts that held up the wooden walkways above.

Destrian sensed her approach, turning to face her as she reached him. His pocket watch was out, the three hands spinning. He shut the watch with the close of his fist before returning it to his pocket.

"I have a new contract," Osiris said before Destrian could say a word.

Destrian blinked a few times, his lips thin. "Are you trying to take my job or do you not like working with me anymore?"

"Both, obviously."

Destrian's cheeks lifted. "Right."

Osiris pulled the satchel off her shoulder, handing Destrian the golden mirror to bring back to their client. "The head knight of Solaris found me."

The satchel slipped from Destrian's grasp, landing on the sand. His mouth was agape. "I-I don't think I heard you correctly, can you repeat that?"

"You heard correctly," Osiris said. She planted her hands on her hips, letting out a sigh. "I already accepted the deal, so you're either with me or you're not."

Destrian reached down and picked the satchel up from the ground. As he answered, he brushed off the grains of sand, "I'm nervous about what deal you made."

"We have to sneak into Captain Hondo's Palace."

The satchel slipped from Destrian's hand once more, shock freezing his body. "By heaven," he cursed under his breath. He snatched the bag off the ground before flinging it over his shoulder. "Why?"

"To retrieve some battle plans. He's offering a thousand silver suns to you, me, and Moriah. Each."

"Moriah? Why is she involved?"

"We're going to need a disguise, and she can have one made –"

"One thousand suns?" Destrian exclaimed, cutting Osiris off as if he had just heard the statement.

Osiris nodded.

Destrian started to mutter inaudible words under his breath. He began to pace up the shoreline, scratching the back of his neck. His shoulders were high, the anxiety exuding from his body language.

"With one thousand suns, you can purchase your passage out of Larkesh," Osiris said.

Destrian's head snapped up. His body froze. "We both can."

Osiris shook her head.

"Why are you holding on to a group of people when you can have your freedom?"

"It's not about the group," Osiris objected, "it's about every Vynx in Larkesh."

Destrian blinked.

"They're our people, Destrian. All of us are the same. I want you to be free, but I won't leave without them."

"And I won't leave without you," Destrian said.

They fell silent. The waves crashed, extending up the shoreline to Osiris's boots. The boats rocked against the pier above, and a distant bell tolled.

"I'm going to find a way to end the Tournament," Osiris said. "One day, our people won't be used for sport."

"It's not a sport," said Destrian. "They think we're cursed, and the Tournament is the only way they can kill us without having to do it themselves."

"I'm well aware." Osiris shifted her weight, her chin lifting. "It's still nothing more than a show."

Destrian hesitated, posing his next question carefully. "Do you think we're cursed?" Destrian's voice was meek.

"I think…" Osiris stopped short. She had never thought about it too much.

Their abilities weren't anything out of the ordinary. She had heard of magic – of the Shadow of Eclipse in Solaris – and what she possessed wasn't anything like that. Heightened senses and the ability to predict weapon trajectory was hardly magic. Destrian didn't have her agility, and her memorization wasn't nearly as refined as Destrian's, so Vynx abilities weren't the same across the board.

Osiris finally answered Destrian's question. "People are scared of the unknown."

"We're no different than they are."

"Not to them," said Osiris. "We're gifted. They can't wrap their small minds around that concept, so all they can do is exterminate it."

Destrian nodded, but his eyes were wandering, meaning his thoughts were running.

Osiris tried to bring him back to the task at hand. "With a thousand suns, we can persuade a soldier to help us break into the prisons. Once we release enough of us, we can fight back."

Destrian wrinkled his nose before running his hand along the back of his neck. "I don't know if you scare me or impress me."

"Some of my many wonderful qualities." Osiris flashed him a smile.

Destrian frowned. "You have a plan for breaking into the Palace?"

A warmth flooded through Osiris. He was going to help her. "No," she admitted.

Destrian straightened his posture, taking a step closer. "It's a good thing I always have a plan."

- 35 -

Kaison

Kaison waited in Nikodemus's office. The expansive room held a circular, marble roundtable in the center. The walls were plastered with white, wooden paneling, and the ceiling arched into a dome with the image of the moorland. On the central roundtable, there was a space for Nikodemus's personal items, and on the other end was a model map with metal figurines and pins. Tiny, model houses marked villages and other shapes marked armies, battalions, and the last places where the Shadow army had struck. Model ships sat on the blue parts of the table, near the islands of Vorinder.

Nikodemus didn't have any books in the room. Instead, the table had shelves underneath it, which held golden scrolls. A stone fireplace was lit on one side of the room, and four torches hung from the ceiling in each corner.

Kaison tried to simplify everything running through his head. He needed to understand why Sir Emmett had blamed Kaison for Seraphina's death. He blinked, trying to put the pieces together.

The door to the head knight's office opened, and Nikodemus entered in swift strides. His clothes were darkened from the rain, and mud splattered off his boots. Theadosia was next to him. She entered behind Nikodemus, just as confused as Kaison, her boots sloshing across the stone floor.

Nikodemus closed the door behind her before giving his full attention to the siblings. They all stood together near the table. "I asked Theadosia to join us. You both need to hear this."

Nikodemus scratched the back of his neck before letting out a sigh. "Please, sit." Nikodemus gestured to about twelve chairs around the table.

Theadosia obeyed, taking a seat, while Kaison chose a chair on the opposite side.

"I apologize for what happened with Sir Emmett," Nikodemus said.

"It wasn't your fault, but thank you," Kaison said. Then he got to the real question on his mind. "Seraphina came here to find Sir Landon…and my father told me I could trust both you and Sir Landon…I need to know. Who is Sir Landon?"

Nikodemus sighed, like he wasn't sure if he should reveal the information. "Sir Landon was a knight for King Arturo," Nikodemus started. His hands moved in big, elegant gestures as he explained the story. "Landon's brother, Mortimer, became the Shadow of Eclipse seventeen years ago. Landon didn't want to be associated with the darkness, so he faked his death, masked his face with a scar, and changed his name." Nikodemus continued walking forward. The clicking of his heeled boots filled the silence in the room.

"Where is he now?" Theadosia asked.

Nikodemus placed his hands on the table and leaned in closer. "Landon now goes by the name Sir Emmett."

A wave of fear flooded over Kaison. His mouth parted to speak, but nothing came out.

"The only people that know he changed his identity are Madame Lucia and me," Nikodemus said.

"But Sir Emmett..." Kaison's voice ran dry.

"Emmett is a good man. He has never agreed with the Shadow of Eclipse," Nikodemus continued.

Kaison disagreed. Sir Emmett was evil. He was plotting Maeve's death in order to get the book. He ordered an attack on Kaison and threatened Theadosia about the pendant. Was it all for his brother – the Shadow of Eclipse?

"That doesn't explain the connection with Seraphina," Theadosia stated, planting her elbows on the arms of the chair.

"Emmett's daughter was kidnapped by the Shadow of Eclipse on the day she was born," Nikodemus explained. "We can only assume that she lived with the Shadow of Eclipse for all this time. I believe Emmett is convinced that Seraphina was his long, lost child. Maybe she escaped from the Shadow of Eclipse."

Kaison ran his hands over his face and shook his head. "No, she didn't escape. Everything was planned. She had a specific message that was mirrored in the sky. That's not a coincidence."

"So what is your theory?"

Kaison began. "Emmett was behind the attack on Maeve's life. He was trying to get the book...but not for himself, for the Shadow of Eclipse. However, Mortimer was 'done waiting' and decided to come take it for himself."

Nikodemus froze. "Are Emmett and Mortimer – the Shadow of Eclipse – working together?"

"It's possible."

Nikodemus's body stiffened. "The Shadow of Eclipse didn't need

Seraphina as collateral anymore," Nikodemus said. "So he got rid of his bargaining chip: Emmett's daughter."

Kaison thought back to his father's letter. He had given him the halberd and led him to the pendant. Was the book the final object that his father had been searching for? Did his father know the Shadow of Eclipse? And why did his father have these objects in this first place?

Theadosia shifted, crossing her legs. "That doesn't explain why Emmett blames you for Seraphina's death," she said to Kaison.

Nikodemus said, "It's because you have the halberd."

"Emmett already tried to take the halberd," Theadosia said.

"Well," Nikodemus replied. "If he was trying to get the halberd for Mortimer, and failed to obtain it, which led to Mortimer taking matters into his own hands, that would explain why he would blame you."

"I was trying to defend myself!" Kaison objected.

Theadosia brushed past Kaison's statement. "Then why didn't Mortimer take the halberd? Why did he take the journal?" Theadosia continued to ask questions, scooting to the front of her chair.

"The halberd and the Ademantum – the journal – must be used together," Nikodemus explained. "So both are needed eventually."

"What do you mean, *used together*?" Kaison asked.

Nikodemus cleared his throat before pulling out a chair from the table and sitting down. "Maybe I should've been honest with you from the beginning – from the moment I saw the halberd. But I didn't know how you would react, or if I could trust you."

Kaison's brow furrowed. "Tell me what you know."

"Your father, Emmett, and I used to work together here at the castle," Nikodemus explained. "Your father was Arturo, the king of Solaris. That makes you Prince Sun."

- 36 -

Kaison

Kaison slumped back into his chair. His eyes stared aimlessly into space before him.

"That's impossible," Theadosia said.

"Not impossible. I helped your family escape to Vorinder."

"There are many people from Vorinder."

"That halberd belonged to King Arturo. Your father." Nikodemus assured them. "That halberd is what your father was chosen to protect. Now, he's passed that duty on to you, Kaison."

Kaison started to come back to reality. "Why does it have to be protected?"

"Because it is a key to something much greater."

Kaison placed his palms on the table and leaned forward. "To what?"

"The door."

Kaison ran his hands through his hair and let out a sigh. "That makes no sense."

"Your father dedicated his life to the door. But knowing that he – the designated protector – would be forced to abscond, he entrusted us to protect the door while he protected the halberd."

"Did you refer to the prophecy?" Theadosia asked. "*The designated protector is forced to abscond*?"

"Yes," Nikodemus said. "The prophecy is real. Both the journal and the halberd must be used together to unlock the door."

"Let's say the prophecy is real..." Kaison muttered, skeptical, "where is this door?"

"The door is hidden somewhere in the labyrinth beneath the castle," Nikodemus said. "It has been protected for centuries."

"Somewhere?" Kaison asked.

Theadosia added, "Do you not know where it is?"

"I haven't been down there since your father's reign," Nikodemus admitted. "It's a maze."

"What's behind this door?" Kaison persisted.

"I don't know."

Kaison was shocked. "You don't know?"

Nikodemus let out a sigh. "The door hasn't been opened."

"Then how do you know it's important?" Theadosia asked.

"This isn't about the door," Nikodemus said. "As King Arturo's son, your job is to protect the halberd with your life."

"I'm not King Arturo's son. I can't rule a kingdom!"

Nikodemus almost laughed. "Who said anything about ruling a kingdom?"

Kaison felt a lump in his throat. "You told me I was heir to Solaris."

"No, I told you that you are Prince Sun," Nikodemus stated. "Your family is only protecting the throne until the true queen arrives."

Kaison's heart pounded in his chest. This conversation only continued to confuse him.

"Now, I must make a plan to protect this kingdom for when Mortimer returns," Nikodemus stated, standing to his feet. He fixed his collar. "You must fulfill your duty and protect the halberd." Then he turned to Theadosia. "You must take care of your brother."

"I'll try," Theadosia muttered.

"Your father would be proud of you two," Nikodemus said. Then he turned to the door and proceeded to the exit.

Theadosia and Kaison stayed in silence while Nikodemus left. It wasn't until the door shut, leaving the siblings alone, did Kaison let out a deep breath.

"If father wanted us to protect the door," Theadosia started, "then we will. It doesn't matter who he was, king or not."

Kaison looked back at his sister before shaking his head. "I can't do it by myself."

Theadosia smiled. "That's why I'm here."

"I want confirmation that father was King Arturo," Kaison said.

"Well there has to be something in the artifact room," Theadosia suggested. "But we shouldn't go around telling people you're Prince Sun yet." Theadosia's nose wrinkled in disgust. "I don't like the sound of that."

"Maybe I'm not," Kaison replied. "Let's go back to the artifact room tonight and look."

"I wonder...," Theadosia muttered, "If the artifact room also leads to the underground labyrinth Nikodemus was referring to. If we found this door, would that be enough proof for you to believe in our father?"

Kaison nodded. "I need to see it for myself."

The siblings rose from the chairs and proceeded to the exit, following after Nikodemus. Once they had exited the head knights' office, they saw Louie and Pandora standing side by side in the corridor outside.

Louie leaned against the wall, his arms crossed casually, but Pandora straightened when seeing the siblings exit. Her ribbons were flattened to her soaked hair, and her dress molded to the shape of her figure.

"Kaison," Pandora exclaimed when she saw him. "I'm so sorry about what happened to you. I should have found you sooner."

Kaison felt the urge to comfort her. "It's all right," he said.

"What did Dux Nikodemus say?"

Kaison debated on an appropriate response, but Theadosia beat him to it. "Dux Nikodemus told us who Sir Landon is," Theadosia paused as she lowered her voice, "it's Sir Emmett."

"What?" Louie blurted out. Remembering the conversation they had at the banquet, he added, "That means Emmett's brother is Mortimer!"

Pandora's doe-like eyes grew larger. "Do you think they're working together?"

"So it would seem," Kaison muttered, "but Nikodemus doesn't seem like he's going to do anything about it. He thinks Emmett has changed or something."

"We have to go back to the artifact room tonight," Theadosia said. "We need to get the halberd, and we need to prove that Emmett is not on the side of Sun Castle. There must be something in that room that can work as evidence against him. Also, there might be information on the journal that the Shadow of Eclipse stole."

Kaison was impressed by the enthusiasm in her voice. Secretly, they had another mission of their own. They needed further confirmation that their father was truly King Arturo. And what about the mysterious door?

"We need to protect the halberd and pendant now that Sir Emmett knows about them both," Pandora was saying.

"The halberd is safe for now, but I don't think I should have the pendant," Kaison said. He withdrew the ruby necklace from his pocket and held it out toward Pandora. "We need to keep the objects separate for now. Mortimer already has the journal."

"Me?" Pandora asked.

"We all know that you have the magic to protect it from Sir Emmett," Kaison said, remembering her powerful shields. He reached out his hand, dangling it in front of Pandora.

"I…" Pandora searched for words to object, but she couldn't.

"Sir Emmett will still think Kaison has it," Theadosia said. "He won't think twice even if he sees a ruby necklace on you."

Pandora nodded. "Alright," she said before taking the pendant from Kaison's hand. She then put it over her neck, letting it rest on her chest.

"We should get ready for the ball," Louie said.

"We can sneak out to the artifact room during the ball," Theadosia suggested.

Everyone agreed. Kaison knew that the ball was the best opportunity for them all to go to the artifact room. The library would be deserted. However, Sir Emmett could have similar plans. They would have to be careful. Kaison needed to know exactly what danger they were getting themselves into. He needed to talk to Maeve about the magic behind the book and what it meant now that Mortimer had stolen it. So he said:

"I'll meet you upstairs. I have something I must do first."

- 37 -

EMMETT

Emmett strode through the castle corridors, anger fuming through his limbs. Fury tingled at his fingertips, and every muscle in his body felt tense. It had taken everything inside him to restrain himself from hitting the boy out in the graveyard. Was Kaison that naive? Or was he playing dumb?

The knight didn't pause for a moment outside the queen's study. The guards on either side bowed before going to open the door, but Emmett wasn't slowing down.

Emmett burst through the doors. He charged down the carpet, leaving behind a trail of muddy footprints, before reaching the desk.

Benedict slowly looked up from the parchment, a feather pen gently flapping between her fingers. "You look terrible," she said.

"Let me kill him."

Benedict let the pen fall from her hands. She clasped her palms together, interlacing her fingers before leaning back in her chair. "I see this has become personal."

"It's not personal."

Benedict inclined her head. "Is that so?"

"We need the halberd. Let me get it."

"How will you justify murdering him?"

"Poison."

Benedict froze. "Not until we have the Ademantum. We still might need the boy."

"Why won't you take any action?"

"I'm waiting for the right time."

"Coward."

Benedict tapped her nails on the desk. "I'm being smart."

Emmett scowled, throwing his hands in the air in anger. "You're not doing anything!"

Benedict slammed her palms down on the table before standing. "Pull yourself together!"

Her voice boomed throughout the room, asserting her authority. Immediately, Emmett slammed his heels together, standing up straighter, and clasped his hands behind his back.

"My apologies, Your Majesty. It won't happen again."

"It better not," she scolded. She paused, clearing her throat in a pompous manner before elegantly taking a seat once more. "I'm worried about Dux Nikodemus."

"How so?"

The queen let out an exasperated sigh. Her nose rose in the air. "You think I don't see every time he frowns when I mention the Ademantum? He's a devout follower of the true bloodline, and he will never accept me."

"He has served you for over a dozen years."

"Now that Kaison's here, I don't think he will anymore," Benedict said. "Kaison has more claim to the throne than I do."

Emmett shifted his weight, pausing for a moment to interpret what the queen was saying. "Again, I can get rid of Kaison."

Benedict picked up the feather pen, flipping it over in her hands. Then she put it back down. Thoughts swirled behind her eyes. She tapped her fingers on the desk, one by one in a hypnotizing rhythm. "Maybe it would be better to get rid of Nikodemus."

Emmett wasn't thrown off by the statement. After all, once the head knight was gone, Emmett would step up to take his place.

Benedict placed her elbows on the table, leaning forward. She raised her eyebrows, waiting for Emmett's response.

"I can take care of it."

A smirk appeared on the queen's face. "That will be all."

Emmett nodded, turning to go. That wasn't the only plan he needed to carry out.

"Emmett." The queen stopped him before he reached the door. "I hope your son is as naïve as you say he is."

Sir Emmett ground his teeth. Without looking over his shoulder, he responded, "He has no idea I'm his real father."

"Will he find out?"

"Doubtful," Emmett said. "He believes his real parents died in his hometown."

There was a moment of silence.

"Good," the queen said. "The last thing we need is for him to learn the truth."

Emmett started for the door once more. "My thoughts exactly."

- 38 -

Kaison

While his friends went to change for the Royal Ball, Kaison made his way back to the medical wing. He had learned some simple medical techniques back in Grovia, and he knew that Maeve was probably still suffering from her injuries. He needed to see if she was recovering, and if she wasn't, he needed to ask her everything she knew about the diamond journal.

Kaison reached the medical wing and entered the waiting area with couches and a large desk. Beyond him were curtains that led to rooms full of cots, potions, and other medicines for the patients. It looked different now, set up with more dividers due to the overflow of patients. People were scattered all around the area, running back and forth between the curtains to help the injured.

He made his way past the front desk, which was unmanned, and spotted the woman who had helped him last night. "Madame Lucia?"

"I don't have any time right now," Madame Lucia said politely.

Her arms were full with blankets and potions.

"Let me take that," offered Kaison.

She let out a grateful sigh, but didn't respond. She handed him half of the blankets she was carrying before setting off again through the infirmary.

Kaison followed Madame Lucia through the patients, handing out the blankets to everyone they passed. "How much longer does Maeve have?" Kaison asked.

"To my surprise, she's made a full recovery. You can go back and talk to her if you wish."

Kaison stopped in his tracks, which made Madame Lucia stop too. "Are you sure? She's going to make it?" he asked.

Madame Lucia spoke in a forced whisper. "Yes. Don't make a big deal about it. Talk to her, but don't ask any questions."

"What do you mean?"

"You're already in enough danger as it is," Madame Lucia said, "as am I now, since I've seen Maeve's recovery take place before my eyes."

Kaison didn't understand.

"Go to her," Madame Lucia said, "but, Great Sun, keep quiet." She leaned her head toward the back wing where he would be able to find Maeve.

Kaison backed away from Madame Lucia. He handed the two remaining blankets to people on his left and right before heading deeper into the infirmary. At the back was where the worst patients were being held. In this section, the foul stench of blood flooded Kaison's senses. When he reached the white curtain, he pulled it backwards and entered.

Maeve was still lying on the cot, this time with a thin blanket over her. She was asleep. The blood had been cleaned up, and her shoulder was completely healed. The skin was perfectly intact, hidden underneath her curly, red hair. Her freckled cheeks were rosy with a beaming energy.

To Kaison's surprise, Simon was sitting on a stool next to Maeve's cot. He was hunched over, leaning his elbows against his knees. His dry wardrobe indicated that he didn't attend the funeral outside. The other cot, where Seraphina once was, was stripped bare. The glass that had shattered during the fight between Nikodemus and Emmett had been cleaned, as if nothing had ever happened.

Simon heard Kaison enter and looked up, his dark eyes grim. But he didn't say anything.

Kaison greeted him with a nod. He entered the room, letting the curtains flap shut behind him. Kaison crossed to the opposite side of the cot. "How is she doing?"

"She'll be fine," Simon said.

Kaison ran a hand through his hair. Now that he had learned that Seraphina was Emmett's long-lost daughter, he had to make a decision whether or not to keep that information to himself. Simon had taken a great interest in Seraphina, and in Maeve as well.

Maeve stirred on the cot, alerting the two boys that she was waking up. She slowly shifted, and her eyes opened. A pair of brilliant blue eyes stared back at Kaison before shifting to Simon.

"Oh..." she started, regaining a sense of her surroundings. She hastily pulled the blanket up over her shoulder and scrambled to a sitting position. "I didn't expect to see either one of you here, let alone both of you." She winced dramatically and clasped her forehead in her palms.

"How are you feeling?" Kaison asked.

"I'm in pain, genius," Maeve snapped, but then she calmed herself with a deep breath. "I'll be fine. Why are you two here?"

“I had a question for you,” Kaison said.

Maeve didn’t look convinced. She turned to Simon. “And you?”

Simon blinked. “I didn’t think anyone would show up for you.”

Maeve wrinkled her nose and slowly nodded. “Thank you.” She said it as if it were a chore. She fiddled with her thumbs on her lap as she searched for the correct words. “I’m sorry.”

Simon shrugged with a shake of his head.

Kaison grew curious about their past but decided not to press them about it. He needed answers of his own.

“Simon, can I have a moment alone with Maeve?” Kaison asked.

Simon remained seated. “I already know all the information you’re looking for.”

“I don’t think you do.”

“You want answers about the journal, right?” Simon asked. “I’m familiar with it.”

Kaison was weary, not knowing if he could trust Simon. Quite frankly, he didn’t know if he could trust anyone.

“I told you about the journal,” Maeve said.

“Not everything,” Kaison replied. Kaison pulled up a nearby stool and took a seat at the edge of Maeve’s cot. “Last night, you asked us for a horse. Did you know Cheyenne was after you?”

“Cheyenne?” Maeve asked. “I had no idea she wanted the journal. I felt the Shadow of Eclipse’s presence, and I knew I had to run.”

“Felt his presence?” Kaison clarified.

Maeve continued, “When I went back inside the castle, Cheyenne came after me, chasing me with the dagger and screaming for my journal. We got into a fight, and then you and Julian appeared. Afterward, as we all know, the Shadow of Eclipse showed up.”

“If only I had gotten there earlier,” Kaison muttered under his breath.

"What made the Eclipse leave?" Simon asked.

"Kaison fought him."

Simon's lips thinned. "I had to save Kaison from Cheyenne," Simon said. "I don't believe he fought the Shadow of Eclipse."

"He didn't fight him," Maeve objected. "He has magic."

"It was nothing," Kaison blurted out, his face turning bright red. "I have something – an object – that can protect me from the Eclipse's magic."

Simon's eyes were dark. "That's convenient."

"Can I see?" Maeve asked.

"No," Kaison replied. "I don't have it anymore." It wasn't a lie.

Maeve's nose wrinkled, and she flipped her red curls out of her face.

"Nevermind that," Kaison said loudly, making sure the conversation returned to the diamond journal. "Where did you find the journal? Originally?"

"It found me," Maeve said, sitting up taller. "One night, it was on my bed – back in my hometown. I thought it was a gift, but no one knew who it was from. I used it as a journal, and soon I realized the powers it held."

Kaison nodded. "So, you kept it?"

"I'm not finished with my story," Maeve stated. She continued, "Nothing I wrote in the book was ever straight forward."

Simon cleared his throat, drawing attention to himself. "Might as well tell him," he said.

Maeve bit her lip. "Simon and I used to be friends when we lived in Wonitu," she muttered. "He was the only one that knew about the journal. One season, he got this disease that…wasn't normal. Every day he was closer to death. So, as the good friend I was," she flashed Simon a glance, "I wished for him to be healthy."

"And?"

"The disease spread like wildfire through the village," Maeve said. "To the point where Simon was the only healthy one."

"A lot of people died," Simon said. "They all blame me for starting the spread."

Maeve frowned. "I only tried to help."

"You didn't stand by me when everyone turned against me," Simon said. "Villages from all over learned what happened, but I still kept your secret." His tone was enigmatic.

"I'm sorry," Maeve said. Her head was down in her hands in her lap.

"That's why I came here to Sun Castle. To find my birth parents," Simon took the ring off of his middle finger. "This is all I have to lead me to them," he said before extending the ring toward Kaison.

Kaison took the ring from Simon and flipped it over in his palm. It was a simple, silver band, but on the inside a name was engraved: *Ivor*.

"Your adoptive parents don't know your real parents?" Kaison asked. Then he handed the ring back to Simon.

Simon slipped the ring onto his middle finger. "Even if they did, my adoptive parents are dead. Everyone else from the village but Maeve and I were killed." He stared at Maeve with his bottomless eyes, though he spoke to Kaison.

"I didn't mean for anyone to die!" Maeve said.

"You killed an entire village? With the journal?" Kaison asked. "Why didn't you get rid of it?"

"I did!" Maeve said. "I threw it in the moat, but it bobbed to the surface, completely dry. Then I threw it in the fireplace, and it wouldn't burn."

Kaison was skeptical, but continued anyway. "If you couldn't destroy it, couldn't you have hidden it away?" Kaison asked.

"I guess," Maeve said, "but then I figured that it was better off in my hands. I didn't want someone else to make the same mistake I did."

Kaison nodded.

"Your eyes…" Simon started. "You've been writing again."

"Little things," Maeve defended herself, "all pertaining to me. I'm trying to learn exactly what has to be written so more people aren't hurt."

"You shouldn't do that," said Simon.

Kaison tried to change the subject. "The Shadow of Eclipse doesn't care who dies," he said. "What could the most powerful man want from a journal that grants you anything?"

Maeve shrugged, brushing her hair behind her ear. Her face was filled with guilt.

Kaison's mind felt as if it was going to burst. Maybe his father sent him to find Sir Landon – Sir Emmett – because he knew Emmett was looking for the diamond journal. Could that be true? How was this connected to the halberd and the pendant? The three objects were definitely some sort of trifecta, and they had to be related to the door Nikodemus had been talking about.

"We need to get the journal back," Simon stated.

"How?" Maeve asked.

Kaison touched his chest, wanting to feel the pendant underneath, but he was woefully reminded that he had given it to Pandora. The pendant was the only thing that kept him protected from the Eclipse's magic. Maybe, with the pendant's protection, he could get the journal back.

He was the designated protector.

Kaison looked over to the cot on the opposite side of the room.

"Dux Nikodemus told me that Seraphina was Sir Emmett's lost daughter," he said, "and that she escaped from the Shadow of Eclipse. She could have given us the exact instructions on how to catch him by surprise."

"What?" Maeve gasped.

Simon stared back at Kaison.

"If only she was alive," Kaison said. "She could tell us so much more."

"Well..." Maeve started. Then she spoke firmly:

"She *is* alive."

- 39 -

Osiris

Osiris was busy training on the outskirts of town. On the cliff edge, Taville could be seen in the distance, as well as the arena for the Tournament. But Osiris didn't pay the sights any attention. She was busy preparing for her mission to raid the Captain's Palace. She had a course set up for agility training and was on her third run that morning. She forced all the energy into her limbs as she started scaling the last wall.

It was going to be one of the hardest heists she had ever pulled off. It would be highly guarded, and she would need someone on the inside.

She didn't want Destrian to stay in Larkesh. She wanted him to be safe. With the money from this heist, he could easily find someone to grant him passage out of this place. Still, she hadn't devised a foolproof plan to free the rest of the people. She didn't want Destrian to stay behind for a plan that may not even happen.

Her mind wandered for a moment, and her foot slipped on

its hold. Before she could grip the wall to save herself, she fell to the ground. Landing flat on her back in the dirt, Osiris's breath was knocked out of her. She let out a groan, staring at the sky as she tried to catch her breath. She placed her hand on her chest in pain, feeling her dual daggers sheathed in her vest.

Then a figure covered the sunlight.

"Need a hand?"

Destrian was hovering over her, his hand extended down. Begrudgingly, Osiris let him help her to her feet. She brushed the dirt off her pants before rolling her shoulders back, feeling the ache in her arms.

"The soldier I mentioned earlier delivered," Destrian said, holding up a rock. He crossed to the cliff edge where the rock was exposed before kneeling down. "This is the entrance." He started carving a map into the earth. "This is most likely where the Captain will keep his battle plans."

Destrian continued to sketch the blueprints he had seen earlier.

Osiris crossed her arms, watching him. She knew he had memorized the map down to its precise measurements. Seeing the expanse of the Palace made her begin to question their heist.

"To make sure he is out of the room, Moriah will be on guard to pull the alarm," Destrian continued, marking a star on the map. "Then she'll meet us around back with the escape boat."

Osiris knelt down beside Destrian, getting a closer look. "How tall is the building?"

"Five stories, but there are balconies on every level. You shouldn't have to free climb the entire thing."

Osiris nodded. She ran her palm against the ground. "How long until Moriah finishes the disguise for you?"

"Eight or nine days," Destrian said.

Osiris's head snapped toward her friends. "We don't have that time."

"She can only work on it when she's not running the store," Destrian defended her.

"We have to have the battle plans sooner."

"I guess I'll talk to her."

Then Osiris examined the sights beyond the cliff edge. The Tournament area was spread over the vast land just outside of the town of Taville. It seemed easy – a trial of three strengths. Swimming, agility, and intelligence. Whoever made it to the end first was the only one given a weapon for the slaughter.

A chill ran down Osiris's spine. She had to stop the atrocities.

Then she sensed something moving behind her. Someone had found their training ground.

In one swift motion, Osiris withdrew one of her daggers as she rose from the ground. She chucked it toward the intruder. The dagger flew at the girl standing there, but it was immediately shifted off course.

Osiris's mind drew a blank, knowing her aim couldn't possibly be that off.

The girl stood there, her jet black hair falling in her eyes. Her skin was ghostly pale, and her bottomless eyes bore into Osiris's soul.

Withdrawing her other dagger, Osiris charged toward the girl. As she lashed forward, the girl countered. Hardly a moment passed before Osiris was flat on her back. The girl's knee was planted into her chest, and she had a hold of both of Osiris's wrists.

The girl slammed Osiris's hand against the ground, forcing her to release the dagger. Then, the dagger magically flew up from the earth and into the girl's palm before she pressed it to Osiris's neck.

Osiris's heart pounded against her chest. She lay on her back, shocked, trying to get a good look at the girl who held her to the ground.

"Hey!" Destrian trotted closer, his arms outstretched.

The mysterious girl's head shot up at Destrian, but her grip remained firm, holding Osiris down.

"There's no reason to kill anybody," said Destrian.

The girl didn't flinch.

"Get off," Osiris said. She tried to push the girl away, but her knee pressed down even harder.

"You're the one who attacked me," the girl spat. She lifted the dagger higher, forcing Osiris to tilt her chin up.

Destrian knelt down. "You can't kill her, she's a Vynx, you'll be cursed."

Osiris's blood boiled. Why would Destrian give them up like that?

The girl's brow furrowed. "A what?"

Osiris pondered her reaction. If she didn't know what a Vynx was, she obviously wasn't from Larkesh.

Destrian tried another tactic. "Let her go. We have money to offer."

"I don't want money," the girl scowled. "I'm looking for Osiris."

Destrian gestured toward his friend. "You found her."

The girl froze. Then she stood, backing away.

Osiris could breathe again. She grabbed her neck, feeling for blood, but the skin hadn't broken. She scrambled to her feet, and Destrian stepped in front of her, preventing Osiris from attacking.

"Dux Nikodemus sent me here," the girl said. She tossed the dagger, letting it clank to the ground in between them. "He said you could help me."

"Help you?" Osiris took a step forward, coming shoulder to

shoulder with Destrian.

"I need a place to lie low for a little while," she said.

Osiris picked up the dagger and sheathed it in her vest. "I don't offer protection to random people."

The girl laughed. "I don't need your protection."

That was obvious.

She continued, "I just need a place to stay for a few days where no one can find me."

"Who are you running from?" Destrian asked.

"My uncle."

"Oh," Osiris wrinkled her nose. "Family problems." It would be nice to have a family.

The girl scowled. She withdrew a note from her pocket. "Nikodemus said this would convince you." She extended her hand forward, palm toward the sky. With telekinetic powers, the note levitated from her hand. It spanned the short distance between the girl and the two Vynx, hovering in the air.

Osiris observed the magic. She had never seen anything like it. That was how the girl took the dagger in her hand so quickly. That was how she knocked the first dagger out of the way. With her mind.

Destrian's hand shook as he snatched the note out of thin air. He blinked profusely, shaking his head as he unfolded the note.

Stepping closer, Osiris read it over his shoulder.

I will raise the initial 1,000 suns to 2,000 each, given to Osiris Saber, Destrian Amir, and Moriah Omanne – only if you agree to protect the messenger.

Dux Nikodemus

Dumbfounded, Osiris's mouth dropped open. He was doubling the payment. Who was this girl? And how was she connected to Dux Nikodemus? How long was she going to need a place to stay?

Destrian disregarded any questions. He crumpled up the note and shoved it into his back pocket. "We have a place you can spend the night, but it isn't anything fancy."

"I don't need something fancy." The girl's voice was dry.

"Great." Destrian took a few steps forward, extending his hand toward her in greeting. "Destrian," he repeated, looking for her name.

The girl was still. Eventually she took Destrian's hand, her black eyes set on him as she introduced herself: "Seraphina."

- 40 -

Kaison

Seraphina is alive?" Kaison asked.

"Yes," Maeve nodded. "When I woke up, Madame Lucia was here, cleaning up broken glass everywhere. Right after she left, Seraphina woke up."

Simon shifted forward. "How is that possible?"

Kaison scratched his head. "Seraphina didn't have a pulse."

"Or…" Simon rose from his stool. "It was so faint we didn't notice it." Simon walked over to the other cot.

"Where is she now?" Kaison asked.

"She created a door with a wave of her hand and vanished."

Simon turned around. "She has Eclipse magic too?"

Maeve's eyes were wide as she shrugged. "I don't know what it was. I was too shocked to even speak."

"How is that possible if she's not the Shadow of Eclipse?" Kaison asked.

"I don't know!" Maeve shouted, but then quickly lowered her

voice again. She flipped her hair out of her face. "Nikodemus came back to take away her body, but she was gone. He also knows that she's alive."

"That doesn't make any sense. They buried her in the graveyard," Kaison objected. "Emmett was at her funeral."

Simon planted his hands on his hips. "Nikodemus must want Emmett to think she is dead."

"Why would he do that?" Maeve asked.

Kaison wondered if he should stay silent. Both Maeve and Simon waited for him to speak, and he gave in. "Emmett is the Shadow of Eclipse's brother."

Maeve and Simon both reacted loudly.

"Supposedly Seraphina was kidnapped," added Kaison.

Everything was starting to make sense, but at the same time it was becoming more confusing. Kaison needed to know the truth and if his father was King Arturo. The only way to do that was going back to the secret room and looking through King Arturo's artifacts. It was time to uncover the remaining secrets of the artifact room once and for all.

"It's possible Emmett has been working with the Shadow of Eclipse – his brother," Simon said. He leaned against the cot that used to be Seraphina's.

"How?" Maeve asked. "They both seemed to be after my journal individually."

"Every once and a while Sir Emmett appears in the stables, coming out of the same empty horse pen," Simon said.

"How does that have anything to do with the Shadow of Eclipse?" Maeve's tone was sharp.

"I used to think nothing of it," Simon said. He spun the ring around his middle finger as he spoke. "Now I wonder if there was something back there, or if he has the transportation magic you said Seraphina has."

Kaison was even more curious. Maybe that was another entrance to the passageways. Maybe Emmett was familiar with the labyrinth Dux Nikodemus spoke of under the castle – the one that led to the door. The door his halberd was a key for. The key he was supposed to protect. That had to be how he and Cheyenne entered the artifact room without using the library.

Kaison rose to his feet, and seconds after, Maeve stopped him.

"You know something else, don't you?"

A lump formed in Kaison's throat. He had to be cautious. He couldn't tell anyone he could be King Arturo's son. But the other things Dux Nikodemus said…about the labyrinth under the castle… that the journal and the halberd were important and had to be used together…Maeve and Simon already knew pieces of that.

"I think there could be a secret door in the stables," Kaison said. "Supposedly there's an entire labyrinth under the castle."

"Secret passageways?" Maeve asked.

"No, a maze to protect something," Kaison said. "There's a magical door. I don't know much about it, but I need to find out more."

"How do you suspect we do that?" Maeve countered.

Kaison cleared his throat. "There's a hidden room filled with King Arturo's things. It could have the answers."

Maeve shot a skeptical glance at Simon, but Simon was attentively listening to Kaison.

Noticing Maeve's hesitance, Kaison continued. "There may be information about your journal."

"What?" Maeve's blue eyes were wide. "Then let's go!" She swung her legs off the cot, ready to bounce off.

Kaison held out his hands to stop her. "I didn't invite you to come."

"You can't be serious!" Maeve yelled. "You can't expect Simon and I to stand by. It's my journal, remember?"

Kaison hesitated. He didn't want to involve anyone else in this mission, but if Nikodemus was right, he would need Maeve eventually. They would be in this together, whether they liked it or not.

"Fine." Kaison gave in. "Not now."

Maeve rolled her eyes, but she seemed to agree. "When?"

"During the ball tonight," Kaison stated. "We will sneak out. Everyone else's attention will be on the queen and the villagers who won the Harvest Banquet."

Maeve glanced at Simon. "Are you with us?"

Simon nodded.

"Then it's settled. Prepare for tonight."

- 41 -

KAISON

Kaison stood face to face with the mirror in his bedroom. He wore a light green, long-sleeved tunic embroidered with tiny, threaded flowers. A blue strip of fabric ran from his high collar down to the center of the shirt, and a black sash was strapped across his side.

Kaison had never worn an outfit like this before, but luckily, Louie had lent him one of his own elite suits. It was made for those close to the high-council of Vorinder. The pants were too short, and the shoulders were baggy, but Kaison was altogether grateful for the kind gesture.

"Let me see how you look," Louie said from behind Kaison.

Kaison turned around to face the knight in training, showing off the outfit.

Louie wrinkled his nose with a tilt of his head. "Well, I don't love it," he said with a shrug. "If only your face wasn't so bruised."

There was nothing much Kaison could do to conceal the bruises from the night that he had been attacked by Cheyenne. A faint outline of purple still circled his eye.

A knock on the door alerted both Kaison and Louie. Kaison was the first to go over to the door and open it.

Theadosia stood in the hallway. Her hair was pulled up into a bun, leaving only her bangs in front of her face. She wore a simple red dress, but it fell to the floor beautifully, creating a slight train.

"I hardly recognize you," Kaison said.

"I know," Theadosia replied. "This is the fanciest gown I've ever worn in my life."

Louie said, "It's beautiful."

"Thank you."

Kaison leaned out into the hallway and looked both ways. "Where's Pandora?"

"She's not walking down with us," Theadosia answered.

"Her loss," Louie said. He slid past Kaison and into the hallway. "What are you two waiting for? I'm sure there will be lots of food!"

Theadosia laughed before saying, "You know we're not staying long? We only need to show our faces and meet up with the others."

"The others?" Louie echoed.

"Maeve and Simon are coming," Kaison told him.

Louie frowned. "They're not a part of our group."

"It was Maeve's journal that was taken, and Simon has saved both Theadosia and me on different occasions," Kaison objected.

"Whatever," Louie let out before starting off down the hallway.

The trio reached the grand ballroom doors alongside other guests. There were two guards posted on either side of the two-story doors.

One of the guards crossed to Kaison.

"Weapons," he stated.

Louie and Kaison shook their heads. Neither one had brought weapons. They both put their arms out to the sides while the guards patted them down. The knights searched underneath their wrists and at their ankles for any small daggers.

When the guards were satisfied, they let them both pass through. They didn't even stop to check Theadosia. Kaison was confident that she was still wearing the hidden blades.

Behind them, the guards stopped the next group. Judging on their clothing, this group had traveled from the North, so they had their swords confiscated and taken away to an adjacent room. Kaison didn't know if these precautions had always taken place, or if they were implemented after last night's fire.

The three entered the ballroom.

They stepped onto a marble floor, swirled with pink. A center chandelier hung over Queen Benedict's fuchsia-tinted crest, which was stamped into the center of the floor. Straight ahead of Kaison was a set of archways leading out onto a glass balcony. The exquisite balcony overlooked the moor, facing the Southern mountains. The balcony's floor and dainty railings were transparent, and aside from the moonlight shining upon it, it appeared to be invisible.

A stunning staircase sat to the left, leading toward the royal chambers through another set of double doors at the top. The queen's throne was on top of the staircase. Around the one edge of the room, there was a second level. Striking, marble columns held up the second level, spaced out by smaller chandeliers. This loft area allowed the guests to view the dancing from private quarters. The wealthier attendees leaned over the railing to examine the others below.

On the level below, a group of instrumentalists played a lively tune next to the staircase. A swarm of people were clumped in groups around the central, pink crest.

"Let's find the others," Louie said.

The three pushed gently through the crowd. There was little space between the couples and groups, due to the women wearing overly large gowns that fluffed outward. No one was dancing yet. They were all chatting wildly, holding the sparkling peach punch in their hands and cocking their heads back in annoying laughter. It was as if the nobles had forgotten about the attack, and the villagers were attempting to enjoy their few moments of fame.

A feeling of urgency crept upon Kaison as he thought of going back to the artifact room and confirming the truth about his father and a supposed magical door underneath the castle. They didn't have much time. The ball would end when the moon was at the highest point in the sky.

The siblings followed Louie and traversed side by side between the mass of people. They had to turn sideways to push their way through the cramped space. It was significantly hotter in the center, and the crowd seemed to congregate around the design in the middle of the room. The queen's crest was stamped into the marble, and the guests' feet covered the outside of the laurel.

Kaison searched for Pandora, Simon, or Maeve. There must have been five hundred people gathered in the spanning ballroom. Guests maneuvered in and out of each other and stood in closed circles with their inner groups.

Kaison craned his neck over toward the windows, but he didn't see any sign of them. Then he looked to the left, where the ballroom stretched on past five paintings that spanned the length of the ceiling to the floor. "Do you see them?" he asked.

Theadosia's head snapped to the left. "Over there."

A girl with fiery red hair stood out from the crowd. She was at the edge of the room underneath a large tapestry that hung from the ceiling. A shimmering, blue bow held her hair back, framing her round face. She wore a blue dress that sparkled as it flew to the floor with white streaks running down on either side symmetrically. Her one arm was held in a sling, releasing the pressure from her shoulder and allowing it to heal. Kaison knew it was an act and that she somehow was already healed from her injuries.

Simon stood beside her, the complete opposite, towering over her with his tall stature and his contrastingly lean build. His dark hair fell in front of his eyes, and he stood with his hands in his pockets. They weren't talking, but rather standing beside one another in silence.

Kaison pushed forward through the crowd. He shifted his body and raised his arms as he side-stepped in between the couples. Then he navigated directly between a group of friends.

"Where are you going?" Louie called.

Kaison pressed ahead toward Simon and Maeve. Kaison was only a few groups away when a force yanked at Kaison's shoulder and pulled him violently to the side. Kaison locked eyes with Julian.

"Look what the rats dragged in," Julian sneered.

Julian wore a decorated outfit, adorned with high-quality, beaded fabrics. His turquoise eyes glistened in the light beaming down from the chandeliers. The sight of him made Kaison's body clench in disgust. He stood beside Pandora, who looked like she belonged in one of the queen's royal paintings. Her golden dress complimented her brown curls, and she had golden bows tied perfectly on either side of her head. Kaison saw his pendant around her neck, and gave a sigh of relief seeing that she still had it on her.

"Hello you two." Louie came up beside Kaison.

"You think you can give Pandora a necklace? Who do you think you are?" Julian growled.

"Julian," Pandora muttered under her breath, trying to calm him.

A burning sensation rippled through Kaison's body. "The necklace is none of your business."

Theadosia was aware of the tension brimming between the two boys and tried to change the subject. She twirled her dress around her as she spoke, "This is the first ball I've ever been to."

"It gets boring quickly," Julian scowled. He returned his attention to Kaison and opened his mouth to speak but was cut off.

At that moment, the music came to a screeching halt, and in unison, the whole crowd turned to look up at the top of the stairs.

"Hello everyone," Queen Benedict called.

Her presence was majestic. She wore a white, diamond-studded dress with lace and exquisite detailing. Her golden hair was pulled back underneath her crown. She seemed to hover elegantly at the top of the staircase.

"Welcome to the Harvest Ball!" she said. The crowd answered with a thunderous applause. "The accident on the moor last night will not stop our celebration," she continued.

Kaison's attention was drawn to Dux Nikodemus who was standing beside her as her guard.

"Now, let's celebrate with a drink and dance!" Queen Benedict called. "The winners will be crowned at midnight. Here's to another plentiful year!"

A joyous applause rose through the crowd before the instrumentalists began again. A jovial tune broke out, calling people to the dance floor. Kaison's group was forced to move out of the way as the dance floor opened up. Guests moved around one another in a mechanical pattern, changing couples and cheering as they danced.

Julian held out a hand to Pandora. "Shall we?" he asked.

“Wait,” Kaison was quick to intervene. “Pandora, aren’t we…?” He had thought she was coming with them to explore the artifact room once more.

“Aren’t you what?” Julian asked.

Kaison ran his hands through his hair in frustration. “Julian, can you give us a moment?”

“Absolutely not.”

Pandora clasped her hands. “What do you need, Kaison?”

Kaison didn’t want to say anything in front of Julian.

Julian retracted his open hand from Pandora’s side and began fixing his cufflinks. “Spit it out, Kaison, let us all hear.”

“Julian, give us a minute,” Pandora said before walking away, expecting Kaison to follow her. Pandora led Kaison underneath the archway that held up the second floor. They were close to the balcony doors, letting the cool air drift inside. The glass balcony sparkled in the moonlight.

“What do you need?” Pandora repeated.

Kaison began. “Um…” Kaison didn’t know how she had forgotten. “We need to go back to the artifact room.”

“Now?”

“Yes.”

“Why?”

“Because it’s important.”

Pandora crossed her arms. “It’s important *right now*?”

“Yes,” Kaison insisted. “That was the plan.”

Pandora let out a sigh.

“Are you mad at me or something?” Kaison asked.

“No.” Her voice lifted up at the end, making it sound more like a question.

“I’m so confused,” Kaison admitted.

"Pandora!" Julian called from a few feet away.

Kaison shot him a glare. They hardly had a moment to talk yet.

Pandora reached into her pocket and pulled out a key before handing it to Kaison. It was the one to the artifact room.

"Are you not coming?" Kaison asked.

"Not right now."

Kaison was at a loss. "Why?"

"Listen," Pandora let out a sigh, "Julian and I got into an argument over the pendant. I can't keep lying to him."

"Seriously?" Kaison's mouth was agape. "This is about Julian being a cry baby?"

Pandora countered, distancing herself from Kaison. "What is wrong with you?"

"He's a jerk. Why can't you see that?"

"You don't know him!"

"I know him enough," Kaison said. "I'm astonished how someone as wonderful as you can't see how terrible he is."

"Don't you dare say that."

"Searching King Arturo's belongings is actually important," Kaison continued. "Julian isn't!"

"Kaison!" Pandora cut him off. She took a step closer. "His sister is dead. Have some respect!" Her hot breath beat against his face.

Mixed emotions clouded Kaison's mind. He wasn't sure if it was guilt or rather disappointment that they had raised their voices at one another.

"By Sun." Pandora shook her head in disappointment. "Think about someone else for *one moment*. You're asking everyone to throw everything to the side to help you on your quest, but you forget that other people have lost family too." Her large eyes didn't blink.

The two stayed there in silence, inches from one another.

"Are you done?" a voice called.

Kaison was lost in Pandora's gaze and didn't see Julian had approached. When he realized Pandora wasn't going to respond, Kaison finally said, "We're done."

"Good," Julian said. He placed his hand on Pandora's lower back. "Let's dance."

Pandora frowned as she brushed her curls behind her shoulder. Then she pushed Julian's hand off her. "I need a moment," she finished, before heading out on the balcony.

"Do you want me to come?" Julian asked.

"No." Pandora called over her shoulder.

Julian addressed Kaison. "What was that about?"

"It's none of your business." Kaison started to walk away when Julian grabbed him by the collar and pulled him back. Kaison stumbled over his footing as Julian yanked him close to his face.

"You don't get to yell at her like that."

"You don't even know what the conversation was about."

"Maybe not, but you need to leave her alone."

"You don't know half of everything Pandora and I have done together," Kaison said. She was the first person at Solaris he trusted. She saved his life in Grovia, and they both discovered the artifact room together. And their moment in Sun Spire…

"Excuse me?" Julian took the statement the wrong way.

Kaison shoved Julian back, relinquishing his grasp around his collar. "Sod off," Kaison said.

"No." Julian took a step forward once more. "You're giving her gifts now? I know the necklace is from you." He started to roll up the ends of his sleeves.

Kaison's eyes narrowed. "So?"

"You think I can't protect her, so you need to give her some magical necklace?" Julian had seen the magic that occurred when the Shadow of Eclipse attacked. "She thinks I don't know it's magical, but I do."

"That's not why I gave it to her."

"Well sod off, she's taken." Julian shoved his palms against Kaison's shoulders, forcing him backwards.

Kaison regained his balance. "You're pathetic," he said. "Pandora deserves someone better than you."

"That someone won't be you," Julian retorted.

"I never said it would be," Kaison said. "Anyone is a better choice than you."

Julian spit in Kaison's face. Kaison jerked backward, and his blood boiled in a rage. He wiped the saliva from his cheek before he grabbed Julian by the collar, ready to clobber him in the jaw.

Julian was swift. He twisted Kaison's arm around his back, sending a sharp pain through Kaison's shoulder. He wailed before Julian shoved him away.

A few people around them were invested. They watched the two boys in alarm. However, most of the guests were still dancing in the center of the room.

Kaison regained his footing. Anger fumed inside him. He whipped around to face Julian, shaking out his arm that Julian had twisted behind his back.

"You'll never be able to fight me," Julian jeered.

Kaison tore forward, ready to punch Julian across the face.

Once again, Julian maneuvered out of the way. He grabbed Kaison's shirt and swung him around, pushing him up against a nearby column. Kaison's upper back slammed into the marble, and the wind was knocked out of him.

Guests were shouting all around them, calling for them to stop, but their voices were muffled to Kaison's ear. One voice that was louder than the rest was Louie's. He ran over and was attempting to pull Julian back and break up the fight.

"Stop!" Louie shouted.

Julian and Kaison were too invested. Julian slammed Kaison against the column once more, holding the top of his shirt in both hands.

Kaison regained his strength and swung his fist as hard as he could at Julian's face. Julian dodged, and the punch met Louie's cheek. Louie stumbled back, clutching his face.

"Enough!"

The booming voice seemed to echo through the entirety of the ballroom.

The instrumentalists came to a screeching halt. The dancers froze and whispers traveled throughout the room.

Sir Emmett appeared from the crowd, his loud voice halting the entire ball.

Julian recomposed himself, standing up straight and fixing his shirt. He began rolling his sleeves down to his wrists once more.

Louie held his face in one hand, massaging his cheek where Kaison had punched him. He straightened slightly as the knight approached.

Sir Emmett grabbed Kaison's upper arm, shaking him. "What were you thinking, child? You're ruining the ball!" Emmett's voice penetrated Kaison's mind like a blade.

Kaison wrenched his arm away from Emmett. "Julian started it." He defended himself. Then he looked at Louie. "I'm sorry."

Louie didn't say a word.

Behind Julian and Louie, Kaison could see Pandora watching the scene.

A sudden wave of guilt and embarrassment flooded over Kaison.

"I will escort you out, child," Emmett continued.

Pandora took a step forward to stand by Julian. All at once, Kaison felt like there was a line separating him from Pandora, Louie, and Julian.

"Louie…" Kaison tried again.

Emmett grabbed Kaison by the arm. "Child!"

Kaison whipped around to face Sir Emmett, wrenching his arm out of the knight's iron grip once more. His gaze burned into Emmett's bottomless eyes.

"I can leave on my own." Kaison dropped his voice to a whisper. "Landon."

- 42 -

Kaison

Emmett froze in his tracks, and his entire body became rigid. His face twisted, and his eyes shifted down over the brim of his nose to burn into Kaison's soul.

Without waiting another moment, Kaison turned on his heel and started for the exit. His body flushed with heat, and the loud thumping of his heart reverberated in his ears. Out of instinct, his hands clenched into tight fists, and his fingernails dug into his palms.

The crowd separated from Kaison, not wanting to be anywhere near the boy who had instigated a fight. The guests whispered, and soft music screeched from a meek violin. The servants were attempting to regain the lively atmosphere of the Royal Ball, but everyone was invested in the drama.

When Kaison neared the ballroom doors, the instrumentalists squeaked again as they waited for the next tune. The conductor tapped his baton on a rattling music stand, but the awkwardness lingered. Guests spoke in hushed tones, and no one continued dancing.

Theadosia ran across the room to catch up with her brother, meeting him as he was exiting the ballroom. She walked rapidly to keep up with his pace, her shoulder beside his. She looked up at him, waiting for him to speak, but Kaison didn't say anything. They both exited into the hallway and retreated farther away from the ballroom.

Finally, Kaison stopped at the opposite end of the long hallway. He could still see the ballroom doors from where they stood, and the music was a distant melody, but he was far enough away to release his anger. He paced back and forth, shaking out his hands and letting out a yell.

Theadosia crossed her arms, sinking into her hip. "You need to stop getting into fights with that jerk."

Kaison ran his hands over his face, trying to steady his breathing. "I called him Landon."

"What? You called Emmett by his real name?"

"Why did I do that?"

The clicking of heels alerted the sibling that someone was approaching. They turned to see Maeve and Simon making their way down the hallway. When they were close enough, Maeve spoke first.

"That was a show," she said. Even with one arm in a sling, she managed to clap her hands together in applause, slow and exaggerated.

"That's not necessary," Theadosia responded.

Maeve shrugged. "I was merely thanking your brother for his service to the ball's entertainment. It was getting boring."

Kaison cleared his throat. "I can't go back in there now."

"Good," Simon said, his monotonous voice unenthused, "because we have another task."

The four of them were in agreement.

***

Kaison pulled back the tapestry to reveal the stone wall. He ran his palm against it, hoping to feel for the one loose stone. Sure enough, one of the stones shifted under his touch. He removed the stone from the wall to reveal a hole. He reached in and pushed the key deep into the lock. A loud click sounded. Kaison removed the key in time to see the lever pop out. After pulling the lever, the stone wall slid to the side and revealed the artifact room.

"This is it," he said.

Maeve's eyes were wide. She held the candle in front of her in one hand and grabbed her ballgown in the other before heading inside the room first. The sling still hung around her arm like some sort of decoration. Simon was next in line, and Theadosia was last.

Kaison stopped his sister in the doorway. "What happens if Nikodemus is telling the truth? That father was…you know…and that I'm…"

"Nothing changes," Theadosia cut him off. "We're still the same people we were yesterday. Are you angry that father didn't tell us about his past, or are you scared about what that means for you?"

Kaison didn't respond. He didn't know the answer.

"Let's go," Theadosia encouraged him and continued into the room.

When Kaison entered, he saw Maeve and Simon were lighting the torches on the wall. The room was not as bright as last time, and Kaison couldn't help the creeping fear that ran down his skin.

Maeve approached the table in the center of the room and began sifting through the pictures and scrolls. "What is this place?" she asked.

"One of the private rooms holding the last artifacts of King Arturo," explained Theadosia.

Maeve turned over a piece of paper on the table. "Well, hopefully the royals know something about my journal."

"That's why we're here," Kaison replied, half in a lie, but secretly he did need to know more about the Ademantum.

Kaison went over to a nearby desk. There had to be a name or something that linked him to King Arturo. He brushed a heap of dust off a manuscript in the center of the table. He picked up the book and examined it.

On one side of the fold was a neatly written page in the language Kaison was familiar with. On the other side was a scribbled jumble of letters and words. There were notes and crosses, as if the manuscript was in the process of being translated. He glanced at it further, but it contained no interesting information. Everything seemed to be about foreign relations, policy, and the War of Worlds.

Setting the book back down, Kaison moved over to a nearby bookshelf. It was filled with scrolls. He peered down the length of the room, knowing how deep it went. They could be searching for a long time.

"This has to be a portrait of the royal family." Simon said.

Kaison grew attentive. He scrambled over to Simon's side. Simon was pointing at a flat object on the top of a shelf. It was wrapped in a sheet, but it certainly did look like a frame.

Simon reached up. He let the object gracefully fall into his grasp. He held it with both arms while Kaison unwrapped it. The sheet fell to the floor, creating a flurry of dust, and the two studied the picture frame in Simon's grip.

Sure enough, it was a portrait of the royal family. The queen was seated holding an infant in her arms. Her crown was stunning, connected to a veil that fell down her back. Standing on her left was a man decorated in royal attire. His hand was placed gingerly on the queen's shoulder. The crown on his head signified that he was the king.

Without a shadow of a doubt, the man in the painting was Kaison's father.

A plaque was attached to the picture frame at the bottom.

"King Arturo, Queen Lidia, and Prince Sun"

Sun…

Kaison pondered the word. It only made sense that after the royal family escaped – after his family escaped – they were forced to change names. Arturo became Arthur. For Kaison, his father simply added Kai to the beginning of Sun.

Unbeknownst to him, Theadosia had come to look at the painting for herself. She made the same connection that Kaison had made once she looked at King Arturo's eyes.

"Too bad we don't know what happened to them," Maeve said from across the room, snapping Kaison out of his trance.

Simon set the painting down gently on the ground, letting it lean against the shelf.

Theadosia and Kaison stood quietly for a moment longer. They were the children of King Arturo. Apparently, that didn't mean they were the heir to the kingdom.

Nikodemus was telling the truth.

- 43 -

THEADOSIA

Theadosia contemplated the image of the royal family. She almost didn't recognize her father, and she didn't know the woman – Kaison's mother. The truth sunk in, and all at once, the person she thought she knew was someone else entirely.

She had never expected her father to tell her about his life before children…but to keep a life such as this a secret seemed impossible. Why hadn't he returned to Solaris?

Vorinder's succession may have been prevented if Arturo remained on the throne.

"Everything he said was true," her brother stated, referring to their conversation with Nikodemus.

Everything.

The siblings met each other's gaze. Theadosia tried to read his expression, to comprehend exactly what he was thinking at that moment. And yet, for the first time in her life, her brother felt more distant than ever.

Half-brother. She corrected herself.

Theadosia broke their eye contact first, turning away and proceeding into the depths of the artifact room. She had her answers. What was she supposed to pretend to be looking for at this point? She had completely forgotten.

She rounded the corner, distancing herself from her brother and leaned against a table, covered by a dusty sheet. She could hear her blood pulsing, and her mind spun. Why did their father keep this a secret from them?

Theadosia finally began to understand. When the new Shadow of Eclipse rose to power, he must have been after the halberd. King Arturo must have decided it was more important to protect the halberd than to protect his kingdom.

The halberd, to the king, was more important than his reputation.

"Are you alright?"

The monotonous voice was quiet.

Theadosia noticed Simon. An orange glow flickered on his face from the distant torch, adding a gleam to his dark eyes. She weighed whether or not to tell him the truth.

"I'm thinking about my parents," she admitted.

Simon kept his distance. "They passed away?"

"They were killed along with everyone else from my hometown," Theadosia stated. Maybe everyone else didn't die. Maybe some people escaped like she and Kaison did, but she had seen her parents die. "Sometimes I wonder why I survived and not them."

Simon was silent for a moment. He let out a deep breath, losing eye contact. "You have no idea how much I relate to that statement."

Theadosia sighed. Her brother remained on the other side of the bookshelf and hadn't followed her to debrief what they had witnessed in the painting. He must have been equally as shocked, being the designated protector and the one gifted with the halberd, but she wished they could have an open conversation about everything that had happened since Grovia. Neither of them had taken time to grieve.

"I'm sure Kaison needs time," Simon said, reading Theadosia's mind.

Theadosia realized Simon was referring to the fight that broke out in the ball, but she knew there was so much more going on.

When another moment of silence had passed, Simon continued, "You could write him a letter."

Theadosia inclined her head, startled. "What?"

"Sometimes communication is easier in writing."

Theadosia tried to contain the laugh, but it escaped her. "My brother and I communicate fine."

Simon nodded. "Right, sorry." He started walking away, but Theadosia reached out and stopped him.

"No, I'm sorry. It's actually a good idea." Theadosia smiled.

Simon's face reddened.

She raised an eyebrow. "You think there's a pen and ink around here?"

"Yes, I think there is."

"Will you help me look?"

Simon didn't blink as he gave a curt nod. "Of course."

- 44 -

Kaison

Kaison remained lost in thought. He continued looking at the portrait for the longest time, hoping that if he stared at it long enough then he would see different faces painted onto the canvas. The face that struck him the most was that of his mother. He had never seen her before. Lidia.

She had a round face, and black hair fell across her dark tan complexion. Even though she wasn't Theadosia's mother, there was a strange similarity about them. Kaison couldn't help but wonder how she died and why his father had never spoken two words about her.

After what seemed like forever, he pulled away from the portrait. It was simply too painful, and he didn't have time to think or talk about his feelings.

He turned in another direction, toward another row of shelves, far away from Simon and Theadosia. Before him, was a large object underneath a dust-ridden sheet. With one swift pull, Kaison tugged the sheet off the object, creating a cloud of dust.

Kaison waved the dust out of his face with his hands. Before him was a white harp. It was completely still, but Kaison imagined what it would sound like.

Maeve came up to Kaison's side. "Do you play?"

Kaison shook his head, coming to his senses. "No," he muttered.

"You look like you're going to faint."

Kaison rubbed his head with the ball of his hand. "I'll be fine."

Maeve placed one hand on her hip. "Are you scared of harps or something?"

"No." Kaison let out a sigh before turning away from the harp. He returned to the center table and planted his hands down, leaning forward. Theadosia and Simon hadn't returned and had gone deeper in the room exploring.

Maeve followed Kaison over to the center table, unconvinced. "Fine, don't tell me," she said. She pulled a book close to her, using the arm that was in a sling. She flipped it open to a random page.

"Fine, don't tell me about why your arm is completely healed."

Maeve's face flushed as white as a ghost. She dropped the book on the table. "I don't know what you mean."

"You healed yourself. Somehow. I don't know how, but it's the only possible explanation. Did you wish for healing powers too? How much have you been experimenting with the journal?"

"Shhh...," Maeve quieted him. "I didn't wish for anything."

"I don't believe you."

Maeve rolled her eyes. "It happens, alright? Ever since I was little. A paper cut, a sore, it all heals. That's why I wasn't afraid of helping Simon when he got sick. No one else would go near him, but I did."

"Are you trying to tell me you're immortal?"

"No. It takes energy and concentration. Depending on the injury, sometimes, it doesn't work at all."

Kaison still wasn't convinced. "The town must have thought you were very brave for treating Simon," he said sarcastically, with a hint of scorn in his voice.

"I'm not brave," said Maeve. "I didn't ask for my powers, alright?"

Kaison scoffed, imagining the ability to heal himself. Anyone would kill for that, and by the sound of it, Maeve was ungrateful.

She faced him. "Those days were the worst days of my life. I lost my entire family too. My parents and my two sisters."

Kaison instantly regretted his tone. "I'm sorry."

"You're not," said Maeve. She wrinkled her nose. "I can tell you don't like me very much." Maeve reached up to her arm and pulled off the bandage, letting it fall onto the table. It shriveled into a wrinkled ball.

Kaison didn't argue. He still remembered her stinging slap to his cheek.

"Even though I can heal myself, I would have died if you didn't intervene with Cheyenne," Maeve explained. "So…thank you."

Kaison sighed. "You're welcome."

Maeve leaned over on the main table. She pulled a large box toward them both, placing it between Kaison and herself. She tried to open it, but it was locked shut. She tilted the box, hoping to find a keyhole, but there seemed to be no way of opening it.

He paused before continuing. "I'm sorry about your family from your hometown. I know how it feels to lose the people closest to you."

"Well," Maeve muttered. "Being responsible for their deaths is an entirely different feeling."

Kaison nodded. "Did you ever recover? From losing your family?"

Maeve shook her head. "You never do. People tell you that it will be alright, or that it will get better, or that you'll be stronger in the end, but those are all words. Empty words from those that can't think of anything else to say."

"I wish you had said it would get better." Kaison forced a laugh.

"It won't," said Maeve, "the ones you lost will always be with you. Death changes your life forever, and it's the hardest thing to accept. But it makes me want to live even more." She stopped.

The sound of footsteps behind him altered them both that Theadosia and Simon were approaching.

"Find anything?" Theadosia asked.

Maeve planted her palm on the box in front of her. "Just this locked box."

Theadosia rounded the table to join Kaison's side. She picked up the box in her hands. It was lighter than she expected. She turned it around and saw a hole in the center of one side. She poked her finger in the hole, but it was hardly deep enough.

"It's probably nothing," Maeve said.

Kaison spotted an inscription on the bottom of the box. He took the box back from his sister. He tilted it to look at the bottom and saw a word written there.

"Ivor," Kaison announced.

Then he looked at Simon before adding, "Your birth parents."

- 45 -

Kaison

Simon stared at the box, and Kaison handed it over.

"Your birth parents?" Theadosia echoed.

Simon set the box down before him. "My birth parents left me a ring," he said. "It has Ivor engraved into it."

"Wait…" Theadosia's voice ran off. She tilted the box back again and examined the hole on the front. "Simon." She pointed to the hole.

Simon yanked the ring off his finger and held it gently in his other hand. The other three watched with anticipation. He delicately placed the ring inside the hole, and it fit like magic. He put the tip of his finger inside, and after a slight turn, the box clicked.

Kaison's breath caught in his throat.

Simon took the ring back and slid it onto his finger before holding the lid of the box in two hands. He let out a deep breath before opening it.

Inside was a small, leather-bound journal. Underneath the journal was a stack of parchment with drawings on it.

Simon picked up the journal in his hands and opened it.

Maeve reached into the box and pulled out the stack of papers that were underneath. She flipped through them, noticing that they were all obscure drawings. She flipped through the five drawings and then laid them out on the table before her so that they were all visible.

"What is this?" She asked the question everyone was thinking.

The two drawings read: *Labyrinth of the Lost* and *The Azure Gateway.*

Simon was too busy staring at the journal. He flipped through each page. "This is a diary," he said, "but it has no signature." For the first time, the disappointment in his voice was apparent.

Theadosia leaned closer to him to read it alongside him.

Kaison was perplexed by the drawings. "These look like maps," he said. He ran his finger down one of the five. In the center of the drawing was an oval, and from that oval, multiple branches reached away from it as though they were pathways. At each end of the branch was either a square or a circle.

"Well, these align." Maeve rotated one of the drawings ninety degrees before holding it a few inches above the one in front of Kaison. Sure enough, the half-circles at the end of the branches connected to other half-circles on the opposite page.

Kaison spotted something underneath the paper Maeve was holding. He took it from her hand and flipped it over. On the back of the paper was the same sun symbol that Nikodemus had shown him. Then Kaison flipped over the adjacent paper that aligned with the one he was holding. It also had a drawing of the sun on it.

"Dux Nikodemus said there was a labyrinth underneath the castle," Kaison explained. "Maybe these are maps."

Maeve flipped over the other three drawings, and the symbol on the back was jarring.

It was of the moon eating the sun – the Shadow of Eclipse.

Maeve looked up at Kaison. "So, these ones are maps of the Shadow of Eclipse's lair or something?" she said it sarcastically, but it wasn't that outlandish.

"This is in a different language," Simon spoke, drawing attention back to him and the leather-bound book. He was on the last few pages of the journal.

Theadosia was peering over his shoulder. "I know that," she said. She looked at her brother. "That's Mysticism."

Kaison was suddenly met with regret. His mother had given him a book to learn Mysticism, and he had never read it.

Theadosia took the book from Simon and examined it. "It's the same sentence over and over..." she muttered.

"What does it say?" Maeve asked.

Theadosia was silent as she tried to translate. "Help my king, help myself, or help my father. No – that's not right." She was hardly audible until she felt like she understood the sentence well enough. Then she looked up from the book. "It says 'Help my king, help myself, or help my brother?' over and over."

Simon leaned into the table. "What does that mean? Why write it in a different language?"

Theadosia looked at Simon sympathetically. "I don't know," she said as she handed it back to him.

Kaison wasn't too interested in the diary written by Simon's family, rather, he was drawn to the maps. He had to investigate. These were definitely the maps that led to the underground door Nikodemus spoke of. The door that Kaison's halberd – key – was made for.

Kaison picked up the two sheets of paper that had the sun on the back of them. "If these are maps...I think it's safe to say that this," he pointed to the large oval at the center of the one sheet, "is the most important."

"How are we supposed to follow these?" Maeve asked, crossing her arms. "They're a bunch of scribbles."

Kaison paused, looking up at the room around him. "There's an entrance here."

Kaison took off toward the back of the artifact room. He remembered where Sir Emmett and Cheyenne had entered and exited. There had to be a hidden passageway there.

Maeve had to run to catch up with him, her small strides quickening. "What do you expect to find?"

Simon and Theadosia followed suit. Simon tucked the leather-bound journal into his back pocket to read later.

"The door," Kaison answered. He took a lit torch off the wall and continued to the back of the room.

Then Kaison stopped at the wall where Emmett and Cheyenne had appeared. If it was anything like the entrance to this hidden room, there had to be a loose stone.

Kaison handed the maps to his sister before running his hand down the wall, feeling for any movement. He moved the torch with him, trying to illuminate the wall.

Theadosia studied the maps while Kaison hastily looked for an opening. "What do the squares and circles on the edges mean?"

"Also, how do we know where we are on the map?" Simon added.

A loose stone moved under Kaison's right grip. He tried to remove it, but it wouldn't pull outward from the wall. Instead, he pressed it and a loud clunk echoed deep on the other side of the stone. Suddenly, a door revealed itself, and a portion of the wall slid to the side.

The four were standing before a hidden passage. A set of concrete stairs led down into darkness. A cold wind blew against them, bringing a foul stench with it.

"This is it," Kaison said. "Hold on one moment."

Kaison left their side. He returned to the place where he had hidden his halberd. Gracefully setting the painting aside, he lifted the sheet and saw the golden staff exactly where he had left it. He swiped it from the hiding spot and latched it to his belt. He couldn't keep hiding it. He wanted it on him at all times.

Then Kaison scurried back to the passageway where all his friends were waiting.

"Well," Kaison said, motioning to the passage. He turned to Maeve. "Ladies first?" he asked. With her healing powers, she shouldn't have much to be afraid of.

Maeve crossed her arms and grimaced.

"Alright then," Kaison replied.

Kaison held his torch in front of him before descending into the passageway. Maeve and Theadosia followed next, and Simon took up the rear. Simon grabbed another torch off the wall before heading down.

Kaison maneuvered down the steep staircase. The number of stairs signified that they were traveling multiple stories into the depths of the castle. After walking for a full minute, he stepped off the last concrete stair and onto a dirt floor. The walls on either side were also dirt, as if the passageway had been carved through the center of the earth. He didn't glance behind him and kept moving forward.

Theadosia and Maeve were close to Kaison, walking between the pools of light cast by Kaison and Simon's torches. Theadosia held her dress up with one hand while holding the maps in the other.

"It looks like no one has been down here." Maeve focused on the dirt floor, examining the nonexistent footprints.

"Emmett has been down here." Kaison was sure.

The pathway winded to a left, and a fork in the road appeared. Kaison halted in his tracks, looking from the left to right at both options.

Theadosia held both portions of the map in her hand, letting her dress fall back to the ground. She carefully considered the drawings and mentally calculated the distance between the varying pathways.

"I don't see a fork in the road," she announced.

"There's one there," Maeve pointed.

"Oh, and one here," Theadosia looked at the other map. "It's closer to the oval."

"Let's go off that one," Kaison said.

"Then go right."

Kaison obeyed. He led the group down the right side of the fork in the road. As he continued, a soft draft blew through the tunnel, as if somewhere in the labyrinth there was an opening to the outside world.

More of the story was making sense in Kaison's mind. It would have been easy for his father to escape using these underground passageways all those years ago.

The group stopped at a 'T' in the road next.

"Which way?"

"Hmm..." Theadosia examined the map and turned it over in her hands. "Left."

Kaison continued to lead the group. They made two more turns until the path curved to the right. Then they stood before another fork, but this time the corridor spanned out in three different directions.

"Now what?" asked Simon.

Theadosia studied the map once more. Then she turned it around again until it was facing another way. "We definitely made a mistake."

"No, we're on this three-pronged path." Kaison pointed to the map.

"No we aren't," Maeve snapped. "We are nowhere near that side. We are here!" She grabbed Kaison's finger and pointed it in another direction.

"These are definitely outdated," said Simon. "Not all of the paths are here. Look, we should be at this fork where there are two paths, but in front of us there are three."

Theadosia turned the map over once more, unsure if it would lead to anything.

"To the mystery path?" asked Kaison. He gestured down the path before them that did not appear on the maps.

"Let's go," Theadosia urged, her eyes fiery with adventure. Theadosia pushed ahead, and all three followed.

After two more turns, they sensed that they were turning back in the direction in which they came, closer and closer to where the oval might be. However, the map was useless to them now. As they continued walking, the labyrinth grew darker, but luckily the torches still provided enough light for them to see their immediate surroundings.

"I can't see a thing up ahead," Kaison called from the back of the group.

"I have a good feeling!" Theadosia's voice was faint, like she was far ahead of them.

"We should go back," said Simon.

"No, I see a light up ahead. Come on!" Theadosia called again, but this time her voice was barely audible.

The three pushed forward faster, struggling to keep up with Theadosia. They put their hands out in front of them to guide their footsteps. Kaison's eyes were starting to adjust to see the darkness beyond the torch light.

"Look!" Maeve breathed.

Up ahead was a soft glow illuminating from around another turn. The light wasn't yellow, but blue.

Kaison followed his friends around the path to the right, and they halted in their tracks. Standing at the end of the hallway was an azure door, brilliantly lit despite the darkness of the passageway. The surface was smooth and shiny, like mesmerizing glass. The door was only slightly taller than Simon, framed by black and gold stones that marked its outline in the wall. The walls directly on its right and left were stone, as if the dirt had magically transformed.

"Is this the door you were looking for?" Maeve asked. She was standing directly before the blue glow.

Kaison took a few steps forward, warily approaching the magnificent door before them. Even though it appeared to be glass, the surface wasn't translucent, and they weren't able to see through the doorway at whatever lay beyond. He held the torch out in front of him, causing the golden detailing around the door to reflect the light. Kaison reached the door and ran his hand along it. The surface was smooth and shiny, and bulged slightly underneath his fingertips, like there was a clear coating covering the true surface.

"There's no handle," Theadosia noted, coming to stand beside her brother.

Maeve and Simon kept their distance.

"There has to be a way to open it," called Maeve.

Kaison thought about his halberd. He unlatched it from his belt.

“This has to be the way to get in.” He held the staff out in front of him, waiting for the willow tree to appear so that they could pass under its lofty branches and enter the door.

“Someone has been trying to get in another way,” Simon said.

Kaison turned around to see Simon shining his torch at an object on the ground. It was a red axe, leaning up against the side of the tunnel. The blade was noticeably dull, and the axe handle was cracking.

Kaison turned back to the door. There were no marks on the door to show that someone had been using the axe to get inside.

“You said Sir Emmett was down here?” Maeve asked.

Kaison nodded.

“If that’s his axe,” Theadosia pointed at the weapon on the ground, “he may intend to sneak down here during the ball.”

Kaison agreed. Then he fixated on the door and the halberd. He pressed his thumb into the red jewel on the staff. The staff began extending in his hand, lost in a flurry of swirling, magic. Once it had extended, the halberd’s large, golden blades exuded from the top and curved slightly, completing the full transformation.

“What?! What is that?” Maeve backed away in shock.

Simon’s gaze was intent on the weapon.

Maeve reached out to touch the handle of the halberd and her fingers became stained in the powdery, magical flakes falling down from the staff.

Kaison waited patiently for a few moments longer, hoping the willow tree would sprout out of the earth. He attempted to envision the physical space on the other side of the door, if it even was a physical space. He imagined the four of them there, in another room beyond the door, hoping the mental image was enough to produce the willow tree. They stood for a few moments longer, but nothing appeared. The golden magic illuminating from the halberd withered.

"What are you doing?" asked Simon, taking a step closer to the door.

"Trying to open the door," answered Kaison.

Suddenly whispers began to circulate through the tunnels. Kaison's hair stood up on his arms in fright. The voices sounded inhuman, but there was something speaking to them. It was obvious that everyone standing before the door heard it too. Ghostly sounds flashed on all sides of the tunnel.

The whispering voices were bone-chilling and pierced through Kaison's mind. He strained to make out the words, but the fading voices flew past him. He wasn't sure if the voices were speaking words or something else more sinister.

"I don't like this. Let's go," Maeve said.

"Wait," Theadosia held out her hand.

"What is it?" asked Kaison.

"Shhhhh…," Theadosia hushed him. "The voices are in Mysticism."

"What are they saying?" asked Simon.

"I can barely make it out."

"Try," urged Simon.

"It says," Theadosia struggled. "Power…" She continued listening to the words, her brow wrinkling as she tried to concentrate. Then she looked warily at her friends and announced:

"The power inside is meant for you."

"Are you sure?" asked Kaison.

The power inside is meant for you…

He could hear the foreign language speaking out to him.

"Yes," Theadosia said.

Kaison continued holding out the halberd. Nothing else happened. They waited for two more minutes as the whispers intensified, but the halberd remained stationary. The slight pull toward an underground willow tree was missing. The halberd only grew heavier in his arm, dipping slightly downward to the floor. The door didn't change in color, and the azure gleam radiated through the tunnel.

Kaison grew discouraged. The voices confirmed that there was power inside the door and that it was meant for someone. Was the halberd not the key? Nikodemus had told him the truth about everything else. It didn't make any sense, especially after all that they had discovered in the artifact room.

Kaison sighed and stepped back from the door. Then he retracted the halberd back into its staff form. The voices were increasing in volume. Something had awakened behind the door, and the sounds were looping faster and faster. Kaison strained once more to make sense of the sounds, but he knew it would be impossible.

"Let's go, this place is scary," announced Maeve.

"Alright," agreed Kaison. For some reason, the key wasn't working, and they were missing a piece to the puzzle. The intensifying whispers surrounding them only confirmed to Kaison that Sir Emmett should never have access to the powers within. They had to tell Dux Nikodemus that Emmett had been attempting to pry the magical gateway open with an axe. They had to get rid of Emmett for good.

The four retraced their steps. The corridors darkened again, and they used the walls to guide them back to the three-pronged fork in the tunnels. Then Theadosia pulled open the maps to retrace their steps.

"Shh!" Maeve's voice forced everyone to halt. "Do you hear that?"

Kaison strained his ears to listen for what she was referring to.

"Music," Simon said.

Sure enough, there was a faint tune playing. It was a bright, jovial folk song.

Kaison spun, pointing his torch in multiple directions.

"This way!" Theadosia exclaimed, gesturing down one pathway. Before she could be stopped, she took off down one corridor at a brisk pace.

Simon and Maeve followed Theadosia, but Kaison was more hesitant, taking up the rear. He didn't want to stray from the maps and get lost down here. He thought once more back to Mortimer, who had stolen the journal – the journal that made anything come true. What if Mortimer wished for the door to be opened? It was a terrifying thought.

The music crescendoed the farther the four of them traveled in the tunnels. After a final turn, they all stopped at a stairwell.

Theadosia looked over her shoulder with a twinkle in her eye. Without another moment of hesitation, she ascended the stairs. The three followed her, circling the winding staircase as the music continued to increase in strength.

When the four reached the top of the stairs, they came to a dead end. Theadosia pressed her hands against the wall and pushed forward. It creaked at a high-pitched tone before creating an alarming scratching noise. Bright light flooded the tunnel, and the wall shifted to the side like a sliding door.

"By plague." Theadosia stepped outside.

The four exited the passageways and found themselves in the hallway outside the ballroom. A set of double doors all the way on the opposite side of the corridor indicated where the ballroom was. Luckily, no one was around to see them step out of the wall.

Kaison stepped out last and made sure to close the door behind them. Once the door was closed, it completely blended in with the wall. Unless someone knew there was a passageway there, no one would ever find it.

"The passageways must have dozens of entrances," Theadosia said. She folded the maps in her hand before concealing them in her dress.

Kaison put his torch in one of the empty sconces on the wall, and Simon did the same. Then Kaison shifted the transformed halberd at his belt. Instead of tying the staff to the outside of the belt, he pushed it up underneath the side of his shirt, using Louie's stiff, long tunic to hide the part with the gemstones. He flatted the tunic against the halberd, and the fabric held it mostly in place. Then Kaison pressed his arm down over it and held the bottom to keep it from falling. Hopefully, this would give him a chance to get it back to his room.

"If I knew about the passageways sooner, I would have used them," Maeve was saying while Kaison fiddled with his shirt.

"I'm sure some people do," Theadosia replied.

Then something caught Kaison's attention. The ballroom doors banged open, and a figure emerged at a quick pace. It was Sir Emmett. He moved with furious speed down the corridor.

The four remained silent as they watched Emmett leave the ballroom. He didn't notice them at first, but when he drew closer, he halted in his tracks. His gaze was set on Kaison.

A tense silence passed through the corridor. Aside from the music and chatter coming from the ballroom, there seemed to be a complete pause in time as Kaison and Emmett stared at one another. His disfigured eye masked his emotions, but his eyebrows were drawn together angrily on his forehead.

That's when Kaison noticed Emmett's sword hanging from his

belt. It was so long it practically touched the ground. Did he have it earlier? The knights surely would have confiscated it at the ball. Without another moment passing, Emmett turned and made a hasty exit down an adjacent hallway. The four remained in silence until Emmett had vanished.

"He's creepy." Maeve broke the silence.

Kaison ran his hands through his hair. He tried to brush aside the uneasy feeling eating away at him.

An unnerving male scream sounded from inside the ballroom. The music screeched to an atrocious halt.

"What was that?" Theadosia asked.

"Come on!" yelled Kaison. His heart clenched in fear as he tore off toward the ballroom, and the other three followed close behind. He held the staff close to his side, careful not to let it fall as he ran.

All four entered through the open ballroom doors and scanned the area. Everyone on the dance floor had stopped dancing. People were chattering under their breath or covering their mouths. They all were looking in the same direction.

Dux Nikodemus stumbled out of the adjacent room with a horrid expression. He was the one who had screamed. A petite figure in a yellow dress hung limp in his arms. Blood spilled from a gaping wound in her stomach and dripped to the ground.

"It's Madame Lucia!" someone shrieked.

Nikodemus collapsed to his knees, and he held Lucia to his chest. He was completely drenched in her blood, and tears formed in his eyes. He swallowed hard before shouting, "She's dead!"

- 46 -

KAISON

Kaison froze. His entire body tensed with fear, which rapidly consumed him like poison. The same urgency from Grovia engulfed his senses. He ran one hand through his hair, keeping the other on the halberd tucked underneath his shirt. He was ready to snap it out at a moment's notice.

Out of instinct, Kaison's hand moved in front of Theadosia and Maeve, creating a barrier between them and those that were rushing toward Nikodemus. One by one, the head knight was swarmed with female guests, who shrank down to his side, their puffy ball gowns extending in perfect circles around them. The male nobles approached more steadily, but stood at his side, offering their condolences to the head knight.

Theadosia's hand flung to cover her mouth. "Not Madame Lucia!"

"This is all my fault," Maeve said. She grabbed Kaison's arm. "Lucia found out about my healing magic." Her neon blue eyes were wide.

"No, it's not your fault," Kaison said. That couldn't be the reason.

"We should leave while we can," Simon said.

Kaison agreed. "We need to go now." The ballroom doors were still open, leading agape to the empty hallway. Sir Emmett had already disappeared. He couldn't have been more suspicious with his timely getaway. Kaison shuddered, remembering Sir Emmett's scowling face.

Kaison pressed forward toward the doors.

At the same moment, Queen Benedict appeared at the top of the second level. "Lock the doors! I will not allow the murderer to leave this room!"

Kaison's body shrunk as he watched the guards slam both of the doors shut, cutting off their escape. He still continued forward, hoping to catch Sir Emmett. When he got closer to the doorway, two guards stepped in front of him.

"Move!" Kaison said, urgency in his voice. "Sir Emmett–"

They pushed Kaison back, making him stumble into his friends.

"No one is leaving!" one of them shouted.

Theadosia, Maeve, and Simon all crashed into Kaison's back. They were trapped.

Fear spread throughout the room like wildfire. All around them, the guests shrieked, running toward the doorway in an attempt to burst open the frames. Men and women were already crying, screaming at the Queen and demanding to be let out of the room. Dramatic nobles had already collapsed on the floor, while the villagers began climbing the columns, attempting to reach the upper levels and escape that way. The knights blocked the staircase with their swords, preventing the villagers from reaching the Queen. The knights pushed the villagers backwards, causing a few to tumble down the stairs. It was a stampede of chaos.

Kaison's group was being shoved closer to the entranceway by a horde of guests that was determined to exit. He struggled to stand upright and teetered back and forth on his feet, being pushed right and left. He had no choice but to move with the panicked crowd.

He could feel Maeve being shoved into his back, until she was pressed directly against him. "Move!" she yelled toward Kaison, although she could barely yell in his ear on her tiptoes.

"I can't," Kaison said. Before them, the knights wouldn't budge. They held their spears crossed in front of the other, and Kaison was only pushed closer into them. A man on his right was pressing into his side, pushing the metal halberd hidden underneath his shirt against his ribcage.

A man shoved Theadosia on his left, forcing her to slam into Kaison as well. They were jam-packed together.

Kaison craned his neck and tried to spot anyone else he recognized. The crowd was like a herd of sheep, waiting to be executed by a lone wolf. Yet Kaison knew for certain the murderer was already getting away. They had to get out of here and stop Sir Emmett. This was the perfect distraction for Sir Emmett to return to the door – or worse.

Guards blocked every exit except for the balcony doors which were still wide open. A few guards joined Dux Nikodemus to carry Madame Lucia back into the adjacent room, attempting to clean up the scene.

Then Kaison spotted Louie by the balcony doors at the edge of the crowd. Before another group rushed them, Kaison grabbed Theadosia's arm and turned around. "That way!" he shouted to his friends. "Come on." His voice was barely audible over the commotion in the room.

Simon led the way, and they moved against the crowd. Kaison had to watch out for Maeve in front of him, who was constantly in danger of being wacked by someone's elbow due to her height. He made sure that they all navigated through the swarm, pulling Theadosia along and holding her tightly so that he didn't lose her.

Shortly, they reached Louie. This side of the ballroom provided a brief respite, and a cool wind blew through the balcony doors. Next to them, more villagers were attempting to scale up the columns. Five were attempting to scale at a time, pushing the next one down and out of their way in a frenzy.

"What happened?" Kaison asked Louie once they reached his side.

Louie was in disbelief. "I thought you left."

"I returned when I heard the screaming."

Louie seemed to forget their previous spat. "Why would anyone kill Madame Lucia? What did she do?"

"Sir Emmett made a timely getaway," Maeve said under her breath.

"Again," Louie said, irritation in his voice, "why would anyone – even Emmett – kill Madame Lucia?"

Kaison was at a loss for words. He took a step back as Maeve and Louie started to bicker. Theadosia also joined in the conversation.

Kaison stood beside Simon in silence. The shattering of a window was heard on their right, and more and more shouting rose in the room. A fight had broken out near the staircase. The queen was nowhere to be seen. No doubt she was rushed out of the room for protection. But without Nikodemus, who still remained sullen near Lucia, they were hopeless.

At least, whatever happened, Kaison had his halberd. He removed it out from under his shirt, knowing that his side would have a pressed, purple bruise in the morning. He put it back on his belt, making sure to be ready to activate the red jewel if necessary.

"Two nights in a row." Simon broke the silence.

"What?" Kaison asked.

Simon shook his head. "There have been attacks two nights in a row. What is happening to Solaris?"

Kaison ran his hand through his hair, distraught. Then something caught his gaze. Out the open balcony doors, the moor was completely visible. Far in the distance was a faint white light. It bobbed, glistening in the shadowy distance.

"What's that?" Kaison pointed outside, drawing Simon's attention.

Simon narrowed his eyes as he took a step closer. He didn't answer.

Kaison tapped Louie on the shoulder, interrupting his conversation. "Louie, look."

Louie followed Kaison's instructions. He peered out at the bobbing light in the distance. "What is that?" he asked, stepping out onto the balcony.

Louie stepped out on the balcony, and Kaison followed. The first step onto the glass balcony took Kaison by surprise. Looking down, he could see the three stories that separated him from the ground. It seemed unnatural to be floating in the air on the glass balcony.

Pushing aside the unease, Kaison walked farther out on the balcony. The screams, cries, and chatter weren't any quieter the more they distanced themselves from the commotion inside.

Louie continued farther than Kaison did and leaned over the glass railing. He squinted his eyes, trying to ignore the hysteria behind him.

The light continued to dance miles away, but it was nearing closer and closer at top speed. Suddenly, hundreds of little specks of light appeared. A distant shouting could be heard over the commotion of the ballroom. The faint sound of horses' hooves rang in the air.

Louie whipped around to face Kaison. "We're under attack!" he said.

Behind them both, a large object was flying through the air. As it drew closer, Kaison's eyes widened as the boulder came into sight. It was coming straight for them.

"Look out!" Kaison screamed.

Louie whipped around to spot the boulder flying toward them from the distant catapult.

Kaison raced back for the ballroom doors. It was as if the whole world started to move in slow motion. His thoughts ran at a mile a minute, and he suddenly became aware of everything around him. He was inches from the open ballroom doors when the giant rock obliterated the side of the castle, smashing a short distance under the balcony.

The boulder collided with the glass balcony supports, shattering them in all directions. The glass began falling out from underneath Kaison and Louie's feet. The entire platform rippled from where the rock hit the supports to where they were standing. The balcony dropped, and Kaison thrust himself forward, jumping to the stable ground beyond the balcony doors.

Kaison whipped around to see Louie farther behind.

"Jump!" Kaison screamed, reaching his hand out as far as he could.

Louie surged everything in his body to launch himself forward, but the glass underneath his boots was already gone. He started to fall, screaming Kaison's name.

- 47 -

Kaison

Kaison reached out farther, barely grabbing a hold of Louie's wrist. Yet, Louie was falling too fast. Kaison dropped to his stomach to ensure he wouldn't tip forward off the edge of the balcony.

Louie grabbed onto Kaison's wrist and swung in his grasp toward the castle. Glass fell around him, slicing his cheeks and hands.

As Louie swung toward the castle, holding onto Kaison's wrist, his forehead slammed against the stone wall. The impact of his hit made Kaison slip forward off the ballroom floor.

The gash in Louie's forehead was instantly visible. Blood rushed from his skull, spreading throughout his dark hair.

At that moment, a body dropped on Kaison's side. Simon was also on his stomach reaching over the side of the castle's edge.

"Don't let me fall!" Louie screamed, clutching Kaison's wrist tightly.

"You're not going to fall," Kaison assured him. He braced himself on the ledge with one hand and tried to pull Louie up with one arm, but he wasn't strong enough to hoist his friend up onto stable ground.

"Grab my hand!" Simon shouted, holding out one arm toward Louie.

Louie didn't respond at first. Instead of reaching for Simon's hand, he slowly touched the caking blood on his forehead. His eyes started to roll back in his head. He was falling unconscious from the wound.

Another boulder hit the castle wall, causing the floor to shake. Kaison's body jerked forward, and he slipped closer to the edge.

"Don't let me fall...," Louie said again. His voice faded, and his eyes closed while his body fell limp. Blood was trickling down his temple.

"Louie!" Kaison screamed. The weight of his friend increased immensely. He started to slip from Kaison's sweaty grasp.

Simon leaned out farther, grabbing Louie's forearm with both of his hands. "Pull!" he ordered.

Kaison tightened his grasp around Louie's wrist and yanked him up. Once Louie was close enough, Simon grabbed him underneath the armpits and hoisted him to safety. All three of them collapsed to their backs inside the ballroom. Louie landed between Kaison and Simon.

"Louie!" Theadosia dropped to the ground, rolling Louie onto his back.

Kaison pulled himself to a standing position.

Somehow, Simon was already on his feet. "Get him to a doctor," he ordered Theadosia and Maeve.

"We can't do that. We're trapped," Theadosia protested.

Maeve was already crouching down beside Louie. "We'll take

care of him." She picked up the corner of her dress and began to dab the blood on his forehead. She gave Kaison a look, and somehow he trusted her.

Simon pointed out the balcony doors. "The Shadows are at the gates. It won't be long before they're knocking down the front doors."

Kaison whipped around to face the cold night. Sure enough, an army of soldiers was making their way over the wall, despite the volleys of defensive arrows headed in their direction. Solaris's archers were already mobilized on the top of the wall surrounding the castle. The Shadow Army approached relentlessly, moving forward with great force as one, collective mass.

Simon put a hand on Kaison's shoulder. "You ready?"

Kaison's thumb found the red jewel at his side. "Yes."

"You don't know how to fight," Theadosia interrupted from her position on the floor next to Louie.

"I will be fine," Kaison told her strongly. "Save Louie."

Maeve's eyes were filled with worry. She could only nod.

Kaison and Simon took off through the ballroom, pushing through the crowd along the way. The room was in complete chaos. The knights had opened the doors so that they could respond to the attackers. The guests were rushing outwards, and people were escaping any way they could. It was mass hysteria.

Nobles that had been enjoying the ball were now grabbing swords and shields from the adjacent room where the security had confiscated all of the weapons. The boys followed their lead and dashed into the room. Simon frantically searched for a weapon. He darted to the pile of swords that was spilling out of the room and grabbed one of the lighter ones.

Kaison stepped into a corner, determined to hide the halberd's transformation. But no one was paying him any attention. He clicked the red jewel and the halberd extended outwards in a second, faster than it ever had before. The sheer force of the transition almost threw Kaison off balance. The staff extended before the axeblade, and the spear transformed in a flurry of sparkling dust.

"Come on!" Simon encouraged him from the doorway.

Kaison and Simon broke through the entranceway of the ballroom and ran through the castle, crashing into many people along the way.

They emerged at the top of the staircase to the grand entryway. The large windows were smashed, and the front door was knocked down. The Shadows filled the room like a dark poison.

They were the Shadow of Eclipse. The ones who had attacked Grovia the day Kaison's parents died.

Simon jumped down the stairs and joined the fight. His sword slashed through one of the Shadows, causing him to disintegrate on impact. Kaison rushed down the stairs after Simon, not taking a moment to think logically.

Before Kaison reached the bottom of the stairs, a Shadow lunged at him. Out of instinct, Kaison blocked with the staff of his halberd. The soldier threw another blow, and Kaison tripped back over the edge of the stair. He struggled to grip his halberd. He hadn't trained for this. He didn't know how to fight.

The Shadow attacked. Kaison was no match for his strength. They locked weapons, and Kaison's arms began shaking.

He wasn't wearing armor. He would be dead in moments.

Kaison kicked the Shadow in the stomach, causing the warrior to stumble into the battle. Kaison backed away, staring at the bloodshed before him. Weapons clanked against one another, and people were yelling all around.

That's when Kaison noticed something familiar. A thick, black smoke began swarming into the main entryway from the outside. It funneled through the cracks in the bricks until it solidified once more into a large, circular mass. The fog descended onto the soldiers and knights, causing them to cough. Then, a human-like effigy rose up in an outline of smoke, spiraling three times as he ascended. The shape moved slowly toward a closed door on the second story and shot forward. Then the mist slithered between the cracks.

The Shadow of Eclipse!

Kaison turned on his heel and sprinted back up the staircase. Quickly, he pressed the red gemstone, and the halberd contracted in an instant, returning to staff form. Kaison sprinted up the stairs, skipping every other.

Kaison burst through the closed doors where the black fog had disappeared, careful not to drop the staff. He found himself in a narrow hallway, and the torches created a dim light. Kaison continued racing down the corridor. He skidded around a corner, past two screaming citizens and saw the grand ballroom doors at the other end of the hallway. The black mass was making its way through the open doors and into the ballroom.

Kaison shoved through another group of running townspeople and entered the ballroom. The swirling black mass had already expanded in the center, spreading out and blanketing the room in a thick layer of vapor. The fumes from the Shadow of Eclipse's cloud made Kaison cough, but he pressed forward into the mist.

Kaison stood firm, wind beating against his face and hair, as screaming villagers tore past him and out the door. He watched as the thick smoke floated over to the staircase and began molding into a figure of a man. The fog formed into a solid state, and Mortimer emerged out of the smoke. Wisps of blackness trickled down the staircase, falling off the man's shoes. The sledgehammer was hooked to his back.

"Where is the princess?"

The voice didn't sound human, but it came from the man on the staircase. It came from Mortimer, the withholder of the Shadow of Eclipse.

Mortimer extended his hand, and all the exits slammed closed. The loud noise caused Kaison to jump in his shoes. Not everyone had made it out. Many people were banging on the doors in attempts to flee. Others were in the far corners and near the balcony. Kaison spotted Theadosia on the other side of the room, cowering behind a column.

"Where is the princess?!" Mortimer's loud, booming noise was heard over all the screaming.

No one responded. They were in too much fear.

Mortimer let out a sigh, and this time raised both hands above his head. The windows on the second floor and the first floor, as well as the glass balcony doors, shattered. The noise was unbearably loud.

Glass shards flew through the air, and Kaison dropped to the ground, covering his head with his arms. Kaison heard glass pieces hit the ground around him, and a few scratched the shirt on his back. Screams erupted from the people who were impaled by large shards. Another explosion sounded, and even more glass piled down onto the guests. Kaison screamed as he felt something puncture his back, causing him to fall flat onto the marble floor.

Another man fell to the ground beside Kaison. A glass shard had also gone through him. Kaison cowered on the ground and shielded his face with his forearms. The last remnants of glass in the air sprinkled down to the ground around him.

A large shard protruded from Kaison's lower back. He gasped as he struggled to re-situate himself on the ground, but the pain was unbearable. He grunted as he turned over from his side to his stomach. Then Kaison cautiously looked at the intruder, careful to avoid more glistening glass on the ground around him. The Shadow of Eclipse stood alone, his bottomless eyes scanning the room, observing the casualties. Between Mortimer and Kaison was a large chandelier that had fallen from the ceiling. It blocked Kaison from view.

Kaison's eyes shot upward.

The halberd!

He had dropped it when he had covered his face. It had rolled a few feet in front of him.

Kaison used his forearms to drag himself over the marble floor. Glass shards pressed into his chest as he pulled himself along the tiles. As he moved, electrifying pain rippled through his back. He guessed the shard in his back was as long as a pocketknife.

"I don't like waiting," Mortimer spoke from the staircase. "I want the halberd and the princess. The girl with the Ademantum."

Kaison continued to pull himself over to the halberd. He winced in pain as he struggled to shift his body so that he could keep his eyes on Mortimer. Finally, his fingers clasped around the staff, and he pulled it tightly to his chest, so that it was partially underneath him. Then his hand grasped around his neck. The pendant. He didn't have it. There was nothing protecting him from Mortimer now.

"The halberd and the girl with the Ademantum," Mortimer repeated. "If it helps, the girl I'm looking for has red hair."

Kaison's cheek was pressed to the floor. The pain was unbearable, and he wanted to scream. From his view on the floor, he could see Theadosia on the far side of the room.

"I'm done waiting," Mortimer continued, repeating the same phrase that had flashed in the sky. He reached out his hand. He looked at one man, and the man straightened up on his tiptoes. The crowd gasped in unison as the man clutched his neck, gasping, choking, and collapsing to the ground.

The Shadow of Eclipse spoke again. "I want the girl with the red hair and the halberd!"

Mortimer extended his hand in another direction. Kaison couldn't see what happened, but a snapping sound resonated in the air, followed by a loud thud of someone falling to the group. The crowd at the doors was screaming, grasping at the wooden frames with their nails in the hope of escaping.

Kaison gritted his teeth and pressed his eyes shut as hard as he could. If he didn't surrender, more people would die. Taking his time, Kaison pressed himself up onto his forearms again. Kaison tried to get to his feet, but the shard sent a shooting pain down his spine. He winced and fell flat on the marble again, the staff pressing into his sternum.

Mortimer turned to another person in the crowd.

"You," he said.

The Shadow of Eclipse was pointing at someone. Kaison looked up once more, trying to get a better view. It wasn't until Mortimer started drawing the person toward him with an invisible force did Kaison see who it was.

Theadosia stood up in the center of the ballroom. She struggled against Mortimer's powers, attempting to dig her heels into the ground. He continued to pull her toward him, shortening the space between them.

"No!" Kaison screamed.

With one wave of his wrist, a purple bolt flew from Mortimer's hand in Kaison's direction. It shot over Kaison's head, impaling the man standing behind him. It burned a hole straight through the man's chest and he collapsed to the ground.

If Kaison were standing, he would be dead.

"I remember you from Grovia," Mortimer said, fixated on Theadosia. He strolled down the staircase.

Theadosia tried to escape the invisible force, but they were only a few paces from one another now.

"Where's your brother and the halberd?" Mortimer's voice boomed throughout the ballroom. "The one with the pendant?"

Kaison pushed himself up into a crawling position, taking a deep breath. Then he held the halberd in his hands. He moved his finger to the red jewel, but his hand was shaking so furiously, that his thumb wouldn't center over it. Sweat dripped down his neck and forehead, dropping on the floor. Blood had already pooled where he had been laying.

Theadosia hadn't answered Mortimer's question.

Mortimer looked around the ballroom once more. "Bring me the halberd if you want to see her alive!"

Mortimer grabbed Theadosia's arm, and black fog began swirling around him again. It encircled both him and Theadosia.

"Thea!" Kaison screamed, dragging himself forward. He managed to put one foot on the ground and stand up. He clutched his side, and his hand was immediately soaked in blood, before he toppled back over again.

Theadosia screamed moments before the black smoke swallowed both her and Mortimer. The darkness ascended into the air, swirling in a mass. It began traveling out the open balcony doors. Those that were near it dodged the black air. Then the fog vanished into the night.

Theadosia was gone.

- 48 -

Kaison

It was dark. The moonlight outside was the only light source that lit the ballroom. Kaison's eyes fluttered open. He drifted in and out of consciousness, laying in a pile of blood and glass shards. He had rolled onto his side, and the movement made the glass shard sink deeper into the lower, right side of his back. Voices echoed around him. Shouting, screaming, whispers. Before him, three sparkling gemstones lay close to his eyes, going in and out of focus. Beyond that, people ran through the open doorways, their faces blurred.

Theadosia. He needed to save her.

Kaison tried to turn onto his stomach and crawl to his knees, but the shard stabbing his back was too painful. He winced and collapsed back on his side. The pain was causing his vision to go completely black, and Kaison was nauseous from the smell of blood. He gasped desperately for air, inhaling as much as possible in one violent gush.

Through his half-open eyes, Kaison saw someone coming toward him. If it wasn't for her fiery red hair, Kaison most likely wouldn't have recognized her.

Maeve dropped to her knees beside him. Blood seeped down her face in a thin line running from her cheek to her ear. If the shard of glass had grazed her an inch higher, it would've taken out her eye.

"Kaison! Are you all right?" Maeve asked. She reached out and helped him to a seated position.

Kaison couldn't speak. The pain was unbearable.

Maeve quickly scrambled around him to get a view of his back. She saw the shard, penetrating his shirt and digging into his flesh. She gasped.

"I'll go get someone to remove the glass," she said and was on her feet in a second. "Don't go anywhere," she ordered, but it wasn't like Kaison could move.

Kaison sat there, surveying the chaos that ensued around him. People limped, hobbled, and crawled to get help. Kaison couldn't find Simon in the crowd. He didn't know if Louie was alive. The crowd was only a swarm of helpless, unfamiliar people.

Then Kaison saw the queen. She was crawling out from behind the staircase, holding her forehead. Her crown had been completely knocked off, but she didn't look injured. She had been in the room the whole time, cowering underneath the stairs.

Kaison's mind sharpened. He had to save Theadosia. He couldn't let the Shadow of Eclipse have her. Mortimer wanted Maeve and the halberd. Theadosia was an innocent bystander.

Maeve returned to his side alone.

"Everyone is busy taking care of other people," Maeve said.

Kaison stared back into her blue eyes blankly. "Can you get it out?" His voice was barely audible, and his face wrinkled in pain.

Maeve's eyes widened. "Me?" she asked. "I'm not a nurse."

"Please."

Maeve was hesitant to answer. She let out a sigh before crawling around him to look at his back again. She paused, staring at the wound, not knowing how to fix it.

"I'm sorry," she said under her breath.

"What –?" Kaison couldn't finish his sentence because Kaison felt her grip the shard in her fingers. She tried to get a tight grip despite the coating of blood.

"I should have stepped forward. Mortimer wanted me," Maeve said. "Now your sister is gone."

Kaison didn't know how to respond. He was as much to blame, for he could have stepped forward and told Mortimer where the halberd was.

Maeve ripped the shard out of Kaison's back.

Kaison winced and grit his teeth in pain, trying to keep in any audible shouts of pain.

"Curses, now it's bleeding more," Maeve said. She looked around for something to wrap the wound, but the only thing that was on the ground were shards of glass.

"Here," Kaison said before taking off his long sleeve shirt.

Maeve didn't object, and took his crumpled shirt out of his hands. Rolling it up into a tight ball, she pressed it against his back, hoping to stop the bleeding.

"I need to save Theadosia," Kaison said.

"You need to take care of yourself first."

"Where's Louie?" Kaison asked.

"Julian helped bring him to the infirmary and wrap his head. No one was there to help. It was a mess," she explained.

"Julian helped you?"

Maeve purposefully ignored his question, continuing to press the shirt against his back. “Louie will survive. Where's Simon?”

“I don't know,” Kaison admitted.

His eyes caught Queen Benedict once more. This time she was talking to someone. Kaison saw a long sword and recognized the man as Sir Emmett. They appeared as though they were in a heated dispute. Sir Emmett was yelling at the queen, using wide hand motions, and the queen was yelling back. Yet they were all the way across the ballroom, so Kaison couldn't make out what they were saying.

“Kaison!” Simon's voice was heard over the loud chatter in the room. He came over to Kaison and Maeve and dropped to his knees before them. He didn't look injured, though there were smears of blood across his shirt. He asked, “What is the plan?”

“I need to save Thea,” Kaison said. “I'm going to the Shadow of Eclipse's castle.”

“What?” Maeve's mouth dropped open. “You're going to get yourself killed.”

Simon ignored Maeve's statement. “I'll join you.”

“While I'm there, I will get your book back,” he promised Maeve.

“It's fine,” she said. “I have something now that no wish would have granted me.”

Kaison wondered what she meant by the vague statement.

Simon moved the shirt off Kaison's back. “This looks bad.”

Kaison could feel the sharp pain along his back from where the shard had been. “Has it at least stopped bleeding?”

“No,” Maeve muttered, scooting around to get a better look.

There was a moment of silence between the three before Kaison looked at Maeve. “Can you…?”

Maeve's blue eyes twinkled back at Kaison. Then Simon put his hand on her shoulder, snapping her gaze to him. “Do it,” Simon said.

Maeve let out a deep breath. Then Maeve placed her hand over the wound. Kaison grimaced as her touch stung, but didn't pull away. Maeve shut her eyes, letting out a deep breath.

At that moment, a tingling sensation began flooding through Kaison's lower back. A warmth started from his wound and slowly extended throughout his entire body. For a brief moment, Kaison felt like he was floating and that the world around him was nonexistent.

Then Maeve pulled her hand back, gasping for breath. Simon placed his arm around her as she fell against his shoulder, breathing heavily.

"You did it," Simon said.

Kaison could no longer feel pain in his back. He touched the wound with his hand, but it was no longer there. The skin was re-formed, and it was as if the injury never happened aside from the crusted, remaining blood.

Maeve smirked. "You're welcome."

Kaison didn't have time to respond, for Sir Emmett and the queen approached in an urgent manner.

"Maeve," Queen Benedict said, catching her off guard. "I need you to come with me."

Simon pulled away from Maeve and rose to his feet, standing up tall in the presence of the queen. Neither Emmett nor Benedict paid him any attention.

Maeve stayed on the ground. "Why?"

"Don't ask questions." Sir Emmett's voice was harsh.

Kaison didn't trust Emmett in the slightest and was not going to let him take Maeve.

"What's going on?" Maeve insisted.

"It won't take long for Mortimer to kill Theadosia and return to the castle," Emmett stated.

"What?" Kaison blurted out. He scrambled to his feet. "We need to save my sister!"

"Silence!" Queen Benedict scolded. "Maeve can't be here when Mortimer returns. You'll thank me for this," the queen said before turning to Emmett. "Grab her and follow me."

"What?" Maeve screeched.

Sir Emmett reached down and yanked Maeve up to her feet in one swift motion.

"Let go of me!" Maeve tried to struggle out of his iron grasp.

"Stop!" Kaison reached out to pull Emmett away, but the queen stepped directly in between Kaison and Emmett. Kaison came face to face with the queen, staring back at her in utter dismay.

"Let the adults handle this," Queen Benedict said.

Sir Emmett dragged Maeve away despite her kicking and screaming. The queen waited a moment, making sure Kaison wouldn't intervene, before she crossed to a set of doors near the staircase. They drew a lot of attention, but the whole room was in too much chaos to care.

"Where are they taking her?" Simon asked.

"I don't know," Kaison replied, "but I need to save my sister. Can you save Maeve?"

Simon's face was enigmatic. "You can't go to the Shadow of Eclipse castle by yourself."

"I'll find Dux Nikodemus, don't worry."

Simon's eyes narrowed ever so slightly. "Alright, I'll save Maeve," he said before turning away. He headed in the direction the queen had taken Maeve, swerving through the crowd.

Kaison scanned the crowd. There were no familiar faces in his view. He needed to find Dux Nikodemus. Nikodemus was the only one he trusted that could help him get Theadosia back.

As if his prayer was answered, Kaison spotted Nikodemus on the opposite side of the ballroom. Julian was with him, and they both held opposite ends of a stretcher. The body on the stretcher was limp.

Kaison swallowed his pride and ignored Julian. He stormed across the room and called, "Dux Nikodemus!"

Julian scoffed.

Nikodemus looked up from the stretcher and acknowledged Kaison with a nod, but didn't answer. He and Julian continued to carry the stretcher toward the ballroom entrance.

"Dux Nikodemus," Kaison repeated. "I need your help saving my sister."

Nikodemus froze. He glanced at Julian and signaled to put the stretcher down. They struggled to set the stretcher down lightly, before Nikodemus let out a huff and stood up straight. "Kaison," he started, turning to Kaison with gentle eyes. "I'm sorry about your sister, but you cannot possibly go to the Lost Lands."

"Why?" Kaison asked.

Nikodemus shook his head. "You're safe here, and we cannot give Mortimer the chance to get his hands on the halberd."

"My sister isn't safe!" Kaison blurted out.

"Theadosia's life is not more important than the lives of Solaris citizens," Julian intervened.

Kaison shot him a glare.

"I'm sorry, Kaison," Nikodemus said, "but this kidnapping actually bought us more time."

"Time?"

"To get Maeve and the halberd far away from the door."

"Emmett and the queen already took Maeve," Kaison said.

"What?" Nikodemus scanned the room, rising on the balls of his feet to see over the crowd.

"Why is she so important?" Julian asked.

Nikodemus let out a sigh. "Only Maeve is able to write in the Ademantum," Nikodemus said, "so Mortimer needs her to write anything."

"Ademantum?" Julian questioned.

Kaison's eyes widened. "That book is the Ademantum? Meaning she…"

"Is the fated queen of Solaris, yes," Nikodemus finished Julian's sentence.

Solaris was destined to be ruled by the one who held the Ademantum. Maeve was the one.

But that didn't mean Theadosia could die.

"Dux Nikodemus," Kaison insisted. "I need to save my sister."

"Kaison, that is a suicide mission," Dux Nikodemus stated. "Now, I need to make a plan for when Mortimer returns, and I need to heal this kingdom." Then he turned to Julian and gestured down to the stretcher. "Kaison will help you. I need to find Maeve."

Dux Nikodemus started off into the crowd, but Kaison stepped in front of him. "I will go with or without you," Kaison stated.

"No, I will not let you get yourself killed," Nikodemus stated. "You are the designated protector, remember?" The knight turned to Julian and pointed at him. "Stay with Kaison at all times and make sure he doesn't get himself killed," he said.

"What?" Julian's eyes widened.

"That's an order, Julian," Nikodemus said. Then, with one last glance at Kaison, Nikodemus started off through the ballroom.

Kaison could feel his heart beat faster in his chest. Nikodemus was letting his sister die!

Kaison met Julian's gaze. "I'm going to save my sister."

He turned away and started through the ballroom. He had no

idea what his plan was exactly, but he knew he had to save his sister. There had to be some way.

The pendant.

Then an iron grasp clamped around Kaison's arm and whipped him around. Kaison came face-to-face with Julian.

"You're going to get yourself killed," Julian spat.

"I will not let my sister die without trying to save her."

"Nikodemus ordered me to keep you here," Julian continued.

"No, he didn't," Kaison replied. "He said don't let me out of your sight."

Julian's eyes burned back into Kaison's, and his hands curled into fists. "I won't," Julian stated. "That means you're staying here."

"I can't, Julian."

Another voice entered the conversation. "Still up for a suicide mission?"

Kaison whipped around to face Sir Emmett. The knight stood with his arms crossed. His bottomless eyes bore into Kaison's soul. He looked so similar to Mortimer, aside from the scar running down his face.

"What do you mean?"

"You want to save your sister, and I want to get the journal," Emmett said. "So, why don't we team up?"

Kaison was taken aback, but he didn't want to argue. The thought of 'teaming up' with Emmett sickened him, but he needed to save Theadosia. He needed his sister back. She was the one person he cared about most in this world.

"I'm only inviting you because you're her brother," Emmett said. "You won't make it out of there alive."

An anger burned inside Kaison. He clenched his hands into fists.

"And why would you make it out alive?" Julian asked, pointing a finger at Emmett.

"I know how to sneak underground," Emmett answered. "It should hopefully lead us directly to Theadosia and the journal. Maybe unscathed."

"The Ademantum?" Julian clarified.

Emmett continued, ignoring Julian, and remained fixated on Kaison. "So, child, care to make a deal with the devil?"

Kaison hated it when he called him that. However, he needed to work with him – this murderer – to get his sister back. Maybe his father had been right all along.

Kaison cleared his throat. "When do we leave?"

Sir Emmett's lips curled into a crooked smile. "Immediately. Get the halberd."

Julian let out a sigh before saying, "Great Sun. I guess I'm going to the Lost Lands."

Emmett wrinkled his nose in disgust. He opened his mouth to speak but Julian cut him off.

"It's not up for discussion," Julian said.

Emmett turned on his heel and walked away.

Kaison wanted to ask why Julian had offered to come, but he bit his tongue, stopping himself. Dux Nikodemus's orders couldn't be the only reason Julian wanted to go on a dangerous mission. Then Kaison shook his head. Julian's motives weren't important at a time like this. He needed the pendant.

"Where's Pandora?" Kaison asked.

Julian took a step closer, puffing out his chest.

"Calm down." Kaison held out his hand to stop Julian from coming closer. "I need the pendant."

Julian let out a huff. "I'll get it for you."

"And risk letting me out of your sight?" Kaison tilted his head.

Julian shifted his jaw, clenching his fists.

A voice sounded from behind Kaison. "Julian!"

Pandora came running up from a few paces away. She stopped before Julian, grabbing his arm. "Are you alright?" she asked. The red pendant shimmered on her neck.

"Yes," Julian replied.

Then Pandora turned to Kaison, her eyes soft. "And you?"

Kaison nodded, relieved she would even ask him after their argument. "I need the pendant. I'm going to save Theadosia," Kaison explained.

Pandora's doe eyes fell. She wanted to object, but couldn't find the words, knowing nothing she said would change his mind.

"I'm going with him," Julian said.

Pandora whipped her attention to Julian, her brown curls flying over her shoulder. "Why?" Pandora shook her head. "I know I can't stop you." She then turned to Kaison before pulling the necklace off over her head.

Kaison extended his hand forward, palm up, to accept the pendant. But Pandora didn't place it in his palm. She reached out and put the pendant around Kaison's neck for him. Once the pendant came to rest, Pandora placed her hands on Kaison's chest.

"I know you will save Theadosia," she said. "Come back alive."

Kaison nodded. "Don't be afraid to use your magic," Kaison said. "Protect Solaris."

Pandora's face went pale. With a curt nod, she turned away from Kaison and took a step toward Julian. She took both of his hands in hers. Julian waited for her to say something, but she didn't. Pandora rose to the balls of her feet and pressed her lips to his.

Kaison cleared his throat, turning away from the kiss and staring at the ground.

Pandora then pulled away from Julian before fixing his collar for him.

"I'll be back soon," Julian said.

"I know." Pandora flashed him a smile before disappearing into the crowd.

"We should go," Kaison said.

Julian nodded. He took a step forward and glared down at the pendant before leaning in toward Kaison. "I think I got the better present," he whispered. Then he started for the exit.

Kaison let out a deep breath.

He was going to save Theadosia. Even if that meant going with the two people he hated the most. Julian and Emmett.

- 49 -

Osiris

Osiris sat in the corner of the cellar, her mind wandering. She was thinking about the plan to break into the Captain's Palace. One wrong move, and she could end up in the Tournament. If it was successful, she would have so many options of what to do next. Especially now that the price was doubled. She would never have imagined having that much money. Now, it was just within reach.

The cellar was quiet. Everyone was asleep. Destrian had the blanket pulled up to his ear, his body facing the wall. Beyond, she could see the people she considered family sleeping soundly.

Osiris pulled up her sleeve, seeing the Vynx symbol there: two diamonds with a line through the center. It was clear as day on her dark skin, announcing to the world what she was. Hastily, she pulled her sleeve back down, concealing it.

Then her attention shifted to Seraphina. The girl was lying flat on her back, one knee propped up, and her hands folded on her stomach. Her eyes were open.

Then Seraphina tilted her head to the side, catching Osiris looking at her.

"I don't need someone to watch me," Seraphina said.

Osiris brought her knees to her chest before resting her elbows against them. "You're a stranger in my home."

Seraphina let out a sigh. She sat upright on the mattress before pushing her hair behind her ear. "Well, I can't stay here. I need to leave."

"Already?"

"I need to make sure my family is safe."

"Your family?" Osiris scoffed. "The one you're running from?"

Seraphina wasn't amused. She stood up from the mattress, and Osiris mirrored her. "Thank you for your hospitality," Seraphina said.

She turned to the grates and extended her hand forward. Directly in front of them, a swirling black portal manifested. A thick mist manifested into a solid oval, swirling with black liquid.

Osiris stepped back, feeling the stone wall against her, a gasp escaping her lips. She hadn't inquired about the girl's magic earlier. Now it was clear. This girl had to be a sorceress.

The fear that rippled through Osiris's body brought her to the stark realization: this is what everyone else felt like when they looked at Vynx.

She would not be afraid of something she didn't understand.

Seraphina took a step closer to the portal. She glanced over her shoulder at Osiris, her black hair flipping. "Do you want to come? Escape this place?" Seraphina offered.

Osiris shook her head. She was not going to step into a dark portal. She had decided long ago that she was not going to leave her people behind, and nothing would change her mind.

"Then I'll see you in another world," Seraphina finished.

Then she stepped through the portal, her body consumed by the swirling darkness. The portal remained only a moment longer before evaporating, and Seraphina was gone.

- 50 -

Kaison

Kaison, Julian, and Sir Emmett set off toward the Lost Lands where the Shadow of Eclipse castle resided. Hopefully, they still had time, because Mortimer planned to use Theadosia as a bargaining chip in exchange for Maeve and the halberd.

The three made their way out to the moor. Once they had traveled a safe distance away from the castle, and found themselves on solid earth, Kaison withdrew the halberd. He pointed it forward, and the willow tree sprang from the ground. The roots easily shot out of the grass and spun around themselves until the structure formed into a weeping willow. Golden sparks rained all around them.

Upon seeing the magic, Julian's mouth hung open, dumbfounded. For the first time, he was speechless. Emmett, on the other hand, did not react to the magic.

On the other side of the willow branches, the trio found themselves on a snowy cliff ledge, overlooking a vast canyon. To their right was a ghostly bridge, extending across a ravine to the Lost

Lands Castle. The stone bridge was supported by massive arches that disappeared down into the misty ravine. The abandoned castle was perched across the bridge on the opposite cliffside. Black and purple jagged towers spiraled up into the sky and blended into the snow-covered, grey mountains. A layer of enchanting fog blanketed the top of the spires. Between the fog, a spectacular display of purple lights danced through the sky around the castle, creating a mysterious and ethereal presence.

The castle itself was black, and flags flashed from the towers. Each flag had the Shadow of Eclipse's symbol. The castle appeared to float in a mix of the polar lights and low-drifting clouds. The only access point was over the rickety bridge.

Kaison focused on the long bridge extending from the mountaintop forest to the castle. He could barely make out two guards standing in front of an open iron gate at the far end of the bridge.

Emmett retreated backward into a meager forest with a few pine trees that offered scanty coverage. "Get back here," he called to Julian and Kaison.

Julian and Kaison retreated back into the trees. Kaison sloshed through fresh snow, which soaked through his boots instantly. Soft flakes that floated from the sky coated his clothes in a white dust. Kaison looked at Julian to read his expression, but it was masked by the darkness. Both he and Kaison didn't argue with Sir Emmett.

Sir Emmett turned to the boys. "You two stay here while I scout the area."

"Scout the area?" Kaison asked abruptly. The castle was apparent in the night sky. The only thing between the trio and the front door was a dangerous hike down the cliff and a trek across the bridge.

Sir Emmett shot him a glare. Even in the night, his disfigured face sent a shiver down Kaison's spine. "Yes, child," Emmett answered. He looked at Julian next. "Don't go anywhere," he finished. Emmett turned away, heading off into the forest behind them, disappearing in the direction where he had gestured. For whatever reason, he wasn't heading toward the castle, which confused Kaison even more.

Kaison stood shivering in the darkness. The nail-biting cold had already chilled his entire body. Fierce wind slapped against his face, and his hot breath formed a puff of smoke in front of him. The halberd's staff was ice cold, similar to the sharp icicles hanging from the tree branches that brushed against Kaison's shoulders. He kept the halberd out and ready.

A moment of tension passed between Julian and Kaison. Neither boy wanted to speak first. They remained still, watching the direction in which Emmett had gone. The silence between them was unbearable.

"It's cold," Kaison muttered under his breath. He knelt down facing the castle and continued searching the horizon, gauging the best way to enter the castle. There were no exterior walls, except for a small square in the front, most likely encasing a courtyard.

Julian clutched his sword. "It's not," he answered.

Julian crouched down beside Kaison. Both boys were next to each other, sizing up the Lost Lands castle and the polar lights that curtained the spires. The phenomenon was common in the wintery South.

Kaison asked the question on his mind. "Why did you come?"

Julian hardly moved. "Why did you keep your magic a secret?"

"It's none of your business," Kaison cut him off. Then he repeated his question. "Really, why did you come?"

"None of your business."

"Yes it is," Kaison answered quickly. "I don't need your personal motives to undermine the main goal of saving my sister."

Julian fixed the breastplate of his armor, considering whether or not he should tell Kaison, before adjusting the strap on his thigh that held throwing knives. A moment passed before he turned to Kaison, his face lighting up as the purple hues flashed on his face. The boys waited in silence for a minute before Julian let the tip of his sword fall into the snow.

"You know...," he began. "It's interesting how days after you show up, everything goes to the sewers in Solaris."

"What does that mean?"

"The attack at the ball. The explosion on the moor." Julian hesitated. "My sister."

"You can't possibly blame me for what happened to Cheyenne."

"You knew about the attack, and you didn't do anything to save her."

"What?"

Julian sighed. "Pandora told me. You knew what was going to happen."

Kaison stood upright. "I tried to stop it."

"You did absolutely nothing."

"I did more than you did!" Kaison objected. "It was mere coincidence you were close enough to hear the screams."

Julian rose to his feet. "Don't even start. I was guarding the castle while you were letting in strangers."

"Letting in strangers? Seraphina was unconscious!"

Julian leaned in closer to Kaison. "You were more focused on a stranger than saving my sister."

"Your sister was going to kill Maeve. She would have been a murderer."

"She's not a murderer!" Julian's frosty breath was now beating down on Kaison's face. "She was my best friend."

"Please," Kaison let out. "You didn't even shed a tear at the funeral."

"Sod off!"

"It's true!"

"I said sod off!" Julian screamed, his face was bright red. "My sister meant everything to me!"

Kaison kept his ground as Julian screamed in his face, but Julian's voice left him. With a shake of his head, he couldn't speak anymore. He turned away before clasping his forehead in his palm, his breathing ragged.

Kaison had no idea if he was supposed to comfort Julian or not. He kept his distance, and the only thing he managed to say was, "I'm sorry you lost your sister."

Julian scoffed. "Well," he clenched his hands to fists. "Remember this moment, Kaison," he began, whipping back around. "Though you didn't save my sister, I'm helping you save yours."

The words penetrated Kaison like a dagger. His face went blank, and he was unable to respond. He didn't know how to respond. He didn't know how to apologize for the death of Julian's sister. Kaison never could have predicted the night would result in Cheyenne's death. If anything, he thought Maeve was going to be the one to lose her life. Would they both be alive if Kaison had warned the others about it?

Julian angrily grabbed his sword up off the ground. He stood like a statue, as if his outburst had never happened.

The bushes rattled, alerting the boys. Sir Emmett returned, stepping out of the shadows. A crooked smile twisted across his face.

"Follow me," Sir Emmett called in a whisper. The knight disappeared once again through the bushes, and Julian and Kaison were left alone.

Julian didn't hesitate. He followed Emmett without acknowledging Kaison.

Kaison let out a deep breath before following them into the darkness. Kaison continued through the trees as the path rounded back in the direction of the castle. They trudged through the snow, pushing aside the spiky pine branches. The pathway steepened, and they had to lean backward as they descended the rock ledges. They skidded down the slopes, small rocks falling with them, until they reached the bottom of the cliffside. Finally, once they had descended about two stories, the land flattened once more. The three stepped toward the pine trees and peered between their branches.

Now, they were directly in front of the bridge. The iron pathway stretched across the ravine, leading straight to the other-worldly castle.

From this angle, the sinister spires were much larger, and spiked at the pinnacles. Phantom figures moved back and forth on the parapets. The purple lights framed the structure, casting shadows across the ravine.

Kaison took a deep breath and wrapped his mind around the fact that the Shadow of Eclipse was waiting inside to take the halberd, and his sister was trapped.

Julian broke the silence. "How do we plan to get inside?" He looked at Sir Emmett for the answer.

"Well," Sir Emmett said, "we cross the bridge."

- 51 -

Kaison

Sir Emmett, Julian, and Kaison stayed low to the ground as they crept up to the cobblestone bridge. When they reached the edge, Kaison glanced off the side of the cliff, checking to see how far the canyon dropped. He couldn't see the bottom of the ravine, for it was covered in white fog. His heart skipped a beat in anxiety, and he shifted away from the edge.

"The towers," Julian said, gesturing to the front two towers on either side of the main gate. He crouched on the side of the bridge.

Shadows stood on guard.

"They won't see us," Emmett said. "Follow me."

Emmett swung his legs over the edge of the cliff and jumped. He disappeared under the fog.

Kaison's stomach dropped as he watched Emmett jump into the canyon. He peered over the edge to see that the fog had parted where Sir Emmett had broken through. Emmett was standing on a lower ledge, easily within distance. Julian was already following Emmett's lead, somehow not questioning the treacherous path. Julian jumped down onto the ledge. The fog closed over them, swallowing them both.

Kaison swung his legs over the cliff-side and dropped down. He couldn't see where he was falling. His legs hit the stone below, and his feet slipped out from under him. He slammed hard onto the ice, and a loud splintering sound was heard as the ice cracked beneath him.

Emmett gave Kaison a disgusted look before turning back toward the bridge.

The knight continued to lead the way, grabbing onto a support beam holding up the bridge and hoisting himself to another ledge. The bridge's supports weaved in and out of each other like a web, creating a lower-tier to the bridge. It was a secondary path hidden by the fog. Emmett started heading across the supports, expecting Julian and Kaison to follow.

Julian began scaling the lower tier of the bridge, and Kaison took up the rear. He grabbed onto the support beam, careful to follow the exact path, before hoisting himself to the ledge underneath the main bridge. It was a horizontal plank, connecting support beams on either side. From here, Kaison noticed that the route before him was a trail of horizontal planks. There was no secure pathway. He would have to leap to each plank and hang onto the supports above. The purple lights from above illuminated the supports. The coating of ice along each beam glistened in the night.

Kaison jumped from the first plank to the next. The planks were wide enough for his footing, but below the planks was the depths of the canyon. His foot skidded on the ice, and he reached up to grab onto the beams above. They were ice cold, and his hands burned from the freezing stone. Kaison held the supports with both hands and looked down. A dreadful feeling crept through his stomach, for even though fog covered the ravine, he knew one wrong step would result in his death.

Kaison continued the journey underneath the main bridge, jumping from each support beam to the next. His heart pounded aggressively in his chest, and he kept his arms outstretched to keep his balance. When he blundered, he reached out to grasp the icy supports.

On the other side of the bridge, the castle rested on a rock ledge. Up ahead, Emmett had jumped from the last support beam to the cliff ledge, landing gracefully. Julian followed suit, seeming unfazed by the mission. They both approached a large, circular grate against the rock wall that appeared to be a vent.

Kaison leapt to the next beam. He only had three more beams to jump to before reaching the cliff side. He lurched his body forward and landed on the next one. His feet slipped slightly on the ice, but he steadied himself. Kaison bent both of his legs this time and sprang forward to the next beam. He fell to the side, and his left arm reached out to lean against the bridge's main arches. There was only one more beam to go.

This beam was slightly farther than all the others. He reached out his right foot and bounded forward, landing one-footed on the plank. His left foot followed, but he felt himself hurling toward the fog. As fast as lightning, Kaison brought his legs together and hurled his body into the cliff side. His upper body smacked hard into the deep snow, but his feet still dangled off the cliff ledge.

Kaison used his upper arms to yank himself forward, grasping onto the snow as leverage. He managed to get his knees under him and scrambled to his feet.

His companions were still at the grate. Emmett dropped to the ground and grabbed two bars of the grate with both hands and attempted to pull it open, but it didn't move. Julian knelt beside Emmett. They both wrenched the gate open, and it made an alarming noise. Kaison winced and tried to make out the Shadows in the watchtowers above, but they were concealed.

"This will take us to the prison," Emmett explained under his breath. "It's possible Theadosia is being held there."

Kaison panted in the snow. He was too worked-up to feel cold anymore.

Julian gestured to the hole in the wall. "After you?" Julian asked, but Kaison knew it wasn't a question.

Kaison peered into the darkness and let out a deep breath before crawling into the vast emptiness. His shoes pressed to a sticky substance along the ground, which Kaison pushed to the back of his mind as he crawled deeper. He held out his hands in front of him while his eyes adjusted. After a few more moments, he could make out the metal ring of the tunnel, leading them further into the crawlspace. They pushed forward even more, heading toward a faint light. It was too narrow to turn back.

Soon, the tunnel opened up into a wider space, and Kaison pulled himself out of darkness. He stood up in the room.

Kaison wiped his hands off on his metal chest plate while Julian emerged from the tunnel.

"Why is there blood on the ground?" Julian asked.

Kaison cringed.

Emmett was last to crawl out of the tunnel and stand up beside the two boys.

"This way," Emmett spoke, his tone dismal. "Stay close."

Emmett headed off down the corridor. Julian and Kaison trailed him, careful not to lose him in the dark. Kaison's shoes clung to the sticky substance on the ground.

Whispers echoed through the hallways. Ghostly voices produced eerie sounds that bounced around the tunnels. The inhuman voices were not like the ones Kaison had heard underneath Sun Castle with Maeve, Simon, and his sister. The ones in Solaris were intriguing, but these voices were horrifying.

The boys continued to follow Sir Emmett, who seemed to have the tunnels memorized. Every once and a while, they would pass underneath a grate which let in moonlight from above.

Then Emmett stopped abruptly. He turned to the wall of the cavern and examined it closely. He ran his hand down the wall and stopped once he felt something. He flashed both Kaison and Julian a chilling expression before pushing the wall, and to Kaison's surprise, a little part of the wall about the size of Emmett's hand shifted backwards. This allowed Emmett to hold onto an indent, ready to pull the wall to the side. With his hand on the formed handle, Emmett spoke:

"I don't know who's on the other side of this wall, so prepare yourself."

Obeying the knight, Kaison grabbed onto his staff and extended the halberd, sending a poof of sparkling magic in the air. Julian obeyed as well, withdrawing his embellished sword. Emmett approved, giving a slight nod with his menacing eye, and pulled the ledge in the wall. It took him all his strength, and the stone wall became a door, sliding open in the direction Emmett had pulled.

It was slightly brighter on the opposite side of the wall. The trio emerged in a small area at the base of a large stairwell. A set of double doors stood opposite them, and two armed Shadows were guarding the doors.

The Shadows, Julian, and Kaison all locked eyes on each other at the exact same moment. Kaison's stomach flipped in anxiety, but he ran toward them regardless. Kaison held the staff of his halberd tightly and aimed it at one of the knights. It clanked against one of the guard's swords, bouncing him backward. Julian went after the other guard with the same amount of determination.

A Shadow swiped his sword at Kaison, and Kaison backed away, barely letting the tip of the sword graze his armor. Kaison tripped on the staircase behind him, falling and landing on his tailbone on the stairs. The Shadow continued after him, lifting his sword up and sending it down in Kaison's face. Kaison blocked just in time with the staff of his halberd, but their weapons remained in fierce contact. Kaison's back was against the stairs. His arms shook, attempting to push up against the knight's sword.

Behind the Shadow, Julian was in battle with the other guard. Julian blocked an oncoming blow before sending his foot into his enemy's stomach. While the guard stumbled, Julian took his sword and sliced the guard's head straight off. The Shadow's head evaporated into black smoke before it even hit the ground.

Kaison's arms were about to give way underneath the strength of the warrior before him. Before he gave in, Julian sent his sword through the warrior's back, and it came out through his stomach, almost reaching Kaison's chest. The pressure of the warrior was instantly relieved as the guard disintegrated into the air like an apparition. Kaison couldn't help but let out a deep breath as his arms collapsed on either side of him.

Julian hovered over Kaison, and he slid his sword back into his belt.

Julian extended a hand to help Kaison up. Kaison blinked, before pushing himself up from the staircase and standing up on his own, brushing past Julian's arm in the process.

Emmett was closing the door. Once the wall was slid back into place, Kaison could hardly see where the door was.

Emmett disregarded the fight that had occurred between the boys and the two Shadow guards, and he turned his attention to the double doors before them.

"That's the dungeon," Emmett said.

The wooden doors had one large, ominous handle. Emmett swiftly crossed to the door and pulled it open. The door made an eerie creaking noise as it opened, revealing the dungeon.

Emmett looked at Julian and Kaison once more. "Find Theadosia, and fast," Emmett said. "I'm going to remain on this side in case any other guards come to this post."

Julian nodded before entering the dungeon. Kaison eyed Emmett carefully, holding his halberd firmly between his clammy hands. Emmett's bottomless eyes stared right back at him with the same intensity. Finally, Kaison followed Julian into the dungeon, bracing himself for what might be inside.

Kaison and Julian entered the room. They were at a crossroads, able to turn left, right, or head straight. Every cell was full. Haunting eyes turned in their direction, and the figures inside the cells began stirring. The prisoners that were strong enough dragged themselves to the front of the cells to view the intruders. The torches lacked sufficient light to fully illuminate their eerie faces.

A loud sound clanked behind Kaison and Julian, making them both jump and turn around. Emmett had shut the door.

"Well, he won't be joining us," Julian muttered under his breath.

Kaison scanned the vast dungeon. It was a maze of pathways diverting between sets of iron bars. The mysterious labyrinth was like a cage, entrapping them both in an awful nightmare. If Theadosia was down here, Kaison needed to find her fast.

"My sister is here somewhere," Kaison said, retracting the halberd and tying the staff to his belt.

"You go that way," Julian motioned to the left, "and I'll go this way," he said.

Kaison considered the pathway, giving Julian an uneasy expression, before heading left.

Not one jail cell was empty. As Kaison walked, a bony hand reached out of the cell toward him, and Kaison shuffled back in alarm. The disfigured bodies were enough for Kaison to deduce the disturbing events that occurred in the prison. Many of the macabre prisoners were unconscious – or dead – their sickly bodies sprawled in horrifying positions on the stone floor. Kaison swallowed his fear and forced himself to study each prisoner, searching for Theadosia. Each cell he passed was more terrifying than the one before.

Something brushed Kaison's leg from behind. A young boy had attempted to touch him through the bars. His bare back showed signs of whippings, and his thin hand looked as if it was going to break off if he reached out farther.

Shaken, Kaison turned away and continued through the winding jail cells. These individuals were not ordinary people. There was something different about them. Broken and disoriented, their disheveled eyes burned into Kaison's, and he tried to look away, but he knew he had to stare at each one of them in turn, hoping to find Theadosia.

These prisoners hadn't been whispering. In fact, these prisoners made no sounds at all. It was petrifying – the eerie silence that filled the room. All Kaison could hear were his footsteps on the ground and the dying breaths of those around him. He shuddered as a tingling sensation spread from his fingers up through his body.

Then Kaison came to an intersection and stopped in his tracks. To his left there was a staircase to an upper level, and to his right, the path wound back around to where Kaison had started. He focused on the staircase for a good amount of time, debating whether or not he should go up. Deciding that he should meet back up with Julian first, Kaison continued searching the maze of jail cells.

When Kaison turned the corner, he noticed Julian at the opposite end of a long hallway. Kaison was relieved to see Julian, much to his surprise.

The boys approached each other slowly, taking their time to look inside the remaining cells. For whatever reason, Kaison didn't call out to Theadosia. He was too scared. Part of him hoped it would be easy to spot her. The fact that they hadn't found his sister among these prisoners filled him with a mixed sensation of relief and dread.

Julian and Kaison met up at another intersection. On their right was a path that led directly back to the entrance. The prison was a circle with a pathway connecting either end.

"Any luck?" Julian asked.

"No," Kaison answered, his voice wavering. "Maybe we should..."

"Shhh!"

"What?" Kaison asked.

"Shhh!" Julian snapped his head left and right, as though he was expecting to find something. "Do you hear that?"

The faint blaring of an instrument could be heard coming from the upper levels.

"Is that a horn?" Kaison muttered.

Julian paused one more moment, listening carefully, before he whipped toward Kaison.

"They're sounding an alarm." His words tumbled out of his mouth quickly. "They know we're here!"

"How?"

"Come on!"

Julian sprinted toward the exit doors, and Kaison dashed after him. All he wanted was to escape this dungeon, but he couldn't leave without Theadosia. He wouldn't leave without her, and Julian and Emmett would have to help him if they wanted to be transported back to Sun Castle alive.

Kaison skidded to a halt.

"I came here for Theadosia, and I'm not leaving without her," Kaison stated. "She has to be here."

Julian stopped inches from the door and whipped around to face Kaison. "She's not here!" he said before turning back to the doors and pushing them.

The doors wouldn't open.

Distraught, Julian attempted to open the doors again. Then he tried pulling. Then he slammed his shoulder into the doors, but they simply rattled.

"It's blocked from the outside," Julian said.

Alarmed, Kaison ran forward and tried to open the doors himself. They didn't move. It was as though someone had forced an object between the two handles on the outside so that they couldn't escape.

Julian backed away from the door, but Kaison persisted, trying to barge through. He slammed his shoulder against the doors again and again.

"This was always his plan…" Julian muttered.

Kaison froze. "What?"

"He set us up!" Julian pointed toward the double doors in reference to Emmett.

Kaison was in disbelief. "No, he didn't."

"You're such an idiot," Julian yelled. "Don't you see? We're a distraction for the Shadows so he can kill Mortimer!"

"He said he was here to help us save Theadosia."

"She's not even here." Julian motioned to the jail around him. "Why do you think he sent us in here alone?"

Kaison was speechless.

"He's not planning to save your sister," Julian said.

All of the sudden, the double doors banged open. Before them stood a dozen Shadows. They held their weapons in hand, and black smoke billowed off their figures. They prepared to charge.

Julian and Kaison shouted in unison:

"Run!"

- 52 -

Kaison

Julian and Kaison tore down the hall, and the Shadows sprinted after them.

Julian withdrew a throwing knife from the belt around his thigh. He stopped for merely a second to throw it behind him at one of the men. His aim was perfect, and he hit a guard right in the throat.

"This way!" Kaison shouted, turning to the left. Kaison remembered the staircase leading to an upper level.

Kaison's heart pounded in his chest. There were too many Shadows to take all at once. Julian had fired another throwing knife, nailing another Shadow, who consequently evaporated.

Kaison reached the staircase first and leapt onto the first step. He skipped stairs as he ascended, saving time. Julian was right on his trail, following his lead.

Kaison turned out of the stairwell onto the second level. He halted in his tracks when his surroundings came into view, and Julian crashed into his back.

They stood in a torture chamber. Guillotines, hatchets, flails, and knives hung on the left wall. On the right wall were shelves full of cages, which were packed with squealing rats. At the center of the room was a large table spread with gruesome stains. A large blade swung above the table.

Julian and Kaison snapped out of their stupor. Kaison sprinted toward a door at the opposite end of the torture chamber, and Julian took up the rear. Kaison maneuvered around the large wooden table and past a rack of axes.

The Shadows charged into the torture room. They let out fierce battle cries, and their loud boots thumped against the stone, making Kaison clench in fear.

Julian pulled out another throwing knife and fired it at one of the many Shadows behind them. It hit the Shadow in front of the group. Then another Shadow came at Julian with a sword in hand, but Julian dodged by rolling on the ground. A third Shadow just behind prepared to strike a death blow to Julian's face.

Kaison charged forward, withdrawing his halberd and pressing down on the red gemstone. In a flash, the staff extended and the blades formed in a flutter of gold. Before Kaison could even come to Julian's rescue, Julian had thrown the Shadow off him and knocked the oncoming knight in the knees. Julian scrambled to his feet and sliced off the attacker's head.

Kaison reached Julian's side, but they were now surrounded. The Shadows slowed their attack as they encircled Kaison and Julian from all sides. They stepped mechanically, closing in their circle and cutting off the boys' escape routes.

Then the Shadows rushed inward.

Julian reacted first and impaled an oncoming Shadow while Kaison struck another attacker, who easily blocked. Kaison retaliated, sending the Shadow's sword flying. The Shadow pummeled into Kaison, forcing Kaison to lean backward onto the giant wooden table in the center. Kaison felt his chest tighten under the Shadow's heavy weight.

Kaison was distracted for a second, seeing the sharp, hanging saws on the ceiling. The Shadow latched onto his neck, bringing him back to his senses, and Kaison rolled over, throwing him off the platform. The Shadow stumbled into a guillotine, and the blade came down on him.

Kaison barely had time to breathe, for another Shadow attacked from the right. Kaison barely dodged in time. Kaison attacked recklessly, but the Shadow blocked with force. The halberd slipped from his sweaty palms and spun across the room.

Seeing his halberd fly from his grasp, Kaison's heart plummeted into his stomach. Before Kaison had the chance to react, a dagger went straight through the attacker's chest. The Shadow disappeared in a flurry of black smoke, and the dagger fell to the ground. Kaison turned around and acknowledged Julian, who had thrown the dagger at the Shadow for him.

Another Shadow charged, and Kaison quickly grabbed a flail off a nearby table and chucked it at the oncoming attacker. Kaison was once again by Julian's side. They were back to back facing the remaining Shadow knights.

Julian kicked a rack of axes, and it fell onto two nearby attackers. Kaison dodged an oncoming sword and kicked a Shadow in the stomach, sending him backward into Julian's blade. Then Julian threw another knife from the belt around his thigh while slashing his sword, taking out two knights at once. Another warrior came toward Kaison, but Julian had already hurled an iron claw in his direction.

The warriors around them were disappearing rapidly into the

air. Julian swerved around the blade of one of the warriors before kicking a Shadow in the knee. As the Shadow took the time to fall, Julian chucked a knife at the warrior behind him, then drove his sword into the Shadow on the ground.

Julian and Kaison both saw the last Shadow, coming toward them from the opposite side of the room. Julian and Kaison simply exchanged a glance. Julian grabbed a pronged device off a nearby table and chucked it across the room. It hit the guard perfectly on his forehead and he fragmented into black smoke. The device clanked to the ground with an unpleasant noise.

Julian and Kaison both stood silent for a moment, panting and waiting for more men to appear. Yet, no other Shadows came.

Julian looked at Kaison, his face red. At first he looked angry, his eyes narrow, but then he laughed.

"We should do that again sometime," Julian said. He fixed his shoulder pad.

Kaison was speechless.

Julian scoffed. "Take a joke." He groaned before beginning to retrieve his throwing knives.

A smile crept across Kaison's face. His halberd was lying on the ground near the wooden table. Panting, he went over to pick it up. Julian stood on the other side of the room, sliding throwing knives into the belt around his thigh.

"Watch your head," he called.

Kaison picked up the halberd and ducked under the blades hanging from the ceiling, which had swung out to the side. Kaison warily stepped away and went over to Julian.

"I know you probably want to get out of here," Kaison said. "You can go, but I need to find my sister."

Julian scowled. "I didn't fight off half this castle for nothing."

This time, a wide smile appeared on Kaison's face. He gestured at the door. "After you," he said. Whatever lay beyond, Julian was more than capable to handle.

The boys made their way through the remaining torture devices, weaving around weapons and contraptions. Julian reached the exit door first, but stopped when he touched the handle.

Julian spoke, "I don't blame you."

Kaison tilted his head in confusion. "What do you mean?"

"Cheyenne," Julian said. He paused for a moment, and his voice lowered. "I don't blame you for her death. The Shadow of Eclipse killed her."

Kaison's face was blank.

"Thank you," Kaison answered.

Julian opened the door.

When they exited the chamber, they found themselves in a dark corridor. This corridor was made of plain stone, and thankfully was not as ominous as the dungeon below. The duo remained quiet as they stepped into the hall and shut the door behind them. Both Julian and Kaison looked down the corridor both ways, contemplating where to start. Julian seemed determined to go one direction, and Kaison followed.

The frigid air from outside seeped through the cracks in the stone. There were barely any torches lit to warm the eerie halls. The doors lining the hallways were closed, and no light pooled underneath them. The vast, abandoned hallways continued, one after the other. Kaison and Julian turned down new pathways, hoping to move toward the center of the castle. It was likely the structure hosted a throne room or central staircase leading to the floors above.

Julian turned another corner, but immediately backtracked, crashing into Kaison.

"Patrol," Julian said under his breath. He sprinted to the closest door on his right. "Come on," he gestured.

Julian opened the door and snuck into the next room to hide from the patrol. Kaison was quick to follow, entering the room and closing the door behind them.

"Who are you?"

A young voice alerted the two. A small girl was sitting on the edge of a bed. They had entered a bedroom. The walls were painted purple, and a toy chest rested at the bottom of the bed. Easels and blank canvases filled up the empty space.

The girl who had spoken sat criss-crossed on the edge of the bed. She was maybe fourteen years old, give or take. Her raven hair was pulled into a ponytail, and her amber eyes scrutinized the intruders.

Julian and Kaison didn't know how to respond.

"Dad doesn't like strangers," the girl continued. She swung her legs off the bed and stood up. She wasn't wearing a dress, but rather black trousers and an oversized shirt. "So, before I scream and get you both in trouble," she crossed her arms, "I repeat, who are you?"

"Julian," he was the first to answer. "This is Kaison."

"I'm here to find my sister," said Kaison. He let his halberd return to the staff form before latching it to his belt.

The girl took a few steps closer. "Nice to meet you," she said. Then added, "I'm Zamara."

Kaison put his hand on Julian's shoulder. "We need to go," he said under his breath.

Julian shrugged, brushing Kaison's hand away. "Can you tell us where we may find your father?"

"Sure," Zamara responded. She shifted her stance. "You have to take me with you."

Julian exchanged a glance with Kaison. Immediately, Kaison

shook his head. They were not going to take the Shadow of Eclipse's daughter with them.

"She's a child," Julian objected, his voice low. Then he turned back to the young girl. "Take us there."

"You promise to take me with you?" Zamara insisted. "Out of this castle?"

"I promise," Julian replied.

"Good," she smirked, "but…we're locked in."

Julian's jaw clenched.

Kaison returned to the door and tried to turn the handle. Sure enough, it was locked. "Why does your father lock you inside your room?" he questioned.

Zamara flipped her hair out of her eyes and gave an exaggerated pout. "I don't know. I've never done anything wrong." She spoke in a high-pitched tone, as if she were lying.

Kaison hesitated. He didn't want to help her and go astray from their mission. Every moment they continued talking was another moment Theadosia was alone with the Shadow of Eclipse. They were not going to take this girl with them.

"Fine," said Julian. He was getting done with the shenanigans. "Take us to your father, and we'll help you get out." He took a step away from the door before bracing himself. In one swift motion, he kicked the door, forcing the lock to break and the door to swing open. He turned to Zamara before gesturing her over. "Lead the way," he said.

A peculiar smile crossed Zamara's face. She sized up Julian before finally starting for the door, but she suddenly froze. "That's pretty," she said, touching Kaison's chest.

Kaison remained still as she moved her hand and grasped the pendant, but Zamara instantly pulled her hand away.

"Ouch," she said. A purple hue burned at her fingertips. She stared at Kaison, neither one of them breaking the gaze, unable to explain what happened.

Zamara led the boys out into the corridor. She walked with her chin up in the air and her arms swinging at her sides. "This way."

Kaison's stomach flipped. The bedroom door was easy to break open, yet Zamara had claimed to be locked inside. Something was off. A spine-chilling feeling rippled through his body. He didn't trust anyone that was related to the Shadow of Eclipse.

Zamara led them through the maze. They backtracked their steps and then entered through a passageway that was hidden by a curtain. They turned two more corners and then stopped at the end of an adjacent hallway. She clasped her hands behind her back and pointed to a wooden door. "Right through here."

"Thank you," Julian said before opening the door.

Both Kaison and Julian were surprised by a blinding light that poured through from the other side. Julian covered his face with one hand, squinted his eyes, and proceeded into the room. Kaison followed him, trying to adjust his eyes to the light.

On the other side, Julian grabbed Kaison's shirt and pulled him around a column. Julian covered his mouth with one finger, silently telling Kaison to remain quiet. Keeping their mouths shut, both Julian and Kaison peered around the corner of the large column.

They were in the entranceway to the castle. It was well lit with candles and chandeliers. The walls and floor were black, and a purple throne sat on a platform. They had entered behind the jagged throne, which was decorated with objects that Kaison would never dare to describe. The large doors leading outside to the courtyard were at the far end of the room, all the way at the other end of a long runner.

Kaison's attention was drawn to one particular scene.

Mortimer stood before the throne on the platform. His back was to the column where Kaison and Julian were hiding. A mist of black smoke followed his boots.

The Shadow of Eclipse. The man that killed his parents.

- 53 -

Kaison

Emmett stood in front of Mortimer, his scarred face flushed and his long sword scraping against the floor. Directly between the two brothers was a small figure. Theadosia was on her knees with her head hanging down. She looked completely broken. Right next to her hand was a blue journal.

Maeve's diamond journal.

Kaison wanted to race forward and rescue Theadosia, but Julian held his arm out to stop him.

"...And yet you come to me bearing no halberd!" Mortimer shouted at Emmett. They were in the middle of a heated argument.

"You went back on our agreement!" Emmett roared.

"I gave you plenty of time to fulfill our agreement," Mortimer responded. His voice boomed through the room, making the ground shake. "When I realized you wouldn't come through, I took matters into my own hands."

Emmett's face was bright red. Then Emmett noticed Zamara

in the doorway where they had just entered. She was watching the scene as though it was her usual entertainment.

Kaison reached out and grabbed Zamara's arm, pulling her behind the column and concealing her from sight.

"Ow," Zamara said under her breath, wrenching her hand from Kaison's grasp.

"Do you want us to get you out of here?"

"Yes."

"Then stay close to me," Kaison ordered.

The yelling continued to echo through the grand hall.

"You killed Seraphina!"

"I did?" Mortimer objected. "I think you have that backward, brother."

Emmett took a step forward. "I would never kill my own daughter!"

Kaison kept quiet behind the column. He knew Seraphina was alive. Maeve said so.

Mortimer continued, "It doesn't matter who killed her. Regardless, I had no need for her anymore, since you didn't get me what I asked for. Face it, brother, you lost her the night she was a baby, just like you lost your wife. At least they'll be together now–"

Upon hearing Mortimer's words, Emmett withdrew his sword. He charged, but the Shadow of Eclipse thrust his hand forward. With one forceful, telekinetic blow, Emmett was shoved backward, landing yards away and skidding on the marble floor.

Kaison grew more alarmed. "We need to get Theadosia and get out of here," he whispered.

Julian nodded in response before peeking around the column once more. Theadosia was on the ground, but her head was down so there was no way Kaison could get her attention from where they were standing. They were close to the throne, so Kaison could make his way closer.

Mortimer stepped down the stairs. He began crossing the room, moving away from the throne and walking across the carpet. He sauntered toward his brother, who was lying directly in the center of the floor. When Mortimer reached the center of the room, he stopped. His back was to Theadosia and the throne.

"We want the same thing, brother," Mortimer called out. "Let us work together."

Emmett groaned, rolling over onto his side. He struggled to a standing position, wielding his sword in both hands. "I'm done working with you!"

Emmett attacked again, and Mortimer repeated the same action, throwing him across the room. He landed harder this time, his armor clamoring on the ground.

Kaison bolted to the next column on the outskirts of the room. Theadosia was in reach now.

Theadosia looked up, and her eyes met Kaison's. They softened in relief.

Kaison prepared himself. He was going to run out to Theadosia and get her out of here. As soon as he had braced himself, Mortimer turned around. Mortimer walked up to Theadosia and paused a few paces away. Then he knelt down in front of her. He snarled in her face and forcefully grabbed her chin. Then he pulled her head toward him.

"I'm sorry, girl, it looks like your brother doesn't care about you," Mortimer said. A soft purple glow started dancing at his fingertips.

Theadosia's brow furrowed. "He's already here." She reached out, extending the hidden dagger from her wrist. The hidden blade impaled Mortimer directly through the chest.

Kaison raced out from behind the column. He withdrew the halberd from his belt in one swift motion. Swiping his thumb against the red gem, the staff extended to its full glory. Sparkling gold twinkled down from the blade, coating the ground in dust. He charged toward Mortimer, raising his weapon in the air.

Mortimer stumbled back, holding his chest right where a pool of blood was forming. In one swift motion, Mortimer extended his hand toward Kaison out of instinct. A purple bolt flew in Kaison's direction, but was met with an intense flash of red light. The heat from the pendant flooded through Kaison's chest, and the blinding light caused him to shut his eyes tightly for a quick moment, but he didn't stop charging. Kaison raised his halberd in the air, swooping toward Mortimer with one grave blow.

Mortimer dodged, and the halberd crashed against the ground.

Kaison shouted. "This is what you want, isn't it?" He gripped the weapon stronger.

Mortimer examined his palm. It was laced with a scarlet burn mark, and steam rose from his fingertips. His other hand was clamped firmly to his chest, trying to contain the crimson liquid. A trickle of blood oozed from Mortimer's mouth and down his chin.

"Give me the halberd," Mortimer said. His eyes were crazy.

Theadosia struggled to her feet, limping to stand beside her brother and face their parent's killer.

Kaison shook his head. "There's nothing you can do now that I have the Crimson Teardrop."

Mortimer's eyebrow rose. "Oh, you're so naive."

He extended his hands on either side of him, summoning the Shadows. Directly behind him, a dozen warriors rose from the ground, forming from thin air. Black dust congealed into armed soldiers, readied with weapons.

Kaison's heart plummeted in his chest.

Mortimer lifted his chin slightly, and the Shadows attacked.

Out of instinct, Kaison blocked the first weapon swung in his direction. Theadosia lunged forward, the hidden blade from her wrist extending into the center of the warrior's chest. A throwing knife flew across the room, impaling another Shadow, and Julian charged forward to join the fight.

Kaison turned to see another warrior coming directly toward Theadosia. He screamed, but she didn't turn around in time. Kaison leapt forward. Before he could reach the oncoming warrior, a giant sword swung and decapitated the Shadow, disintegrating him.

Sir Emmett.

Emmett lunged again, his long sword swooping and slaying two Shadows simultaneously.

Julian was on Kaison's other side, his sword in hand as he fought back the onslaught.

Mortimer watched them. He stood peacefully at the center of the chaos, and the blood dripped down the front of his body.

The Shadows kept coming. Kaison couldn't fight them.

He saw the diamond journal on the ground and dove for it. He scooped it up in his grasp before locking weapons with another Shadow.

Theadosia was already limping out the front door. Julian was in front of her, defending her.

"Mortimer!" Emmett's voice could be heard screaming over the clanking of metal.

Mortimer's eyes were filled with rage. He took a step back, summoning more of the Shadows around him.

There were too many.

Kaison saw the silver blade of a sword coming out of his peripheral vision. He couldn't block in time.

To his relief, the Shadow was flung across the room with a telekinetic force.

Kaison turned over his shoulder, seeing Zamara – Mortimer's daughter – with her hand outstretched toward the Shadow. Her amber eyes twinkled with delight, and a smirk plastered across her face.

She had the Eclipse magic too.

"Run!" Kaison yelled to his friends. He handed Theadosia the diamond journal, who grabbed it hastily, before he put his arm around Theadosia's back. Helping her, they raced toward the exit.

Zamara ran ahead of them, and Julian stayed behind, fending off any Shadows that followed.

Sir Emmett was in the middle of a crowd of Shadows, slaying every single one and advancing closer to his brother.

"Zamara!" Mortimer's voice boomed over the clashing of iron.

Kaison supported Theadosia's weight, and she leaned against him. She was hardly able to put pressure on her right leg.

Julian was the first to reach the exit and yanked the handle. He pulled open the front door, revealing the outside courtyard.

For a brief moment, Kaison hesitated in the doorway, turning around to take another look at Mortimer. He met Mortimer's gaze in the distance, over the Shadows that were fighting Emmett. This wasn't over. Kaison would be back to kill him once and for all.

Two more Shadows appeared out of thin air, directly in front of Kaison.

"Come on!" Theadosia screamed, yanking his shirt.

Not wasting a second longer, Kaison turned on his heel and fled. The frosty air outside choked him. A flurry of snow poured down from the sky. Up ahead, Zamara charged across the courtyard, with Julian flanking her.

Kaison and Theadosia dashed after the others, running toward the iron gate that was far across the courtyard. It was a jousting field away from them. He felt his sister struggle to put any weight on her right leg. She let out a shriek of pain as they picked up speed, but she pushed herself to run faster. She still clutched the Ademantum to her chest.

When they were halfway across the courtyard, a horn was blown somewhere on the premises. Kaison had no idea where it came from. An ear-piercing screech followed.

Kaison snapped around. On either side of the front doors were two iron gates. They were closed but slowly lifting. Behind them were Shadow warriors, holding various weapons, preparing to charge out of the gates and attack the intruders. It was an overwhelming number of soldiers.

There was no way Kaison and Julian could take all of them.

"Keep going!" Julian shouted. He turned in the opposite direction and returned to the sibling's side.

Kaison stood frozen, staring at the iron gates that were slowly lifting.

"I'll hold them off," Julian said. He withdrew his sword from his belt, stepping between Kaison and the iron gates in the distance. "Now run!"

"Are you crazy?" Kaison asked Julian.

Zamara was a far distance in front of them, sprinting toward the exit. "Don't die, you promised to take me with you!" she called over her shoulder.

Kaison grasped the halberd in both hands, bracing for an attack. "Theadosia, go. Can you run?"

"I'm not leaving you," she said.

Julian was slowly backing away from the gates, attempting to create as much space as possible between him and the onslaught of warriors. He stayed close to Kaison in the event that they could make a run for it.

More Shadows appeared from behind. They scaled down from the watchtowers at the front of the castle courtyard. They stood in front of Zamara and withdrew their weapons, blocking the main entrance and the pathway across the bridge. They stood blocking their only escape route.

Then the iron gates completely lifted, and with a battle cry, the slew of Shadow warriors charged out of the castle. Warriors rushed them from all sides, and there was nowhere to run.

The group was surrounded. Julian grasped his sword tightly in his hands, his mind frantically strategizing as more and more Shadows came straight at their group. Theodosia was limping backward, closing the distance between her and Zamara. Kaison's mind was clouded by the battle cries, and his arms shook as he attempted to hold the halberd.

Kaison couldn't transport them out of this situation. They were standing on solid stone, and the willow tree only grew out of the earth. Nevertheless, he tried to picture Sun Castle, but the willow tree didn't emerge, no matter how hard he concentrated.

The Shadows reached them.

Julian started to fight. He threw a knife at the first warrior before blocking the next attack, going down in a brave fashion.

To all of their surprise, a black doorway began to manifest out of thin air. A swirling portal appeared, and a girl stepped out of it. Her cape lapped in the wind, and her black hair blew across her face. She turned to look at the oncoming knights on Julian's side. She outstretched her hand, and a wave of purple magic shot forward.

The wave hurled into the front rows of soldiers, throwing them back and causing every single one to vanish into thin air. With one wave of magic, dozens of soldiers were killed.

The girl then turned to the exit. Using both hands, she shot her arms forward. A thunderous noise clapped as a purple bolt flew from her palms. Every soldier that was between Kaison and the exit was incinerated, leaving Theadosia and Zamara unscathed.

Hardly out of breath, the girl locked eyes with Kaison.

It was Seraphina.

Kaison stared back at her helplessly.

The portal still swirled behind her, fluttering her cape. "Zamara, come," she said, gesturing to the young girl.

Zamara didn't move.

Seraphina snapped her fingers before extending her palm once more. "Come."

Obeying the second time, Zamara walked forward, taking Seraphina's hand.

Julian was awe-struck. "What was that?" he asked, holding his sword in his hands.

Seraphina nodded her head in the direction of the castle exit. "You better go while you have the chance," she said.

With that, she took Zamara and pulled her through the portal. Zamara took one last look over her shoulder at Kaison, her amber eyes glistening, before disappearing into the darkness. The gateway swirled in a black mass before evaporating.

They were gone.

The pathway to the exit was clear, but they could still hear the clanging of swords inside the castle. Kaison retracted his halberd once more before coming back to Theadosia's aid. Then they started for the exit. Julian raced after the siblings, not questioning the magic he had witnessed.

So, it was true. Seraphina was alive. She saved their lives.

- 54 -

Kaison

Kaison, Theadosia, and Julian crossed the deadly bridge, this time venturing straight across it. When they reached the other side, they hiked up the hill, pushing away the pine trees and stepping into the clearing. As they walked, Theadosia leaned up against Kaison, limping.

"What did Mortimer do to you?" Julian asked. He replaced his sword in its sheath.

Theadosia shuddered. She took a moment to stop her head from spinning before she replied. "He…" she gripped the book tighter in her hands, remembering.

"We can talk about this when we're safely away from the castle," Kaison intervened.

"Here." Theadosia handed the diamond journal to Kaison. "I don't want anything to do with this anymore."

Julian was peering through the bushes at the castle in the distance. "They're sending more Shadows after us," he said. "We need to go now."

Kaison withdrew his halberd. He pointed it in front of him, imagining the castle. They were now over solid earth. Instantly, the trees began to move in front of his eyes. In a glistening golden sparkle, the willow tree grew. The branches hung low, creating a curtain of magic. Without another moment's hesitation, Kaison moved forward under the tree.

Kaison emerged on the other side, readjusting his eyes after being exposed to the blinding light. They were standing right before the castle gates. It was very early in the morning, but it was still dark. They had been out all night.

Once he was aware of Theadosia and Julian behind him, Kaison pressed on the red gem and tied the halberd back to his belt. The willow tree shrunk back into the ground.

Julian shrugged. "I still don't know how that's possible."

"Magic." Theadosia smiled softly.

The three quickened their pace and walked forward toward Sun Castle. Theadosia pushed through the pain and stood away from Kaison to walk on her own. The throbbing spasms were reflected in her facial expression, but she didn't complain.

When they reached the iron gate, they noted that four knights were standing guard. Upon the sight of the intruders, the knights' hands flew to their swords.

"Halt!" One of the guards exclaimed.

Julian recognized the knights. "We're returning from the Lost Lands," he said.

"We know," one of them answered. "You've been instructed to come with us."

"First my sister needs an infirmary," said Kaison.

"No. You must come with us."

"Why?" asked Julian.

"We're following orders."

Kaison didn't want to argue. He offered his arm out toward Theadosia, but she brushed him aside. In his other hand, he maintained a hold of the diamond journal.

The three waited for the knights to raise the gate, and they all stepped onto the grounds. They entered the pink garden, now red and reeking of death. All around them, knights were lining up the dead bodies from the ball. A group of villagers were gathering together, handing out shovels before heading out on the moor.

The sight troubled Kaison. He had witnessed dreadful events, but seeing the once pristine castle gardens in a desolate state, full of mourning villagers, hurt him more than anything. In Grovia, he had never witnessed the aftermath and the grieving. He had escaped everything and left it behind. Now, he would have to try and help pick up the pieces. A pang of guilt fluttered through him, for he regretted not staying in Grovia longer to search for survivors.

The four knights around them had maneuvered into a diamond shape. There was one knight at each point, surrounding the three as they entered the grand hall.

They crossed the mosaic on the floor of the grand hall. Instead of going up the stairs, the knights led them all down a corridor. They were traveling a long distance, and Theadosia was now struggling to keep up with their pace, which seemed to grow brisker. She held her stomach as she limped along.

Julian countered, changing to the other side of Kaison as he walked. He spoke under his breath. "Something's wrong."

Kaison kept his gaze forward as to not draw attention. "What?"

Julian hesitated, unsure how to respond.

Then the knight in the lead turned down an adjacent hallway.

Julian stopped dead in his tracks. "Why are you taking us this way?"

Kaison had no idea where they were. He had never been to this part of the castle. However, the alarmed tone in Julian's voice jolted him into action.

"Grab them," the knight at the front commanded the three others, who obeyed immediately.

"Stop!" Kaison screamed. He went to attack the man holding Theadosia, but he was pulled away. Theadosia was wrenched from his grasp. The knight yanked both of Kaison's arms behind him, and the diamond journal fell to the ground.

"Don't struggle, and she will be fine," the knight said. He reached down to pick up the diamond journal from the ground.

Kaison obeyed when he saw Theadosia stumble. The knight that was holding her practically held her up. She didn't even try to struggle in his arms.

Julian didn't back down. He pulled out of a knight's arms and swung at him, clobbering him against the jaw. The fourth knight grabbed Julian and slammed him against the wall, face first, clamping his arm down behind his back.

"Don't fight us!" the knight shouted in Julian's ear.

Julian huffed, wriggling underneath the knight's grasp. Soon, the knight that had punched Julian composed himself and pushed Julian further into the wall, slamming his face once more into the stone. With two knights on Julian, and one on both Kaison and Theadosia, they were hopeless to escape. Furiously, the knights pulled them into the next room.

They were forced down a flight of stairs into the dungeon. To their right and left, was a row of jail cells. Most of them were empty. However, one of the jail cells held a tall, lean figure.

It was Simon!

Simon was trapped inside the cell. His hands were tied in front of him, and he sprawled on the ground. When Simon saw the others approaching, he scrambled to his feet.

"Kaison! Don't let them take you. You have to get out of here!" Simon called.

The knight holding Kaison opened an empty jail cell before shoving Kaison inside. The knight kept the diamond journal in his hands. Kaison didn't fight him, hoping that they would take care of Theadosia as promised. The following knight pushed Theadosia inside, and she slammed into Kaison's chest.

"I will not be put in jail!" Julian shouted. He threw his head back, head-butting one of the two knights that was holding him. The knight released him enough so that Julian could free his one arm. Then Julian clobbered the other knight.

Now free, Julian went after the two other guards. He slammed one against the jail cell, who was instantly knocked unconscious. The next guard came after Julian, but Julian ducked. He rammed his shoulder into the knight's stomach, throwing him over his shoulder. The knight landed on his back on the ground with a loud thud. Julian braced himself for the next guard when a loud voice rang throughout the dungeon.

"Silence!"

Julian froze.

Queen Benedict stood at the end of the hallway, her expression fierce.

"Your Majesty," Julian stammered, composing himself.

The queen's crown rested on her head elegantly, but her stance was aggressive. Before her, she held Maeve. Maeve's arms were tied behind her back, and the queen tightly held her forearm. A gag ran across Maeve's mouth, preventing her from crying out.

"Let her go!" Kaison said, running to the doorway of the jail cell.

Simon pushed himself to his feet and ran to the iron bars that separated him from everyone else.

Maeve met Kaison's gaze. Her red hair was frayed in many directions, but her face was still visible. Her blue eyes were filled with fear and tears welled at the corners.

"Where's the journal?" Queen Benedict asked.

One of the knights sluggishly got up from the ground. He extended his arm forward, displaying the diamond journal.

"Thank you," the queen said, taking the journal from the knight. A crooked expression appeared on the queen's face. She flipped the book over in her hands, examining it. "Put him inside," she ordered.

The three knights that were standing all grabbed Julian at the same time. They shoved him inside the jail cell, knocking Kaison back in the process. Then they grabbed the cell door and slammed it shut.

Both Kaison and Julian ran to the bars and grabbed on. They were in the cell opposite Simon, along with Theadosia. Theadosia leaned up against the wall at the back of the jail cell, unable to fight. In the space between them, the queen was holding Maeve.

"That journal doesn't belong to you," Kaison shouted. "You're going to get us all killed!"

"And you can't throw us in jail for no reason," Julian added.

The queen looked at the unconscious knight on the ground. "Take him and leave us," she ordered.

The three knights did what they were told. They picked up their friend and carried him away, leaving the queen alone with the rest.

Then the queen kicked Maeve in the back of the knee, forcing her to fall to the ground.

"Don't hurt her!" Simon shouted, his face burning into the queen's. He must have been in the jail cell all night.

Queen Benedict shot Simon an annoyed glare. Then she looked down at Maeve on her knees. "Now, are you going to cooperate?"

Maeve emitted soft sobs from the ground, her chest heaving up and down. Her attention remained on the floor in front of her.

Queen Benedict dropped the book in front of Maeve. It landed with a thud on the concrete floor. She then withdrew a quill from the pocket of her dress and let it fall beside the book.

Then Queen Benedict turned to the jail cell. She walked forward until she was inches from Kaison's face. The iron bars still separated them. She pulled out the keys to the cell from the pocket of her dress. "I will let you out," she said, "if you cooperate."

"What do you want?" Kaison's expression hardened.

"That's the spirit." Benedict smiled. She replaced the key in the pocket of her dress. "Now, give me your halberd."

Kaison glowered at the queen. He was the designated protector. He was supposed to protect the halberd with his life, exactly how his father had done. His father had died trying to keep evil forces away from the objects and the door. There was no way he was going to hand the halberd to the queen.

Maeve shook her head, trying to say something, but the gag in her mouth made whatever she was saying inaudible.

"If you don't give me your halberd," the queen said, "I will order every one of your deaths." She paused, taking a step over until she could see Theadosia. "Starting with her." She pointed at Kaison's sister.

"You won't touch her," Kaison said.

The queen sneered. "Try me," she said.

"You'll have to go through us first, then," Julian stated. He took a step to the side, standing directly in the sightline the queen had to Theadosia.

"Fine," the queen said. "Then I'll start with Simon over here." She turned away from Kaison's cell and walked the narrow corridor to the jail opposite them. "Let's see if your friends care about you, Plague Boy."

Simon didn't answer. His bottomless eyes were dark.

"Guard!" the queen called.

Soon a knight responded to the queen's call and approached the cells.

"I want him executed," the queen stated, pointing at Simon's cell.

The knight nodded before pulling the master key off his belt and unlocking Simon's cell.

Maeve screamed, trying to say something again, but the gag prevented her.

"You can't kill him!" Kaison called, his sweaty palms grabbing the iron bars firmly. "He has nothing to do with this!"

The knight opened Simon's cell door.

Simon stepped away from the knight, but the guard grabbed him roughly by his tied arms and dragged him out.

"Stop!" Theadosia's voice rang out.

Maeve was screaming from behind the gag, and even Julian pounded on the iron bars, telling the queen how inhumane the execution was. But the words they shouted fell on deaf ears. The knight threw Simon down in the center of the aisle. Then the knight pulled his sword from his sheath, and it made an awful scraping noise as the blade extended. The knight used one foot to press down onto Simon's chest.

Everyone else in the room continued shouting as loud as they could until their throats hurt. Julian and Kaison yanked at the bars, shaking them so hard that the gate rattled.

Then the knight raised his sword high into the air. He looked to the Queen for final approval, and she nodded.

"Stop!" Kaison yelled, louder than everyone. He withdrew his halberd, untying it from the side of his belt and extending it through the iron bars. "Take it. Please, leave him alone!"

The queen put her hand up, and with one hand gesture, the guard froze in his tracks. He lowered his sword, but he kept his foot down on Simon's chest, moving it up to his neck.

Queen Benedict cautiously approached Kaison. "Good boy," she said. She took the transformed halberd out of his hands, holding the staff in her grasp. She ran her finger down the gemstones, examining the craftsmanship. "What a beautiful key," she whispered. She gently squatted and placed the staff on the ground beside Maeve and the book. "Now," she clasped her hands together once more. "I need you to write a little something for me."

Maeve didn't move, but her arms and body shook out of fear. She remained focused on the diamond journal and halberd before her.

"Don't try anything, or your friend will be killed," Benedict threatened. She reached around to Maeve's back and began to untie the ropes that held her hands together.

Kaison continued to watch Maeve. In his head, he was frantically running over one million potential plans. Thoughts shot in and out of his mind, but he couldn't see a way out of this – at least not where everyone survived. He stole a glance at his sister behind him, and she was still leaning up against the back wall. Then there was Julian, Maeve, and Simon. Maybe, if they could escape the cell, they all could take Benedict and the guard.

The Queen finished untying Maeve. The ropes fell down from

around Maeve's wrists. Maeve rubbed her wrists gently, before she took off her own gag.

"What do you want me to write?" Maeve asked. As she spoke, she focused on Kaison. Her eyebrows raised, as if she was trying to silently communicate.

Benedict stood up from the ground, hovering over Maeve. "Pick up the quill," she ordered.

Maeve let out a sigh. Then she grasped the quill in her hands. She flipped open the journal to a clear page before adjusting the quill on the page.

"Now write, 'As the light diminishes–' "

Maeve sprung up from the ground. She shoved Benedict backward with all the strength that she had. Benedict stumbled and slammed against the bars directly in front of Kaison. Kaison reached his arm through the bars and wrapped it around Benedict's neck, pressing his forearm against her throat as he pulled her tighter against the bars.

"Get the key!" Kaison shouted.

The guard holding Simon released him and sprang forward to save the queen, but Simon intervened. He jumped up and using both his hands tied together as a weapon, clobbering the guard on the side of the head.

Queen Benedict pulled against Kaison's arm, trying to break out of the choke hold. She gasped for breath.

Maeve scrambled forward and reached into Benedict's pocket, pulling out the key. She lunged for the cell and started to unlock it. Julian was encouraging her to move faster.

The knight turned on Simon and hit him against the jaw. Simon lunged forward and pummeled the knight to the ground, but the knight easily rolled on top of Simon, holding him down. The sword had spun down the hallway.

"Faster!" Kaison shouted at Maeve.

"I'm trying!" Maeve yelled.

The queen scratched at Kaison's metal armor furiously, her strength wearing thin.

"Maeve!" Julian screamed.

"I'm trying!"

A loud click alerted everyone that Maeve had unlocked the cell. She opened the door wide, and Julian was the first one out. He threw the knight off of Simon, clobbering him in the head with his foot and knocking him unconscious.

Kaison continued to hold the queen. He needed his friends to be safe first. "Run!" he shouted.

Maeve turned to pick up the book but stopped.

"Kaison," she said, her voice filled with dread.

Julian reached out a hand to help Simon up from the ground, but he too looked horrified.

Theadosia covered her mouth with her hands.

Then Kaison realized. The queen had stopped moving. Her head and arms were limp, and she was only being held up by Kaison's forearm.

Kaison released his grasp, and the queen collapsed onto the dungeon floor. "I didn't…I…" Kaison struggled for words. He exited the jail cell and rounded to the other side. He dropped to the ground beside the queen and pressed his hand to her neck, feeling for a pulse.

The queen was dead.

Kaison rose from the ground and turned to face everyone. They were all too terrified to move.

Finally, Theadosia touched Kaison, her hand trembling.

"You killed the queen," Maeve muttered.

Kaison was frozen.

"She wasn't the true queen," mused Julian.

"What do you mean?" Theadosia asked.

Julian cleared his throat. "Maeve's the true queen. The journal chose her."

"How do you know that?" Maeve asked.

Julian frowned. He began untying the ropes that bound Simon's hands together. "I'm not an idiot," he said. "Though I may disagree with the book's choice," he shot Maeve a glare, "the light lineage must be restored." The ropes fell from Simon's hands, freeing him.

"I didn't know you believed in the prophecy," Simon said.

Julian shrugged. "I didn't, but Pandora is convincing."

Maeve's face flushed. She picked up the diamond journal from the ground. "I never asked for this."

Kaison reached down and picked up the halberd. "And I didn't ask for this," he said.

"Designated protector," Theadosia muttered, staring at her brother.

The five felt a brief moment of relief. Theadosia was safe from Mortimer. The queen was dead, and Maeve and Simon had also been rescued.

Suddenly a horn sounded in the distance. All of them jumped at the noise. The blaring sound sent a chill down Kaison's spine.

"We're under attack again," Julian said. He was the first to start charging out of the dungeon.

Kaison, Theadosia, Maeve, and Simon raced after him. They burst out of the dungeon, coming into contact with torch light. The events at the ball and their journey to the Lost Lands had taken all night, and now the torches had been lit for the morning. All five sprinted down the corridor, retracing their steps exactly the way they came, and froze once they entered the Grand Hall.

A mass of people faced the doorway, watching something on the moor. The windows had broken in the battle earlier, and an aggressive wind blew through the open frames.

When the five entered the space, Kaison covered his face, trying to keep his eyes open against the wind. The air pushed against his chest and caused his hair and shirt to blow. He felt as if he was fighting back the force of an ocean wave. Kaison pushed his body forward into the gust in order to get a better look outside.

The sky was black. The morning sun was covered in darkness. Leaves and flowers swirled in from the garden, creating mini tornados, and black fog rolled along the ground. The moon was consuming the sun, and an eclipse was forming in the sky.

The Shadow of Eclipse.

Simon, Maeve, Theadosia, and Julian struggled to stand beside Kaison.

"By plague…" Maeve said.

"What is that?" Theadosia asked.

Kaison's jaw dropped in astonishment. In the far distance, an army of knights in black were racing out of the forest on horses. Black smoke lapped around the horses' hooves, and although they were on the horizon, Kaison could hear their battle cries. It was the Shadow Army in its terrifying glory.

"They've come back for the book and Maeve," Julian said.

Kaison whipped to face Maeve. "You have to go and hide."

"Hide?" Maeve was taken aback. "I don't think so."

"The Shadow of Eclipse will kill everyone in the castle until he finds you," Julian said. "He won't take the wrong girl this time."

"They're after the halberd too," Simon interjected. "We all saw what happened with the queen."

Kaison's body flushed and his heart beat anxiously. "Maybe we can stop them."

"Stop an army?" Theadosia asked.

"Can't I wish for the battle to stop?" Maeve pleaded.

"No," Simon said. "You know how dangerous that could be. You could kill everyone here. Including us."

Chaos was breaking out all around them. The nobles and knights that remained were grabbing swords and pieces of leftover armour from the ground. They were shouting out battle plans and rushing out into the gardens. Outside, at the wall, knights lined up cannons on the parapets.

"Go to Sun Spire," Kaison told Maeve. "We will do what we can to hold them off."

"I'll come with you," Theadosia said.

"Here." Julian unstrapped the belt filled with throwing knives from around his thigh. He came over to Theadosia and clipped it around her waist. "I have a feeling you're a fighter," he said.

A smile almost crept on Theodosia's face.

Simon moved closer to Theadosia. "Please be careful," he said, his eyes longing. Then he turned to Maeve. "Both of you."

Maeve rolled her eyes. "We're not fighting an army. We're hiding in Sun Spire."

Julian surveyed the moor. The Shadow Army was charging forward at top speed. They would reach the wall any minute. Julian spoke warily, "If we're fighting, we need to take defensive positions now."

Kaison's heart raced even faster. He pulled the transformed halberd off his belt and ran his thumb over the red gemstone.

"Kaison," Maeve said. Something was on the tip of her tongue, but she said, "Don't get yourself killed."

Kaison paused. "I'll try not to."

Theadosia grabbed Maeve's arm. "Come on," she said, taking one last glance at her brother.

Maeve clutched the diamond journal to her chest, and she took off with Theadosia, heading to Sun Spire. Theadosia limped along the way, struggling to keep up with Maeve.

Kaison watched them go until they completely disappeared into the crowd of frantic knights, nobles, and villagers. Then Julian nudged his shoulder, getting his attention.

"Are you with us?" Julian asked Kaison.

Simon cleared his throat and said matter-of-factly, "You're not a knight yet, so you don't have to go."

Kaison turned back to the moor. The army had reached the front gates of the castle. Shadows and Solaris knights clashed with one another. That wasn't all. Rain started pouring down from the black sky. A single lightning bolt flashed, penetrating the thick black fog. The battlefield and the Eclipse above had been drawn out of his worst nightmare.

Kaison pressed the red gemstone, and the halberd transformed. He said:

"We fight together."

- 55 -

Kaison

Kaison threw himself into the thick of the battle. Rain pounded down from above, immediately soaking them from head to toe. The trio had lost the opportunity to find defensive positions. The Shadows were already overrunning the line at the wall.

A mace flew inches from Kaison's nose, and hit the earth in front of him. The spikes indented the ground. Kaison bounced back out of shock and faced his opponent. Even though his opponent was a Shadow, he still appeared to be a man until death took him. Kaison took a few steps back to prepare for his attack while the Shadow picked up his mace and spun it.

Instead, the Shadow was sliced in half by Julian and evaporated into the air. With another spin, Julian continued to aggressively fight the attackers, never missing a single slash.

Kaison turned to the next Shadow. He was carrying a battle axe and shield. The shield was engraved with the Shadow of Eclipse symbol.

Kaison lunged forward, only to be shoved back by the shield. Kaison was forced to hang onto his halberd tightly so it didn't fly out of his hands when he lost his footing. The warrior prepared himself for another attack. Kaison ducked quickly as the battle axe flew over his head. The knight was impaled by a weapon, but it wasn't Kaison's weapon, it was Julian's. The knight dissipated into the black fog that surrounded them.

From behind Julian, a spear flew through the air.

"Look out!" Kaison screamed, grabbing Julian's shirt and throwing them both to the ground.

Right before the spear flew over their heads, it was derailed from its course in a flash of light. Kaison could see the trail it left in the fog.

From the soggy earth, Kaison looked up to see Pandora on the battlefield, her hands glowing with a white light. "Pandora!" Julian shouted. He scrambled to his feet, slipping on the wet ground. "You're going to get yourself killed!"

On Julian's right, another Shadow was approaching. With one swift move of her hand, Pandora placed a glowing barricade between Julian and the Shadow's incoming sword. The Shadow bounced off the magical shield, falling back onto the ground.

Julian's face melted in shock.

Pandora flashed Julian a smile and let the magical field disappear. Julian leapt forward and killed the Shadow with one swift blow.

Kaison sprung to his feet and locked weapons with another enemy. The blow came too strong. Kaison's halberd was knocked straight out of his hands and slid across the mud. Kaison stared back at his opponent, and his mouth dropped open, but the warrior didn't hesitate. Kaison ducked before the sword would have cut off his neck. Kaison tried to look for his halberd through the curtain of rain while keeping his eyes on his opponent. It was only a few paces away in the distance.

Before the warrior tried to kill him again, Kaison dove for his halberd. His stomach skidded on the muddy ground, and Kaison grabbed his weapon. Kaison flipped over onto his back to brace himself for the oncoming attack. Yet when Kaison turned over, all that was before him was a multitude of black particles evaporating into the air.

Simon was standing behind where the soldier used to be, and Kaison knew he had been saved. Simon reached down to help him up, and Kaison struggled to get to his feet even with Simon's assistance. Their hands were slippery from the mud and rain.

All of the sudden, Simon was struck by an arrow on his right shoulder. A screech escaped Simon's lips and he held his shoulder in pain, the arrow still protruding from him.

Kaison turned in the direction of the arrow to see a Shadow loading up his bow once more. He fired again, but the harsh wind sent it into the soldier behind Kaison. As he was loading his next arrow, a spear went straight through the Shadow's head. Kaison wasn't about to question or thank who killed the Shadow for them.

Kaison spun around, expecting to see Simon, but he was gone. Kaison's heart plummeted in his chest. He scanned the clearing outside the castle doors and saw Simon lying on his back, struggling to hold up his sword and protect himself from a Shadow. Kaison raced over, terminating the Shadow by slicing through him with his halberd. Consequently, the warrior evaporated into the air

Kaison went to help Simon up but was confronted by a horrible sight. The knight had struck Simon's right arm above the elbow, grazing down his entire forearm. Blood was gushing from the open wound, and the bone was almost visible. Kaison couldn't mistake the exhaustion and intense anguish that was written all over Simon's face.

"Behind you!" Simon said quickly.

Kaison turned around, about to be executed by one of the Shadows, but all of the sudden, a spear came through the shadow's chest. The Shadow evaporated, revealing the killer that was behind him. Kaison recognized the face immediately.

"Miss me?" Louie winked. He had a dressing wrapped around his forehead like a headband.

"Louie!" Kaison exclaimed in joy.

"Get him inside," Louie yelled, motioning to Simon. He flipped his spear in his hand. "I've got this," he finished before turning to the oncoming Shadows.

Obeying, Kaison dropped to the ground beside Simon and scooped a hand underneath his back. Kaison pulled out the arrow that was lodged into Simon's shoulder and Simon winced. Whatever was left of Simon's arm Kaison strung over his shoulders. Simon let out a horrifying cry. Kaison grunted as he helped Simon to his feet. Both Simon and Kaison held their weapons in their outer hands. Kaison tried his best to lead Simon into the castle.

Kaison turned over his shoulder to look back at the field. In the distance, he could see Louie meet up with Julian and Pandora. Louie and Julian flanked Pandora on either side with their swords outstretched, and Pandora was creating a magical shield around them.

Kaison returned his attention to the front doors, but a Shadow lunged at them. Kaison blocked out of instinct. Before Kaison had a chance to make any other move, Simon had already sent his sword through the soldier's stomach. They acted as a single person, wielding two weapons.

They were limping through the open castle doors when a loud rumbling sound crashed through the distant forest. Everyone on the battlefield froze and turned to the source. Kaison also looked at the monster on the horizon.

A wall of black smoke taller than the trees was moving across the moor along the battlefield. Both the Shadows and knights began running away, as fast as they could, but as soon as the smoke touched them, they either disappeared into the smoke or they grabbed their necks and collapsed to the ground, dead.

"What is that?" Simon gasped for breath.

The wall of smoke was strangling everyone it touched and killing the Shadows on impact. Everyone on the battlefield was in awe of the image. Part of the smoke broke away from the wall and floated at a fast pace toward the castle. It flew in the air, and Kaison squinted his eyes to see it against the black sky.

Kaison released his hold on Simon and took a step back onto the battlefield. Knights were running in all directions, some back inside the castle, but the deadly wall of smoke was evaporating. Kaison focused on the independent mass of fog flying over their heads and levitating above the castle. With one swift motion, it flew through the stained-glass windows of the Sun Spire, magically leaving the windows perfectly intact, and disappeared.

Kaison's eyes widened.

"Maeve and Theadosia!" Kaison let out.

Simon was holding the remains of his arm and leaning up against the door frame for support.

"Mortimer's here!" Kaison shouted.

Kaison pushed past one of their own knights and ran through the entryway of the castle. Simon stumbled after him, and they took off down the hallway that would lead them to Sun Spire.

"Wait!" Simon screeched from behind.

Kaison skidded to a halt and turned around, seeing Simon limping after him. His ghostly face was full of pain, for he was losing so much blood. Kaison ran back to him and looked at his arm. The bone was clearly visible.

Kaison handed Simon his halberd, who took it without question. "Here," Kaison ordered in a panic. Then Kaison unbuckled his belt and whipped it out from around him. Kaison wrapped it around Simon's bicep, and he screamed in pain as Kaison pulled it tight. The tourniquet wasn't much, but it would stop at least some of the excessive bleeding.

"Come on," Kaison said, taking his halberd back from Simon before continuing to Sun Spire.

Simon held his arm with his other hand and raced after Kaison, biting his tongue in excruciating pain.

Kaison skidded around the entryway to the stairwell and stepped inside. Multiple stairs wrapped endlessly in a spiral to Sun Spire.

"By plague…" Simon let out, seeing the intimidating number of stairs.

A scream pierced the stairwell.

Kaison started up the stairs, skipping every other one. Simon raced after him as fast as he possibly could. Kaison couldn't let Mortimer kill Theadosia and Maeve.

About three-fourths of the way up the extreme staircase, when his thighs were burning with agony and he was completely out of breath, Kaison heard Simon fall. Kaison snapped around and saw Simon face flat on one of the stairs. Kaison raced back down the staircase to him and dropped down. Kaison rolled Simon onto his back to see that his eyes were hardly open. He had left a trail of blood along the entire stairwell.

"Go…" Simon choked. He was losing too much blood.

Kaison nodded, grateful for his permission. Kaison turned away and continued up the last few stories. As soon as Kaison saw the door to Sun Spire, his blood turned to ice. When Kaison reached the top, he burst through the door only to come to a standstill.

Sir Emmett was standing in the middle of Sun Spire with his arm around Maeve's throat. Maeve was easily a foot smaller than he was, and she was standing on her tiptoes to try and breathe. She grasped his arm, attempting to escape, but his hold was too tight.

Sir Emmett? How was he the victorious brother?

"Let her go!" Kaison shouted, keeping his distance.

"Oh, we have a visitor." A disgusting, crooked smile appeared on Emmett's disfigured face.

Theadosia was on the ground, her back to where Kaison entered, but she didn't look injured.

Emmett threw Maeve to the ground, and she choked for an ounce of air. It was then that Kaison noticed Emmett had a hold of the diamond journal.

"I thought you were dead," Kaison spat.

"Dead?" Emmett laughed. "No, child. I killed the Shadow of Eclipse."

Maeve remained on the ground trying to regain her bearings. She inched closer to Theadosia.

"Don't try anything, child." Emmett noticed Kaison's eyes darting to his sister. "I have more power than you can ever imagine."

Kaison was at a loss for words.

"Give me the halberd, or else," Emmett ordered, his disfigured face wrinkling. A purple glow danced at his fingertips.

Kaison moved toward his sister. He knew exactly how Emmett would try and threaten him. Kaison lunged to try and block Theadosia with the Crimson Teardrop, but he wasn't fast enough. Emmett extended his hand out, and a purple bolt grazed Theadosia's side, burning a wound into her skin.

She screamed, grabbing her ribcage on the ground.

"Stop!" Kaison screamed. He slid to his knees, holding Theadosia upright with one hand. With his other, he slid the halberd across the room toward the Shadow of Eclipse. "Take it!" Kaison shouted.

"Thank you," Emmett flicked his wrist, and Kaison's halberd flew into his grasp.

Theadosia gasped for air, clutching her side where blood was already gushing from the gash.

Kaison pressed his palm to the wound, trying to stop the bleeding. Maeve needed to heal her.

Emmett kept a hold of the halberd but dropped the diamond journal on the ground in front of Maeve, making her jump. A feather pen rolled out from between the pages.

"Open the journal," Emmett commanded.

Maeve was on her knees while Emmett loomed over her.

"Do it yourself," she retorted.

Emmett squatted beside her to be closer to eye level. "Feisty," Emmett spoke. "I won't tolerate it."

Emmett snapped his fingers. The journal on the ground flipped open, the pages creating a gentle breeze. Emmett examined the letters that were written on the open page.

"Oh, this will be good," Emmett grinned. Emmett picked up the book in his hands. Slowly, he took the page and began ripping it, tear by tear.

Maeve screamed and clutched her face.

Then, Emmett let the ripped page float to the ground. It swayed once in each direction before it landed on the floor of Sun Spire.

Maeve managed to open her eyes, pleading with Kaison for help. Her green eyes, hidden behind her palms, were flooded with tears. Emmett had ripped her wish from the book.

"You're a monster!" Kaison shouted.

Emmett extended his hand toward the siblings, and the purple bolt was met with a brilliant flash of red light. Kaison squinted his eyes against the blinding magic, feeling the warmth ripple from the rock at his chest.

"Try taking off that pendant. See how long you survive," Emmett said.

Emmett threw the diamond journal to the ground, inches from Maeve. "Now write!" he ordered.

Maeve had no choice but to obey. Hesitantly, she reached out for the book and opened it, fastening her quill on a clear page.

"What do you want me to write?" Maeve growled under her breath. Her red curls fell in her face.

Emmett began to speak:

> *"As the light diminishes and the stars ascend, the shadows, darkness, and evil will descend.*
> *Bedlam will ensue and tears will form, but the most horrifying is the eye of the storm."*

Maeve scribbled on the clear page of the journal. Kaison watched her write, second guessing what they were doing. Wasn't there a way they could prevent this? Was there any way they could stop the Shadow of Eclipse?

Theadosia shifted, withdrawing one of the blades from her belt. Her breathing was raspy. She gave it to Kaison with a blood-soaked hand.

Kaison took the knife from her.

Emmett continued:

"I am aware of the consequences, so listen now as I speak in confidence.
Transform what we have to what we need, to fulfill what previously was decreed."

As Maeve wrote Emmett's last words, she shut her eyes, wincing in regret. She finished the last word and added a period to the sentence.

Sir Emmett fixated on the halberd in his hand. Before their eyes, the halberd began to glow. The staff exuded a vibrant golden light, and the three gemstones on the handle illuminated their individual colors: red, green, and purple. Tiny twinkles of light sparked off of the handle, flickering in all directions.

Emmett smiled. He rose to his feet with his palm open, displaying the halberd, now activated with the magic required to open the door. He tightened his grip on the staff before scowling at Maeve.

"Thank you, my queen," Emmett said.

Kaison lunged, jumping up from his feet with the knife in hand. He drove it into Emmett's side with as much force as he could.

Emmett let out a shrill yell, dropping the halberd to the ground. It clanked loudly on the stone.

Maeve dove across the room to go to Theadosia's aid.

Flashes of purple and red lit the air again, blinding Kaison. The Eclipse magic was blocked by the Teardrop every time. Then Kaison felt iron knuckles across his jaw, nearly knocking him directly off his feet.

When he regained his balance, he saw the halberd on the ground.

Kaison swooped his father's weapon into his palms. It was glowing, exuding magic in multicolored hues that flashed all over Sun

Spire. He faced Emmett, raising the halberd high above his head to bring down a death blow.

Then a sword protruded from the front of Emmett's stomach.

Kaison froze.

Emmett was still as he looked down at the tip of a sword, red with blood, that had penetrated his abdomen. The sword was withdrawn as quickly as it entered, and Emmett collapsed to the ground. As Emmett fell, Simon was revealed behind him.

Simon held his sword in one hand, for his other arm was simply a skeleton along his forearm. Simon looked like a complete mess. Mud covered his face, but his bottomless eyes were still clear. The makeshift tourniquet was caked in blood, and his clothes were drenched from the rain outside. He was panting, and his hand that held the sword was shaking.

Kaison slowly lowered the halberd, and Maeve helped Theadosia up to her feet.

Emmett looked up at Simon, his legs paralyzed. The side of his face that wasn't scarred raised slightly into a crooked smile.

"I knew…" Emmett choked, barely audible. "You're just like me." Emmett's voice shook as he tried to speak, but blood was filling his lungs.

"No," Simon said, his voice grim. "I'm nothing like you."

A deep laugh rumbled through Emmett, but it ended in a bout of coughing. Once he regained his strength he spoke again. "Like father, like son."

Simon's expression was indiscernible. "What?"

"You and Seraphina look so much alike," Emmett's voice was barely audible. "But I chose to protect the royal family, and you were gone." Emmett growled. "I failed at being a knight and a father."

"You're not my father!" Simon screamed.

Emmett lifted a shaking hand to point at his son. "Ivor. That ring was mine."

Simon's silver ring glistened.

Emmett continued, "Enjoy your power, my son."

"No!" Simon screamed, sending his sword straight through Emmett's heart, killing him. "You liar!" he cried. He released his sword, leaving it sticking out of Emmett's chest. His body was shaking, and his face was even paler than normal.

Emmett began evaporating into thin air. His body turned into black flakes before ascending and disintegrating. Simon's sword clanked abruptly to the ground.

A purple hue began forming around Simon's hand. He looked down at it in shock, and he was instantly filled with fear.

Maeve, Theadosia, and Kaison kept their distance.

"What's happening to me?" Simon asked.

Theadosia was the first to take a step forward.

"Stay away from me," Simon said, his voice quivering. He backed away, trying to distance himself from the purple hue emanating from him.

"Please, stay calm," Theadosia said. She reached her hand out toward Simon.

"Stay back!" Simon shouted.

Suddenly Theadosia was thrown backwards. She was propelled into the stone wall with more force than the previous Shadow of Eclipses combined. Her head smashed into the stone, and she collapsed to the ground like a ragdoll.

"Thea!" Kaison's scream rang through the tower. The halberd fell from his grasp. He raced over to his sister and dropped to the ground. Blood was pouring from her skull, and she stared blankly into the sky.

She choked once. "Open it…," she forced, barely audible. Then her body fell limp.

"Thea…," Kaison breathed. He picked his sister up into his arms, holding her close to his chest. "No!" Kaison cried, rocking back and forth with her. "No!" The scream erupted from deep within. He pulled her closer, shaking her, hoping she would move. He held the back of her head, feeling the blood coat his entire palm. Maybe he could stop the bleeding. Maybe he could bring her back to life.

"By plague…," Simon said. Tears began forming in his eyes. "I'm a monster." He tried to distance himself even more, but his back met the stained-glass window behind him.

Maeve shook her head, but kept her distance. "You're not a monster," she said. "This is all new and you're scared."

"I killed her!" Simon screamed. A thunderous bolt exploded from his body.

Maeve ducked, dodging the oncoming bolt.

Simon's arms were shaking. The purple glow was extending even further up his arms. Slowly, the power was entering every limb of his body.

Kaison held Theadosia tightly, and tears streamed down his face. "You…you killed her."

Simon stared back at Kaison. "I'm sorry…"

Kaison pulled Theadosia closer as he screamed. "You killed her!" His entire body felt numb. "Why…," he choked, tears pouring down his cheeks. "Why her?"

The purple glow was emanating from Simon's body. "I'm so sorry…," he said, shaking his head.

Maeve took another two steps toward Simon. "Take a deep breath," she said.

"I don't want to hurt you too," Simon said.

"You're not going to," Maeve said firmly. She was close to him now.

Simon saw his remaining hand. It was quivering, and the purple glow was moving along his arm as the Shadow of Eclipse magic entered his body. His father's ring was almost consumed in a purple hue.

"Stay back," he warned Maeve.

"No," Maeve said.

Maeve reached out toward Simon, touching his arm. Alarmed, Simon jerked away, but there was nowhere for him to go. He tripped over the ledge of the stained-glass window and fell into it. The stained glass shattered, and he tumbled out of the frame.

"Simon!" Maeve screamed, reaching out to grab him, but she was too late.

Simon fell through the window.

Simon screamed as he plunged down the side of Sun Spire. Kaison waited, listening intently to the sound of his cries.

Suddenly the screaming stopped.

Everything was silent.

- 56 -

Kaison

Sun Spire was still. The black sky outside began to lighten, and the furious wind calmed.

Kaison stayed on the ground, holding Theadosia in his arms. The blood was spilling from the back of her head, creating a pool as it dripped down Kaison's armor. Tears flowed down Kaison's face, and he whipped around to look at Maeve. "Please heal her."

Maeve stood at the window frame. She turned to face Kaison, her face melting in sorrow. "I can't…"

"Please!" Kaison pleaded.

Maeve ran over and dropped to her knees beside him. "Kaison," she said, cupping his face in her palms. "My magic doesn't work that way. I can't bring someone back."

Kaison's face was wet with tears. Maeve let go of him, and he looked down at his sister. Kaison slowly rested Theadosia on the ground in front of him. She stared blankly at the ceiling above. Delicately, he shut her eyes with his hand, setting her to rest.

"She's gone," Kaison muttered, barely audible.

Maeve wrapped her arms around him and rested her head on his shoulder.

"I'm sorry," she said.

Kaison didn't pull away from Maeve's embrace. "I don't know what I'm going to do without her," he said.

Maeve continued to hold Kaison. "I know. Nothing I say will make it better," she said.

Kaison tilted his head to rest it on Maeve's. They remained in silence for a little while, letting the wind lap in through the open window.

Maeve eventually pulled away. "You're the heir to Solaris," she said.

Kaison remained seated on the ground. "No, I'm not."

"Yes," Maeve said. "You are Prince Sun."

"That doesn't matter."

"Yes, it does," Maeve objected. "With the queen dead, the kingdom needs you to step up."

Kaison shook his head. "Don't you understand?" he asked. "I was a placeholder. The designated protector. My entire family line was put on the throne until your family line came along to claim it. The Ademantum decided you were the true heir."

Maeve hesitated. She spotted the journal and the glowing halberd across the floor of Sun Spire. They rested nearby, unscathed. "I can't step up and rule," she said. "No one would listen to me."

"Yes, they will," Kaison said. He wiped away the tears from his eyes. "You were chosen. I know it doesn't seem like you can step up now, but you can and you will."

"I can't do it alone."

"You won't be alone."

Maeve smiled.

Noises rang from the stairwell. Julian, Pandora, and Louie entered Sun Spire. All three were drenched from head to toe and coated in a thick layer of mud. They came to a halt at the entrance to Sun Spire when they saw the shattered glass and Theadosia's limp body.

"Great Sun," Pandora said under her breath.

Louie shoved his way between Pandora and Julian before kneeling beside Theadosia on the ground. "By plague...," he muttered.

"Are you two all right?" Pandora asked, taking another step into the room.

"No," Maeve said.

"All the Shadows disappeared at the same time," Julian said. "Is it over?"

Kaison nodded. "Simon killed Sir Emmett."

"Where is he?" Pandora asked.

Maeve nodded in the direction of the broken window.

They group let a moment of silence pass between them.

Julian cleared his throat. "The Shadow of Eclipse is dead. We're safe now."

Kaison's fingers grazed the pendant at his neck. A wave of realization flooded over him. "The prophecy," he said.

Maeve tilted her head. "What do you mean?"

"It's all coming true."

Pandora took another step forward. "I don't understand."

"When the lineage of darkness begins from beyond," Kaison quoted, "that was the rise of the Shadows with Mortimer's reign," he explained. "The designated protector is forced to abscond... that was my father when he left Sun Castle."

The group surrounding Kaison nodded in turn, taking in everything Kaison was saying.

Kaison took off the pendant and held it in front of Maeve. "This. A teardrop shaped ruby pendant. It's 'a teardrop of blood as defense.'"

Maeve's face flushed. She looked to where Simon's sword remained after he slayed Emmett. "The sword wins the war at a friend's expense," she quoted.

Kaison nodded. He closed his fingers around the ruby pendant.

"We're living the prophecy," Louie muttered.

"That means we are far from done," Pandora added.

Julian didn't seem fully convinced, but let out a deep breath. "What do we do now?"

The halberd was still glowing. The magical chant that Maeve had cast over it remained. Kaison reached over and picked it up off the floor. He said, "We should find out what everyone was after."

Julian, Louie, and Pandora exchanged a glance.

Maeve's green eyes twinkled. "Yes."

Kaison thought of Theadosia's last words. The only way to keep the halberd and the door protected was to know what he was protecting. His mother, father, and sister had died for the halberd and the secrets that it protected deep in the labyrinth of Sun Castle. Kaison's face hardened, and he spoke with determination:

"We're opening the door."

Shortly, the five arrived at the door in the tunnels. Kaison held the halberd firmly in his hands, the glow bright enough to illuminate the space around them. Maeve stood directly beside him, close enough for their shoulders to be touching, holding the diamond journal close to her chest.

Pandora and Julian stood hand and hand beside them, mesmerized by the blue doorway. A glowing orb floated before Pandora, lighting the remainder of the tunnel that Kaison's halberd was unable to reach.

Louie remained a few feet behind, keeping his distance between the magical gateway and himself.

"So, this is what all those clues were leading us to?" Pandora asked.

"Yes." Kaison's palms started to sweat, and he felt his heart beating faster in his chest.

"I don't have a good feeling about this," Louie muttered. "Are you sure this is a good idea?"

Kaison nodded. "This is what everyone was after – the queen, Mortimer, and Sir Emmett," he said. "I need to find out what's inside."

Kaison took a step forward moments before Maeve grabbed his arm.

"Wait," Maeve said, her voice dropped to a whisper. "I don't hear the voices."

"What voices?" Kaison asked.

"Remember when we were here earlier, they said: 'the power inside is meant for you,' " Maeve recalled. She paused for a moment to let the words sink in. "Now, it's silent."

"I don't like the sound of that," Louie chimed.

"Listen, are you using the halberd, or do I have to do it?" Julian sneered.

Kaison glared at Julian. He let out a deep breath. "No, I'm opening it."

Kaison took a step forward, the distance between him and the door shortening. His heart continued to thump in his chest, anticipation overwhelming his senses. Maeve was right behind, approaching the door beside him.

The blue door was blank. There was no handle nor keyhole. As

Kaison drew closer, he could feel the halberd in his hands begin to shake. The tremors increased in intensity. The gemstones cast colored hues on the tunnel around them.

When Kaison was within a few paces, the door began to shimmer. A silhouette of the halberd appeared on the front of the door, coated with glittering, golden magic. The halberd in Kaison's grasp shook as if it was being drawn to the designated spot on the door.

Kaison extended his arm, raising the halberd up to match the dazzling imprint on the door. In one jolt, the halberd was pulled into the silhouette by a magical force. A sprinkle of luminous dust fluttered to the ground. The magnitude of the colors continued to intensify.

Something grazed Kaison's fingertips. He looked down to see Maeve interlacing her hand with his.

"Whatever is inside, we do this together," she said.

Kaison nodded.

The brilliant rays were intensifying, and the floor rumbled underneath them. A sharp wind lapped around them, creating a furious noise.

Suddenly a piercing glow electrified the tunnel. Kaison's vision went white as magic beamed outward from the door. Kaison was blinded by the light for a moment, completely consumed. He felt lost, spinning somewhere away from his friends as if he had been transported to a different realm.

Then the grip on his hand tightened. Maeve stood beside him. Kaison was brought back to his senses. He observed his surroundings, and the light diminished. Slowly, the wind died down to nothing, and the rumbling of the floor ceased.

Then everything was extinguished. All that was left was the glowing light from Pandora's magic orb. Kaison blinked, regaining his sight.

The halberd rested at his feet, perfectly intact, and in its staff form. The gemstones were radiant, but it was no longer glowing like before.

The door was wide open.

Kaison couldn't move, for his entire body was frozen. All he could see from his position was a red room on the opposite side of the door. A faint glow of a symbol flashed in the doorway: two diamonds with a line through the center. Then, the mysterious symbol faded.

Kaison's eyes narrowed.

"Let's go."

- 57 -

Simon

Rain poured down from the night sky, turning the moor into a muddy wasteland. Clouds covered any glimmer of light from the moon, leaving the land in hopeless darkness. On the outskirts of the graveyard was an unloved grave. No flowers rested on top of the mound of dirt.

A thick smoke congealed into a young man, aggressively dropping him to the ground. He landed forcefully on the mud, splattering his face in more dirt. He groaned, rolling over onto his back. The rain pelted down on him from the sky above, feeling like rocks against his face.

How was he alive?

He looked to his right, where his forearm was only skin and bones. He could no longer feel past his elbow.

He dragged himself to his feet, slipping on the wet earth. He knew what he had to do. There was something he had to be certain of. He began taking the long walk across the moor. Then he trudged through the cemetery toward his desired location. He passed an open grave, picking up a wooden shovel. He would need it.

When he reached the grave, he examined the wood that marked the location, making sure he was at the right place. Unable to use his right arm, he started digging with his left.

The sloshing of the earth was unpleasant, and the rain made the shovel heavier. He used the shovel to remove pile after pile of dirt from the grave.

The darkness around him was shrinking. The smallest bit of light began peaking over the tallest pine trees. The boy had dug four feet down into the earth, before planting the shovel into the ground with the handle sticking up to the sky.

He examined the crater he had created, before sitting back on the wall made from mud and dirt. His boots were two inches deep in the rainwater that had pooled around him. The water from the earth seeped deeper into his black armor. He held onto his scarred wrist, now aching, and let out a deep sigh.

The grave was empty. No one in their right mind would bury a body deeper than four feet, especially an individual that no one knew or cared about.

The boy let out an angry yell, his voice spreading through the graveyard. The cross marking the grave flew out of the ground and landed a couple yards away. The crater got wider as his voice pushed the earth away from him, and the shovel, too deep in the ground to move, splintered. For a moment, it was as if everything around him tried to escape.

He panted, feeling his throat close and his head spin. A black smoke pooled around him, fanning off him like steam from a hot spring. A purple hue began to cloud his eyesight.

Footsteps alerted the boy, making him jump to his feet. He withdrew a dagger from his belt and turned around quickly to face a girl.

She was tall and thin, with tight trousers that went seamlessly into black boots. She wore a leather corset, and a black coat that was high in the front and almost touched the ground in the back.

Beside her, stood a younger girl, maybe fourteen years old. Her amber, beady eyes scrutinized the young man in the grave.

The boy's dagger shook in his hand. He watched the tall girl slowly pull back the hood of her coat. Her bottomless eyes connected with his. He had dug up her grave only minutes ago, meaning she had to be alive. However, if he didn't know this information, he would have questioned if she were a ghost.

He swallowed hard before speaking, looking up at the figure that was standing on solid ground. "Seraphina?"

Her expression was enigmatic. "I can help you."

"I don't need help!" The boy's hand quivered around the metal handle of the dagger.

The fourteen-year-old crossed her arms and frowned.

Seraphina hovered over him. She opened her palm, and it was as if the dagger was yanked toward her. Slipping out of his measly, sweaty grasp, the dagger flew to Seraphina, and she caught it a foot away from her. She didn't even blink.

The girl slid the dagger into her own belt, disarming him.

"How did you...," the boy uttered, looking at his own empty palm.

"Let me help you."

Simon asked his twin, "You have the Shadow of Eclipse magic too?"

"Not exactly," Seraphina said.

"Then how...?"

Seraphina took a step closer to Simon and lowered herself to a squatting position. She extended her hand toward her brother. "We can help each other."

Simon hesitated, not because he was skeptical, but because he was in disbelief at how perfect this arrangement might be. "Who is that?" He gestured to the young girl behind his sister.

"I'm Zamara," the girl said, flipping her raven hair out of her eyes. "Nice to meet you, cousin."

"Zamara," Seraphina snapped, cutting her off.

Zamara rolled her eyes in an over-exaggerated manner, shifting her weight onto her other leg.

At that moment, the rain cleared. The sun shone magnificently in the sky, forcing Simon to squint against its brilliance. In the distance, a beam of light fired into the air from the Sun Spire. Sun Castle lit up, the light extending into the heavens. The trio turned away from the light, unable to look directly at the beam. It remained lit for a few moments, shining across the moor and beyond. There was no doubt the light could be seen from all of Morbaeda.

The beam faded. Simon opened his eyes again, refocusing on Sun Castle. It was coated in a magical, twinkling aura.

A trio of doves flew over them, heading to Sun Castle.

Simon stared in stunned silence.

"What was that?" Zamara asked.

Simon glared at the castle on the moor. "They opened the door," he said.

Disregarding the light magic that spread across the kingdom, Seraphina reached down once again. "Let me help you."

Simon assessed her. He needed her. Solaris hated him before. He would always be Plague Boy. Why would they let him back into Sun Castle now that he had manifested the worst evil of their world?

Finally, Simon grabbed his sister's hand, and she hoisted him out of the grave and onto solid ground. He slid on the muddy earth, but Seraphina's strength was pleasantly surprising.

They looked determinedly at one another, the resemblance uncanny.

Simon spoke, "Lead the way."

ACKNOWLEDGMENTS

The world of Morbaeda has been in the works for over ten years, and it is beyond exciting to be able to finally see it in book form. Thank you to everyone who has made that possible.

First and foremost to our family, who have been supportive every step of the way. To Mom and Dad, who have always encouraged us to pursue anything and everything. To our sister Emily, who is an inspiration, and has shown us that you can achieve any dream you set your mind to. Also to our extended family. Grandma, Barbara, and everyone else. And, of course, we cannot forget Dan.

Thank you to all our beta readers. You've helped shape the story to what it is today.

A huge shoutout to our gorgeous cover designer, Stefanie, who worked with us until it was perfect.

Finally, thank you to our readers. Thank you for embarking on this journey - we wouldn't have this story without you.

Please consider leaving us a review on Amazon, Goodreads, Facebook, or anywhere. As indie authors, it means the world to us.

We appreciate your support as we continue to write Kaison and Osiris's stories, and cannot wait for you to keep reading!

KEEP READING FOR A SPECIAL SNEAK PEEK!

10 YEARS BEFORE THE DEATH OF KING SUN

- 1 -

Osiris

A shallow breath escaped Osiris's lips as she pressed her back into the wall, hiding in the shadows. Two voices were heard on the other side, and as long as they didn't step out on the balcony, it would be safe.

"Go place my wager on the small one," a deep voice said. "I think she will outsmart him."

"Yes, Captain."

The sound of footsteps started again, this time heading away from the doorway that led to the balcony.

If the footsteps belonged to Captain Hondo, that meant he wasn't in his quarters.

Osiris waited a moment longer before deciding it was safe. She moved away from the wall and back to the railing. Looking up, she noted there was still one more story to climb.

Hoisting herself on the railing, Osiris leveraged herself using the post that held the above story up. Then she proceeded to free climb the column.

Lights flickered in the distance coming from the town center, but the outside of the Captain's palace was nearly pitch black. This side of the palace faced the open sea. The water lapped against the structure of the building stories below, and the smell of salt water filled the air. The elite part of the city was built against the sea, and the overpopulated kingdom of Larkesh became poorer the farther inland one traveled.

The palace was a multi-tiered building. Captain Hondo's study was on the top floor.

There was too much money involved. They couldn't fail.

Osiris reached the next balcony, her biceps aching from the climb. She glanced behind her, seeing the ocean far below. Then she grabbed the railing, hoisting herself over it and landing on stable ground.

There was a pair of glass doors in front of her, leading into a room. She approached them quietly, making sure she remained light on her feet. She glanced inside.

It appeared empty, but she couldn't be certain. Inside was a circular room with wooden walls. An archway led into the bedchamber, and a dark red door blocked the entrance. The desk was raised on a platform in the center, with two stairs leading up to it. A large map was draped from the ceiling, and the Larkesh flag hung on the opposite wall.

Just then, a key rattled in the lock of the door. A gasp escaped Osiris's lips before she moved away from the glass doors and pressed up against the outside wall. Osiris listened intently, hearing the door open and someone enter. The footsteps were heavy. No doubt it was Captain Hondo.

The footsteps continued before stopping abruptly. A clattering was heard, and Osiris tried to make out what was happening.

A sound rang in the distance. It was soft and muffled, but was a relief to hear.

"Thank you, Moriah," Osiris said under her breath.

The footsteps started again, and Osiris knew Hondo was leaving the room in response to the noise. Osiris waited until she heard a door slam before moving again.

She came to the balcony doors, pulling her pick from the inside of her vest. Dropping to her knees, she inserted it into the lock. With careful focus, she moved it until she heard a click. Osiris stood, putting the pick away, before entering inside the room.

She was quiet, closing the glass door behind her so that it didn't make a sound. Osiris quickly crossed the room to the front door, knowing they didn't have much time. Unlocking the main entrance to the study, Osiris opened it to find a young man standing in the hallway.

"Destrian," she said, acknowledging one of her two accomplices. He looked different in a soldier's bright orange uniform.

He gave a curt nod, pulling a pocket watch out and flipping the top open. "We're twelve seconds ahead of schedule," he said, not making eye contact.

"Come on." Osiris gestured into the room.

Destrian entered, taking in the room before him.

Osiris shut the door, relocking it. She crossed to the bedchamber, knowing her part in the plan, while Destrian maneuvered over the desk in the middle of the study.

Osiris entered the bedchamber. Captain Hondo's bed was covered by a large canopy. It was next to two side tables. A wardrobe was on the opposite side of the room with an ornate seating area. The other wooden wall contained a floor-length mirror.

First, she went to the side tables. She opened each one in turn, examining the objects inside. Nothing out of the ordinary. She proceeded to check underneath the pillows, but there was nothing there.

"Osiris."

Upon hearing her name, Osiris turned and faced the doorway. She could see Destrian through it, standing at the desk on the platform in the center of the room.

He held up a piece of paper. "Our names are on this."

Osiris's eyes widened. "What is it?"

"I'm not sure," Destrian said. "It's just a list of names."

"Well, memorize it. We will look into it later," Osiris said. "That's not why we're here."

Destrian nodded before skimming the page. "Done." He placed it down and continued rummaging through the desk.

Osiris brought her attention back to the room. She scanned it again. She had to be missing something.

Then her gaze settled on the mirror on the wall. Something was off about it. Why was it extended from the wall like that?

Osiris walked forward until she was standing in front of the mirror. She tilted her head, her eyes narrowing. She rested her finger against it.

It was a double sided mirror.

Osiris immediately scanned the border of the mirror. There was nothing on either side, and no cracks in the paneling signaled a hidden door. Then she looked at the floor.

There was a rectangular shape that would have blended in perfectly with the beams if she hadn't been looking for it.

Osiris pressed her foot against the shape and heard a click. The mirror slid to the side, revealing a hidden room. It was a small room that could only fit four or five people inside.

She examined the opposite side of the mirror. Sure enough, it was a window.

Osiris turned back to the hidden room.

The room contained weapons of all kinds, and on the back wall was a shelf with a golden box.

Osiris's heart skipped a beat. She entered the room and stood before the chest, which had no lock. She opened it gently, uncovering a diamond ring.

Nikodemus was right.

"I have it!" Destrian called.

Osiris grabbed the diamond ring and put it into her vest pocket. She quickly left the hidden room, sliding the double mirror closed.

She dashed across the bedchamber and back into the study. Destrian was hunched over, examining a piece of paper.

"Will he want the copy with the Captain's seal?" Osiris asked.

Destrian tapped his temple with his pointer finger. "I have it."

Osiris raised her eyebrows. "That wasn't the question."

"We don't want him to know it's gone," Destrian said.

Osiris shrugged. "He will know someone has been here anyway." She gestured in the direction of the bedchamber where she had found the ring.

Destrian blinked, his mind racing.

The doorknob rattled, notifying them that someone was unlocking the door.

Osiris grabbed the map off the table before Destrian could object and raced back to the balcony. Destrian charged after her, and they burst through the balcony doors.

Osiris shoved the map into the waterproof pocket on her vest before grabbing the railing. Her eyes scanned the dark water three stories below. The only light source came from the moon.

There was no boat.

“Where’s Moriah?” Destrian asked.

A sound alerted them that the door was opening.

“Jump!” Osiris said. Without hesitating another moment, she hopped over the railing, plunging toward the water below. She crossed her arms against her chest, preparing for the impact.

Osiris only fell for a few moments before her body hit the water. She plunged underneath the sea, feeling the impact against her entire body before she began swimming toward the surface.

She broke through the water, flipping her dark braid backwards. She kicked her hands and legs furiously, feeling the waves attempt to push her underneath the first balcony.

Destrian emerged from the water, gasping for breath.

“This way!” he called.

He started swimming furiously toward the nearest dock. The lights flickered on it, masked by smaller boats.

Osiris followed him quickly behind, feeling the current pull her body backward.

Once Destrian reached the dock, he leveraged himself with his arms before hoisting himself out of the water. He spun around, reaching his hand toward Osiris. They grabbed each other’s wrists, and he helped her pull herself up onto the dock.

“We have to find Moriah,” Osiris said, whipping around and preparing to run up the dock.

But Osiris froze in her tracks as she faced three soldiers. They were blocking their path.

Osiris instantly withdrew the dagger from her belt. She lunged forward, swiping at the first soldier’s chest. The blade barely grazed him. The soldier withdrew his rapier in one slice, but Osiris ducked.

“Osiris!” Destrian screamed, weaponless.

Osiris kicked the soldier in the knee, causing him to buckle to the ground, before sending the dagger into his chest. Then she whirled around, withdrawing another blade from her belt, and stabbed the soldier that was approaching her accomplice with a death blow.

She sensed something behind her, and whipped around just in time to see a blade coming for her face. She was unable to completely dodge, and a sharp sting sliced her cheek from the very tip of the blade. Osiris grabbed her attacker's wrist, sending her knee up into his elbow and breaking his arm. The soldier reeled in pain, and Osiris knocked her shoulder into his chest, sending him off the dock and into the water.

She turned back to Destrian, seeing he was unharmed. "Run!"

They both started down the dock once more, but before they had sprinted a few paces they came to a halt.

Captain Hondo's large stature took up the most space. His leather armor only covered half his chest and ran down his fighting arm. A dagger in his hand dripped with fresh blood.

"Your friend is dead," Hondo stated, soldiers coming up behind him and flanking him, "and you will be next."

A gasp escaped Osiris's lips, and she was consumed with anger. She lunged forward but was immediately blocked.

The soldiers were already on them. Osiris tried to fight them, but both of her arms were bound tightly behind her back before she could defend herself.

"You can't kill us!" Destrian shouted.

The soldiers holding Destrian froze.

"Check him," Hondo said.

One of the soldiers rolled up Destrian's sleeve, revealing a symbol on the inside of his wrist. It was a branded symbol of two overlapping diamonds with a line through the center.

The soldier holding Osiris did the same, seeing the same symbol on her wrist as well.

"Well, I should have known," the captain said.

The soldiers held Destrian and Osiris before the Captain. One of the soldiers patted down Destrian, looking for any weapons on him. Of course, he had none. But the soldier pulled out Destrian's pocket watch, examining the craftsmanship.

"T-Thats..." Destrian started, but then cut himself short.

The soldier yanked the pocket watch off the chain before handing it to Captain Hondo, who put it in his own pocket.

Osiris could hear Destrian let out a slight gasp.

Then the soldier came up to Osiris. He patted her down, noticing the pockets on her vest. Immediately he opened one, withdrawing the diamond ring.

Osiris shifted her jaw, trying to wrench herself from the two men holding her, but it was no use.

The soldier handed Captain Hondo the ring. Then he found the waterproof pocket. He pulled out the two papers inside and handed them to the Captain as well before finally backing away.

Hondo looked the thieves up and down. "Who hired you?"

Osiris stared back at the Captain, remaining silent.

First he unraveled the paper that Osiris and Destrian had stolen, seeing his own map. He eyed the thieves curiously, attempting to interpret their orders.

"Who do you work for?" the captain asked.

Osiris and Destrian remained silent.

Captain Hondo stormed forward until he was standing right before the two of them. "I asked you a question!" he raised his hand up, ready to bring it down on Osiris's face. When he started swinging, a bright glow lit up the night sky. Everyone froze as they turned to face the light.

Far in the distance, somewhere in the Northwest, a beacon of light shot up into the heavens. It was blinding to look at and far more powerful than any of the stars in the sky.

Osiris's mouth dropped open in awe, her eyes widening. It couldn't be possible. She thought it was only a story.

Then she turned to meet Destrian's gaze. His eyes were wide, and she knew he was thinking the exact same thing she was.

Then Captain Hondo took a step toward the light. "It's real," he said. "The Light of Solaris."

ABOUT THE AUTHORS:

Originally from Lancaster, Pennsylvania, Amanda and Hope grew up in the arts world. They started writing stories at a young age, and Amanda completed her first mystery novel in middle school. They both wrote a musical together, Royal Shadows, which is also a fantasy with sorcery! Now, Amanda lives in New York with her finacé. She manages a non-profit organization, which allows her to engage with an international team working in 10+ countries on a day-to-day basis! Hope Abrom is a film editor and 3D artist working at an award-winning production house in LA. However, they still both write in every moment of free time! Don't forget to follow their writing on tiktok, instagram or facebook @abromauthors!